TITLES BY DAWN ADDONIZIO

Novels Of The Faerie Realm:

A RISKY PROPOSITION, Book 1 of
The Third Wish Duology

SOUL SEDUCTION, Book 2 of
The Third Wish Duology

PASSIONATE MAGIC

GREY'S MAGIC

Published by Nouveau Ventures Unlimited
3606 Woods Walk Blvd
Lake Worth, FL 33467

Edited by DM Eburn

A RISKY PROPOSITION
Book 1 of The Third Wish Duology

Copyright © 2012 by Dawn Addonizio
ISBN 978-0-9648418-4-0

First paperback printing November 2013

For information contact:
Dawn Addonizio
DawnsBoutique@Comcast.Net

This is a work of fiction. All of the characters, organizations, locales and events portrayed in this novel are either products of the author's imagination, or are used purely for fictitious purposes.

The Third Wish Duology is dedicated to:

Dr. Amy Kaufman – Who read it first as both a friend and an English professor, and kept me going with a priceless combination of encouragement and good feedback. I couldn't have done it without you!

My Mom – Who has always encouraged me to think bigger and better and to believe that anything is possible.

My Husband – Who inspires my fantasies…and makes them come true.

Ann C. Crispin & the attendees of her 2008 Writers Workshop at Dragon*Con (which was Amy's idea) – Thanks for the feedback & encouragement!

Much Love & Faerie Blessings Upon You All!   -Dawn

Table of Contents

Chapter 1 - Careful What You Wish For

"What the hell am I doing here? Ugh, I wish I was dead," I muttered as I shoved the ladies' room door open with more force than necessary. A dark-haired man at a nearby courtesy phone jerked his head in my direction. I looked down and quickened my step through the doorway, my pale cheeks heating in embarrassment.

I wasn't usually prone to such outbursts, but I had just found out that my husband was cheating on me.

Jeremy and I had been married seven years and I'd thought everything was fine between us. We still talked…laughed…had semi-regular sex. Money was okay. We could have used a little extra, but who couldn't?

And he had to go and screw it up by sleeping with some vapid little tramp that made eyes at him at the office.

I fought a fresh bout of angry tears as I stomped from the restroom and crossed the ritzy hotel lobby in search of the bar. My heels struck a sharp echo against the polished marble tile and I pushed my long brown hair past my shoulder, doing my best to ignore my discomfort over the near-indecent length of my cocktail dress.

Relief coursed through me as I escaped the naked space of the hotel foyer and made my way into an intimate corner lounge. I positioned my short skirt beneath me on the burgundy leather of a barstool and glanced up as the bartender approached from the dim wooden depths of his post.

He gave me a mocking look as I tugged at my hem. "What can I get for you this evening, madam?" he sniffed.

My expression hardened and I ordered a Grey Goose martini, foregoing a 'please' and my usual ready smile. I wasn't in the mood for his attitude. So what if he worked for one of the most exclusive hotels in the country?

My lack of friendliness seemed to have the opposite effect on him. His frosty demeanor warmed as he handed me my drink, and he was downright solicitous as he offered me a choice of two crystal bowls filled with bar munchies. Sad that being rude actually makes some people treat you nicer.

I sighed and sipped the icy vodka, realizing that this encounter wasn't helping my current, less than favorable, view of humanity. I managed to swallow without pulling a face, which would have ruined the sophisticated image I was attempting to cultivate.

No one here had to know that I was in a place I would normally never go, wearing a dress that was far more revealing than anything I would normally wear, drinking a drink I would normally never order.

I picked up the frilly pick with the olives and slid one free with my lips, chewing slowly as I glanced around the bar to give myself a break from the alcohol.

A couple sat in a booth off to one side. A generous sprinkle of salt and pepper dusted the man's hair at his temples. The obviously younger woman had not an ounce of fat on her, with platinum blonde hair and a red dress that clung to her tanned, surgically enhanced curves like a second skin.

Blech. His wife of fifty years, and the mother of his children, was probably waiting for him at home while he was out hoping his wealth could buy him a newer model.

A maddeningly fair voice in my head insisted that my opinion of men might be just a bit skewed at the moment. I nearly stuck my tongue out at it.

A guy closer to my age, several barstools down from me, caught my eye and raised his glass in a friendly salute. His eyes twinkled as if we were sharing a joke and I found myself smiling back at him. He made a questioning motion toward the seat next to me.

I gave a shrug of assent and he picked up his glass and moved to join me. Polite, but confident; I liked that. There wasn't anything not to like about his looks either—tall, lean and muscular, with chestnut hair and vivid green eyes. No sign of a wedding band.

That was lucky for him. I was in the mood to perform a Bobbitt on the next married guy who showed signs of cheating.

"Good evening. My name is Balthus." His voice was rich and cultured, with a faint accent that I couldn't put my finger on.

"I'm Sydney." I smiled and took his extended hand, wondering what kind of parents named their kid Balthus.

I had a firm handshake. Some men seemed to take it as a challenge and squeezed my hand painfully in return. But Balthus' grip was almost sensual, lingering for just a moment longer than necessary before he released me.

"Balthus—that's an interesting name," I commented, trying to ignore the tingling sensation that traveled up my arm at his touch.

"It's a family name," he explained, his mesmerizing eyes never breaking contact with mine. They appeared molten, almost as if flames burned within their depths.

If there was such a thing as vampires, they'd probably have eyes like this guy's, I thought.

"I'm pleased to make your acquaintance Sydney," he said in a velvet tone, "and I appreciate you allowing me to join you. Solitary drinking is never as entertaining as imbibing with a companion."

Ooh bonus—cute and well-spoken. I shook my head and chuckled at myself. Vampires—what a crazy idea! Besides, he was far too tan to be anything of the sort.

"Are you staying here at the hotel?" I asked.

"Yes. Just for the weekend, on business."

"And what type of business are you in?" I took a small sip from my glass, giddy that I was actually doing this: sitting in a posh bar, drinking a high-end martini, making small talk with an attractive stranger. I really hadn't been sure that I could pull it off. Years of faithful marriage can make for rusty flirtation skills.

"Oh, mostly trading and commodities," answered Balthus with a vaguely amused gleam in his eyes. "And what do you do, Sydney?"

"Well, a little management, a little advertising, a little bookkeeping," I responded with a dismissive wave. My job truly wasn't that interesting.

"Like a free-lance consultant," he surmised.

"I guess you could call it that." I grinned. It sounded better than Administrative Assistant, or any of the other titles I usually gave myself when people asked me what I did for a living.

"And are you here on business, or do you live in the area?" He took an easy swallow from his glass.

"I actually live about a half hour's drive away, but I work here on the island."

"And what is a beautiful woman like you doing here alone on a Friday night?" His voice was warm, but his smile was deliberately teasing. "Where is your husband this evening?"

"What makes you think I'm married?" I asked, playing along with a surprised tone.

He reached over and softly traced the faint tan-line on my ring finger. I forgot how to breathe for a moment as pure electricity crackled between us. It sent waves of awareness traveling across my skin and my gaze involuntarily jumped to his, finding a knowing look behind the heat in his eyes.

I took a gulp of vodka to steady myself, and as an excuse to look away. After seven years of monogamy, I wasn't used to even entertaining the sorts of feelings I was beginning to have about this man. My fingers played nervously over the stem of my martini glass as I decided how to respond.

"We're separated," I said finally. Not officially true, but I promised myself that it would be soon enough. Oh, Goddess—what were we going to do with the house? I shoved back a fresh pang of hurt at Jeremy's betrayal and looked up with shielded eyes to find Balthus staring at me.

"And what was it that separated you?" he asked, his voice just above a whisper.

My brow furrowed as I thought about whether I wanted to discuss this with a complete stranger. I supposed I was already well on my way past reckless this evening, considering the skimpy dress and the hotel bar. And talking to Balthus was cheaper than therapy—although not much, at Palm

Beach drink prices.

"He no longer possesses the qualities that I require for a relationship to work," I muttered.

A lazy smile spread across Balthus' face, its effects on my body stealing my breath once more. "And what might those qualities be?" His voice brushed over me like an intimate caress.

I hesitated, inhaled, and then said in a rush, "Respect and loyalty, for starters." I attempted to even out the breathless defiance in my tone.

His eyes held mine for a long moment, as if he was drawing the truth from me. They bathed me in heat, leaving me unable to look away.

"How could anyone be disloyal to you?" he asked, almost as if he was talking to himself. I could detect no guile in his manner, and the question hit so close to the center of my pain that I felt tears prick at the backs of my eyes.

Shit. I shouldn't have started talking about this.

Balthus broke our eye contact and cleared his throat, then took a long draw from his glass. I was embarrassed that he felt the need to give me a moment and I made a valiant effort to swallow back my tears.

"You know," he said, staring down into the ice-cubes at the bottom of his glass, "there is one sure way to forget about that type of disloyalty." Balthus' gaze captured mine again and the teasing warmth in his eyes, combined with his slow, sexy grin, seemed to help dislodge the lump in my throat.

"I'll admit," I began unsteadily, "I wish I could forget about my problems, even if only for a night. But don't tell me that you're suggesting I... reciprocate my husband's disloyalty with someone I just met," I continued in a chiding tone. "I hardly think that would do anything but complicate matters further."

Balthus laughed then—a deep, rich bass that seemed to resonate throughout my entire body. "Oh, Sydney, you are delightful," he chuckled with a shake of his head. "I think I'm going to enjoy getting to know you better."

"Oh really?" My brows rose at the assuming tone of his statement. A prickle of unease touched my spine, but I shrugged it off and told myself that I was being childish. I just wasn't used to interacting with men this way.

"That is, if you'll consent to conversing with me for a while longer," he replied smoothly. "You don't seem to be enjoying your drink." He pointed to the now-warm liquid that still filled half my glass. "Share a bottle of champagne with me?"

I hesitated as an increasingly fuzzy corner of my brain warned against accepting his offer. But my reserve faded and my inner alarm bells dissolved into a pleasant, carefree haze. Champagne sounded fun! And I was here to have fun, right? And to forget about…something.

Frowning, I looked up to find Balthus' expectant gaze centered on me. "So what do you say, Sydney?"

I blinked and gave him an uncertain smile. "Champagne sounds good." I suddenly felt as if I'd been holding my breath for hours and was finally letting it all out in one big rush. The relief was dizzying.

Balthus shot me a devilish grin and signaled the bartender.

An hour later I found myself a few shades past tipsy, and laughing merrily at something Balthus was saying as I accompanied him up to his tenth floor penthouse in a heavy marble and bronze elevator that opened directly into his private outer foyer.

As I waited for Balthus to unlock the penthouse door, however, that annoying, rational inner voice intruded once more. I scowled as it pierced my cloud of contentment, demanding to know what the hell I was doing getting drunk and going to some strange guy's hotel room. This was not normal behavior for me. Maybe I should slow things down and forgo Balthus' offer of a nightcap…

My thoughts stalled out as Balthus turned to me with a disarming smile and beckoned me through the door.

I trailed behind him, gaping at the most luxurious hotel room I'd ever seen. Balthus strolled forward into the suite's sitting room and halted behind an elegant freestanding bar trimmed in tawny leather and burnished metal rivets that matched the room's over-stuffed leather sofas.

Everything in the space, from the speckled fawn carpet to the ultra-modern fixtures to the Impressionist style paintings on the walls, had been chosen with exquisite care and taste. But it all paled in comparison to the breathtaking ocean panorama visible through the room's wall of expansive sliding glass doors.

"This view is incredible!" I made my way across the plush carpet toward the sprawling balcony. "Do you mind if I open the door?"

"No, go right ahead." Balthus indulged my enthusiasm. "Would you like another glass of champagne?" he called.

I turned, prepared to politely refuse, just as he popped the cork and began tipping some into a delicate crystal flute. My refusal died on my lips. I shook my head and found myself agreeing to a drink I knew I didn't need as I wandered out onto the balcony.

The night was warm, but the penthouse was high enough that the breeze took the edge off the heat. I breathed deeply, the tang of salt from the ocean air helping to clear my head. I leaned over the railing, enjoying the feel of my wind-tousled hair teasing the sensitive skin on my bare shoulders.

I felt Balthus' presence behind me and turned to accept one of the chilled crystal flutes he held. He gently reached to tuck a few strands of hair behind my ear, his fingertips gliding down my neck to linger warmly on my shoulder. His touch amplified the sensations I had already been enjoying, and I had to close my eyes and force myself to remain still against the wave of desire that blossomed through me.

"It's beautiful here," I prattled.

"It certainly has its charms," Balthus agreed with a smile. "I come here quite frequently, actually."

"This penthouse is fantastic. I wish I could live here." I shivered with growing anxiety.

Balthus' fingers tightened on my shoulder and I felt that odd prick of unease in my spine again. But then his fingers began a slow massage, dissolving away my tension as if by magic. He took my glass from my nerveless hand and placed it beside his on a nearby table.

"Why not?" he whispered. "Surely a woman as lovely as you deserves to live in such a beautiful penthouse. What else do you wish, Sydney?" he asked, his breath softly stirring the hair near my temple as he moved closer.

I leaned into the warmth of his body. "I wish…" Hmm…I was sure I wished a lot of things…but I could only seem to think of one desire as I stared up into the fiery depths of Balthus' eyes…

"That's enough," a disembodied voice interrupted from the darkness.

The words I had been about to speak died on my tongue.

A man appeared, as if he had melted away from the shadows of the wrap-around balcony to assume solid form.

I froze, furious with myself for having been so stupid as to go somewhere this private with a man I'd just met. Actually, it was more terror desperately trying to work its way up to fury—until I noticed that Balthus looked every bit as stunned as I did.

Holding onto the small morsel of relief provided by that, I clutched at his hands where they rested on my shoulders, trying to dissolve back into him and away from the other man.

My relief was short-lived as my gaze shot to the man's hand. He was pointing something at us. My breath caught in my throat and my brain screamed *Gun!* Panic swelled, excluding all other thought. Yet for some reason, my eyes kept trying to break in and signal my brain that something was off.

I didn't know much about weapons, but the one this man was holding looked rather odd. It seemed to be made entirely of tarnished bronze, and the finger loop at the back looked more like a handle than a trigger.

"Miss, step away from the djinn."

I had the distant thought that the stranger's tenor brogue sounded Irish. He stared at me expectantly, impatience tightening his features when I didn't immediately obey his command. My brain finally kicked into gear as I realized that, despite my attraction to Balthus, I didn't know him well enough to stand between him and a bullet. The thought eased my guilt as I began to inch away from him, my mind registering distractedly that the stranger had called him…the djinn?

I didn't get far before Balthus' grip tightened painfully on my shoulders.

"Stay where you are Sydney," he commanded. His cultured voice belied the unpleasant manner in which he held me. "She is mine, by right." He glared at the other man.

I stiffened, not liking the sound of that at all. "Um, I'm not sure what's going on here," I began, raking Balthus with an indignant glare, "but I really wish the two of you would just…"

"SHUT UP!" growled the man with the gun. "Not one more word if you value your pathetic life at all!"

My mouth snapped shut at his vehemence. "Ow!" I gasped as Balthus' fingers dug deeper into my shoulders, my own fingers scrabbling helplessly against his in an attempt to pry them out of the indentions I was sure they were making in my skin. It felt as if they were beginning to burn brands into my flesh. My panicked gaze flew to the man in front of us as his voice rang out with authority.

"Balthus of King Moab's tribe of the Ifrit djinn, in the name of Impellier, I sentence you to imprisonment for crimes against the Realm. In the name of Impellier, I summon you into containment until such time as the Realm sees fit to free you." He broke into the lilting syllables of a strange foreign language, his words taking on the tone of a well-practiced chant.

Not that I understood much of what he'd said in English.

But I did notice that, as the man continued speaking, Balthus' grip on me weakened. I took the opportunity to duck away from him and scramble back into the corner between the wall and the railing of the balcony, as far away from the both of them as I could get without taking a dive off the tenth storey.

The bizarre, chanting man blocked the escape I longed for—back inside the penthouse and into the elevator, down and away from this stupid, over-priced hotel full of assholes.

This whole night had been a mistake.

"She is mine by right!" Balthus insisted, a note of pleading breaking through his demand.

His words might have galled me more, if I hadn't been so damned scared, and if my brain hadn't started to register the fact that Balthus seemed to be…fading. His legs were going smoky and transparent, and the phenomenon was spreading slowly up his body. I blinked as my obviously damaged mind tried to convince me that the Balthus-smoke was drifting toward the barrel of the gun that the other man was pointing at him.

No. Not a gun, I realized. It was an old-fashioned, metal oil lamp. I couldn't do anything but stare—it was either that, or pass out. Come to think of it, unconsciousness might have been preferable, but I'd never been the type of girl to swoon.

"Sparrow, she's mine!" Balthus let out a thin, petulant wail, the smoky remains of his upper body drifting toward the opening in the lamp's spout and disappearing, as if he was being sucked into it by a vacuum.

"Shut it, Balthus," the man replied, sounding irritated. "You know damn well that if she'd completed the contract, you'd have already claimed her."

And with that, Balthus' smoky head vanished, and he was gone. I felt a mad giggle rise up into my throat as I watched the last of him get sucked into the narrow metal spout. My eyes rose disbelievingly to the stranger's face. He was gazing intently at the lamp, making a complicated hand gesture over it and whispering a series of unintelligible words.

Then he tucked the lamp into a pocket inside his jacket, where it disappeared without leaving so much as a lump or a crease. Surprising, but hardly worth comment after what I'd just witnessed. That task completed, he focused his attention on me.

I was hoping he'd have forgotten my presence, but no such luck. All the air left my lungs and the old phrase 'like a deer in the headlights' suddenly took on a very personal meaning. I searched desperately for a third option to my innate fight or flight response. I was trapped in the corner with him blocking the door, and somehow I didn't think I'd come out on top in a contest of strength.

The man had about a foot on me and he looked *solid*.

His eyes pierced mine for a long moment, and then he waved over the railing. "If your life means so little to you, you could just jump."

Then he turned and went inside the penthouse.

Chapter 2 - Contractual Obligations

Still frozen in place, although relieved to be alone on the balcony, I stared after the man who had vaporized my date for the evening. I wondered why his less than appealing escape suggestion had left me feeling more insulted than terrorized.

"*Asshole,*" I muttered, knowing damn well I wasn't brave enough to say it to his face.

I watched him through the sliding glass door as he performed a thorough search of the sitting room. He felt in the cracks of the sofa and chair cushions, and then dropped into a rather impressive push-up to peer beneath the furniture, before disappearing behind the bar.

I tried willing him to grab a bottle and drink himself unconscious, but apparently my Jedi mind trick needed some work. He reappeared from behind the bar and strode away unaffected. Oh yeah, I was supposed to make the suggestion out loud. Well, forget that—I wasn't getting any closer.

He proceeded to stick his head beneath each of the living room's lampshades, tracing the inner fabric with his hand. He even went fishing inside an opaque vase containing a tasteful arrangement of silk flowers.

I scowled when he upended the contents of my little black handbag over the dining room table. But he didn't appear to find anything of interest, so I stayed put. Riiight—like I would have gone after him just because he stole my favorite lip gloss.

Finally he appeared to be finished with the room and moved down an adjoining hallway.

I waited another minute in indecision, and then crept toward the sliding glass door. He'd left it open just far enough for me to squeeze through. I sucked in my stomach and shimmied past as silently as I could, then tiptoed over to the table. I quickly scooped my keys, lipstick case, cash, credit card and license back into my handbag.

I made a move for the front door, but froze when I heard him walk back into the room behind me. I slowly turned to find him watching me with an expression of tight disdain. I clutched my satin handbag in front of me, as if it might provide some protection.

"Erm," I gurgled, clearing my throat before I tried to speak again. "Can I go now?" I asked uncertainly, trying to decide what insanity had possessed me to stop my retreat toward the door. I could only guess that it was some instinct about not running and triggering a predator's chase response.

"You can do whatever you want, Miss," he said blandly.

I felt a modicum of tension leave my body at his words. He didn't seem to be the least bit interested in me—which, I reasoned, probably meant that he had no immediate plans to commit any heinous acts against my person. I started to feel a little braver, and fingers of curiosity poked at my brain.

"Would you mind telling me what happened out there?" I asked, trying for a polite, inquisitive tone.

He stared at me coldly. "I arrested Balthus."

"I gathered that—'imprisonment for crimes against the Realm' and so forth," I parroted, doing my best to temper my sarcasm. "I meant the part about…well…did I hear you call him a djinn? As in genie of the lamp?"

He sighed as if I was a tremendous source of annoyance, and then answered, "Yes Miss, Balthus is a djinn, and as you *clearly* saw, I confined him to a lamp for holding."

My remaining fear dissipated with the growing frustration his tone was causing. "Look, I don't mean to be dense, but I can't believe I'm having this conversation. Until tonight, I would have thought you were crazy if you'd suggested that djinns were real. If I hadn't seen it myself…well, I'm still not sure that I didn't hallucinate it. And why did he keep insisting that I was '*his by right*'?"

"Miss," he began, his condescension making my teeth grind so hard I expected to taste powdered enamel.

"Sydney," I interrupted, forcing a determined smile. "My name is Sydney. And you are?"

He closed his eyes briefly as if it was a great effort to be civil. "I'm Agent Sparrow. And Balthus insisted that you were his because you damn near were—you're two-thirds his already, and you were about two words away from sealing the contract."

"What contract?" I demanded in irritation.

"Balthus is a death djinn," Sparrow explained, slowly emphasizing each word as if I was mentally deficient. "You were one wish away from him granting your death wish, at which point your soul would have belonged to him."

"What!" I exclaimed. "My soul…*death wish*?" I spat incredulously, "I didn't wish for anything! What the hell are you talking about?"

"Look Miss…Sydney…" he corrected, palms up to prevent my interruption, "I have little patience for those who would throw their lives away so carelessly. You wished for death, Balthus intercepted that wish, and the contract was created. He first had to grant three wishes of your choosing. At the completion of the third, he would have granted your death wish and your immortal soul would have belonged to him."

No matter how much I would have liked to believe he was kidding—or maybe just clinically insane—considering the recent scene on the balcony, I had the sinking suspicion that he was deadly serious. My knees buckled and I stumbled backward, dropping onto the thick cushion of a nearby chair.

"I can't believe this," I muttered. "I didn't wish for death! I didn't wish for anything." I blinked at Sparrow, feeling increasingly faint.

He gazed at me, a flicker of uncertainty moving across amazingly blue eyes. "That's not possible. Not even Balthus can bend the rules that much. You must have wished aloud for death within his hearing at some point recently. I watched him stalk you to the bar. There's no other reason he would have been interested in you."

I shot him a glare, stifling the offended response that sprang to my lips. This was so obviously not the time to indulge my battered ego.

"I…I *jokingly* may have said out loud to myself that I wished I was dead earlier this evening," I murmured, remembering my words by the ladies room.

The more I thought about it, the more I realized that the man by the phones who'd overheard me had looked a lot like Balthus.

Sparrow gave me a look that said I had just proved his point. He walked past me and headed into the unexplored room opposite us.

"Wait a minute!" I exclaimed, following on his heels through a well-stocked kitchen and down a dim, lushly carpeted hallway.

When we hit the bedroom, I stopped in my tracks. The most gorgeous bed I'd ever seen dominated the space, its offer of tranquility almost too inviting to resist. A fluffy cream comforter was surrounded by four posters of glowingly polished cherry-wood, draped with gossamer silk curtains that sparkled in the muted light.

The surrounding furniture, also gleaming cherry-wood, was carved with a delicate and dreamy touch. Deep blue carpet, thick and soft, had me resisting the urge to slip my shoes off so that my toes could sink into it.

"Just one minute, Sparrow," I demanded distractedly, forcing my gaze away from the sliding glass doors leading out onto the room's private balcony. "Are you telling me that some stupid words I spoke to myself in a moment of…uncertainty…were enough to bind me to some crazy contract just because Balthus overheard them?"

I was going to say 'moment of weakness', but settled on 'uncertainty' because it irked me to add to Sparrow's obviously low opinion of me.

"You must have meant it when you said it," he insisted, his attention now focused on a thorough search of the bedroom.

"Oh, come on!" I threw my hands up in exasperation. "That's crazy. I was talking to myself, for Goddess' sake. Do you honestly mean to tell me that you've never voiced a thought, in a moment of anger, or grief, that you didn't really mean?"

I watched him and waited for him to deny it. If he did, he was either lying or he wasn't human…which, considering the experiences of the evening, was a frighteningly plausible possibility.

He paused in his search and eyed me in a considering manner. "Are you

Wiccan?"

"*What?* No…what does that have to do with anything?" I asked in baffled annoyance.

"You said, 'For Goddess' sake'—an unusual turn of phrase for most humans. I wondered if you were Wiccan. It might explain Balthus' attraction to you, especially if you have an aptitude for spell craft."

"No," I shrugged uncomfortably, "I don't follow any particular religion. It's just my way of balancing things out. I've never found much creditability in the popular assumption that the creator of the universe is a man."

Sparrow's lips twitched, the twinkle in his eyes making him appear genuinely amused. I found that I was smiling back at him in spite of myself.

"What do you mean when you say it's a weird thing for 'humans' to say? Does that mean you're not human?"

"I'm half human, half sidhe," he answered, turning to continue his search of the bedroom.

"She?" I repeated in confusion.

"It's Gaelic: s-i-d-h-e, pronounced 'she'," he explained. "We're a race of human-sized faerie folk from Ireland. I wouldn't expect you to know of us—few people do, especially outside of the homeland."

An unrestrained smile of wonder stretched my lips. "There are really faeries?"

Sparrow straightened from his perusal of a drawer to smile grudgingly at my excitement, "Is it so outlandish after seeing a djinn get sucked into a lamp? Yes, Sydney, there are really faeries."

I couldn't help it. I giggled. I'd always loved faeries.

"That's awesome. But I'm pretty sure you were about to tell me how Balthus could have overheard me talking to myself and turned it into a contract to take possession of my soul."

"Persistent little witch, aren't you?" He curled his lip at me, but his eyes held barely restrained laughter.

"I just told you I *wasn't* a witch." I snorted.

"Alright, Sydney, you win," he conceded with a helpless chuckle. "Balthus is obviously a criminal. Maybe it's not such a stretch that he didn't play fair. But the fact remains that, although he may not have followed the spirit of the law, he was most definitely bound by the letter of it. Even if only for a moment, deep within your soul, you had to have meant to wish for death."

His words knocked all of the wind out of my sails. The defeat must have shown in my eyes, because he looked at me with the first hint of sympathy I'd seen from him. "I'm sorry, Sydney," he said quietly.

Dejected, I wandered over to sit on the side of the bed. It wasn't just beautiful—it was the most comfortable thing I'd ever felt, like sitting on a cloud. "What are you looking for, anyway?" I asked morosely.

"Any objects that were magically tied to Balthus," he replied, his voice muffled by the door of the walk-in closet. "Such things can be dangerous to unsuspecting humans who find them. It's just a precaution—I doubt there's anything here," he continued as he stepped into the bathroom and flicked on the light switch. "He only checked in today."

After a moment he reappeared and took one last appraising look around. Then he strode over to gracefully lower himself onto the bed beside me. He sighed, his muscular arms distributing his weight as he tested the tension of the mattress. "Quite comfy, isn't it?"

His proximity sent awareness cascading through me, and for the first time I noticed just how attractive he was. His eyes were an incredible shade of deep blue, and they radiated warmth and kindness when he smiled. His tanned skin glowed with health, his dark hair looked touchably soft, and his broad chest appeared toned beneath his white shirt.

He smelled good too—a warm and woodsy scent that stole over me and set all my senses tingling.

Stubble roughened his features and the edge of a tattoo peaked from beneath the sleeve of his sports jacket, hinting at a ruggedness beneath his polished appearance. And that Irish accent of his definitely wasn't a turnoff.

Sparrow rubbed a hand wearily across his shadowed cheek. "Listen Sydney, I know you've had a rough night here. And I'm sorry if I made it worse by being hard on you earlier. You didn't deserve it. Is there anything I can do for you before I take off?"

I dismissed the absurd vision of him suddenly taking flight over the balcony railing. I hesitated to ask, but I needed to know—"What would Balthus have done to me if you hadn't shown up?"

Sparrow studied me before answering, a shuttered look dimming the warmth that brightened his eyes. "He would have claimed ownership of your mortality and your soul. You'd have died a mortal death and returned as an immortal slave, at Balthus' beck and call for eternity. If you had a talent for spell craft, he may have used you for that purpose."

Sparrow's gaze pierced mine as he continued, "But seeing as you claim no connection with that discipline, and judging from the interplay between you this evening, his interest was probably more...sexual in nature."

I blanched, visions of being forced into an eternity of sexual slavery filling my mind.

"That doesn't seem like much of a deal to me," I mumbled. "Three wishes and then I get to spend eternity wishing I was dead? How is that 'granting a death wish'?"

Sparrow exhaled harshly. "You make a good point, Sydney, and an objection that has been put forth many times. However, I believe that the implied death is that of your mortality and the accompanying loss of your soul. The granting of your additional three wishes and the gift of immortality is considered a fair trade.

"Not to mention that it becomes the responsibility of the djinn in possession of your soul to keep you in relative health and comfort, if only to protect his assets—an arrangement that some find preferable to the uncertainties of mortality, believe it or not. Granting of wishes aside, souls are valuable commodities. The death djinns' contract to gain them is ancient and cleverly worded."

I snorted. "Sounds convoluted and dishonest to me. And I still don't think Balthus should have been able to interpret what I said as a real wish." I couldn't help wanting to avoid the unsettling fact that, apparently, some part of me had truly wished to die tonight.

Sparrow placed a hand on my shoulder, his eyes glowing with a curious intensity. "I, for one, am glad you didn't really intend to wish yourself dead this eve," he replied, sincerity whispering through his lilting brogue.

My entire body shivered to life at his touch. His voice and his nearness were doing wicked things to my libido, and I mentally chastised myself for my shameless reaction. You'd think that after Balthus, my sex drive would have shut itself down for the night—if only out of self-preservation.

Sparrow stared at me for a moment longer and then stood, breaking the tenuous connection. Nonetheless, I couldn't help noticing the way the thin material of his shirt molded the muscles of his chest when he pulled his shoulders back. And my glimpse of a darker image beneath the taut white cotton had me heatedly imagining where else he might have tattoos.

"Well, I'm exhausted, and I've still got one hell of a report to write before I go home for the night. You should probably go ahead and get some sleep, Sydney," he advised as he pulled his jacket straight and made to leave the room.

"Sleep?" I asked in confusion. "You mean here?"

"Why not?" he asked over his shoulder.

"This is Balthus' hotel room, not mine," I called, thoughtfully keeping the 'duh' to myself as I pursued him through the penthouse and out the door into the foyer.

Sparrow snorted in amusement as he pushed the button for the elevator. "Not anymore. Haven't you been listening, Sydney? This penthouse is yours now. It was your second wish."

I was so astonished, my jaw dropped. "Are you sure?" I whispered.

"Yes, Sydney, I was standing right there." He laughed at my shocked expression. "You wished you could live here. The key's on the bar."

I could only stare; speech was a traitor that had deserted me.

"And by the way," he added as the elevator arrived and he stepped in, "I wouldn't make any more wishes out loud if I were you. You have an open death djinn contract—any one of them can fulfill it if you make your third wish within earshot.

"And they tend to have excellent hearing," he called out loudly just as the doors slid shut.

"*Of course they do,*" I muttered as I watched the tiny blue lights on the wall panel blink their way from 10P down to L. Mind reeling, I slowly turned and made my way back inside the penthouse.

<u>Chapter 3 - Ironing Out the Details</u>

The key to the most luxurious penthouse in Palm Beach was on the bar—just as Sparrow had said.

I plunked down on the buttery-soft leather couch and tried to collect my thoughts. Could I really stay here? Even if Sparrow was wrong about the wish thing, it wasn't like I would be charged for sleeping here. The hotel had Balthus' info, not mine. And for some reason, the thought of going home made me a little nauseous.

I tried to pinpoint why, but my brain kept going blank when I reached for an answer. With a sigh, I gave up and looked around the well-appointed living room instead. The silence was a little creepy, so I set my mind to figuring out how to turn on the huge, flat screen TV that eclipsed the wall.

The remote was easier to navigate than I feared, and the channel line-up appeared to be about the same as mine at home. I kicked off my heels and wiggled the circulation back into my toes as I flipped through the digital music stations. I debated over Salsa, and then settled on Light Classical.

It's hard to be freaked out when you're listening to something as upbeat as Salsa, but right now I figured I was more in need of serenity. I turned it up and pushed myself off the couch for a little barefoot exploration of the place.

The penthouse had a split level design with a spacious second bathroom and guest room down the hallway opposite the kitchen. I wandered back into the living room and ducked my head into the mini-fridge behind the bar, grinning when I found the half-full bottle of champagne.

It had been a rough night—I figured I deserved it.

I opened the sliding glass doors to the balcony so that I could hear the ocean and turned down the A/C to counter the warm air. Then I dimmed the lights and sank back into the supple cushions of the leather sofa, crystal flute of champagne in hand.

Waterford, and probably worth about $75 a glass, I noticed with weary amusement.

I let my mind drift as I sipped the champagne, enjoying the lyrical instrumentals that sighed from the speakers in soft counterpoint to the waves gently rolling onto the beach below. Before I knew it, I was finishing the bottle.

Stifling a yawn, I tipped the last of the champagne past my lips, savoring the bubbles on my tongue before I swallowed. Then I pulled myself up off the couch, determined to make use of the huge canopy bed.

A hint of Sparrow's clean, woodsy scent lingered in the air, and I wondered if I'd be seeing the handsome Irish detective again. Probably not if he could help it. Although, he *had* seemed to warm up to me a bit toward the end of our conversation.

I made my way through the kitchen and down the hall to the master bedroom, pausing to indulge my urge to sink my toes into the thick carpet. I wandered over to the bathroom, hoping to find some toothpaste so I could at least swish it around my mouth. I was pleased to discover both the paste and a new toothbrush wrapped in plastic.

I took off my jewelry and laid it on the vanity, dimmed the lights, then stood by the bed for a moment debating about the vulnerability of being naked. In the end I chose comfort and pulled my dress over my head, dropping it on a nearby chair.

I climbed between the soft, silky sheets and pulled the thick, cream comforter up beneath my chin, luxuriating in the feel of being snuggled in a warm cocoon. My eyes drifted closed and I smiled, exhaling deeply as I released the tension from my body.

Amazing...an actual genie...and three wishes, I mused. *And this penthouse was incredible.* I had one more wish to go; too bad I couldn't make it without losing my immortal soul. I frowned. That meant I had already made two. Sparrow said the penthouse had been my second.

What had been my first?

I began replaying the evening, my mind winding back up out of the comfortable peace it had settled into. What had I wished for between my first fateful comment to myself in the hotel lobby and my wish to live in the penthouse? My brow furrowed and my eyes shot open.

"What the hell did I wish for?" I whispered in consternation, my hands gripping the comforter anxiously.

"Relax, Sydney," chimed a tinkling voice from somewhere in the vicinity of my right ear.

I rolled to the left, nearly toppling off the bed as I frantically searched the room for intruders.

There, hovering just above the pillow next to mine, was the loveliest creature I had ever seen. It was a tiny woman, her delicate wings fluttering slowly and shimmering in the subdued light. She laughed at me in delight, and I felt a blissful grin spread across my face.

She stood approximately three inches tall, her shining dark tresses falling in cascading waves over her shoulders and down her back. She was barefoot and wore a knee-length iridescent dress that seemed to shift from blue to purple to green. Her skin glowed with silvery light, and her small, pointed face shone with happiness.

Somehow, in some deep place that defied memory or explanation, I knew exactly who and what she was.

"Lorien?" I whispered incredulously.

Her smile widened and pleasure lit her violet eyes as she nodded her tiny head in assent.

I had never seen her before, but I had *felt* her. I had spoken to her almost every day for as long as I could remember. I had never heard her answer, but some part of me had always believed that she was real and not just a product of my over-active imagination.

A distant memory tickled the back of my mind, of a time when I had simply accepted that faeries existed. I didn't have any sisters or brothers, and floating just beyond my grasp were vague memories of the tiny winged beings acting as my playmates when I was a small child. A haunting, unearthly music accompanied the vision, but sound and sight faded away before I could coax them into solidity.

I had no problem conjuring my very real recollection of trying to explain the faeries to my disbelieving older cousins. I had been teased mercilessly. In embarrassment and desperation to fit in, I had quickly abandoned my attempts to convince them. And in a way, I guess I had abandoned the faeries as well. But deep down, a piece of me had preserved the knowledge that they were real.

And some instinctive part of me knew that this being's name was Lorien, and that she was my faerie guardian.

"It took you long enough," she said with a grin.

"Hmm?" I mumbled dazedly, still staring at her in wonder as bright little spots of color began to dance across my field of vision.

"Sydney? Hellooo!" She waved both hands in front of me, but my body felt too relaxed to bother with a response, so I just smiled.

"Snap out of it!" she demanded, multihued sparks flying from her fingers as she darted toward me and snapped them in my face.

"Ow!" I exclaimed, my hand coming up to cover my nose against a sudden onslaught of prickling explosions. It felt like I'd snorted Poprocks and soda.

"Ooh, sorry about that Sydney," she breathed contritely. "Let me see."

I cautiously lowered my hand and went a little cross-eyed as she zoomed in closer to my nose and sprinkled a fine, silvery dust over the skin. I let out a violent sneeze, reaching up too late to cover my mouth. I searched for Lorien with a rueful expression, but she had darted out of the way before the blast hit her, and stood watching me again from the pillow.

"Faerie magic," she explained apologetically. "Sometimes it makes humans a little loopy. I wanted to snap you out of it before it made you too spacey to talk. Is your nose okay?"

"Yeah, it's fine," I sniffed, rubbing my fingertips over the tip. "It didn't really hurt, just gave me a shock. What was that anyway?"

"Fire dust." She shrugged in chagrin.

I stopped rubbing my nose and sat up straighter against the headboard, pulling the comforter against my nakedness. "I can't believe you're real!"

"Hmph," she rolled her eyes at me. "You *almost* believed more times than I can count. *I* can't believe all it took was that hunk of a half-faerie, Agent Sparrow, telling you faeries were real to push you over the edge."

I blinked at her and then laughed in disbelief. "Do you mean to tell me that all I had to do to be able to see you was to believe in you?"

"That's the way it generally works," she said dryly. "Even your popular fairy tales will tell you that much."

"Unreal." I chuckled, shaking my head in amazement.

She floated closer and looked me in the eye, sounding offended when she spoke. "You talk to me every day, Sydney. You've heard me when I was trying to lead you away from danger—remember last month when you took the long way to the office, even though you were in a hurry, and you just missed that horrible accident on the interstate? You even guessed my name—although I suppose it could have remained in your mind from childhood."

"I knew I remembered faeries from when I was little!" I cried triumphantly.

"Big whoop," Lorien muttered. "Children are natural believers. But no matter what I did, you couldn't bring your adult self to believe I was real until you heard it from that half-sidhe." She shook her translucent wings out in an indignant gesture.

"Actually, I think it was watching the djinn get sucked into the lamp that did it for me," I pointed out wryly. "If I hadn't seen that, I don't think Sparrow telling me faeries were real would have had nearly the same impact."

Lorien snorted. "Well, at least I'll win my bet with Eleanor."

"Who?" I shot her a confused look.

"Never you mind," she said with a pleased expression, "Just a friendly wager between sprites."

"Sprites?" I repeated questioningly.

"Yes, sprites," she replied in exasperation. "That's what we…what *I* am."

I kneaded my forehead. "I thought you were a faerie."

"A sprite is a type of faerie." She scoffed. "But I'm not here to give you a lesson on the faerie races. What we need to be discussing is this rather nasty situation you've gotten yourself into with Balthus. I tried to warn you about him, you know…several times, in fact!"

I sighed in frustration. "I knew something wasn't right with him. There was a kind of prickle in my spine when he said certain things to me, but I didn't want to believe it."

She nodded at me reprovingly. "You, of all people, should know better than to ignore that sort of intuition, Sydney."

"Yeah," I grumbled. "I remember feeling it the day of that accident, when I decided to get out of the turning lane for the interstate. I wish I'd…" My thought was interrupted by a violent sneeze.

"Shhh...Hush Sydney!" Lorien admonished in alarm, a sparkling red cloud of faerie dust drifting behind her as she flitted away from my nose and back to her perch above the pillow.

I sent her a watery glare.

"No more wishes for you," she announced, returning my glower.

"I doubt there's a death djinn hiding in the closet," I sniffed crossly.

"It doesn't matter! There might not be one for ten miles or there might be one ten feet away! The point is—you won't know until it's too late. You need to remove that word from your vocabulary until we figure out how to get this situation under control." She shook one tiny forefinger at me, her wings buzzing in agitation.

I pursed my lips sullenly and nodded in grudging agreement. I knew she was right, but being told what to do always activated my stubborn streak.

"I still don't think it was a fair contract," I grumped.

"Fair? Hello—death djinn! Since when has anyone trying to gain possession of someone's immortal soul ever played fair?"

She zoomed to the foot of the bed and looked back at me with a grin. "It's not all bad though; just look at this place!" she exclaimed, trailing iridescent green fairy dust around the room.

"It is pretty cool," I admitted.

"Oh, it's better than that!" she teased. "And you've not only wished yourself into physical luxury, but you did a pretty decent job of wishing yourself into an equally satisfactory mental state," she giggled.

"What does that mean?" I demanded, pushing myself upright again and fighting the bed's cushy invitation of softness.

She clasped her hands behind her back, her expression mischievous as she recited my forgotten words to Balthus, "I wish I could forget about my problems, even if only for a night."

I stared at her blankly. "What did I forget?"

Lorien bit her lip. "You spent a wish on forgetting it. Far be it from me to force the memory back on you."

"But what if it's important?" I argued with a pleading look.

Her gaze softened. "It's nothing you need to think about tonight, I promise. And the way you worded the wish means tonight is probably the only reprieve you'll get from it."

A weight settled in the pit of my stomach and an inexplicable wave of depression moved through me.

"It's no good worrying about it now," she said with a sad smile. "You made two rather clever wishes, I thought. You mortals have a nasty habit of creating pandemonium when given the freedom to make three wishes come true. But you've done amazingly well so far."

"Well, I guess I could have done worse than to lose a memory and gain a penthouse," I muttered.

"That's the spirit," she agreed merrily. "Just remember not to make any more wishes."

I frowned at the remnants of red dust on the comforter. "Yeah, I could do without you shoving more pepper up my nose," I said with a sniff.

"It's not pepper—it's faerie dust." She crossed her arms over her chest and looked at me with a disgruntled expression. "And if you can come up with a quicker, more effective way for me to shut you up, let me know."

I grumbled at that and then changed the subject. "I'll be able to see you from now on, right?"

"You'd be amazed at how much you can see when you actually *look*," she retorted.

"Hey, it's not my fault that life beat the belief in fairy tales out of me," I said with a yawn. "So what do we do now?"

"*I've* got somewhere to be, and I think *you* should try to get a good night's sleep."

My gaze followed her warily as she hovered above me. "I'm not sure I *can* sleep after everything that's happened." I yawned again. "It's not every night that I hook up with a death djinn and almost lose my soul." My eyelids began to feel heavy and I blinked. "And finding out that faeries really do exist…"

I noticed the deep blue dust that was slowly sifting down from Lorien's wings to sprinkle over me. "Hey," I mumbled feebly, "What are you…"

The last thing I heard before I drifted into unconsciousness was a soft tinkling laugh, and Lorien's voice echoing in my head, "Sleep well, Sydney. We'll talk again soon."

<u>Chapter 4 - The Daily Grind</u>

The rest of the weekend passed in a blur. On Saturday my first wish apparently expired, because the memories of Jeremy's betrayal came rushing back. I spent most of the day crying as I loaded up my station wagon with things from our house that I was bringing to the hotel, including my cat, Jasper.

Sunday I unpacked and decorated the penthouse with some of my stuff to make it feel more like home, and then I set up my office on the dining room table. I usually ate on the coffee table in front of the TV anyway, and I wanted to keep the guest room open for company. Not to mention I probably wouldn't get much work done in a room with a bed.

Now here I was, ready to jump back into work like a normal person, with no hint of faerie magic or death djinns anywhere in sight. It was a wonder that I wasn't cowering in the closet or wallowing beneath the covers in depression. I couldn't decide whether it was residual forgetfulness from the wish, or just my amazing aptitude for denial.

I'd lied to Jeremy and told him I was staying at my boss Hannah's spare apartment. It wasn't as if the truth was an option.

Hannah was a jewelry designer from France who owned a little couture shop called Haute Hannah's on Worth Avenue—the most exclusive place to shop in Palm Beach. She was a tiny spitfire of a woman in her fifties, the top of her head barely coming up to my shoulders. I had never seen her anything other than perfectly coiffed, and bedecked with as many of her most mammoth jewelry designs as she could cram into her ensemble for the day.

And she adored expensive French perfumes. Her small shop was permeated with an amalgamation of her favorite scents, ranging from spicy to flowery to cloying. The paperwork that I'd picked up from her a week ago still reeked of it. I worked from home doing her bookkeeping, making her travel arrangements, and taking care of her administrative needs.

Unfortunately Hannah's was only a part time job, so I also worked for Cindy, a permanently frazzled woman with an abusive husband named Leslie and an ungrateful teenage son named Mickey. Her husband was her 'boss' at their store, Designer Jewelry Direct, and he made her call him 'Mr. Horowitz' at work.

Mr. H, or 'The Horrorwitz' as I called him, was well known around Palm Beach for verbally flaying both innocent employees and customers who didn't spend enough money at his store. D.J.D. only stayed in business because he constantly advertised to bring in new clients and usually held his tongue for the big spenders.

He was a compulsive gambler who siphoned all the profits from the store during season, and kept things running during the summer off season by only paying the rent and utilities. Employees and vendors were left unpaid for months at a time through a campaign of Cindy's sob stories and Mr. H's threats.

This made things difficult with Hannah because she was one of their vendors. Whenever her bill came too far past due, she begged me to talk to Cindy for her, who would only give me empty reassurances to pass along. It always made me feel guilty and stuck in the middle.

I often thought about quitting my job at D.J.D. But it was convenient to work from home, and I did their online banking, so I always managed to get paid. Not to mention the fact that I felt sorry for Cindy, even though she sometimes drove me crazy.

Each time Mr. H scared away their office manager the responsibility fell on her to keep up with things until she found a new one. I was the most recent in a long series of them and she'd agreed to let me report directly to her so that I never had to deal with 'The Horrorwitz'.

I wrinkled my nose and settled back into the cream cushions of a heavy dining room chair, staring moodily around my new makeshift office. My laptop and printer were set up on the polished wood table, along with my fax machine and a cordless phone. My working file boxes were stacked neatly along the rear wall and my cache of office supplies resided in one of these.

There was a constant whisper of scratching sounds behind me, due to the fascination my cat, Jasper, had developed with the row of open boxes. He had an inordinate fondness for rubber-bands and paperclips, and seemed to have decided that this was some sort of breeding ground for them.

The first words out of my mouth that morning had been a rude result of my stepping on the pointy end of a bent paperclip that he'd managed to liberate onto the carpet. Jasper was smart enough not to be anywhere in sight when it happened. He no doubt knew that the earlier it was, the less charitable my mood tended to be.

The cordless phone rang and I frowned because I hadn't given the number to anyone yet. The caller ID read 'Cleaning Svcs' and my spirits soared immediately at the reminder of one of my new perks as a hotel resident.

"Hello Miss Corrigan, this is Angelica. Would it be convenient for me to come by to clean now? If not, I could come by later this afternoon." Her voice was sweet with a hint of huskiness, and an odd impression of warm, drizzling caramel flashed through my head. I blinked at the image and at her use of my maiden name.

The guy at the front desk had also called me 'Miss Corrigan', despite the fact that no one at the hotel should have known me by that name or any other. I guessed it must all be a part of the living in the penthouse wish.

I realized she was waiting for a reply and cleared my throat, "Um, yes, now would be great. Thank you."

"Sure thing. I'll see you in a minute."

She hung up, and soon after I heard a soft knock at the door.

I opened it expecting a woman in a subdued hotel uniform, but standing there was a six foot blonde in a French maid's outfit. And she made it look like naughty lingerie without even trying. I couldn't help gaping at her. It was like having a Victoria's Secret model show up to clean the house.

"Is there anything in particular you'd like me to focus on today, or should I just give everything the once-over?" She offered me a smile, and between her luminous blue eyes, perfectly straight white teeth, and infectious warmth—the effect was dazzling.

"Uh, the once-over would be great," I stuttered.

"No problem, Miss Corrigan," she replied cheerily, turning to pull some cleaning supplies from her cart.

"Thanks." I returned to my 'office', shaking off a strange reluctance to leave her side.

"Ooh, I love what you've done with the place!" she exclaimed as she stepped into the living room. "These pre-furnished rooms can feel so cold without a few personal touches. This is a lovely coffee table—so much nicer than that formal hunk of metal that was here before," she remarked as she began Windexing the scratched, glass surface of the table I'd brought from home.

"Thank you," I replied, taken aback by her friendliness. "Uh, the base was hand-crafted from driftwood by an artist that collected his materials from the beach. My Mom bought it before I was born."

"It's so *primal*," she commented, her voice dropping into a soft growl. "I love it! And look at all these adorable frogs!" She smiled at one of my figurines as she picked it up to dust it.

"Yeah, I've always loved frogs—as evidenced by their sudden take-over of the room," I added self consciously.

"It's important to surround ourselves with the things we enjoy. Did you know that there's a yoga pose called 'frog'?" she asked.

"Really? I've taken a class or two, but I don't know much about it," I answered as she paused in her dusting to glance up at me.

"The frog pose works to open the pelvic region. It's been known to initiate spontaneous orgasm in some women." Her eyes sparkled with contagious humor.

"Wow," I chuckled.

"Mmhm. Gave me one of the best orgasms I've ever had. Yoga can be an extremely enlightening practice. You may want to think about exploring it further." She grinned.

My eyebrows rose. "Maybe I will."

"Will it disturb you if I vacuum?"

"Not at all; thanks for asking."

I watched her disappear into the outer foyer, amazed at how comfortable she was discussing orgasms within the first five minutes of meeting me. Her openness felt natural and unassuming, though, and I couldn't help liking her.

She returned pushing a fancy vacuum with multiple attachments. As soon as she turned it on, Jasper went streaking from his hiding place behind the couch and gave her a baleful glare before he shot down the hallway toward the guest room.

I had set up his litter box behind a large potted palm on the main balcony, and the cat door was hidden behind the window treatments on the unused end of the sliding glass door—both purposely out of sight.

I had a suspicion that the hotel didn't allow pets, but now the cat was out of the bag, so to speak. Angelica switched the vacuum off and stared after the frightened feline.

"That's Jasper," I said in chagrin. "I wasn't sure if he was allowed, so I kind of snuck him in." I watched for her reaction.

Angelica blinked at me, reading the concern in my expression. "Oh, please don't worry Miss Corrigan. I would never abuse your privacy by talking about something I'd seen in your home! Be it your cat or something more *personal* in nature." She grinned suggestively.

I laughed in relief. "Thanks Angelica. And please call me Sydney."

"You're welcome. He looks like a beautiful animal. And what interesting markings! Is he black all over, except for one white spot on the tip of his tail?"

"Yep, pitch black except for that one speck of white ruining all his witchy-ness." I smirked.

She gave me an odd look and I got the feeling it was the witch reference. I made a mental note: *sex talk okay, but ixnay on the itch-way.*

"Anyway," I continued hurriedly, "thanks again for not ratting me out."

"Think nothing of it—I believe everyone should have the right to privacy and to conduct their lives the way they see fit...Sydney," she added with a belated smile.

She switched the vacuum back on and began a thorough sweep of the penthouse. I watched her for a moment, wondering at her odd choice of words, and then I decided I'd better get to work as well.

I called Cindy to give her my new phone number and the banking update. I rolled my eyes and jotted down some things she wanted me to do, like printing and faxing her emails to her, and checking the results of a horse race for Mr. H, who was screaming at her in the background.

Then I listened to her complain about money for a while before reminding her that the electric and telephone were past due. I knew she didn't want to hear it, and therefore it was the quickest way to get her off the phone. It worked like a charm.

As we hung up, I could hear Angelica humming softly from the hallway. "You know, Sydney," she commented as she carried the used bedding to her cart, "depending on your partner's height, that tall bed of yours would be perfect for certain standing positions."

I blinked after her in confusion, exhaling in amusement when her words sank in. She disappeared back into the bedroom, apparently unconcerned with receiving a reply to the observation.

She moved into the kitchen next, which I had barely touched, but she found my tea mug in the sink and stuck it in the dishwasher. She emptied all the wastebaskets and wiped down the balconies; she even dusted the ceiling fans. When she was finished, not a fleck of dirt or clutter was left anywhere. And it had taken her less than an hour.

"Well, I think that's about everything. I saw your laundry basket, but I wasn't sure if you were ready to do a wash. Would you like for me to start one?"

"No, thanks—I should do something myself or I'll be *completely* spoiled. I'm not sure I'll ever be able to survive without you again as it is," I joked.

"It's my pleasure," she replied sincerely. "I actually enjoy cleaning. There's something calming and almost sensual about the repetitive physical movements. So if you need anything, just put a call into Cleaning Services and ask for Angelica. Otherwise, I'll plan to come by again on Thursday."

I thanked her again as I saw her out the door and she pushed her cart into the elevator. I wasn't sure about the sensual properties of cleaning, but I fully intended to let Jeremy cover our mortgage for a while and redistribute some of my freed-up cash into tips for Angelica.

∞∞∞∞∞∞∞∞∞

After forcing myself to concentrate on work for a couple more hours, I made my way down to the garage and hopped in my station wagon to pick up some paperwork from Cindy and do the grocery shopping for the week.

Staying at the hotel cut my usual half hour commute down to five minutes. It was great, but there was no way I was telling Cindy or she'd have me running errands all day. I called to let her know I was outside and pulled up near the rear entrance. I waited for a moment before I saw her bustle backward out the door, calling, "Yes, Sir!", no doubt to Mr. H. My not having to go inside and risk a confrontation with him was part of our working arrangement.

Cindy was a plumply attractive woman in her fifties with dark blonde hair and grey eyes. She struck me as someone who'd probably been a cheerleader in high school.

When I saw her, she usually sported a smile and kept up a rash of convivial chatter. And she never seemed to stop moving, although that might have had more to do with avoiding her husband's tirades than anything else.

Her clothes tended to be rumpled, but she was never without at least one piece of expensive jewelry—supposedly borrowed from D.J.D. to be worn for advertising purposes. I wasn't sure how many of those 'borrowed' pieces actually found their way back to the store to be sold, though.

She rushed forward when she saw me. "Hi, Sydney, what's up? What a day! Mr. Horowitz is on the war path. You brought my checks? Good. Thanks. Here's your stuff. Was there anything else...no, I don't think so. I'll talk to you in the morning." She handed me my bag of paperwork for the week and hurried back inside in usual frenzied Cindy fashion.

As I was getting back into my station wagon, a black Hummer pulled up next to me. I smiled and waved briefly at Mickey, Cindy's seventeen year old son. The teenager waved back instead of giving me his usual sulky nod, then leapt down from his vehicle and began heading toward my driver side window.

As opposed to the tattered black wardrobe I expected to see hanging from his lean frame, he looked neat in crisp blue-jeans and a red polo-style shirt. His hair was trimmed so that his blue-grey eyes were visible, and although it was still dyed black, it shone soft and clean, instead of lank and greasy. He had even removed his facial piercings, leaving only a single stud in his right ear.

He hovered about a foot away grinning at me and I had no choice but to roll down my window.

"Hey, Mickey, you look a little different than the last time I saw you," I said with a chuckle of disbelief.

"Hey, Sydney, what's up?" he asked eagerly.

"Not much, just dropping something off for your Mom."

"Oh. That's cool." Mickey bent down to rest his elbows on my windowsill and peered around the inside of my station wagon with interest. "Nice car, Sydney. All leather interior?"

My eyebrows drew down together as I stared at him. "Thanks. Yeah, it's leather. Did you need something?" I hoped that didn't come off as rude, but his sudden interest in me was strange.

"Well, actually," he said, giving me a coy smile that looked wrong on his sallow face, "I was wondering if you'd have a cup of coffee with me sometime. I mean, I know you're working right now, but maybe after you get off, or some time this weekend?"

I bit my bottom lip and studied him, working out how best to phrase my response. "Mickey, you seem like a nice kid. But I'm not sure your parents would approve of us spending time together on a personal level." *Was he asking me out on a date?*

"Aw, come on Sydney. It's just coffee. I won't tell them if you won't," he cajoled. He grinned at me in what I was sure he thought was a charming manner.

I snorted. "I'm almost twice your age. Why would you want to hang out with me? Is there something you want to talk about, or…?" I trailed off, unsure what else to say.

"I just think you're really nice." He smiled and took a step back from my car. "I thought we could talk about my parents and stuff. I bet they drive you crazy too."

My eyes widened. Of course they drove me crazy, but I was their employee, and I wasn't about to discuss it with their son!

"Sorry, I just don't think it's a good idea," I replied in a choked voice. I hit the button to close my window. "See you later, okay Mickey?" I called as I reversed out of the lot.

"Could my life get any weirder?" I muttered.

I turned in the direction of the supermarket and tried to shake off the encounter by focusing on my grocery list. I wanted to make sure I had extra supplies since my friend Sunny was due to fly in from Boston on Friday afternoon. We had been planning the visit for several weeks, since before the whole Jeremy thing and all the craziness that followed.

I hadn't seen Sunny for about a year and I was really excited. The trip wasn't only about me—her cousin Rachel was due to have a baby and if she didn't go into labor by Friday they were going to induce. But Sunny had promised I could have her to myself for the rest of the time.

I would definitely need to pick up some coffee. Despite the 'greet the day cheerfully' picture her name implied, Sunny required an infusion of strong, black coffee to dezombify herself in the mornings. There was no way that my usual tea was going to do it for her.

I ran over my list in my head as I pulled into a parking space and prepared to do battle with the afternoon brigade of wealthy Palm Beach shoppers. This was the only grocery store I'd ever seen that offered valet parking, and the attitude of entitlement carried over from the parking lot into the store.

Sure enough, a stiff-lipped woman in huge sunglasses and chunky gold jewelry swept past me to grab the last cart. I sighed to myself and wondered if driving to the less affluent supermarket across the bridge wasn't worth the extra time.

I decided against it and walked around to the exit doors to grab another cart. I was already here, and besides, it wasn't the woman's fault that the surgeon had pulled her face too tight for her to smile.

When I passed her again during my first sweep down the dairy aisle, I saw that her expression had turned even more sour. She was attempting to ignore the fact that the wheels of her cart were intermittently making an awful screeching noise.

I smirked as I reached to grab a tube of cinnamon roll dough, and froze when Lorien suddenly appeared hovering there next to the image of the Pillsbury Dough Boy.

She grinned and whispered, "See, Sydney—you didn't want that cart anyway."

"So nice to see Karma in action," I mumbled sarcastically.

"Sometimes it just needs a little nudge." She winked and then she was gone.

I'd seen neither hide nor hair of her since Friday night and was beginning to wonder if I had imagined her.

I snorted quietly and finished up my shopping in a considerably lighter mood.

Chapter 5 - Revelations

"So, do you want to talk about it?" asked my friend Sunny as she stepped off the elevator into the outer foyer of the penthouse, each hand laden with a mismatched overnight bag.

"Not really," I answered dryly, knowing the 'it' was my husband's infidelity, since I hadn't told her about the death djinn situation yet.

She was going to be the first person I told about my recent foray into the supernatural. I was nervous about how she'd react. I only hoped she wouldn't decide that my mind had cracked along with my marriage.

She followed me through the door, tossed her bags onto a nearby chair, and then assaulted me with a bear hug. She knocked me backward, despite her smaller frame, as I laughingly returned the embrace.

"Ooh, I missed you so much, Syd. And this place is amazing!" she exclaimed with an excited twirl that sent her colorful patchwork skirt billowing.

"How did you end up staying in a penthouse at the most exclusive hotel in Palm Beach? You promised to tell me when I got here. You were so mysterious on the phone!" She brushed a dark curl from her mouth and placed her hands on her hips, narrowing her smoky green eyes at me.

I chuckled. "Why don't we sit down and have a drink while I tell you? That way, if you decide to call the nice people in white coats to come take me away, I can just blame it on the alcohol."

"I would never!" She gave me an indignant look and looped an arm through mine, hauling me over to the freestanding bar in the corner. "So, what's good for inducing insanity? Oh, hello Jasper!" Sunny bent down to briefly scratch behind Jasper's ears as he twined himself between her legs in greeting.

I had few close friends that I'd kept in touch with throughout the years, and Sunny was one of them. We'd known each other since middle school, but had become best friends in high-school. There was a measles scare and all of the students whose vaccination records weren't up to date had been quarantined in the school gym for two days while they arranged for mass inoculations.

Sunny and I spent the entire two days huddled side-by-side on the bleachers, comparing boys, books and music we liked, and talking about everything else under the sun. I'd never made another friend like her since.

Sunny began rattling glass bottles around as she explored the fully stocked bar. She whistled in appreciation. "This is the stuff they keep in the locked cabinet *above* the top shelf. You've finally won the lottery, haven't you! That's it, isn't it? I can't believe you didn't tell me!"

"How I got into this place is *way* more unbelievable than hitting the lottery. Champagne?" I suggested, pointing to the mini-fridge built into the bar cabinet.

I had been ecstatic to discover an entire case of the stuff in the small utility room near the kitchen. Sunny pulled a bottle from the fridge as I grabbed the Waterford flutes and motioned her over to the sofa.

"Sinfully rich, darkly handsome, wickedly sexy and enormously endowed sugar daddy?" she asked hopefully, plopping down beside me and removing the foil from the cork.

I snorted. "Sort of. If you want to put an extremely euphemistic spin on it."

Balthus had been all of those things. Granted, I hadn't had a chance to find out about his endowments—but as he was a creature with the ability to make wishes come true, it was probably a safe bet he wasn't lacking in that area. Unfortunately, trying to steal my soul trumped any of his desirable qualities.

Sunny stared at me expectantly, her expression shifting to a frown at my hesitation to elaborate. I watched in amusement as she popped the cork, filled the expensive crystal glasses and then placed them next to the bottle on the scratched glass of my old coffee table.

Then she turned to me and her hands snaked out to grab my shoulders and shake me. "Enough!" she yelled. "Spill, Spill, SPILL, you insufferable wench!" She unerringly found the ticklish spot on my side and set upon it without mercy. "NOW!"

In response to my screech of protest, Jasper, who had curled up on a nearby chair, raised his head to glare at us. I could almost see his black brow twitch in disdain at our childish antics.

When I could breathe again, I haltingly began to tell Sunny about coming to the hotel Friday night and how I met Balthus at the bar and then followed him up to his room. She grinned appreciatively at my description of him and kept interrupting me with suggestive questions and innuendos.

When I finally got to the part about Sparrow showing up on the balcony with the lamp and Balthus going all smoky and disappearing, she just laughed in an 'Oh, that's a good one Syd—you got me!' sort of way.

When it slowly dawned on her that I wasn't kidding, she downed the rest of her champagne in one gulp and silently got up to retrieve another bottle. After that she didn't say a word until I'd completed the story, including Lorien's appearance on my pillow later that night, and how I completely forgot about Jeremy until the next morning.

By the time I finished we were on bottle number three.

"That's some tall tale, Syd," she said at last, her speech slurred.

"I wish that's all it was," I said blithely. Not only was I high on the champagne, but it felt damn good to tell a fellow human what had happened to me after keeping it to myself for a week.

Sunny stared at me wide-eyed and I giggled at her expression for a moment before I realized I'd spoken the forbidden word. I slapped a hand over my mouth just in time to cover a sneeze.

"I *told* you not to say that word!" grumbled a tinkling voice. "And if you're going to get sloshed and talk about me, the least you could do is invite me. Ooh, champagne, my favorite!"

I swung my head toward the sound, waited for my blurred vision to clear, and then smiled at Lorien through a sparkling red haze of faerie dust. "Lorien, Sunny" I gestured, "Lunny, Sorien. Um, sorry, you guys know what I mean."

I gazed expectantly at Sunny, who was looking somewhere off to Lorien's left with narrowed eyes and an expression of utter confusion adorning her heart-shaped face. My head tilted back toward Lorien to find her dipping a thimble-sized earthenware jug into my champagne flute.

She took an experimental sip and sighed in approval before carefully settling on the edge of the glass tabletop with her bare feet swinging over the side.

"She can't see me," Lorien said smugly.

"What? But you said believing is seeing!" I settled my eyes back on Sunny, who was watching me with an air of concern.

"She thinks you've taken a spin on the loopy locomotive," giggled Lorien, already helping herself to a second jug of my drink.

I snatched my glass away indignantly and turned to Sunny. "I have not taken a ride on the *loopy locomotive*," I insisted. She licked her lips and looked at me as if she thought it might be time to call the nice folks in white coats after all.

Jasper leapt nimbly from his chair to the carpet and stalked around the coffee table. He deposited himself directly in front of Lorien, his bright jade eyes fixed on her and the stark white tip of his black tail twitching. An indulgent expression crossed Lorien's face as she reached out and sprinkled a light peppering of green faerie dust over his dark muzzle. He promptly began to purr and rub his head against the driftwood base of the coffee table.

I huffed in annoyance. "Apparently Jasper can see you. Why can't Sunny?"

"She doesn't truly believe?" Lorien suggested, gazing longingly at my glass.

I jerked back to face Sunny. "You don't believe me!" I accused in a wounded tone.

"Of course I do!" she claimed defensively. "It's just a lot to take in— death djinns, and hot half-faerie detectives, and faerie guardians...I'm trying," she mumbled.

"Can't you sprinkle her with faerie dust or something to make her see?" I begged Lorien.

"That'll just make her sneeze," she smirked. "She has to really believe."

I thought for a minute. "Okay, Sunny. Lorien's going to make you sneeze."

Her eyebrows shot up skeptically and I ignored the added insult to my sanity.

"What I mean is, she's going to sprinkle you with faerie dust and it's going to make you sneeze. Will you believe me then?"

"You want me to believe faeries exist because I sneezed?"

"No," I said with as much dignity as I could muster, "I want you believe that faeries exist because faerie dust is going to make you sneeze exactly when I predict. And because I'm your best friend and I *say* faeries exist."

"How do you know faerie dust will make me sneeze?"

I blinked at her. "It makes *me* sneeze."

"Maybe you're allergic to it," she suggested, unconvinced.

I looked imploringly at Lorien, who was in the process of sneaking jug number three from my glass.

"What?" she said innocently.

"How do you know faerie dust will make *her* sneeze too?" I asked, ignoring the fact that my faerie guardian was apparently a lush. In my present state, I was in no position to judge.

"Oh, faerie dust makes *all* humans sneeze," she assured me with glee.

"Lorien says it makes all humans sneeze," I relayed. Then I narrowed my eyes, "Unless, of course, you've been hiding your non-human origins from me all these years?"

Sunny snorted.

"Right," I breathed. "Okay then—Lorien, do your stuff!"

Lorien plunked her faerie-sized champagne jug on the coffee table and zoomed crookedly over toward Sunny's nose.

"Sneeze!" I directed in smug amusement a split second before Sunny broke out in a sneezing fit, right on cue. A thick cloud of green faerie dust hung in the air just in front of her face.

I waited a moment, but it didn't seem to be dissipating and Sunny's sneezing was becoming more violent. I waved my hand briskly to clear the air, succeeding only in brushing the cloud toward myself and instigating my own sneezing fit.

I attempted to glare at Lorien through watering eyes. "Lorien! You used too much!" My complaint was cut short by three exploding sneezes in quick succession.

The sparkling cloud finally dispersed to reveal Lorien laying back on my coffee table, her overturned jug dripping miniscule drops of champagne onto the glass top as she rolled around in hysterical laughter. A cluster of small, iridescent bubbles drifted around her, swirling away in all directions as she flailed from side to side.

Jasper echoed her movements, rolling playfully on the carpet beneath her and batting lazily at stray bubbles with one fluffy black paw. His eyes were bright and intense, as if he was zonked out on some particularly high-grade catnip.

"It's not funny," I wheezed. "And where are all those bubbles coming from?"

Lorien hiccupped delicately between guffaws, emitting a stream of the tiny shimmering spheres.

"You hiccup bubbles?" I asked in disbelief.

She only laughed harder.

I gave up trying to obtain a response from the obviously intoxicated faerie and turned back to Sunny with an apologetic sniffle. She was perched on the edge of the sofa, leaning forward with her mouth gaping open in amazement as she stared at the coffee table.

"You can see her!" I exclaimed in delight.

"Wow," she whispered, "that's a faerie."

I harrumphed. "Gold star for you."

"What's the matter with her?" she asked me out of the side of her mouth. She reached forward as if she intended to poke Lorien, who was still lying prone on the coffee table, clutching her sides in fading mirth as the last of the hiccup-bubbles popped out of existence.

Lorien guessed Sunny's intention and darted upright and away from her to hover next to my glass with a fierce glower. "Hey! Watch the poking there, Sunshine!"

"Sorry!" Sunny said contritely, jerking her hand back, but continuing to stare at Lorien in fascination.

Lorien brushed herself off and righted her jug on the table with a disgruntled expression.

"So sparkly…so pretty," whispered Sunny in a fawning voice.

I looked at her askance as she made another grab for Lorien, who again darted out of the way.

"Oh, for the love of the Seelie Court! She's a grabby one, isn't she?" Lorien, apparently having recovered from her inebriation, zipped over to hover in front of Sunny's face. She made a snapping motion and a colorful burst of sparks exploded from her fingertips, making Sunny blink in rapid succession.

"What the…" Sunny muttered, her eyes sharpening into focus. She shook her head as if to clear it. "What happened?"

"Faerie magic." I grinned. "Makes us humans go a bit addle-brained. You just needed a little fire dust to jolt you back into reality. You're lucky you didn't get any up your nose."

Sunny's eyes followed Lorien with avid curiosity as she scooped up another jug of champagne and settled herself back on the edge of the coffee table.

"Don't you think you've had enough? Just a minute ago you were rolling around on the table spewing bubbles and cackling like a lunatic," I pointed out.

"I have a quick metabolism." Lorien shrugged.

I followed her lead and topped off both the Waterford flutes with the remaining champagne, gently placing Sunny's in her hand. She looked a bit stunned and I knew exactly how she felt.

"What was that you said before…'for the love of some kind of court'?" I asked, wondering about the unfamiliar phrase.

Lorien looked at me without comprehension for a moment, then said, "Oh, you mean 'for the love of the Seelie Court'? Right. That's an expression you might hear me use when, say, some lumbering human comes along and tries to crush me in her sticky, oversized hand."

She shot a dirty look at Sunny, who had the grace to appear chagrinned.

"What's the Seelie Court?" I asked.

Lorien blinked at me in astonishment and shook her head. "Sometimes I forget how woefully ignorant you humans are."

"Thanks," I drawled. "I guess I neglected to read that comprehensive guide to the faerie world you gave me."

"You have a 'Comprehensive Guide to The Faerie World'?" Sunny whispered in amazement.

I gave her a half shake of my head to let her know I was kidding. She looked a little crestfallen.

"Here's a lesson, then," Lorien drawled. "The Seelie Court is the most powerful body of faerie folk in existence. Simply stated, its members are responsible for keeping the balance of good and evil in check. Without them, the magical entities aligned with evil would take control and chaos would overcome all the realms. You humans wouldn't stand a chance." She snorted derisively.

Lorien intercepted the look of shock Sunny and I shared and folded her arms over her chest, her still-dangling bare feet twitching out an annoyed rhythm. "What—did you think faeries just flitted about all day watching to make sure you got a good parking spot? Humans," she grumbled, "they always think they're the center of the universe."

"What kinds of evil entities?" I asked, ignoring her slight.

Lorien took a swig from her jug, throwing her free hand up as if to indicate that there were too many to list, and then surreptitiously using it to cover another bubble-inducing hiccup.

"There are a few races that are predisposed toward evil…trolls and goblins, for instance, are generally rather nasty creatures." She wrinkled her nose in distaste. "But anyone or thing can align themselves with evil—mortal and immortal alike."

"Well, death djinns must be evil, right?" I asked slowly, a thought beginning to form in my muddled brain.

"Yeah," Sunny agreed, catching on. "Anyone who tries to steal your soul *must* be evil. I bet this Seelie Court would overturn Balthus' contract in a flash!"

Lorien pursed her lips and gave us an apologetic look. "I'm afraid it doesn't work that way. Balthus' contract for Sydney's soul was legal. And the Seelie Court isn't like one of your human courts of law—they don't deal with such mundane matters."

"Mundane?" I sputtered.

"As much as I don't want to see you lose your soul, Sydney, I guarantee you the Seelie Court isn't going get involved in the details of a standard death djinn contract," she replied ruefully.

"But Balthus was arrested—he's a criminal!" I insisted.

"And for that, he'll go before the king of his tribe and a tribunal assigned by the Court to answer for any laws he's broken. I have it on good authority that he was arrested for being in possession of an unaligned soul. It was just lucky for you that Agent Sparrow stopped him when he did." She shot me a meaningful glance.

"Unaligned soul?" I asked, shuddering at the reminder of how close I'd come to becoming Balthus' eternal sex slave.

"A living soul that's lost its ties to a mortal body—kind of like a lost soul, I guess you'd say. There are strict guidelines for the soul trade. A soul can only be legally taken if a mortal has willingly given it up. It's *possible* to take an unwilling soul, of course, but only a dark mage would attempt such a thing. Possession of an unaligned soul is a serious crime."

"Sydney wouldn't willingly give up her soul!" Sunny cried. "And you just said that if it's not willingly given, no death djinn can legally take it. They can't hold her hostage forever to a wish she doesn't even want, can they? Can't we talk to the king of the tribe, or whoever, and get the contract cancelled?"

Lorien grunted, earning frowns from both of us. "You want to appeal to the king of the death djinns in order to overturn a contract for which he himself created the terms? His people have been profiting from the soul trade for millennia. You can bet your sweet wand that he's not going to do anything to jeopardize the legal status of their standard contract."

My shoulders drooped at her words. I had begun to believe that we were on to something.

"Can't you at least put a spell on her to keep her from saying the word 'wish'?" asked Sunny.

I brightened. "That's a great idea! Why didn't I think of that?" I beamed at her.

"It would violate the terms of the contract," Lorien said with a sigh, dashing my hopes yet again. "And before you start racking your brains for more clever little loopholes, she can't *wish* for anything that will interfere with the contract, either."

I was suddenly ashamed that I hadn't spent the last week thinking up witty third wishes that would outsmart the death djinns and leave my soul, and preferably also my new penthouse, intact and in my possession.

"Well, how *are* we going to get Sydney's contract cancelled, then?" Sunny demanded in frustration.

"I'm still working on it. I've been researching death djinns and their involvement in the soul trade. I haven't found anything that I think will help us to void the contract yet, but I'll figure something out. Just because it's never been done, doesn't mean it's impossible!" Lorien enthused.

But her wings seemed to lack some of their zip as she headed toward my glass for another refill, hiccup-bubbles trailing behind her.

Sunny and I exchanged glances. She took a deep breath and gave me a smile that I knew was intended to bolster my confidence.

Jasper leant his support by choosing that moment to leap into my lap. I grunted at the sudden impact of his weight and helped him to curl into a position that was comfortable for both of us.

"So, what's with the hiccupping bubbles, anyway?" Sunny asked Lorien. I was grateful for the change of subject, but I couldn't stop thinking about the danger I was in.

"It only happens when I drink champagne," Lorien explained, looking embarrassed.

"What about absinthe? They call it the 'Green Fairy'—any connection to real faeries?" Sunny asked.

"Actually, humans gave it that nickname because it allowed them to suspend their disbelief long enough to get a peek into the faerie realm," Lorien answered. "But even when they do glimpse one of us, most humans just chalk it up to hallucinating when they come down from the stuff."

"Really?" Sunny queried, her gaze sharpening on Lorien with genuine interest. "That's fascinating! I smoked some laced pot once in college and I could have *sworn* I saw a leprechaun eating a sandwich under the oak tree in our back yard…"

I sat quietly sipping the golden liquid remaining in my glass and absently stroking Jasper's silky fur, as Sunny quizzed Lorien on the effectiveness of various mind-altering substances at heightening human sensitivity to the faerie realm. It was a discussion that would have normally intrigued me, but I was beginning to feel distinctly discouraged about the likelihood of figuring out how to hold onto my soul.

I couldn't rely on Lorien alone to get me out of this mess, I realized. I needed to have my own plan. The problem was, I knew nothing about death djinns and somehow I didn't think a few hours at the library or surfing the web was going to help.

The one thing I did know was that if I ever saw Balthus again I was going to keep my mouth shut and let my feet do the talking—right from my shoe to his crotch. Maybe if I kicked him hard enough he'd wish he never met me and it would solve both our problems.

<u>Chapter 6 - Infatuations</u>

"Mmm…peppermint mocha," I sighed, inhaling the minty, chocolaty, caffeine-packed wonder. I wasn't usually one to jump on the corporate bandwagon, but Starbucks made a damn good coffee drink.

Sunny grinned at me from the passenger seat of my station wagon. She was on her third dose of the black jet fuel she drank, the first two cups at my penthouse having barely brought her out of her morning coma. Now we were both riding the high from the caffeine, and the sugar rush from cinnamon rolls drenched in gooey cream-cheese icing.

"I'm not sure how long this visit's going to last—Rachel sounded exhausted on the phone," Sunny commented between sips.

"Well, she did just pass a ten pound human being through her body. I'd be exhausted too."

"I'm *never* having kids," Sunny stated with an adamant head shake.

I chuckled, ignoring the twinge of sadness I felt. Jeremy and I hadn't been sure if we were ready for kids either, but we'd been thinking about it.

Best to put that out of my mind—along with the message from him I'd retrieved earlier that morning, quietly asking for me to come home, or at least meet with him to talk.

I'd been returning his calls so he wouldn't worry, but only when I knew he was at work. The cheerful "Hi! You've reached Sydney and Jeremy!" on the voicemail was a real kick in the ass, but it was better than the inevitable sob-fest that I knew talking to him would bring.

Maybe it was juvenile, but as far as I was concerned, there was no excuse for what he'd done, and nothing left to say.

I turned into the parking lot for the hospital, commencing a slow drive through one of the parking rows near the entrance.

"Looks pretty full," Sunny observed.

"Yeah, but if I can find a space here we won't have to hoof it from B.F.E. in this ninety degree heat. One more pass-through—maybe someone will be leaving."

"You realize no one says 'B.F.E.' anymore," Sunny informed me in a dry tone. "Oh wait—there's a guy!" She pointed to a man getting into a white pick-up truck.

I sped up and made the U-Turn into his row, putting on my blinker to signal my intention to park there. A split second later, a surly looking woman in a dark blue sedan pulled up facing me and put her blinker on for the same spot.

"Beeyatch," Sunny exhaled in annoyance.

The man in the truck began pulling out with his rear bumper angled toward me, giving surly-blue-car-woman the first shot at my space. I resigned myself to giving up gracefully, but just as she moved forward, her engine sputtered and her car shuddered to a halt.

Sunny let out a burst of surprised laughter as I whipped my wagon into the parking space. I spared a 'you win some, you lose some' sort of shrug for blue-car-woman as we got out and walked toward the hospital entrance. She glared at me over the painful noise of her starter grinding.

"Poor thing," Sunny said with mock sympathy.

The faint tinkle of faerie laughter rang in my ears.

"I guess they just don't make enough good parking spaces for *everyone* to have a faerie guardian," I smirked.

We stopped at the front desk to sign the log and get our 'Visitor' stickers, and then headed up in the elevator to the maternity wing. I wrinkled my nose at the antiseptic odor in the hallways as we followed the room number signs that mapped our way to Rachel.

When we found the right number, we peeked our heads through the doorway of a small, private room with a hospital bed for Mom and a corner fold-away cot for Dad. An infant's Plexiglas crib on wheels rested in a pool of sunshine beneath the window, but the baby was in Rachel's arms.

"Rachel!" Sunny whispered excitedly as she moved forward and made room for her greeting card and gift on the bedside table. Rachel didn't seem to notice any of it as she gazed down at her daughter.

"Meet Molly," she said with a radiant smile, tucking down a soft white blanket to give us an unobstructed view.

Rachel's husband, Brian, greeted us with a, "Hi guys, thanks for coming." He looked dazed but happy.

Lorien appeared just above my shoulder and I jerked my head in surprise. "Ooh, she's *so* cute...I love babies! How could anyone resist that pinched, purple wittle face?" she cooed in a sugary falsetto.

I did an admirable job of schooling my expression, but Sunny made a choking sound that almost ruined my efforts. Rachel and her husband beamed at Sunny, and she recovered quickly with a heartfelt, "She's precious!"

"She's beautiful," I agreed.

We fussed over Molly for a while, Sunny and I doing our best to ignore Lorien as she flitted around making fawning noises. I could have sworn that the baby was cooing back at her. But when Sunny and Rachel started in on the family gossip, I decided to give them some time alone to catch up.

"I think I'll go for a walk and maybe browse around the gift shop. Can I get anybody anything?" I offered as I stood.

They all declined and I stepped out into the hall with Lorien alighting on my shoulder to accompany me. "I don't suppose you know where the gift shop is?" I whispered as we reached the elevator.

"Try the second floor," she suggested.

I smiled at a cute male nurse in black scrubs as I stepped on and we rode down in silence. I stepped off and waited for the doors to close before muttering "Now where?"

"Go to the end of this hallway, then take a right," Lorien answered promptly.

I made my way down the corridor and glanced around before speaking again. "So, you really have a thing for babies, huh?" I whispered.

"What are you whispering for?" Lorien asked with a smirk.

"Because people who roam hospitals talking to themselves usually end up in the psych ward," I griped, snapping my mouth shut to smile at an elderly woman as she tottered out of the doorway in front of me wearing a paper-thin hospital gown. The nurse at her elbow gave me an odd look.

I glared at Lorien and she smothered a laugh.

"Hilarious," I whispered. "I'm glad you get such a kick out of making me look like a lunatic. And do you have any idea how hard it was to pretend you weren't darting around making goo goo eyes at Molly up there? If Rachel and Brian hadn't been so preoccupied with the baby, they would have thought Sunny and I were both nuts."

"You need to relax and worry a little less about what other people are thinking, Sydney," Lorien pronounced. "Besides, who can resist making 'goo goo eyes' at babies? They're so sweet and guileless with their little newly aligned souls. They're beings of pure love, and that's a rare and special thing. It only lasts so long before the world teaches them differently."

I pondered that depressing thought as I trudged to the end of the hallway and hit a dead end. I frowned. "There's no right at the end of this hall. It's a patient's room. Lorien?" I looked around for her, but she had disappeared.

I sighed, wondering if I'd done something to drive her away.

My eyes settled on the occupant of the room to my right. A woman lay pale and unconscious in the bed, lifeless but for the machine that was forcing breath into her body. She had long, light brown hair, much like mine, and similar features as well. I took an involuntary step forward, but froze when the light clicked off in the bathroom and a man crossed the scratched tile floor to stand at her side.

He bent over her, his black t-shirt stretching across well-defined shoulder and back muscles. He wore faded jeans and his tanned arms were covered in tattoos of runes and Celtic symbols. His startlingly blue eyes expressed surprise as he glanced up to find me staring at him.

"Sydney?" he asked as he straightened, his voice rough beneath his thick Irish brogue.

"Agent Sparrow?" I croaked, shock, and something warmer, traveling across my nerve endings at the sight of him. He'd starred in a few of my more explicit fantasies over the past week, but seeing him here was the last thing I'd expected.

"Do you know her?" he asked softly, indicating the girl in the bed.

"No. I...I'm visiting someone else," I sputtered.

"What are you doing here then?" he asked, his cobalt eyes narrowing in a mixture of confusion and suspicion.

"Lorien said...I mean my friend said...I was looking for the gift shop," I finally managed, cringing at how awkward I sounded.

A slow smile dawned across his face and my stomach quivered in response. "Lorien?" he queried, one dark eyebrow cocked in a knowing expression.

"You know Lorien?" I asked uncertainly.

"I've had the pleasure," he said dryly.

"Oh. I wasn't sure if you could see her," I replied, and then winced at my stupidity. Of course he could see her. He was a half-faerie policeman who arrested death djinns.

He chuckled at my obvious discomfort. "How would you like to have a cup of coffee with me, Sydney?"

My pulse quickened. "Sure," I answered, suppressing the urge to grin like an idiot. It was hospital coffee, for Goddess' sake, it wasn't like he'd asked me out on a date.

"Good. I have a feeling it was Lorien's intention that you and I have a chat. Just let me finish up here."

He reached out to gently place his hand on the unconscious woman's head. He whispered a few words that had the sound of ritual, and then slowly removed his hand, his strong fingers brushing her brow in a regretful caress. The dim light reflected faintly off of something silver in his palm before it disappeared into his jeans pocket.

Then he left her side and exited the room, towering over me as he motioned me to join him. I fell into step beside him, inhaling his spicy, woodsy scent.

"Who is she," I asked in a subdued tone, hoping she wasn't his wife, or sister, or some other close relation.

Sparrow sighed. "I'm not sure. She was found unconscious by the side of the road about a week ago. She's been in a coma ever since."

A tension that I hadn't known I held left my body at the discovery that he didn't know her.

"What happened to her?" I asked as we stepped onto the elevator and began to descend.

"I think it's quite probable that someone stole her soul." Sparrow's anger hung in the air as we stopped on the first floor and waited for the doors to open.

"But I thought that when a death djinn claimed a soul the person became an immortal slave," I said in a low voice, hurrying to keep up with his long strides as we turned a corner to find the brightly lit cafeteria. "Why would she be in a coma?"

"I didn't say it was a death djinn, nor did I suggest someone claimed her soul legally; I said it was probably stolen. There's a difference." I digested that as we moved down the empty buffet line, past some dry mashed potatoes, questionable looking meatloaf, and myriad small bowls filled with green Jell-o squares. He stopped at the drink station and filled a white ceramic mug with steaming hot coffee, which he then offered to me.

"No, thanks. I'll just grab some iced tea."

Sparrow paid the tired-looking cashier and we moved through the sterile, fluorescent space toward a quiet corner alcove. He pulled an ugly plastic chair away from a table adorned with a cheap vase of fake flowers, and held it out for me to sit. The chivalry of the gesture felt odd in the midst of the inelegant surroundings.

As soon as we were settled, I heard someone call my name. I looked up to find Mickey, of all people, heading straight for me in his gangly teenage stride. He'd abandoned the Goth thing completely and dyed his hair brown. "I knew we were destined to have coffee together..." he dropped into silence as he rounded the corner and saw that I wasn't alone.

"Hi, Mickey. What are you doing here—is everyone okay?" I asked, ignoring the disappointed look that flashed across his face at the discovery of Sparrow's presence.

"Um yeah, no, I'm just visiting a friend," he fumbled, his eyes darting from Sparrow and back to me.

"Well, I hope your friend's alright. Tell your Mom I said 'hi' and I'll talk to her Monday, okay?"

"Alright, I guess I'll catch you later."

"Bye, Mickey." I gave him a smile and a wave as he hurried away.

Mickey looked back once before he darted out a side exit into the hallway and Sparrow's eyes followed him until he was gone.

"Who was that?"

"Oh, just my boss' son," I smirked. "I think he might have developed a crush on me. He's seventeen. I'm sure he'll get over it in a day or two."

Sparrow raised a dark eyebrow and gave a noncommittal nod.

I tore open a pink packet of sweetener and carefully sprinkled half into my iced tea, stirring it with my straw as the questions I wanted to ask percolated in my mind.

"So, when you arrested Balthus, you're saying it *wasn't* for stealing that woman's soul?"

Sparrow combed his fingers through his dark hair with a sigh of frustration, leaving it charmingly disheveled. "I shouldn't be discussing the details of the case with you, Sydney. She is very much his type, though.

I don't know if you noticed, but she bears quite a bit of resemblance to you."

I *had* noticed, and the idea that it could have been me lying in that hospital bed made my stomach lurch. "Lorien said he was arrested for having an illegal soul…unaligned, or whatever," I replied in discomfort. "I just assumed it was hers."

"Bloomin' faeries," he mumbled. "Incapable of discretion, every last one of them."

I frowned at him. "I take it that means you're the one who told Lorien about Balthus. You know she only told me because she's trying to help with the whole death djinn thing. Besides, I thought *you* were half-faerie."

"I'm half-sidhe; Lorien's a sprite," he corrected flatly. "And as it happens, I did tell that little loud-mouth why Balthus was arrested. In confidence. And only because she's been a pint-sized pain in the ass about it all week."

I smiled. "She can be very persistent."

"That's an understatement," he muttered.

"She says she's been researching death djinn contracts. And that there's no record of anyone ever getting out of one," I added with a grimace.

A look of regret passed across his handsome face. "I'm truly sorry, Sydney. I wish I could help you…"

My eyes widened at his choice of words and he stared at me for a moment before a slightly queasy look overtook him.

"See how easy it is to slip up?" I asked with a despairing laugh.

His tanned, symbol-entwined arm moved toward me, as if he wanted to touch me, but he pulled back at the last moment. Something within me strained toward him, disappointed that he'd changed his mind.

The silence went on for a beat too long and I cleared my throat. "What kind of tattoos are those?" I asked to fill the void.

He glanced down at his arms, flexing his muscles so that they shifted smoothly beneath his skin, giving the intricate designs a life of their own. "Ancient Celtic runes and symbols of power and protection. A gift from my sidhe kin, who've passed down the art from generation to generation."

"Cool," I breathed. "Can they really protect you when you're in danger?"

"That they can—and have many a time," he added with a grin that ignited sparks in his eyes and sent my heart into a quicker rhythm.

"What's that one?" I asked, pointing to a particularly striking design high on his thick upper arm.

"Ah, that's one of my first and one of my favorites," he answered with a nostalgic smile as he pushed up the edge of his sleeve so that the inking was fully visible. "It's quite a traditional design, and very powerful—it's called an Aegishjalmur. It gives its bearer protection and irresistibility in battle."

I think it's giving you irresistibility in more than just battle, I thought.

"It's beautiful," I whispered aloud, reaching forward to trace it with my forefinger before I realized what I was doing. A shock of electricity passed between us and for a split second the tattoo glowed red through the black ink, bathing my palm in heat.

I jerked my hand away and anxiously met Sparrow's eyes. They blazed a radiant sapphire.

"I'm sorry," I said uncertainly.

"It's alright, Sydney." He took a deep breath. "You did no harm. As I said, they're powerful symbols."

I gave him a tentative smile. He slowly returned it, making my stomach do queer little flips. He looked away and took a swallow of his coffee. My mind raced along with my pulse. I was achingly attracted to him. But I couldn't allow that to get in the way of the more important fact that I needed his help.

"I was thinking," I began cautiously, "if Balthus really has been stealing unaligned souls, maybe there's a way to cancel my contract by getting him discredited."

Sparrow gave me a considering look. "It might be possible," he admitted. My heart leapt, but his next words dampened my enthusiasm.

"I don't want you to get your hopes up, though. Lorien's right, there are no recorded instances of a death djinn contract ever being cancelled."

I opened my mouth to protest and Sparrow held up his hand. "Impatient little witch," he taunted. "I wasn't finished. There are extenuating circumstances in your case. If I can prove that Balthus has been trading in unaligned souls, I can make a good argument that some, if not all, of his existing contracts should be nullified—especially an uncompleted one like yours."

He paused, as if deciding whether to say more, and his eyes turned serious. "But you should know that, so far, I've only discovered the one unaligned soul in Balthus' possession. He insists that he won it from a goblin during a game of dice, and that it appeared to be aligned when he received it."

I gave him an incredulous look. "Now you're telling me that there are *goblins*, and that they gamble with death djinns using human souls as currency? And that's *legal*?"

Sparrow sighed. "I've never endorsed the soul trade, Sydney. But as long as the human receives some sort of payment in return and their soul remains aligned, it's considered legal. The official position of the Seelie Court is that if a human wants to sell their soul for fortune, fame, protection...whatever it may be...that's their business."

I shook my head in consternation. "How can you tell the difference between an 'aligned' soul and an 'unaligned' one?"

"Aligned souls are still connected to their human host in some manner. Unaligned souls have been ripped completely free of their host."

Sparrow exhaled wearily. "And a human cannot survive for long once their soul has been completely cut free."

My eyes widened. "Is that what happened to the girl upstairs?" *The one who looks so much like me,* I thought, but didn't say it. "Is she going to die?"

He gave me a measured look and the sorrow in his expression was answer enough.

"Christ, Sparrow!" I whispered. "And you think Balthus did that to her?"

His jaw tightened. "Balthus swears he'd have no use for an unaligned soul, and that hers must have been tampered with to make it appear aligned."

"And you believe him?" I scoffed. "How could he not know? Wouldn't he have figured it out as soon as he realized there was no human host for him to boss around?"

His lips turned up in a derisive twist. "He says he only had the soul for a few days and that he stuck it in his vault and hadn't bothered to check in with the host yet."

Sparrow drained his cup and his gaze turned considering. "There *are* minute traces of magic on the soul. We haven't yet discovered what that magic was designed to do, but if the soul appeared aligned when he received it, whatever made it appear that way has clearly worn off now."

"You really think it's possible that he didn't know?" I asked.

Sparrow was quiet for a moment. "I don't believe that Balthus can be trusted," he said finally, "so it makes it difficult to gauge whether there's any truth to his story."

I worried the corner of my lip between my teeth as I tried to assimilate everything Sparrow had said and find a way to make it work to my advantage. "I need to talk to him again," I muttered with a soft shake of my head.

"Pardon?" Sparrow said incredulously.

My eyes flew to his. I hadn't realized I'd spoken aloud, but I wasn't taking it back. It was the only way I could see to move forward. "I said I need to talk to Balthus again," I repeated, working to keep my voice confident despite my apprehension.

"I'm not sure that's such a good idea, Sydney," Sparrow replied.

"Balthus and I have a connection," I pressed. "You said it yourself at the hotel that night—I'm two thirds his already. I want to hear what he has to say. I *need* this Sparrow. I can't just sit by and wait for your investigation or Lorien's research. Meanwhile, if I screw up and say the wrong thing, I lose my soul forever. You saw how easy it is to say that word by accident."

"I still don't see the point." He crossed his arms over his chest and leaned back until the plastic chair groaned. "What exactly do you think you're going to get out of Balthus that trained investigators and magic haven't already?"

"Who knows? He won't be threatened by me, so maybe he'll slip up and say something he wouldn't say in front of you. Or maybe I can appeal to his sense of fair play and get him to admit that I didn't really make a 'death wish'. Maybe he'll cancel my contract as a gesture of good faith since he's in such a legal tight spot with the unaligned soul you found."

A range of emotions played across Sparrow's handsome face as he stared at me. "Balthus doesn't have your sense of fair play, Sydney. He'll try to trick you, and he's exceedingly good at what he does. If you slip up and make a wish in front of him, I won't be able to help you."

"Please, Sparrow," I pleaded, sensing that I almost had him convinced. "I have to do this. I'm well aware of the stakes, and I promise I'll be careful."

He closed his eyes and his jaw tightened. Then he let out a long breath and said briskly, "Fine. It'll probably be about a week before I can get you approved for a visit."

I smiled in relief. "Thank you, Sparrow. It'll be okay, I promise."

He gave a resigned chuckle and said, "How did we end up with you trying to reassure me? And it's Patrick, by the way. But you can call me Pat."

"Syd! There you are—I've been looking all over for you! Oh..." Sunny skidded to a halt as she realized that I wasn't alone. "Sorry. I didn't know you had company. Who *is* your company?" she eyed Sparrow with interest.

"Sunny, this is Agent Patrick Sparrow. He's the one who arrested Balthus last weekend. Sparrow, this is my best friend since high school, Sunny."

Sparrow snorted. "Great. Just how many people have you told about our world?" he asked with futile amusement.

"Only Sunny," I said, trying not to sound defensive. "Was I really supposed to keep the most unbelievable thing that's ever happened to me a secret from everyone I love?"

"No. Of course not," he sighed. "Nice to meet you, Sunny." He extended his hand.

Sunny accepted it, shooting me a sideways look that clearly accused me of not mentioning how hot he was.

"So, what are you doing about this Balthus guy?" she asked.

Her voice was friendly, but Sparrow didn't mistake it for anything other than a demand. He stiffened and switched back into policeman mode as he answered her. It made me miss the more relaxed Sparrow from moments before.

"Sydney and I have just been discussing that at some length. I am currently conducting an investigation into certain allegations against Balthus. I have agreed to give Sydney the opportunity to interview him, as she feels that his incarceration may allow her some leverage over the status of her soul contract. I'm sure she'll be glad to tell you all about it," he said, rising.

"However, right now I'm afraid I'm pressed for time and must return to the office."

"Well, it was nice to meet you, Patrick. And we'll be counting on you." She grinned, clearly unfazed by his official demeanor. "Cool tattoos, by the way."

"Much appreciated." He nodded at Sunny and then winked at me. "Sydney, I'll be in touch."

"Bye, Sparrow. And thanks."

His lips twitched with humor. "I said you could call me Pat."

I cocked my head and smiled up at him. "I think I'll stick with Sparrow. It feels better, somehow."

"Stubborn little witch," he whispered. Then he turned away and was gone.

"That man is no sparrow," Sunny muttered. "A falcon or a hawk, maybe, but definitely no sparrow."

I nodded, nibbling my lip with a wistful sigh.

Chapter 7 - Monday Blues

The haranguing buzz of my alarm jerked me from sleep and I groaned, nearly sobbing in frustration. Not only was 8 am an ungodly hour to be awake, but a quickly fading dream—involving Sparrow, and me running my fingers over his magically glowing tattoos—left me wanting to smash the evil, unrelenting piece of machinery to bits.

Even in the best of circumstances, I'd never been a morning person.

I forced myself into a sitting position before sliding the alarm switch to 'Off', knowing that I ran the risk of drifting back to sleep if I lay down again. The thick aroma of coffee wafted through the closed door of my bedroom, along with the sounds of Sunny puttering around in the kitchen. I angrily swiped at an unexpected tear, realizing those simple morning rituals reminded me of Jeremy.

I told myself I'd feel better after a quick wash in the sink and my usual double-decker mug of hot tea with honey.

As I passed through the kitchen, Sunny grunted and gave me a weak semblance of a smile in response to my weary, "Morning." She then returned to watching the coffee pot's progress, one hip resting against a cabinet. She folded her arms across her chest and her black silk robe drifted open to reveal a crisp cotton tank top and shorts in a pretty shade of melon beneath.

I dropped a tea bag into my favorite mug and filled it from the hot water dispenser to steep. I glanced down with a grimace at what passed for my own customary sleeping ensemble: a ratty old Grateful Dead t-shirt and boxers whose material had been washed into perfect softness, but whose elastic had disintegrated. The swell of my hips was the only thing that prevented them from falling down around my knees.

I shuffled forward into my dining room/office to turn on my computer and blinked numbly at the screen as it booted up. Sunny and I knew each other well enough to appreciate that attempts at conversation were futile before caffeine.

An hour later we were both more coherent as we sat in companionable silence, working on our laptops, with Salsa music pounding through the flat-screen's speakers. Sunny was writing a syllabus for the medieval history class she would be teaching next semester at Boston College, and I was plugging away at my usual data entry after having gone my morning rounds with Cindy.

Jasper was curled up on a chair by the sliding glass door, basking in a patch of late morning sunlight. Nothing supernatural here—just your ordinary every day Monday. Thank Goddess for small favors.

I could get used to this, I thought with a twinge of regret. I was going to be lonely after Sunny left.

The phone rang and I saw on the caller ID that it was Angelica. It had only been a week and I could barely contemplate the thought of returning to a life without maid service. I was really becoming spoiled.

"Good morning, Angelica," I said brightly.

"Good morning, Sydney! Shall I come by now or later?"

"Now's good."

"Who was that?" asked Sunny as I hung up.

"That was Angelica, from the hotel's cleaning staff. She's on her way up now. And just to prepare you, she's about six feet tall, looks like a supermodel, and wears one of those French maid outfits. She's really sweet, and she's amazing at cleaning. Oh—and she likes to talk about sex."

I snickered at Sunny's bewildered expression as I got up to answer Angelica's soft knock.

"Hello Sydney! Just the usual today?" she asked, glass cleaner and duster in hand.

"That would be great." I smiled as I stepped to the side so she could enter.

"Salsa music—what an invigorating way to begin the day! Oh—do you have company?" she inquired, glancing at one of Sunny's suitcases on a nearby chair. "I hope it's a handsome man," she whispered conspiratorially. "It would be a shame not to properly break in that bed."

"Nope, just me," Sunny commented.

"Oh, I beg your pardon!" Angelica colored, the rosy tint making her even more lovely. "I didn't see you there. And I didn't mean to presume you required a man to break in your bed, either," she told me with a wicked grin.

I laughed. "Angelica, this is my best friend, Sunny. She's visiting from Boston for the week."

"Nice to meet you, Angelica. And believe me, I would be just as pleased as you to see Syd break in her bed with a handsome man," Sunny teased. She dodged as I swatted at her.

"Lovely to meet you, Sunny," Angelica replied as she continued into the sitting room to begin her cleaning routine. "Maybe, then, your combined powers of attraction will draw a pair of beautiful men to you before the week is out. Or at least one for you to share—when approached correctly, that can be a truly bonding experience between friends, you know."

I swallowed and shook off the unbidden image of Sunny, Sparrow and myself sharing my new bed. Sunny's snort of mirth mirrored my own, and I said, "I'm not sure our friendship has a need for that type of bond, Angelica."

She shrugged as she bent over to dust one of my frogs. "Suit yourselves—a pair of men it is, then." She grinned suddenly as she added,

"Maybe hot Latin lovers, who'll appreciate your taste in Salsa music."

"I like the way you think," Sunny said.

Angelica continued about her work as Sunny and I returned to our own. I couldn't help but envy her unconscious sex-appeal as she matched her movements to the beat of the music. If I hadn't liked her so much, I probably would have had a hard time not hating her. I was willing to bet that men fell helplessly at her feet wherever she went.

She disappeared into the back rooms for a while and then began returning supplies to her cart. "Thursday?" she inquired cheerfully.

"Yes, please," I agreed.

"See you then, Sydney. It was nice to meet you Sunny. I hope you enjoy your stay."

"Thanks—we'll let you know how it goes with the Latin lovers!" Sunny called.

Angelica paused and pursed her lips thoughtfully. "The angle and depth of that couch might be conducive to some interesting seated positions, especially if you enjoy being on top." She gave it an appraising once-over and nodded before turning to push her cart into the elevator.

"You know, I think she might be right," Sunny mused a moment later.

I shook my head and went back to work.

∞∞∞∞∞∞∞∞∞∞

Later that afternoon Sunny came for a ride with me as I made my rounds to pick up paperwork from my employers. Mr. H appeared at the back door to scream obscenities at Cindy for taking too long to talk to me. I grimaced and slammed the car door to drown him out.

Sunny whistled. "That is one nasty little man."

"Ugly inside and out," I agreed.

I snapped up an empty parallel parking spot right in front of Haute Hannah's on crowded Worth Avenue, and made a mental note to ask Lorien if she was responsible for my good parking fortune again.

"You should come in with me. Hannah has a really nice shop, and you'll get a kick out of her," I told Sunny.

"Sure, why not?" she agreed with a shrug. "She won't try to get me to buy anything though, will she? I doubt she's in my price range."

"I don't think you have to worry," I replied. "Hannah's a consummate saleswoman who knows her clientele. She generally saves her sales pitch for the ladies in Chanel suits—or at least *designer* jeans." I glanced down pointedly at our casual attire as we crossed the sidewalk.

"Hey! I paid thirty dollars for these at The Gap," Sunny argued with a laugh.

"Twenty bucks at Ross," I countered smugly, indicating mine.

"Nice."

The spotless glass door glided open with the tinkling of a bell, and we stepped into the cool, bright interior of Hannah's shop. Soft French jazz drifted over us, and brilliant shimmers of light dazzled our eyes as they reflected off of the precious metals and gemstones displayed throughout the store. The glittering intensity was relieved by pastel blue and white walls, delicately sponge painted to resemble a tranquil sky.

"Oh! Hello, Sydney! I am so happy to see you!" Hannah rushed forward, a compact force of nature, sparkling with jewels and floating in a cloud of rich perfume. I leaned down so she could kiss me once on each cheek.

She took my hands in the manicured fingers of her own, spreading them out to get a look at me. "You are looking good, no? You have lost weight! And who is your lovely friend?"

I grinned, always a little overwhelmed by Hannah's enthusiastic personality. "This is my good friend Sunny. She's visiting from Boston for a few days."

"You look beautiful as well, Sunny!" Hannah complimented as she reached to squeeze Sunny's fingers in greeting.

"Why thank you," Sunny smiled, reclaiming her hands just in time to stifle a sneeze.

"À vos souhaits!" Hannah called out in response to Sunny's outburst, as she bustled back behind a display case of multi-hued crystal perfume bottles to retrieve my paperwork.

"So, you girls will hit the town tonight and paint it *rouge*, yes?" she continued, a mischievous twinkle in her eye as she glanced up from gathering files. "*Les hommes*, they will find you irresistible!" She spread her arms in a grand gesture as she sashayed forward to hand me my work.

"That's the plan!" I agreed. Actually, we were going to stay home and get takeout, but I wasn't going to disappoint Hannah with the boring version of our plans.

She tapped my arm and gave a delighted laugh. "Oh, to be young again!" she sighed dramatically.

Sunny attempted to subdue another sneeze, and Hannah's brows drew together as she gazed at her in concern. "But your friend, she is maybe coming down with the cold, no? Perhaps you should take it easy. You do not wish to chase the handsome men away with a dripping nose."

Hannah reached out to give Sunny a motherly pat, and she immediately sneezed again, retreating toward the door with a strangled, "I don't want you to catch anything from me Hannah, but it was so nice to meet you, and you have a beautiful store! I'll just wait in the car, Syd." She exploded with a final sneeze as she fled.

"You should see that your friend gets the rest. We are much susceptible to illness when we travel, yes?" I swallowed my laughter and thanked her for her concern as I left with the files.

I dropped into the driver's seat to the sound of Sunny purging her nose into a Kleenex. "Holy hell, Syd!" she sniffed. "What does that woman do—take a morning dip in a pool of perfume? That was worse than sticking my head in a vat of faerie dust! I'm going to have to change and wash my hair just to get the stench off."

"Hannah likes her perfume like she likes her jewelry," I shot her a grin as I pulled into traffic and turned down a side street toward the nearest bridge spanning the inter-coastal, "outrageously expensive and displayed in overwhelming force."

"Well, she's very sweet, but I'm surprised she doesn't asphyxiate all of her customers. You've got allergies—how do you stand it?"

"I seal off my nose and start breathing through my mouth as soon as I walk in the door."

"Really? Thanks for the forewarning," Sunny intoned sarcastically.

I snickered. "It'll wear off soon, I promise."

Sunny groaned. "I guess it's kind of fading already."

"Enough that you'd come to a restaurant with me instead of bringing home takeout?" I coaxed.

"Sure," Sunny replied with a shrug.

"City Place is close."

"Sounds good." Sunny sniffled again and I hid a smile.

We parked in the garage and walked over to one of the more casual eating venues with dim lighting and big leather booths. We shared a huge French fry appetizer dripping with cheese and bacon, and split a pitcher of their freshly brewed beer. We justified the calories by having salads on the side.

Pleasantly sated, we decided to make a detour by Starbucks before going on to browse the bookstore. Sunny ran to the bathroom while I waited to pay. The store was abuzz with jonesing caffeine addicts, and a flustered cashier rang me up, noisily breaking open rolls of change into her drawer while I stood there with my credit card out.

"I've got it," a voice said behind me, handing the cashier a ten over my shoulder before I could get a word in.

"Really?" I smiled in confusion and turned to find Mickey standing there. The cha-ching of the cash register sounded before I could refuse.

"Uh, thanks Mickey," I said half-heartedly. I was beginning to feel a little stalked.

"You're welcome," he said with a grin. He followed me to the other end of the counter, his face falling when he saw that my order contained not one cup, but two.

"Gimme, gimme," Sunny demanded greedily as she returned to retrieve her coffee.

She inhaled her undiluted brew and I took a sip of my Chai, closing my eyes in bliss at the spicy sweetness. I wanted to ignore Mickey, hovering there behind us, but decided I was incapable of being that rude.

I sighed. Sometimes civility was such a burden.

"Sunny, this is Cindy and Leslie's son, Mickey," I said with a false smile, shooting her a meaningful look as I turned to include him in the conversation.

I'd mentioned seeing him at the hospital and the little crush he'd apparently developed on me. She'd made some joke about the stamina of properly-trained seventeen year old males that I hadn't dignified with a response. This was Mickey we were talking about, fruit of 'The Horrorwitz's' loins.

"Mickey, this is my best friend, Sunny. Mickey was nice enough to treat us to our coffees."

Sunny sent me an amused glance before saying, "Thanks! That was so sweet. I'll bet the high school girls just love you."

Mickey's face flushed red as we navigated a swarm of bodies and exited back out into the heated dusk.

All the chairs were taken, so I led the way to a nearby fountain, where Sunny and I sat side by side on the wide, stone rim. I didn't want him following us to the bookstore. Mickey perched himself beside me after a moment, looking uncomfortable.

"So, we sure have been seeing a lot of each other lately," I observed.

"I just stopped by to get a cup of coffee on my way out for the night," he replied with a shrug.

Sunny elbowed me. "Syd was telling me you used to go for the Goth look. What brought about the change?" she asked.

A lost expression played over his face as he mumbled, "I dunno. I guess I just wanted to do something different."

He seemed suddenly vulnerable and I felt like a jerk for being callous about his interest in me. "Well, it looks good, right Sunny?" I said brightly.

I didn't want to encourage his attentions, but maybe he just needed someone to be nice to him.

"Very handsome," she enthused.

My attention strayed toward the eye-candy that walked past us. It was almost Angelica's fantasy come to life—two tall, muscular, Latin men with smoldering dark eyes.

Mmm. Didn't quite do it for me the way a certain Irish half-sidhe did, but not bad at all.

I glanced at Sunny, who sent a soft whistle of shared appreciation my way. But what really surprised me was the look on Mickey's face. His eyes were also hungrily following The Latin Sexuality Twins. Sunny noticed too and smirked at me.

Apparently I'd been totally off base about him.

Mickey reached into his pocket and pulled out a handful of change. He rubbed a penny between his fingers and closed his eyes, murmuring something about how he wished his parents understood him as he tossed it over his shoulder into the fountain.

He smiled sadly as he placed pennies in each of our hands. "Your turn, ladies."

My heart went out to him as I pictured what it must be like to have Mr. H as a father. I almost echoed his wish, when I caught myself. I dropped the penny on the flagstone pavement and glanced at the thick crowd of people surrounding us.

One of them could easily be a death djinn. And I'd nearly slipped up and made a wish out loud. I could have lost my immortal soul while hanging out at the equivalent of the mall.

It was a horrifying thought.

I looked over to find Mickey staring at me with disappointment and hurt.

"Syd's allergic to copper," Sunny fabricated apologetically as she tossed her own coin into the fountain. "Pennies give her a rash."

"But I still hope your—you know—comes true," I added lamely.

He rose, looking upset. "Well, I guess I'd better get going."

I stood and tried to thank him again for the coffee, but he was already striding away.

"Smooth, Syd," Sunny intoned with a snicker. "You still think he has a crush on you?"

Before I could come up with a suitably sarcastic reply, a hand grabbed my shoulder and I let out a muffled shriek. I leapt forward and my knees met the stone lip of the fountain with a painful thud. I overbalanced, my arms flailing as I teetered toward the shallow pool.

Just as I was about to go for an unwanted swim, a thick arm hooked around my waist and yanked me back against a wall of muscle. Shaking, I squeezed my eyes shut and released the breath I'd been holding, both hands clinging to the solid, bare forearm that circled my mid-section.

"Easy there, little witch," murmured Sparrow, his Irish brogue heavy with amusement. His breath warmed my ear and the heat from his body curled through me, making my muscles turn to water.

"Good goddess, Sparrow," I mumbled unsteadily, "you scared the crap out of me!"

His arm tightened and his thumb brushed the underside of my breast. Unintentionally, I was sure, but I shivered with awareness anyway.

"You're trembling," he said in concern. "I'm sorry. I didn't mean to frighten you." He disentangled himself and urged me to sit on the fountain ledge. I used the moment to collect my brain, since his touch had apparently short-circuited it.

His deep blue eyes searched mine and I let out an unsteady laugh. "It's not your fault—I'm just a little on edge. I guess I'm imagining death djinns around every corner."

"That's perfectly understandable, given the situation." He frowned and my fingers itched to smooth the crease between his brows. "Maybe it's not such a good idea for you to meet with Balthus after all. He won't hesitate to exploit any weakness he senses in you. And if he can keep you off balance, you might trip up in front of him."

I stiffened and scowled at him, ignoring his lack of explanation for his unexpected presence. "No way, Sparrow. Talking to Balthus might be the only chance I get to make some sense out of this mess. You promised you'd get me in to see him."

"You are so stubborn." He shook his head at me.

"She's our little Aries ram," Sunny intoned. "She'll smack her head against the wall until she either gets what she wants, or she knocks herself out trying."

"Ah, an Aries, well that explains it." He winked at Sunny.

I scowled at her. "I'm serious, Sparrow. I thought we already had this discussion. It could help your investigation, and it's definitely going to help me wrap my head around what I'm dealing with."

"I'm only trying to do what's best for you, Sydney," he said quietly.

I softened at his words. "And I appreciate that Sparrow, but I think what's best for me is letting *me* decide what's best for me."

He chuckled. "Why does that not surprise me?"

I leaned into him playfully. "So does that mean I get my interview with a death djinn?" I asked, tilting my head back against his shoulder to bat my eyelashes at him.

His hooded gaze travelled slowly over my upturned face, and my breath grew shallow. A smile twitched on his lips and I suddenly realized how much I wanted him to close the few inches that remained between us and put his mouth on mine. He bent forward to place a light kiss on my forehead.

"That's what I came to tell you. Your interview is on Saturday, little witch."

I lifted my head from his chest, my heart racing. His kiss was chaste, but his eyes were full of sensual promise. I raised my gaze to his again, needing to make sure I hadn't mistaken seeing it there.

His smile widened and he fixed me with a look that was teasing, yet knowing. Then he leaned forward and my eyes fluttered closed as his warm breath caressed my ear. "You're welcome," he said softly.

"Thank you," I murmured belatedly.

His lips lingered, brushing against the sensitive shell of my ear, and making me shudder with need. Then he reached for my hand and gave my fingers a regretful squeeze as he rose.

"I'll be by on Saturday to pick you up. I'll get in touch with Lorien about the details. I'm afraid it's going to be a busy week and I won't have much time to check in—but I'll be there if you need me."

I nodded. "Thanks Sparrow. I'll be ready." I was aching with need for him now, but I didn't say it.

He disappeared, and my eyes darted amongst the faces around us, but no one else seemed to notice.

I turned to Sunny. "Wow. Saturday." I couldn't decide if it was too long to wait, or too close for comfort. My face fell. "Oh crap! You fly out on Saturday!"

Sunny made a face. "Yeah. That sucks. On the bright side though, I think the hot Irish guy really likes you."

I grinned at her.

"Ready to go, little witch?" she asked mockingly. She jumped up, dodging my elbow, and laughing as I chased her across the courtyard.

Chapter 8 - A Square Peg

"So, Syd, I've been thinking," Sunny mused aloud.

I looked up, granting my full attention to her reflection in the mirror over the vanity sink. "Gya?" I mumbled around my toothbrush.

It was Saturday and I had been puttering around, lost in thought, all morning. I was a little depressed that Sunny was leaving, and more than a little nervous about my impending meeting with Balthus—not to mention seeing Sparrow again.

Sunny plunked herself onto the unmade bed behind me and pulled a pillow into her lap. Her fingers fidgeted with the edge of the pillowcase as she watched me.

"Well, I don't have any classes to teach for another six weeks. My bills are all on automatic withdrawal from my checking account, and my fish died last month and I haven't had the heart to replace him. I signed up to take that Latin course online over the summer, but I can do that from anywhere. There's really no reason I have to fly back home today.

"I mean, I don't want to overstay my welcome, but if you wanted, I could postpone my flight for a week or so. I could stay and, you know, try to help figure out how to get this ridiculous contract cancelled..."

I spat a mouthful of foam into the sink and hurriedly rinsed, my eyes wide as I stared at her.

"It's just a thought," she shrugged, "I'll understand if you don't want the company."

I swiped at my mouth with a towel and sprinted the short distance to the bed, pouncing on her with a grateful hug and knocking us both off balance.

"I'll take that as an invitation to stay," she laughed.

"Of course!" I exclaimed happily. "You can stay as long as you want!"

Instead of driving to the airport we ordered lunch, and two hours later we were sinking back on the couch, empty edamame pods and the colorful remnants of sushi rolls littering the coffee table in front of us. I leaned into the soft leather armrest and coaxed Jasper over to take a bit of salmon from my fingers.

Sparrow was late to pick me up for my meeting with Balthus, but I was trying not to think about it because it made my insides churn. The sushi was delicious going down, but now it was sloshing around my stomach. I stared out through the wall of sliding glass doors at the waves lapping onto the beach and tried not to draw a comparison.

"Where is he?" I muttered edgily.

"He'll be here," Sunny soothed. "Patrick wouldn't leave you hanging, he's not the type."

"Yeah, well I didn't think Jeremy was the type to do what he did either, and you can see how brilliant my intuition turned out to be in that regard," I replied.

Sunny's eyes filled with sympathy. "He'll be here," she repeated.

Jasper suddenly leapt into the space between us with his ears perked. I followed his green gaze to the back of the couch and found Lorien hovering there, bent over and sprinkling yellow faerie dust as she tried to catch her breath.

"Whew, that was some flight," she wheezed.

"I got the impression you could just snap your fingers and end up wherever you wanted," Sunny remarked.

Lorien sent her a glare of irritation between huffs. "I was at the police station, smack dab in the middle of Seelie City. You can't just blink in and out of there. You have to have the proper authorization. Otherwise, every unbound goblin, troll and death djinn they brought in for questioning would disappear as soon as their attention was turned."

Sunny shrugged and gave me a pained glance that asked how she was supposed to have known that. I bit my lip in amused commiseration.

"Where's Sparrow?" I asked.

"He got tied up with some big police raid. He sent a message that he wasn't going to be able to meet you and asked me to bring you to the station."

"Oh." My gut clenched in both anxiety and disappointment.

It had taken me twice as long as usual to get ready since I knew I was going to see Sparrow again, and now he wasn't even coming.

"Can I go with you?" Sunny asked hopefully.

"Sorry, Sunny. Agent Sparrow had to fill out a mountain of paperwork just to get Sydney in, and Seelie security is no joke. I don't think I could sneak you in even with an anti-detection spell hand-cast by Lauringer herself."

"Who?" asked Sunny.

Lorien rolled her eyes in exasperation. "Titania's wand. Lauringer! Any school-child can tell you that she's the most powerful mage alive!"

Sunny glared at her in annoyance, "Human here! No clue about the inner workings of Seelie City, or wherever, much less who gets their own page in the faerie history books."

Lorien blinked at her. "Yeah, sorry," she mumbled, clenching and unclenching her small fists. "I guess I'm just a little on edge about Sydney's meeting with Balthus. Speaking of which, we have to go!"

She flitted over to hover in front of me, faint purple shimmers of faerie dust falling from her wings as she motioned for me to rise.

Sunny stood up to give me a hug. "I wi...I mean, I'd really like it if I were coming with you. Good luck, and whatever you do, don't wish for anything!"

I chuckled nervously and turned to follow Lorien.

"Close your eyes, Sydney, and don't open them 'til I tell you. I don't want you getting dizzy and passing out on me."

The last thing I saw before my eyelids fell shut was her pulling a tiny silver pouch from an inner pocket of her color-shifting dress. A strange tingling began at the top of my scalp and she commanded from above my head, "Lock your knees!"

The tingling sensation quickly spread downward, sweeping over my body in a rush like a bucket full of ice-water. I gasped in shock as I felt a heart-stopping jerk, like I'd been perched at the top of a roller coaster and had coasted over the edge. My muscles tightened in panic against the sudden ruthless demand of gravity.

I remembered with alarm that Lorien had told me to do something… lock my knees! I tried to persuade my legs to comply with my brain, and they shook in protest as I finally managed some semblance of a knee-lock.

Suddenly the sickening momentum of falling ceased and I was floating downward as if the air itself had decided to cushion me. My muscles slowly relaxed and all thoughts of locking my knees were swept away just as my feet made contact with something solid. I collapsed heavily to the ground which, lucky for me, was soft and spongy.

I opened my eyes in surprise, despite Lorien's admonition to wait for her say-so, and found myself on a grassy slope between the arms of towering twin mountains. The air was cool and cleaner than anything I'd ever tasted. I blinked dizzily at my surroundings, taking deep breaths in an attempt to ward off unconsciousness.

A slender waterfall spilled down a rocky outcrop in the mountainside nearest me. It flowed into a little spring, rushing to merge with the waters of a crystalline lake that sprawled at the feet of the mountains. The spot where I had landed was carpeted in soft, vibrant green.

Dandelion tufts drifted on the breeze, and tiny yellow and purple flowers sprouted everywhere. Enormous jewel-toned dragonflies hovered and darted around me, while a sweet chirruping sound gave counterpoint to the faint buzz of their wings.

As I strained to identify the sound, I noticed a small movement in the folds of greenery at my fingertips. I looked down to see a miniscule, golden-brown frog, its round eyes blinking up at me curiously, irises tinted with gold-dust.

It was so cute that I scooped it into my palm to get a closer look. It didn't seem afraid, it just looked back at me, its throat swelling as it let out a trilling chirrup. Joy bubbled up from deep within me and I realized that I was surrounded by frog song.

I lay my hand flat on the ground and gently nudged the creature. "Go sing with your friends." It blinked at me once more and then hopped away.

"Thank Titania you didn't pass out!" I looked up to find Lorien hovering above me with a worried expression.

"Where have you been? And what is this place? It's amazing!" I pushed to my feet and brushed the dirt from my jeans. I noticed with a grimace that the damp vegetation had left an embarrassing wet spot right over my butt.

"Welcome to the faerie realm, Sydney," she said as she flitted higher to avoid a stray piece of moss I flicked off my hand. "We're just beyond the outskirts of Seelie City—and not too far from my home."

"It's just…amazing," I breathed a laugh, unable to find a better word to describe it. "But how come I got here before you did? I thought all you had to do was blink in and out."

She blushed. "Oh that. Well, I seem to have miscalculated a bit. I meant for you to land right by the mountain pass. But don't worry—it's only a short climb down to get there."

I narrowed my eyes. "Short climb?"

"Um, yeah. Not too bad. Come on, I'll show you." She darted away before I could voice my concern about climbing anything in jeans and sandals—not to mention my silk top.

I followed her past the lake, stepping carefully to avoid the frogs, and around the perimeter of a craggy rock formation. Lichen and spiky pink flower-buds covered its pitted surface and its lip rose from the ground, creating a small cave.

I stared inside it, but couldn't see very far before the light disappeared into blackness. I got an odd impression of depth, as if it weren't simply a depression beneath the rock, but delved deep beneath the mountain itself. I shook off the urge to crouch lower and peer into the gloom, and turned to catch up with Lorien.

Soft echoing laughter floated up behind me. I spun around to see a chubby faerie child galloping out of the darkness, riding on the harnessed back of a tiny golden frog. He giggled and gripped the threadlike reins in his plump little fists, shaking them with each leap.

A glowing bluish bubble drifted along after him. As it faded into the light of day I realized that it was a lantern, held by a beautiful faerie woman with long, dark hair and a striking resemblance to Lorien.

I watched the scene unfold, frozen in awe. The faerie woman smiled up at me serenely as the child continued his cavorting frog ride. He didn't seem to notice the giant human towering above him.

"You must be Sydney," the woman spoke, fluttering up to greet me at my level. She wore a color-shifting dress like Lorien's, but in pastel shades of pink, blue and yellow. "I'm Lorien's sister, Eleanor. And that's my son, Obie, and our frog, Buster." She gestured down toward the frolicking pair with an indulgent roll of her eyes. "Obie, say hello to Miss Sydney," she called.

Obie pulled the reins and said, "Heel, Buthter." When the frog settled to a stop, he raised his dark head to stare at me, violet eyes growing wide in his chubby pink face. He waved and lisped, "Hello, Mith Thydney. You're big!"

I giggled. "Hello, Obie. You and Buster look like you're having fun."

He gave an exuberant nod. "Can I ride thumore?" He looked to his mother for permission. She nodded and he kicked his heels, laughing as the frog leapt back into a gallop.

"I see you've met my sister and nephew."

I tore my gaze from Obie with a helpless smile and turned to look at Lorien.

She made a tsking sound. "Ellie, I know I promised I'd introduce you to Sydney, but we have an important meeting now."

Eleanor gave a placid shrug. "You're the one who brought her to our doorstep. I told you how precise the measurement had to be for the transport powder. I thought we'd practiced all this."

"Give me a break, Ellie! You know it was my first time. It's not like I sent her into the goblin territories!" Lorien was visibly flustered.

"No. You're right." Eleanor's nose twitched in amusement. "I suppose it could have been worse. But you're going to have to call a peg up here to get her down—she's not going to be able to make that climb."

"Aw, Ellie! You know how testy they get when you ask them to fly someone! The climb down isn't *that* bad," she insisted.

"Don't be ridiculous, Lori," Eleanor chided.

"Alright," Lorien agreed sourly. "Sydney, follow me to the edge and I'll try to find a peg to fly you down."

She buzzed off in a huff, orange dust sprinkling a quickly fading trail behind her. "She's just jealous because I won our bet," I heard her grumble under her breath.

"A peg?" I asked, wondering at the strange term as I turned back to Eleanor.

"You'll see," she answered, amusement lighting her eyes.

I gave her a dubious look. "Uh, I guess I should go, then. It was nice to meet you and Obie."

Laughter danced in her expression. "It was nice to meet you too. You're Lorien's first human charge, you know. I'm quite proud of her, despite my teasing. She takes her guardianship of you most seriously. Good luck with your meeting—I hope to see you again." She glided down toward her son and I turned to follow Lorien.

As I approached the rim of a small cliff, the discordant notes of arguing voices drifted up to greet me.

"No! Of course I don't think you're some kind of pack mule! I simply made a mistake and I'm asking for your help. I'll double your fee."

A response came in the form of a heavy snort, followed by an angry-sounding voice clearly enunciating the words, "I. Don't. Fly. Humans."

I looked over the edge in time to see a beautiful horse with a gleaming chestnut coat and long, feather-tipped wings. It turned its back on Lorien and trotted away, tossing its head in annoyance.

"Bloody faerie, why don't you sprinkle her with dust and fly her down on your own back," it muttered.

"Peg. Pegasus," I whispered to no one in particular, a hysterical laugh gurgling up into my throat.

Lorien threw her hands up in aggravation. "Stupid donkey," she mumbled, but not loud enough for the departing creature to hear.

I studied the sheer rock face beneath me. It dropped about fifteen feet to the ground below, which was littered with fragments of broken boulders. I agreed with Eleanor—there was no way I was climbing down that. But I kept the thought to myself, not wanting to further antagonize Lorien.

She flitted upward to meet me, heaving an irritated sigh. "I'm not sure what to do, Sydney. The pegs have this stupid notion that it's demeaning to carry someone on their back when they fly. They'll trot you up and down the road all day for the right fee, but ask them to fly someone a few measly feet and they act like you just called their mother a mule," she grumbled.

"Hmm. Can't you sprinkle me with some more of that transport powder stuff and just transport me down?" I asked.

She drooped in frustration. "That only works for transportation between realms. And I don't have enough to send you to your realm and bring you back here again."

I stared down at the rock wall dubiously. "Well, maybe I could try to climb down. It's just that if I fall, I'm not exactly going to have a soft landing." I gestured unhappily at the jagged rocks below.

"I have healing dust that would soothe any cuts or bruises," she offered.

"You got anything for broken bones?" I asked with a grimace.

Lorien sagged. "Oh, you're right Sydney. You can't climb this."

"What seems to be the problem, ladies?" drawled a deep voice.

I looked down to find another winged horse blinking up at us. His flanks were thick and heavily knotted with muscle and his coat was a handsome blend of golden tones, offset by the white feathered tips of his immense wings and his matching white mane and tail.

"Good day to you, Master Peg," Lorien said in a polite tone as she zoomed down to hover near the pegasus. "I'm Lorien, and this is my human charge, Sydney." She gave him a pleading look. "And I've made a mistake and could really use your help."

The creature made a rumbling noise that invited her to continue.

"You see," she rushed on, "I meant to transport her to the peg station down the hill so we could buy a ride to the police station in Seelie City for an important meeting. But it was my first attempt at inter-realm transport, and I miscalculated and sent her to the wrong spot. So now we're going to be late for our appointment because I can't figure out how to get her down."

"I see," the peg answered with a nod.

"I would never ask if it weren't an emergency," she said imploringly, "but could you possibly fly her down and then get us to the police station? I'll pay extra for your trouble."

He blinked up at us, a rolling thunder beginning deep in his chest, growing into a full-fledged laugh that vibrated the air around us. Lorien and I glanced at each other uncertainly.

"Everyone makes mistakes, Mistress Lorien," he rumbled finally. "I'm Titus. And I'd be glad to bring Miss Sydney down and take her wherever she needs to be." He unfolded his wings, their colossal span robbing me of breath as he gracefully leapt up to land beside me with one powerful thrust.

I wondered why he had agreed when the other peg had been insulted by the very idea, but I was too grateful for his aid to question it.

"My thanks, Master Titus." Lorien smiled, her wings buzzing happily as they filtered emerald dust.

"Climb on, little human," Titus boomed, giving me a horsey grin as he sank to the ground and lifted his wings so that my legs could rest beneath them. "Pull yourself up with my mane."

"Are you sure?" I asked uncertainly, striving to climb up without pulling too hard. I ended up hanging onto the coarse tresses for dear life to keep from sliding back down the barrel of his side as I tried to right myself atop him. But the tugging didn't seem to bother him.

It was painfully obvious that I was no equestrian. I was damp with sweat by the time I positioned myself to sit high astride his back, my hands resting on his neck. "Thank you so much, Mr. Titus," I said finally, heaving a sigh of relief.

"Hold on now!" he warned.

I barely had time to tighten my fingers in his mane as he rose with dizzying speed and leapt over the edge to glide smoothly down to the ground below. I heard a high-pitched squeal and belatedly realized it had come from my own throat.

"Piece of oatcake," Titus said with satisfaction. "Now, Miss Sydney, if you would kindly lift your feet for a moment so I can refold my wings."

I slowly released my white-knuckled grip on his mane and exhaled a breath I hadn't realized I'd been holding as I obliged his request.

"Thank you, ma'am," he drawled as he cantered down the hill to the mountain pass, Lorien darting along behind us.

A group of four pegs came into view. One of them was the chestnut from before, while two of them were warmer shades of cinnamon and the fourth boasted an eye-catching mix of black and white patching. They all looked sleek and trim, giving an impression of youth next to the mature bulk of Titus' physique. They whispered amongst themselves as we reached the bottom of the hill, glancing at us and letting out snickering little neighs as we approached.

The black and white bared his teeth in a sneer and flicked a disdainful glance at us. The others scoffed in agreement.

Titus ignored them, until the chestnut said the words 'pack mule' a little too loudly. Then he stopped in his tracks. I instinctively rewrapped my fingers in the long white hairs of his mane.

The chestnut's three companions whickered in amusement. It was a mistake. Titus shot forward like a massive bullet. I squeezed my eyes shut and prayed I wouldn't fall—even though we weren't in the air, it was still a long way to the ground. He stopped just short of the group and pawed in the dirt before them, his head tossing wildly. The four pegs backed up with their eyes rolling in fear.

"Now you listen to me!" Titus roared. "There's pride, an' then there's foolishness. And if you weanlings aren't old enough to know the difference, then you'd better hoof it back to your mothers' sides and learn it before coming back to work at this station."

He snorted. "If they're not too ashamed to have you. Leaving a guest to our realm, and a *lady*, stranded in order to preen your own feathers," he accused in disgust. "Just because we don't take flying jobs, it doesn't mean we refuse to help out when someone's in a tight spot. If I *ever* hear that any of you have been so insufferably rude again, you'll find yourselves on haulin' detail in the goblin mines. Do you understand me?" he growled.

I had never heard a horse growl; it was a surprisingly frightening sound.

"Yes, Titus," they gibbered in unison, their eyes still rolling, expressions humbled.

Titus stared them down for another long minute, then snorted and turned away.

Lorien and I kept our mouths shut.

"Sorry about that," Titus apologized after we had traveled a distance from the chastened pegs. "Sometimes the younguns need to be put in their places. I hope my outburst didn't startle ya', Miss Sydney."

"Uh, not too much," I lied.

"We're just thankful that you came along," Lorien chimed in.

"My pleasure to serve, ladies," he said, tipping his great head. "Next stop, Seelie City." His laughter rumbled through me as he increased his pace to a rolling gallop.

I held on tighter and prayed I wouldn't bounce right off of him.

Chapter 9 - Balthus Bound

"Ugh," Lorien groaned, "I'll never get used to flying into bound space."
I shot her a questioning look.

"We just crossed the border into Seelie City. I told you, you can't blink in and out of here without special authorization. Remember?"

"Yeah, I remember, but I didn't realize you'd be able to feel it as soon as you crossed the border."

"Of course I can feel it," Lorien said testily. "It's like having your insides all bound up." She flicked her wings as if trying to rid them of the orange dust sprinkling from them.

A low chuckle resounded through Titus' chest, which I felt as much as heard. "You always know you've crossed the border when you're traveling to an' from Seelie City with faerie folk. But the binding's for good reason, Mistress Lorien."

The faerie dust trailing behind her abruptly changed to a bright shade of melon. "You're right," she said contritely. "It's a small inconvenience compared to the problems they had before it was put in place."

"What problems?" I asked, craning my neck at a line of buildings in the distance, their mismatched heights glittering white in the sun, proclaiming the imminent arrival of the approaching city.

"Well, it makes law enforcement kind of difficult when prisoners have the ability to blink out of custody. Most officers have the ability to bind a prisoner's powers with spells. But those individual bindings take constant monitoring and some of the more powerful prisoners were able to escape by waiting for the bindings to weaken during shift changes or other distractions. It was a real problem. So the Seelie Court petitioned the mages of the faerie realm to help them come up with a solution."

Titus made a disgruntled sound, and Lorien paused in her dissertation to glance at him.

"What?" I asked.

"Nothin'. Just don't trust mages overmuch is all," he rumbled.

"Why not?" I asked.

"Well, don't get me wrong, a lot of them have put their cleverness to good work. But they don't just use spells, mages; they invent 'em. That kind of power can easily fall into corruption." He tossed his head.

"But you don't need to hear the prejudices of an old peg like me. Please continue, Mistress Lorien."

"Uh, thank you," Lorien said politely. She cleared her throat with a small, delicate noise. "So it was Lauringer, a relatively unknown mage at the time, who suggested binding the entire city. The highest members of the mage council ridiculed her idea, insisting that such a spell would be too massive and that it would never take permanent hold, if it could even be performed."

"Why didn't they just bind the prison?" I interrupted, my eyes still canvassing the looming city.

The buildings all seemed to be made of the same rough white stone, rife with sparkling quartz, and peppered with deep green curtains of climbing ivy. When the sunlight reflected off of them, the effect was magical. Ahead, the median of the main thoroughfare was populated by gnarled, ancient-looking trees. Their branches reached out to shade both sides of the street beneath a thick, leafy canopy.

Lorien grunted at my question. "They tried binding the prison, but it wasn't any more effective than the individual bindings. It seems that magical prisoners have an uncanny ability to figure out how to escape buildings. And once out, they would blink away before the guards could recapture them."

"Oh."

"Anyway," Lorien continued, "Lauringer ignored the high mages and requested a meeting with the Seelie Court, asking them to give her a chance. That in itself took great courage, because a failure would not only discredit her in the eyes of the mage community, but it would leave a less than stellar impression upon the governing body of the Realm.

"As soon as The Court agreed, she went straight to the center of Seelie City to begin weaving her spell. She gradually moved outward in widening spirals, until the last circle encompassed the outskirts of the city. A huge crowd gathered to watch her progress, probably the whole of the city's population and then some. It took her a day and a half, and when she finished and spoke the final words of binding, it was as if the entire city held its breath to see what would happen." Lorien paused for effect.

"So what happened?" I asked.

"Nothing," she answered with a small chuckle.

"What do you mean, nothing?" I snorted in disbelief, my gaze drawn to a handsome black peg as he trotted past.

"I mean, nothing happened. No big bang, no flash of light, nothing. The throng that had watched her in near silence for a day and a half suddenly discovered its voice. Some of them were embarrassed for her, and some of them found satisfaction in her failure. Lauringer just stood there, mute and exhausted. The crowd began to disperse, returning to their daily lives, already beginning to dismiss the name of a little known mage called Lauringer—until a single sprite attempted to blink out."

"And?" I prodded after a moment.

Lorien grinned widely. "At that moment, a tremendous shockwave of power swept across the city, rattling the windows of every building and leaving a burning afterimage of magelight upon the eyes of everyone who saw it. Lauringer collapsed to the ground, and the sprite who had tried to blink was nearly stunned out of the air. Lauringer had done it, although it took her almost a month to recover from the expenditure of power.

"From that point on, no one disputed that she must be the most powerful mage alive. She could easily have become the head of the mage council, but their ridicule had left a bad taste in her mouth. She helps the community when called upon, but other than that, she mostly keeps to herself."

"Wow," I commented faintly. I realized that I sounded preoccupied, but I was fascinated by Seelie City. My eyes were attempting to soak everything up faster than my brain could process it.

We had reached the city proper and I was trying to figure out why there seemed to be a profusion of alarmingly massive anthills between each of the white stone buildings. Not to mention that the streets were scattered with other pegs—with and without riders such as myself. And a colorful haze filled the air, which I quickly realized must be faerie dust residue from the multitude of faeries flitting about. Other than that, it seemed a pleasantly clean and orderly city, albeit with more trees and foliage than any human city I'd ever seen.

"You have quite a knack for story-telling, Mistress Lorien," Titus complimented in his rumbling bass. "Do you have any other questions about our fine city, Mistress Sydney?" he asked me over his shoulder.

"Um, yeah actually," I replied, my eyes still drinking in the surreally familiar environment through which we passed. Somehow I had expected it to appear more alien. "What are those huge anthill things between all the buildings?"

Titus snorted in soft amusement, while Lorien peered confusedly between two buildings as we passed. "Anthill things? I don't see any… wait…those aren't ant hills, they're faerie mounds! Lumbering human," she muttered in affront.

"Well how am I supposed to know? What exactly are faerie mounds?"

"They're like apartments," she replied in a sullen tone. "Seelie City is populated by all sorts of folk, from your size to mine. Sizes of living accommodations, therefore, vary as well."

"Oh, that makes sense," I said, taking note that some of the buildings had entrances only large enough to accommodate a human child. "But I've read myths that said faeries lived in giant oak trees. Where did they get that?"

Lorien rolled her eyes at me and sighed. "A tree is a living entity. Wood nymphs, or dryads, will live in certain trees—but they're more like spirits. They can manifest a physical form if they choose, or become insubstantial and morph into the tree itself.

"If a sprite and a dryad are friendly, we'll sometimes heal their tree if it develops a blight. That's probably where the rumors associating faeries with trees began. But you try living in a tree—it's not the most stable of environments. Although, certain petrified tree stumps do conceal the entrances to our homes.

"We prefer to live in natural caverns beneath the earth. The closest ones are beneath the mountains we just came from, but they don't extend this far, so the sprites who work and live in Seelie City build faerie mounds. They're a bit like above ground caverns, supported by rock beneath the earthen exterior."

I inspected a mound more closely and realized that beds of tiny flowers surrounded it, some even beginning to grow up the packed dirt sides. A group of sprite children, probably a little older than Obie, suddenly shot out of the opening at the top of the mound. The mismatched troupe raced down toward a patch of large toadstools growing in the shade of one of the buildings. They began jumping up and down on the spongy caps as if they were trampolines, giggling and using their wings to gain height.

I smiled and shook my head as they passed out of sight. "So, where do pegs live?" I asked Titus.

"We live in the open fields beneath the skies, little human, wherever our wings can carry us," he replied in a deep rumble. "But entertaining as it has been, I believe my part in your lesson for the day is over. Here we are."

Titus came to a stop before an official-looking white stone building. Large silver letters posted above the entrance labeled it 'Seelie City Police Station'. He lowered himself to the ground so that I could climb down, my fists again bunched in the long hairs of his mane to keep from falling. I looked up in time to see Lorien sprinkle an oddly lumpy, blandly colored dust over his wide nose.

She bit her lip regretfully. "I'd give you more for all your help, Master Titus, but I'm afraid that's all the oatcake spell I can spare. Otherwise I won't have enough to pay for Sydney's ride back. You've been so kind to us. Allow me to do something else for you. If there's anything that's been paining you, I could heal it," she offered.

"Not to worry, Mistress Lorien, the spell will be fine," he replied in a kindly voice as he rose to his feet.

"Please?" she entreated.

Titus was silent for a moment. He seemed to be struggling with his pride. "Well," he said finally, "I suppose my back left hoof has been troubling me a bit of late. Probably just a stone bruise, but maybe a little healing wouldn't go amiss."

Lorien was already at the site of his complaint, gently sprinkling a fine silvery dust over the area. He lifted his heavy rear leg, gingerly stamping his foot into the ground, an expression of satisfaction spreading down his long face.

"Why thank you Mistress Lorien. That did the trick right nicely."

"Nothing to it," she said, sounding pleased.

"If you have need of me again, just ask any of the pegs. They'll know how to reach me. It was nice to meet both of you ladies—pleasure to serve." He nodded as he began to trot away.

Lorien and I echoed our gratitude and turned to enter the police station. I automatically prepared to hold one of the glass doors open for her, then noticed that she had already flown through another miniature door high in the wall. I smiled faintly as I pushed open the door designed to accommodate someone my size, and was assaulted by a chaotic rush of sound.

A harried little man with dark, wizened skin and a grizzled, brown beard sat on a high stool behind a long counter. He was surrounded by haphazard piles of papers. A distinguished-looking older gentleman stood before him in a tailored suit, quietly arguing about something. His hand gestures were an elegant enforcement of his dispute. But the volume of the many voices spilling from the unseen room beyond prevented his words from reaching my ears.

He glanced over at us as we entered, his fiery green eyes piercing me from a maturely handsome face, framed by salt and pepper hair, and sporting a neatly trimmed goatee. Three small, gold hoops pierced his left ear. The corners of his chiseled lips raised slightly when he saw me, but I found no comfort in his semblance of a smile. His attention only rested on me briefly, but it made me feel like an insect being pinned for study.

Lorien darted in front of me, trailing red dust as she motioned me to a seat in the far corner. She flew closer to whisper in my ear, "That's King Moab, ruler of the death djinns. Please Sydney, just sit here quietly and don't say a word. I'm going to try to sneak past Galen, while he's occupied with the king, and find Agent Sparrow. I'll be back as soon as I can."

My stomach lurched at the discovery that I was sitting several feet away from the king of the death djinns. Lorien disappeared into the chaos of the room beyond and I was left alone with the morbid desire to gape at him. I realized that something about him reminded me of Balthus, and I wondered if I could learn how to recognize death djinns by sight. Now that would be a useful skill, especially for someone in my position.

The door to the back room suddenly flew open and out stormed Sparrow, cursing under his breath in Gaelic. My heart fluttered and I resisted the urge to jump up and run across the room to him. He looked angry, and exhausted, and sexy as hell. His tie was pulled loose around his collar and his white button-down shirt was rumpled, the sleeves rolled up to his elbows to expose the tattoos inked into his tanned forearms. One of them was pulsing with a yellow glow. Lorien whizzed out after him, her wings dropping purple faerie dust.

"Ah, Agent Sparrow. Just the man I wanted to see. What is the meaning of this attack against my people?" King Moab's voice was calm and refined, but his words created a tension so thick he might as well have drawn a weapon.

My eyes widened as I watched the lines of one of Sparrow's tattoos expand and go blacker into stark relief against his skin. When he spoke, his tone held a composure that belied the fury radiating from him.

"King Moab," he nodded. "My apologies for your wait. I'm afraid all I can tell you at the moment is that we have charged several members of your tribe with the possession of unaligned souls—which as you know, is a very serious offense. I assure you that this is not meant to be an attack against your people, and that only those found guilty will be punished."

Moab's jaw clenched beneath his salt and pepper goatee. "This is ludicrous. The death djinns have lived by the terms of the soul contract for millennia. No member of my tribe would knowingly deal in the trade of an unaligned soul. I promise you, our council's punishment for doing so is far more...*unpleasant* than anything that would be inflicted by the Seelie Court."

"Be that as it may, possession itself is grounds for arrest. I will take your words under advisement, and if it is discovered that your djinns were unaware of the illegal status of the souls in question, they will of course be released." It was impossible to ascertain Sparrow's opinion on the matter from his carefully modulated tone, but I could guess that he thought the djinns' innocence unlikely.

"Mmm," King Moab responded with a razor-thin smile. His gaze sliced to me and I froze. "This is an interesting specimen to find in the waiting room of Seelie police headquarters—a non-magical human with an open contract. I don't suppose she has anything to do with your inquiries into the legitimacy of the affairs of my people."

Suddenly King Moab was towering over me. I gasped—I hadn't even seen him move. "Pretty little thing, isn't she? Bright, shiny soul too. I could find several uses for this one."

His emerald eyes burned into me, leaving me cold with fear. A faint whisper began in my brain, dissolving my growing terror and fogging my thoughts. I heard a voice softly murmur, "I wish..." and was horrified to find that it was my own.

"Yes, my lovely, what do you wish?" King Moab urged in a husky purr, gently caressing my cheek and sending unwanted desire cascading through my belly.

"Her business here is none of your own." It was a growl, low and menacing. The sound tore my eyes from King Moab's, and I was shocked to discover that it had come from Sparrow.

Lorien positioned herself between me and the king, sooty black dust filtering heavily from her agitated wings. Other than the glowing yellow design, all of Sparrow's visible tattoos had now thickened into a pulsing, nearly indistinguishable blackness that bled across his skin.

King Moab stepped casually back from me, giving me a slow smile that chilled me to the bone. "I was merely testing her resolve. No law against that. I would be careful if I were you, Agent Sparrow. You don't want to be accused of allowing your personal feelings to cloud your judgment during this investigation. I would hate for you to be reassigned due to any old grudges you might be harboring."

He faded into a smoky outline and was gone.

Sparrow muttered another harsh string of Gaelic curses and Lorien turned to face me anxiously, the dust from her wings changing from black to purple.

"Are you okay, Sydney?" she asked worriedly.

"I thought he couldn't just disappear from here like that," I said in a faint voice.

"He's a king, Sydney. He has close ties with members of the Seelie Court and standing authorization to do pretty much whatever the hell he pleases," Sparrow spat angrily.

Lorien's wings flickered faster for a moment, giving off a high-pitched buzz. Sparrow closed his eyes and sank into the chair next to me. "I'm sorry, Sydney. Lorien's right. Are you okay? If that bastard enspelled you, I swear I'll kill him."

My fingers reached out to soften the tension in his jaw, the desire to taste his lips so visceral that I almost wondered if *he* hadn't somehow enspelled me. I jerked my hand away when I realized what I had been about to do. It wasn't the time or place.

"No, I don't think he did," I denied softly. "I think he was doing exactly what he said—testing my resolve. He tried to persuade me to make a wish, but in the end he left it up to me."

Even if Moab had enspelled me, I didn't think I would have admitted it to Sparrow at that moment. I fully believed he would go after the djinn, and somehow I didn't think it would be a good idea for Sparrow to threaten the king.

His blue eyes were searching, but he seemed to accept my answer. "Are you sure you want to go through with this? Balthus is bound to try the same thing. He's not as powerful as the king, but he's a close second."

"We've already had this discussion, Sparrow. I need to do this."

"Dragon dung, Sydney! I've had my doubts about this idea from the beginning. And don't tell me your *resolve* wasn't swayed just now—I could see it in your face!" His voice was low and desperate.

The comment rankled, but I did my best to ignore it. "First of all, *dragon dung?*" I repeated teasingly. "And second of all—I've made up my mind, Sparrow. The only thing that Old Moby did was help me prepare for

Balthus' tricks. Don't back out on me now." I gave him an irreverent smile.

Sparrow groaned a reluctant laugh. "Fine Sydney. You win. Again. Just do me a favor—don't ever call the king *Old Moby* to his face."

"I'll try to remember that."

"Incorrigible little witch," Sparrow muttered.

∞∞∞∞∞∞∞∞

Sparrow led the way past Galen, the dwarf manning the front counter, and into the organized chaos beyond. Wooden desks populated an open area, punctuated on two sides by closed doors and windows with drawn blinds.

Uniformed and plain-clothed officers filled the room, the larger variety draped across chairs and perched on the sides of desks, while the more diminutive variety hovered in the air between them. They were all joking and laughing companionably over different-sized steaming mugs of coffee. The thick, heavy aroma was a palpable presence.

They whooped and cheered as Sparrow passed through, some of them reaching out to pat him on the back. He gave everyone a forced smile and a hearty wave.

"Great raid, Pat," chimed a thin, graceful woman. She was breathtaking, with watery turquoise eyes and wavy red hair that seemed to billow in an unseen wind. I struggled to subdue a surge of jealousy.

"Who's that?" I whispered to Lorien, trying to sound casual.

Her knowing smirk told me she hadn't been fooled by my off-handed tone. "That's Daisy. She belongs to the tribe of the Marid djinn."

She grinned at the look of horror that passed across my face. "She's not a death djinn, Sydney. The Marids are water djinns, and they don't deal in the soul trade. Death djinns belong to the Ifrit tribe—they're fire djinns."

I repeated my mantra for the day: "Oh."

We followed a brooding Sparrow down a long hallway and through a locked door. It opened onto a covered walkway that led across a stark grassy courtyard, ending at a shiny metal gate in a grey stone wall. Burly guards nodded at Sparrow as we passed through the gate, beyond which crouched a stone bunker, imposing in its sheer massiveness.

After clearing the silent efficiency of prison security, we were buzzed through another locked gate. This led onto a brightly lit, sterile hallway, lined with modest cells whose bars were set into a clear Plexiglas. The only comforts provided were a flimsy-looking cot, a lidless metal toilet, and a small television bolted into a high corner near the ceiling. I was surprised to see how many of the cells were inhabited only by an old-fashioned bronze oil lamp sitting on a narrow table.

Apparently the death djinn raid *had* been successful.

The single living creature I saw within one of the cells was a squat, ugly man curled up on a cot, snoring loudly. His skin was mottled and his light reddish hair was thin and wiry. He had a broad, flat nose and a grotesquely wide mouth.

"Goblin," whispered Lorien in distaste.

Sparrow stopped before one of the cells containing a table with an oil lamp and unlocked the door. "I've made arrangements to send you in—I think it will make for a better interview than forcing him out to talk to you."

I swallowed. "You can do that?"

"It's a complicated spell, which is one reason why it was so difficult to get authorized, but yes, I can do that. He won't be able to harm you—as long as you don't wish for anything," he added pointedly. "Are you ready?"

"I guess," I answered, my eyes glued to his.

"I need you to be certain, Sydney, because I'm sure as hell not."

I cleared my throat and looked at the lamp, unable to lie to Sparrow's face. "Yes, I'm ready."

"You've got twenty minutes," he said abruptly. "You already know he'll use every tactic he's got to try to persuade you to make a wish. Stay focused on what you want to ask him and remember why you're there, and you should be fine. This talisman is keyed to you." He held up a bright silver coin, slightly larger than a quarter, and depicting an intricately detailed tree on one side.

"If you want to come out before the twenty minutes are up, all you have to do is touch this and you'll instantly be transported back here. I'm going to slip it into your pocket, because I've spelled it to be very sensitive and I don't want it to react to your touch before you need it. Is that alright?"

I nodded mutely and lifted the hem of my silk shirt above my right front jeans pocket. Sparrow stepped toward me and leaned down, using two fingers to carefully pull the edge of the pocket forward. He tucked the coin inside, pushing it deep enough so that it wouldn't fall out, but leaving it easily accessible.

I inhaled shakily. I'd forgotten how good he smelled. His heady scent, combined with the brief intimacy of his touch, erased my growing fear. For an instant, only Sparrow and I existed, and I didn't care why he was touching me, as long as he kept doing it. He glanced up at me, straightening slowly, his blue eyes growing hot. He lingered for a moment before gently slipping his fingers back out of my pocket, the movement a tantalizing caress.

His gave me an unhurried smile and whispered, "Come back to me, Sydney."

Then he turned away, stepping toward the lamp to begin a soft chant. My nerve endings felt like live wires as my gaze left his back and drifted to Lorien. She was so studiously ignoring us, I wouldn't have been surprised to find her whistling.

"It's ready," Sparrow said. "When you touch the lamp, you'll be transported inside. He won't be allowed any physical contact with you. Just watch what you say, and we'll be waiting here for you when you come back out. Remember—twenty minutes."

"Good luck, Sydney—and no wishing!" Lorien cautioned.

"Thanks," I muttered as I stepped forward and grasped the lamp before I could change my mind.

I shut my eyes against the sudden blackness, and when I opened them again I was standing in a small, rounded room that glowed with soft, pleasing light. The trip was much more agreeable than the one using Lorien's transport powder, albeit to a much less agreeable destination.

I looked around to find Balthus reclining on an overstuffed love seat. He was elegantly dressed in dark slacks and a navy silk shirt, and disturbingly handsome, considering the threat he posed.

"Sydney—what a pleasant surprise! I wouldn't have thought it possible, but you look even more enchanting than I remember. Won't you have a seat?" He scooted to one side, offering me the space next to him.

I hesitated for a moment, then perched myself on the edge of the room's modest bed, deciding its intimate associations were preferable to the proximity of sharing the love seat.

"Hello Balthus," I said politely, trying to match his easy self-assurance and take control of the situation. "How are you doing?"

He gave me a mocking smile, his eyes sparkling with emerald fire as he re-centered himself on the love seat. "You mean other than being falsely incarcerated? I'm doing fine, thank you, Sydney. These accommodations are rather restrictive, although I suppose that they are…adequate, considering the situation. And you? How are you finding your new accommodations?"

"Uh, they're lovely, thank you," I answered, trying not to squirm at the obligation that question implied.

"I am pleased to hear it. I did my best not to cut any corners on that particular wish. I wouldn't have gone to the trouble of granting full ownership of the penthouse and arranging for complimentary use of the hotel's perks for just anyone, you know. I have special plans for us, Sydney. You will find that I can be an extremely desirable companion—quite literally what or whomever you wish."

The seductive intensity of his gaze pulled at me, and I found myself leaning forward, my breath coming a little faster.

"With only a few simple words, you can become immortal, Sydney," he whispered, his tone increasingly hypnotic. "Have you even stopped to consider the meaning of that? You would never age or grow sick. You would remain in eternal beauty, forever able to enjoy the endless pleasures I am offering you."

His voice was warm silk, gently entwining me with promises, both spoken and unspoken. I shuddered against the tendrils of desire swirling through me, and the effort it took to ignore them. When I pushed them down, they coalesced into a low ache.

"I don't want immortality Balthus." I forced the words out with difficulty. "And no matter how enjoyable you insist it would be, I have no desire to become anyone's slave. I came here for answers. I would appreciate it if you would stop trying to trick me into making a..." I clenched my teeth, stubbornly refusing to say the word. "I've already had my *resolve* tested once today, and it didn't falter then either."

Balthus grinned. "So, one of my cohorts has been attempting to persuade you to spend eternity with them instead of me? Well, I suppose I can't blame them. I can only hope that you weren't too tempted. You should know that, as the prince of my people, there are certain advantages I can offer you that most others could not."

I blinked to conceal my shock at the discovery that Balthus was the damned prince of the death djinns. No wonder Moab had reminded me of him; Balthus must be his son!

"Well, considering it was your *king* who attempted to persuade me, I think that my resolve will remain intact—prince or not," I answered.

A look of cold fury passed across Balthus' face before he smoothed his expression back into a semblance of charming amusement. "I think you would find spending eternity with me much more palatable than you would find spending it with Father. He is well-known for the ruthlessness of his appetites; I fear you would discover the true meaning of being a slave beneath his tutelage.

"I, on the other hand, have always found the infliction of pain—although sometimes necessary—much less satisfying than the sharing of pleasure. And I must admit that I have developed something of a fondness for you, Sydney. Though any of my people have the right to seek the completion of your contract, I have declared my intention to do so myself. I am most displeased that my father would disrespect my wishes in this manner. Thank you for letting me know; I must remember to speak with him about it."

Oh great, just what I needed—to have the attention of the death djinn king drawn toward me again. This was going swimmingly.

"I wouldn't concern myself with it too much if I were you. I got the feeling he was just toying with me to piss off Sparrow. He said something about old grudges?"

Genuine humor sparked in Balthus' eyes. "Is that so? Yes, Father's presence does tend to put Agent Sparrow on edge. And seeing Father in active pursuit of a contract would certainly have *pissed him off*, as you so eloquently put it. Maybe I will forgive Father for his interference with my claim on you after all. If Agent Sparrow was in attendance, he was probably unable to help himself."

I resisted the urge to ask Balthus about the history between Sparrow and King Moab. My twenty minutes were ticking, and I was sure his version would be skewed anyway.

"Well, I am happy to have helped resolve a possible family conflict." I did my best to temper the sarcasm in my voice. "But I'm running out of time to chat, and I was hoping you would be willing to answer some questions for me."

"Your wish is my command, love." Balthus' voice was a guttural purr that sent shivers of anticipation down my spine. His effect on me was becoming damned annoying.

"I was hoping you could tell me something about the woman whose soul you were arrested for being in possession of," I continued doggedly.

His eyes widened. "Now I wonder what your interest in that would be. Not jealous are you, my pet?"

I tried to school the disgust from my expression, but Balthus' chuckle told me that I hadn't been particularly successful.

I shrugged, hoping he would take my inquiry for innocent curiosity. "Well, I saw her in the hospital. She did look a bit like me."

"Merely a coincidence, I assure you. As I have already explained to Agent Sparrow and his associates, I won that soul during a game of chance with a goblin. It was the only thing of worth he had left to offer. Goblins tend to have a penchant for excessive gambling, you see," he added instructively, "and this one was no exception—but he was particularly incompetent at it. He was quite pitiful, actually.

"Anyhow, when he gave me the soul, it seemed perfectly normal. I was able to detect that the woman didn't have any spell casting ability to speak of, but I found her physical form rather lovely and could have made use of her in another, equally enjoyable manner. So I took her."

I wrinkled my nose in distaste, but remained silent.

"When I parted ways with the little cheat of a goblin, I believed I was in possession of the newest addition to my collection of souls. It was only later, when I called the woman to me and she didn't appear, that I discovered her lamentable condition.

"I suppose it would have been wise to question how she came to be in such a state—but I'm afraid that, at the time, I wasn't able to see past my fury.

"My only thought was to find the little swindler and take my satisfaction in some other way, but to no avail—I hadn't bothered to ask his name." Balthus heaved a sigh, anger darkening his features for a moment.

"I was determined to salvage my loss in some manner, and it was then that I came across you, Sydney. Your resemblance to that unfortunate woman may have been what drew me to you initially. But I was quite taken with you from the moment I began following you.

"And when you wished for death, why it was music to my ears! I couldn't believe my luck. I knew immediately that we were meant to spend eternity together, you and I. So you see, any physical similarities you share are merely a coincidence. Or perhaps, if you look at it from my perspective, surely fate must have been at work."

He fixed me with a heated look that whispered an endless promise of wicked pleasures. I dropped my gaze, trying hard to ignore him.

"So, you had no idea that the woman's soul was unaligned from her body?" I asked, forging ahead with growing difficulty.

He was quiet for a moment. "Look at me, Sydney," he said softly.

My eyes rose of their own accord.

"I wonder, my love, if you are attempting to prove my guilt or my innocence. I have no need to steal souls. Throughout the years, countless mortals have been eager to trade their souls for the wishes I grant, the immortality I bestow, and the security of having their comforts provided for throughout eternity. It is no idle boast when I tell you that, in your current mortal state, you are incapable of comprehending the extent of the pleasure I can offer you."

He gazed at me steadily, the flecks of green light in his eyes like sparks igniting flames of desire throughout my body. I sucked in a breath as I felt a gentle caress move down my cheek and across my jaw to linger over the sensitive expanse of my neck. My eyes never left his. I knew that he hadn't moved to touch me. And the knowledge that he was doing it with his mind somehow made it infinitely more erotic.

"I want you, Sydney." His words were a dark seduction. "Tell me what you wish and I will give it to you. I can give you more than you could ever imagine."

The caress moved lower, lightly tracing my collar bone, and lower still, dipping into the valley between my breasts and then dividing to spread enticingly across their upper curves. The sensation was mesmerizing, and my lust-drenched brain was suddenly having trouble remembering why it shouldn't allow something that felt so wonderful to continue.

"Oh, Goddess," I murmured. "I wish…"

I felt an uncomfortable tug at the core of my being. It jerked me back to awareness and sent me straight into panic mode. My twenty minutes were up and I was about to be pulled out of the room. I huddled into a ball, reflexively wrapping my arms around my midsection in an attempt to resist the pull.

"Balthus, I have to go now. Tell me how to find this goblin—you must remember something that could lead me to him—please!" I pleaded desperately.

There is another who was witness to our bet. I will tell you how to contact her, if you swear not to reveal her identity to the Seelie police.

I realized with shock that he hadn't spoken aloud. I had heard him in my mind.

"I swear!" I whimpered, the force of the pull becoming painful.

Her name is Ophelia Jameson. You will find her in the 8th floor penthouse at your hotel. She was with me that night; she may remember something.

I sobbed in relief as I released the tension I held in my body, no longer able to resist the tug of the magic attempting to transport me.

I only tell you this as an act of faith. I intend for you to spend eternity at my side, Sydney. Do not disappoint me.

Balthus' voice faded to silence as everything went black. I opened my eyes to find myself standing in the glaring brightness of the cell with the bronze oil lamp sitting on the table. It was disorienting to realize that I had just been inside something so impossibly small. Lorien hovered over me in concern, shedding purple faerie dust, and Sparrow supported me by my elbow, a furious expression tightening his features.

"Damn it, Sydney! Why did you resist the transport spell?" he exploded, his brogue thickened with irritation.

"Why didn't anyone bother to tell me that Balthus was the damned king's son?" I sputtered. It was the first thing that popped into my head to deflect his question.

Sparrow's grip on my elbow loosened, his gaze raking me uncertainly. "It didn't seem that important. I didn't think it would serve any purpose but to frighten you. How could it possibly have helped?"

I snorted. "A girl likes to know what she's getting into, especially when she goes for a solo interview with an amoral death djinn trying to gain possession of her soul!"

"You knew what to expect—and you nearly let him have you anyway! You started to make a wish just before I tried to pull you out, and then you resisted leaving him!" Sparrow dropped my elbow and turned away, swearing softly.

"You don't know..." I was going to tell him he didn't know what it was like to try to resist a death djinn in full seduction mode, but I realized it probably wouldn't go over too well. Then I replayed what he'd said and felt my face flush scarlet. "You were watching?"

He glared at me. "Of course we were watching. This is a prison; Balthus is an inmate."

Comprehension dawned as I glanced up at the small television in the corner, and mortification silenced me as I replayed all the intimate things Balthus had said to me. I tried to recall if I'd said anything embarrassing in reply, but all I could remember was the heat of his invisible touch and the way I'd responded to it.

Sparrow sighed and ran his fingers through his dark hair. "He didn't tell you anything he hadn't already told us, Sydney."

I briefly surfaced from my self-torment to consider that statement. Balthus had obviously known we were being observed, which must have been why he'd spoken to me in my mind when he'd told me about Ophelia Jameson in the 8th floor penthouse. And I'd sworn not to lead the police to her, which meant not telling Sparrow.

Goddess knew I shouldn't feel any loyalty toward Balthus, but for some reason I was still reluctant to break my word to him. Bending the truth was one thing, but lying outright had always made me uncomfortable. Not to mention the fact that I questioned the wisdom of breaking an oath to a death djinn—especially one who was already two thirds of the way to gaining possession of my soul.

What could it hurt just to talk to Ophelia on my own? If I found out anything of use, I could always take the information to Sparrow without revealing her identity. I realized Sparrow was speaking again.

"I can't even believe I agreed to this. We gained nothing, and almost lost you in the process," he railed, pacing the confined length of the cell. "You knew what could happen—and you still fought to stay with that bastard!"

I glanced over to find Lorien hovering silently in a corner, watching us with a troubled expression. I lay my hand on Sparrow's forearm as he passed, coaxing him to a stop. He stared stonily at the wall as I looked up at him.

"I didn't want to stay with him; I wanted to get information out of him. I was hoping he'd tell me something to help us find the goblin he claims gave him that woman's soul. I did almost make a wish, alright? But you know he used magic to persuade me. It wasn't real. And it wasn't useless. It was something I needed to do for my own peace of mind. If I had to do it over again, I'd do the exact same thing."

Sparrow finally lowered his eyes to mine, something akin to pain flickering within their blue depths. "I don't want you around any more death djinns until we get this resolved. With your contract two-thirds complete, their hold on you is too strong."

"Fine by me. Faeries are far better company than djinns, anyway," I teased, hoping to lighten his mood.

He shook his head at me, a faint smile playing around the corners of his lips. "How do you do that to me, Sydney? You say you're not a witch, yet you always seem able to make me fall under your spell."

My small chuckle faded as he covered my hand with the warmth of his palm, his fingertips sliding across, then beneath mine. He grasped my hand in his and brought it up to his mouth for a kiss. It was a charmingly old-fashioned gesture, but there was nothing old-fashioned about my body's response.

"I think it's past time to call it a day," he said, giving my hand a gentle squeeze and trailing his fingers across my sensitive palm as he released it. "I'll let you know if anything relevant turns up with regard to Balthus."

I could still feel the tingle of his fingertips as he led the way out of the cell and back up the long hallway. Lorien was being so quiet that I glanced back to make sure she was trailing behind us. She sent me a troubled half-smile. "I'll go find us a Peg," she murmured, darting past us toward the exit.

"Sparrow?" I began uncertainly as we passed a pair of security guards. I was trying to work up the courage to broach the subject of his history with King Moab. Although it probably wasn't any of my business, I was dying to know.

"Hmm?" he answered, sounding lost in thought. He held the door for us and I waited to speak again until he fell into step beside me as we approached the outer gate.

"What happened between you and King Moab?" I asked on a rushed breath.

His expression remained remote as he led us through the courtyard and around the outside of the police station, along white stone walls that glittered in the sun. When he didn't answer, I resolved to let it go—at least temporarily. But then he stopped me as we were almost to the street.

He put his hands on my shoulders and looked down at me, his gaze intent.

"It's been a long day, Sydney. I promise I'll tell you about King Moab, but some other time, okay?" he said, weariness breaking through the strength in his voice.

"Okay," I sighed my agreement. His palms were steady and warm against my upper arms, and my eyelids fluttered closed as I inhaled his spicy scent, struggling to restrain the urge to lean into him.

He let go of my shoulders and I felt one of his hands come up to softly cup my chin, his thumb brushing over my bottom lip. Muscles clenched low in my belly and I stifled a moan as my lips parted in response.

"Take care of yourself, Sydney," he said in a hushed voice as he released me.

Disappointed at the loss of his touch, I opened my eyes…but he was gone.

<u>Chapter 10 - The Price of Passion</u>

"I've never been so sexually frustrated in my life," I groaned.

I held the silver coin Sparrow had given me in one palm, keeping it in contact with my skin in the same way I would have worn one of his shirts to surround myself with his scent. The man made it shockingly easy to forget about Jeremy's betrayal—*probably too easy*, I thought. But I wasn't ready to give up such a pleasant distraction.

I'd found the coin in my pocket when I took off my jeans last night, pulling it out before I thought about what I was doing. Luckily, it hadn't transported me back to Balthus' prison cell. I studied it curiously now.

I had never seen its like. It had an ancient feel to it somehow, yet it was as bright and flawless as a newly minted dime. On one side was a full, lushly blooming tree, depicted in meticulous detail, with hundreds of tiny leaves that glinted in the light. On the other was an intricate representation of a sun, with curving scroll-work arms and a swirling, energetic mass of Celtic knot-work throughout its center.

It made me think of Sparrow's Aegishjalmur tattoo.

I'd slept with the stupid thing under my pillow simply because it reminded me of him. I couldn't decide what was more embarrassing—my sudden regression into acting like a teenager with a crush, or my recent difficulty with controlling my body's response to every half-sidhe or death djinn who came within ten feet of me.

Sunny made a strained sound that I took for commiseration.

"My brain is turning to mush," I complained. "I almost sold my soul into eternal enslavement for the promise of 'endless pleasure', such that I am apparently 'incapable of comprehending in my current mortal state'—not once, but twice yesterday.

"Goddess Sunny, I haven't gone this long without sex since I started having orgasms! And I can't remember ever wanting it this much. Why did Jeremy have to go and cheat on me? My life was so simple and comfortable before all this."

Jeremy—I'd been trying to avoid all thoughts of him, but in my current state of mind I couldn't help reflecting on the fact that, for the most part, I'd enjoyed our sex-life. He hadn't always made sure I finished before he did, and often his idea of foreplay had consisted of tickling me into laughing submission—which was fun sometimes, although admittedly, it could get tiresome.

Well, okay, I guess the sex could have been a little better. But at least it had been regular. I hadn't realized how much I'd miss it.

"Uh, Syd?" Sunny croaked.

Sunny's tone made me look up from my self-pity party...and up some more, to take in the gorgeous, six-foot blonde woman who hovered uncertainly over me.

"Angelica?" I squeaked. "How did you…"

"I am so sorry Sydney! I did not mean to invade your privacy in such an unforgivable manner. I will just go now." She began a rigid walk toward the door, her graceful fingers clenched into fists at her sides.

"Wait! Angelica, no, please sit with us," I stuttered.

She cringed and glanced back at me.

"Please," I reiterated with calm acceptance. In the last week my mind had gotten about as blown as I thought it was possible to get. The sudden unexplained appearance of my supermodel housekeeper in the living room was just par for the course.

She sighed and moved stiffly into a chair, crossing her long legs primly and looking uncomfortable in the extreme.

"How did you get in here?" I asked.

Angelica remained awkwardly silent, her blush slowly staining her cheeks a deep shade of crimson.

Sunny grunted, apparently unable to contain herself, and burst out, "She just appeared there, standing next to you—right out of thin air!"

I looked disbelievingly from her back to Angelica.

Sunny rolled her eyes. "What? You're going to question *me* now, faerie girl? Tell her, Angelica," she demanded.

"Sunny is correct," Angelica finally murmured, seeming to resign herself to an inevitable fate. "I was drawn to the intensity of your sexual yearnings, Sydney. I tried to resist the call, but I was unable to."

Sunny and I exchanged a baffled glance.

Angelica groaned in misery, looking like she'd have rather been anywhere else. "I am a succubus, you see. By my very nature, I am inextricably linked to the sexual desires of mortals. I have been experiencing some difficulty lately, however, with controlling my response to the call of passion."

"Uh *huh*," grunted Sunny, eyeing Angelica dubiously. "So, someone decides they're in the mood for a booty call and you just snap your fingers and show up. And then what?"

Angelica's expression turned earnest. "Well, usually I would grant their every sexual fantasy and desire, until they were limp with satisfied exhaustion."

Sunny's eyes grew comically wide, and I was pretty sure mine were about to pop out of my head as well. I guessed that's what I got for assuming my mind was incapable of being blown further.

"But after millennia of being at the sexual beck and call of countless aroused mortals," Angelica continued, "one begins to wonder if there isn't more to life. I began to resent the invasions of my privacy and gradually reduced the number of calls I answered, until I ceased answering them altogether. Many of my kind have shunned me for my decision to embrace celibacy, but it is my life and I feel I should be able to live it according to my choosing." Her voice had taken on a decidedly stubborn tone.

Unable to peel my eyes from her, I cleared the dryness from my throat as I tried to form a response. "Of course you should," I agreed hoarsely. So that was where the whole 'right to privacy' and 'conduct our lives the way we see fit' rant had come from when she'd agreed not to reveal Jasper's presence to hotel management.

"So, how come you showed up for Syd's little moaning session about not getting any?" Sunny asked, her voice falling somewhere between sympathy and glee.

I tossed a throw pillow at her. It missed and landed next to Jasper, who looked up from his interrupted nap with a green glare.

Angelica frowned helplessly. "It seems my decision to deny my natural tendencies has had an unexpected side effect. The longer I go without sexual gratification, the harder it becomes to deny the call of passion—any call of passion. Normally succubi and incubi are able to pick and choose which calls they answer. And we generally will go to a mortal during the dream state, so that they believe they have simply experienced an unusually erotic dream.

"But the intensity of Sydney's sexual frustration called to mine and I was unable to resist. So far, I have been able to conceal my presence when this has happened—however it becomes more and more difficult. I have not yet figured out how to resolve this problem," she explained in an apologetic tone.

"Um, I can see how fulfilling everyone else's desires all the time could get pretty tiresome," I offered, "but although celibacy can be good for certain people, it seems like maybe it's a rather drastic approach for someone like you. Have you considered having a relationship with just one person? You know—someone who's aware that you're a succubus and doesn't mind helping you ignore all those...calls of passion?"

"Yeah," Sunny enthused, "someone who'll get together for your steamy little trysts at times that are convenient for both of you!"

Angelica stared at us with an expression akin to horror. "Monogamy?" she whispered, her pert nose wrinkling in disgust.

Sunny snorted.

"Well, yeah," I chuckled. "How much worse could it be than celibacy?"

"Succubi are *not* monogamous creatures," Angelica denied vehemently.

"Well, apparently they're not celibate creatures either." Sunny was laughing openly now.

I shrugged. "You could at least give it a try. It might ease some of that pent-up frustration that has you popping up unexpectedly in people's living rooms," I said with a pointed smile.

The look on Angelica's face reminded me of the first time my Grandma had scooped a pile of creamed spinach onto my plate. I couldn't believe I was actually supposed to put something that disgusting-looking into my mouth.

"You might be right." She sounded shocked that she was even considering such a thing. "I suppose I could give it a try."

"I bet you could have any man—or woman—you wanted," Sunny offered.

"I'm sure you could," I agreed with a glance at her perfect figure.

"Just do me a favor," I added, "and don't choose a half-human, half-sidhe named Patrick Sparrow. I don't think I could take another man cheating on me."

Whoa. Where had that come from? Sparrow and I weren't together—i.e. it was none of my business who he slept with. I really needed to get a handle on the teenage crush thing.

"So you *do* have a handsome man to bring you many orgasms!" Angelica said, regaining some of her usual spark. "I hope you have allowed him to stand and enter you from behind while you knelt on that bed of yours. And the couch! You must have lowered yourself onto his beautiful erection while he sat on the couch. Tell me, which did you prefer?"

I choked, feeling heat suffuse my face until I was sure it must be glowing candy-apple red. Sunny howled with laughter, tears streaming from her eyes. Angelica looked at us in bewilderment. "What?" she asked.

"I'm afraid Syd hasn't had the chance to experience Patrick's beautiful erection yet," Sunny wheezed. "Hence, her sexual frustration."

"Oh, right," Angelica frowned. "Well, why has this man not granted you the fulfillment you deserve?" she asked in an affronted tone. "Does he prefer men?" She gave me a look of sympathy.

I closed my eyes in mortification.

"Uh no, I think it's quite possible that he prefers Syd," Sunny interjected on my behalf, still chortling gleefully.

In deference to my crush, I had described all of my Sparrow encounters in minute detail for Sunny. She agreed that, although he seemed to be holding back, he acted as if he was interested in me.

"Some humans tend to be a little more reticent about their sexual practices than you are, though, Angelica," Sunny continued with a snigger. "They go through this whole ritual of getting to know each other first— maybe a little kissing here and there, then some hot and heavy foreplay— before they actually jump into the sack together.

"Syd and Patrick have only met a few times and they aren't to the erection sharing stage just yet. Plus, Syd has been a little preoccupied lately with finding her way out of a death djinn contract. Not to mention that she's still married to her loser of a cheating husband."

"Why don't you just lay it all on the table," I grumped.

I felt a soft, warm probing, like a spot of concentrated sunlight hitting my chest. "But your soul is still intact, Sydney," Angelica informed me, concern etching her voice. "How can you have completed a contract with a death djinn?"

"Oh, it's not completed yet," I assured her. "I have one more wish to go."

"Oh Sydney, this is no good! You must not give in and make that wish, no matter what they promise you. Nothing is worth the eternal enslavement of your soul!

"Certain of my kind have been known to deal in the soul trade, using their powers to bestow ultimate pleasure as their bargaining tools. It is an evil business. Death djinns will promise the same; you must remain strong. I know several very talented and upstanding incubi who would be happy to relieve your sexual frustration, so that you will not be as tempted by the death djinns," she offered.

"Uh, thanks, Angelica. That's very kind of you—but I think I'll hold off on going that route until the situation becomes a little more desperate," I declined, trying my best to sound appreciative.

Come to think of it, I probably would have taken her up on it if I hadn't had Sparrow on the brain—or more aptly, other parts of my anatomy. Who was I kidding—how much more desperate could it get?

"Well, if you're sure," she said doubtfully. "Why do you not simply enjoy sexual congress with the man you have married, then? Is that not what humans do?"

"I told you—he cheated on her," Sunny interjected with a sympathetic wince in my direction.

Angelica looked at both of us in confusion.

"The monogamy thing," I mumbled.

"Oh," Sunny said in sudden comprehension.

She began a hasty explanation for Angelica, presumably so that I wouldn't have to.

"Syd's husband had sex with someone else. Generally when two humans marry, they both expect the other person to remain sexually faithful only to them for as long as they're married. It's like a promise they make to each other. If one person breaks that promise, it's a serious betrayal. Some couples work it out, but others are unwilling to accept the betrayal and can no longer be happy remaining in the marriage."

Angelica nodded slowly, as if she was trying hard to grasp the concept. "It is not in my nature to embrace this monogamy you seem to prize so highly. But if you claim that your husband engaging in acts of sexual pleasure with another was a betrayal, then I will accept your judgment.

"I know some rather vile little imps that delight in causing mayhem and destruction. Would you like for me to send them to his home to wreak havoc as punishment for this betrayal?"

Sunny watched me with horrified amusement. And I found myself pausing in serious consideration, before letting out a regretful sigh.

"That's very sweet of you, Angelica, but the house is half mine, so I really don't want it destroyed. Plus it would probably give me bad karma, and Goddess knows I don't need any more of that.

"Although," I added thoughtfully, "maybe it wouldn't be *too* bad if they wrought just a *tiny bit* of havoc at his office. Not only on him, but on that little tramp he cheated on me with."

Sunny's eyes widened and I shot her a wicked grin.

"Hmm," Angelica mused, "I don't think these particular imps would be good for such a job. They would be very difficult to restrain once released. But I will think about it and let you know when I have come up with a more appropriate reprisal for your husband and this…'tramp'."

Sunny snorted.

"So, you forgive me for intruding in this manner?" Angelica asked uncertainly.

"Don't give it another thought," I assured her, "you're welcome any time. But I still think you should try the monogamy thing—if only to regain your control."

"I thank you for the advice." Angelica grinned. "I should probably go and leave you to your plans for the day. Do you mind if I just blink out instead of using the door?"

"Doesn't bother me in the least," I said. "Sunny?"

"Uh, no, fine with me—but can I talk to you for a second before you go?" Sunny asked hesitantly.

She rose and motioned for Angelica to follow. I watched in bemusement as they whispered to each other briefly in the corner. Sunny returned to the living room with a secret smile as Angelica gave a final wave and blinked out.

"What was that about?" I asked with a bland expression.

"I'll tell you later, I promise," Sunny answered with glee.

"Hey—I'm your best friend—we're not supposed to keep secrets from each other! Was it about me?" I demanded.

"No," she tsked at me. "It was a personal sexual concern and I wanted the unique perspective of a succubus. I'll let you know how it works out after I try her recommendation."

"I can't believe you're not going to tell me. After all the years we've known each other," I said in a wounded voice

"Oh, fine. Have it your way," she said sulkily. "I asked her about sending those incubi to me, since you didn't seem interested in taking her up on the offer. I would have told you about it afterward."

"Unique perspective of a succubus, my ass." I dissolved into helpless laughter. Sunny struggled to hold onto her sulky expression for a moment, but couldn't quite manage it and erupted into giggles.

"I haven't had this much fun in ages!" she gasped finally. "Who knew Palm Beach was such a hotbed of supernatural activity?"

"Does it really surprise you?" I groaned, my stomach hurting from the laughter.

"So what's next on the agenda?"

"Well, we might as well pay a visit to Ophelia," I suggested, still wiping away tears of mirth.

"Sounds good to me," Sunny agreed. "Think it's too much to hope that she'll be as entertaining as Angelica?"

"Only one way to find out," I replied, heading for the phone.

∞∞∞∞∞∞∞∞∞

"Hi, could you connect me to Ophelia Jameson in the 8th floor penthouse?"

"Certainly, one moment please," came the polite reply.

The line clicked during the transfer, then began ringing. Sunny watched me expectantly.

I huffed in disappointment after the fifth ring. "She's not answering."

"Maybe she's out." Sunny shrugged.

I continued to hold onto the stubborn hope that she would pick up, but after the tenth ring Sunny said, "We'll just try her later, Syd."

I was about to give in and hang up, but just as my finger was over the button I heard a muffled, "Hello?"

I quickly pulled the phone back up to my ear, butterflies winging around my stomach. "Ophelia Jameson?"

Silence greeted me on the other end. "Uh, hi. My name is Sydney. Balthus suggested I contact you…"

"The Master?" a breathless voice responded.

"Uh, yeah, I guess." The Master? What kind of crap was that?

"You have spoken to Master?" she crooned. "Is he alright? Has he a message for me?" Her tone held something approaching rapture.

"Well, I saw Balthus yesterday…"

"You lie!" she interrupted, sounding enraged. The transformation was so startling that I wondered if a different person had grabbed the phone. "The Master has been falsely imprisoned! He would have come to me if he had been released!"

"He hasn't been released," I explained in the soothing voice of someone trying to calm a cornered animal. "I was allowed a brief interview with him inside his prison cell. He told me how to get in touch with you because he thought you might be able to answer some of my questions."

"You saw Master?" she breathed on a sigh. "Who are you?" she asked, her tone sharpening again.

"My name is Sydney...Corrigan," I answered. I was still trying to get used to using my maiden name. "I live upstairs from you in the 10th floor penthouse."

"You!" she accused.

"Uh, me?" I responded in confusion.

"You are the mortal whom Master covets, and for whom he broke our last date before he was betrayed and wrongfully arrested! I have been Master's favorite for over two centuries—you will not usurp my place in his affections!" she informed me angrily.

"Whoa—I have no intention of usurping Master's, I mean *Balthus'* affections. As a matter of fact, I have no intention of having any further contact with him at all. That's kind of why I need to talk to you. I was hoping you had some information that could help me...break my ties with Balthus, so to speak."

She was silent for a moment. "I will not be fooled by your tricks," she warned, her voice turning childish. "Master is powerful and much desired by many. But he prizes me above the others. Only I have been able to perfect the art of pleasing him."

"And he's all yours," I agreed. "I'd just like to meet with you for a few minutes, if I could. You're welcome to come up here if you like, or I could come to you."

I waited. She gave no response.

"The Master did suggest this meeting himself," I urged with a silent grimace at my tactics.

She huffed. "Fine. You will come here. You must give me one hour to prepare."

The line went dead and I stared dubiously at the receiver.

"What did she say?" Sunny demanded, tapping her foot in impatience.

"She said I should come over, but she needs an hour to 'prepare'."

"What does that mean?" Sunny frowned.

I shook my head slowly. "Damned if I know. Hopefully all it means is that she has to get dressed and tidy up for visitors. Although, she seems to have gotten it into her head that I'm some sort of threat to her relationship with Balthus. And she sounds like she's the psychotically jealous type."

"I'm coming with you," Sunny stated flatly.

I snorted. "Damned right, you are."

∞∞∞∞∞∞∞∞∞∞

An hour later I called Ophelia again. After about the twelfth ring she picked up and churlishly agreed to grant me access to her elevator stop. I didn't mention that I was bringing Sunny—I figured I'd deal with that when we got there. Ophelia's moods seemed to be unusually volatile, and I didn't want to jeopardize her reluctant agreement to meet with me.

Sunny and I stepped off the elevator into an outer foyer blooming with fresh cut flowers—roses of every color, combined with lavender and white daisies, and some type of delicate purple-blue blossom. Fresh herbs had been used for the accenting greenery—soft licorice traces of fennel mingled with something light and citrusy.

The door to the penthouse slid open in front of us, and there stood a petite brunette in a clinging, floor-length dressing gown of gleaming copper silk. Everything about her had a strange, artificial perfection— from her artfully tousled curls, to her flawless makeup, to her freshly manicured fingers and toes. Her placid smile faltered for a moment when she realized there were two of us, but she quickly pasted it back into place.

"Let me guess," she purred, "you must be Sydney." She indicated me with a delicate lift of her chin.

"That's right," I said, trying to appear friendly and non-threatening.

She arched her back in a sultry movement that thrust her obviously enhanced breasts forward, widening the vee at the neck of her robe. Then she leaned casually into the door frame and gave me haughty smile. "The Master is very predictable. He always chooses the same type of mortal for his brief dalliances. I have seen him go through countless women like you over the years. Although, I must say his taste is slipping a bit." Her disdainful gaze traveled over my t-shirt and jeans.

I forced myself not to rise to her bait.

"And who is your friend? I hope you don't think to gain The Master's favor as well. You are most definitely not his type," she informed Sunny arrogantly.

"This is my friend, Sunny," I interjected in haste, glancing at Sunny's tell-tale raised eyebrows and pursed lips, and trying to avoid the verbal onslaught I knew was coming. "She's staying with me, so I brought her along. *Neither* of us have any interest in Balthus. I only want to talk to you."

Ophelia tipped her head into her raised shoulder. "Fine. Come in, then." She turned and glided deeper into her den.

Heavy burgundy curtains were drawn over the sliding glass doors to block out the sunlight, and a multitude of tiny flames from a host of candles and glass oil lamps cast a warm glow over the room. Flower arrangements similar to those in the outer foyer were scattered throughout the space, but the warm smell of baking pastries overpowered their scent.

Sunny and I followed Ophelia into a sitting room inhabited by deep velvet couches in a rich claret that complimented the drapes. Ophelia indicated we should have a seat, waiting for us to take our places on one couch before she lowered herself onto the other. Then she reached toward the coffee table and a formal silver tea service, with a set of antique china teacups and saucers in a delicate rose pattern.

"Your place is beautiful, Ophelia. And that's a lovely tea service," I commented, hoping to appeal to her pleasant side—assuming she had one.

"It is so seldom that I have visitors," she confided, nibbling her lower lip with a shy smile. "I wanted everything to be perfect. How do you take your tea?"

"Oh, I'm fine," I began. I hastily reconsidered at the lightning flash of anger that flickered across Ophelia's face. "Actually, some tea would be very nice. Two lumps of sugar and a splash of milk, please."

Ophelia fixed my tea as I requested and carefully handed it to me, her shy smile returning as quickly as it had gone. She looked questioningly at Sunny.

"Uh, the same for me, thanks." Sunny glanced at me, pursing her lips in a silent whistle that questioned the sanity of our hostess. She didn't drink tea, being of the opinion that it was a pointless waste of water that could have been used to brew coffee instead, but she was perceptive enough to realize that raining on Ophelia's little tea party would be a bad idea.

Ophelia hummed a toneless melody as she handed Sunny her cup and then fixed one for herself. I was relieved to see that she added both milk and sugar to hers as well, the possibility of her trying to poison us with something from the gleaming silver tray not having escaped my attention.

Her humming faded to silence as she raised her cup and smiled at us brightly in toast. "Now, what shall we talk about ladies?"

I waited for Ophelia to swallow before I took a sip. I had the strong suspicion that Sunny faked her accompanying sip and murmur of approval.

"Well, Ophelia, I wanted to ask you about something that happened several weeks ago. As a matter of fact, it has to do with the reason Balthus was arrested. He told me that you were with him recently when he won a soul from a goblin during some sort of bet?" My voice faltered as I watched Ophelia's hands begin to tremble. A look of pain passed across her face.

"Are you alright?" I asked, casting a worried glance toward Sunny.

"What? I'm fine," Ophelia snapped, seeming to recover from her brief reaction. "You ask me about a goblin? I do not associate with such creatures."

"Yes, I've heard that they can be rather unpleasant," I replied. "But nonetheless, I need to find this one. He gave Balthus the illegal soul that got him arrested. And Balthus says you were there when it happened."

Ophelia dropped her teacup, the pale liquid spilling out onto the buff-colored carpet at her feet. She clutched her middle and moaned, sweat breaking out across her forehead.

"Bad cramps?" Sunny asked sympathetically.

"The Master," Ophelia whimpered, "I need The Master." Her eyelids fell shut as she grimaced in pain and began rocking back and forth.

I knelt to retrieve her cup and mopped at the spilled tea with a napkin, looking up at her in concern. "Can I get you anything?"

"Why does Master not come to me?" she whispered pleadingly.

"Ophelia, is it getting bad again, honey? Here let me help," offered a kindly voice.

I started at the sudden appearance of a sprite hovering above Ophelia. Her color-shifting dress was a study in muddy browns and grays. Her wings looked tattered and her violet eyes were dull in her sallow face. She sprinkled a silvery dust over Ophelia, who slowly straightened and sighed in relief as her eyelids fluttered open.

"Who are you?" demanded the sprite, taking notice of Sunny and me.

"Interlopers!" cried Ophelia, seeming to have returned to her former unpleasant self. "This is the woman who has led Master astray with her wicked wiles! He promised me I could have the 10th floor penthouse as soon as it became available—yet he gave it to *her*. This companion of hers no doubt harbors hopes of worming her way into Master's affections as well." She pointed at Sunny.

A buzzer sounded from the kitchen. "Ooh! Scones!" Ophelia exclaimed in delight, jumping up and skipping into the other room, accusations against us forgotten.

"Wow," Sunny commented, raising her eyebrows at me. She twirled her finger beside her ear in the universal signal indicating that someone had flown over the cuckoo's nest.

"Who are you?" the sprite insisted, her hands on her hips as she hovered before us, tattered wings giving off a sad buzz of agitation.

"Sorry. I'm Sydney, and this is my friend, Sunny."

"And why are you here? It's been hard enough to keep Ophelia calm without Balthus' groupies coming by to rile her up!" she said angrily.

"Whoa, hold on sister. We are *not* Balthus' groupies," Sunny said, affronted.

The sprite looked peevishly from Sunny back to me, weariness radiating from her entire being.

"We had no intention of upsetting Ophelia, and we certainly don't want anything more to do with Balthus than is necessary," I said quickly. "Balthus did give me the 10th floor penthouse—it was my second wish. I haven't made a third, and I'm trying to figure out how to get out of his contract. That's why we're here. We need some information from Ophelia."

The sprite grated out a weak laugh. "Ophelia's the last person who'd be able to help you get out of your contract. She entered into hers quite willingly."

"She was with Balthus the night he won the unaligned soul that got him arrested," I explained.

"Or so he claims," Sunny said dryly.

"He says he got the soul from a goblin," I continued. "I need to find that goblin, and Ophelia may have seen him."

"And how will that help you?" the sprite asked, settling tiredly onto the polished metal edge of the coffee table.

I gazed at her steadily for a moment before answering. "If I can prove that he knew the soul was illegal, my contract may be deemed unlawful as well. I want it cancelled. And the goblin is my only lead."

"Sounds like a long shot, honey," the sprite sighed.

"It's the only shot I have." I smiled at her, but I couldn't keep the desperation from my voice.

"You realize that Ophelia's memory is fragmented. She's half mad with the loss of her soul," the sprite said, her expression pained.

"Is that what's making her act so...uh...erratically?" Sunny asked.

"That, and the withdrawal," the sprite answered, gazing toward the sound of humming spilling from the kitchen.

"Wait, losing her soul made her start to lose her mind?" I interrupted. "I thought the death djinn contract made you immortal and impervious to sickness and all that."

The sprite grunted. "Honey, immortality is a tricky concept. Even immortals can be killed, if you put their bodies through severe enough punishment. And as for mental suffering, immortality just gives you that much longer to experience it. A mortal who's traded their soul for immortality is usually fine for the first couple hundred years, but then the long separation from their soul begins to wear on their sanity. The immortality that death djinns grant is a weak version of what true immortals are born with."

"Can't anything be done to help?" I asked with a grimace.

The sprite nodded her head with a mirthless smile.

"Sure. Creatures like Balthus, who trade in souls, have the ability to grant their charges a sort of temporary repossession of their soul, to help drive away the madness. But even if he wanted to, he can't do it from a prison cell. And the sad truth is, after a couple of centuries, even the most intriguing of playthings can become tiresome—especially to a creature such as a death djinn," she said bitterly.

"By the time the madness hits, djinns rarely remain interested enough to keep their charges sane. Why bother, if they've got a stable full of newly acquired souls to keep them entertained? Or they'll find that the madness adds a fresh spin to an old relationship and won't *want* to do anything to alleviate it." She grimaced.

"Now, if we were able to get our hands on a vial of *true* immortality—not just the unnatural immortality granted through the contract—it would halt the madness altogether. But true immortality is a rare and costly thing." She shook her head sadly.

"No, I'm afraid there's not much we can do without Balthus. Ophelia suffers mentally from the extended separation from her soul, and physically from the withdrawal caused by her separation from him."

"Withdrawal?" Sunny repeated.

"Yes," the sprite sighed. "She gets worse with every day that she has no contact with Balthus. That's how he keeps them in line, you know—he gets them hooked on a pleasure that only he can provide. It's a powerful physical addiction, and it becomes painful when it's not sated." She looked at me pointedly, as if she knew I had nearly given in to Balthus' temptation.

"You mean *sex*? If she doesn't have sex with him she goes into withdrawal like some kind of heroin addict?" Sunny asked in disbelief.

The sprite gave a bleak nod of confirmation.

"What a miserable bastard!" Sunny exclaimed in disgust.

The sprite snorted her agreement. "I've done my best to get Ophelia over the worst episodes. But if Balthus isn't released soon, I don't know what will happen to us."

"It looks like it's been taking its toll on you too," Sunny said with a wince of commiseration.

"I'm her faerie guardian." She shrugged simply. "Once a sprite chooses to make that bond, it lasts for a lifetime. Our destinies are linked until one of us dies."

"I guess in a normal situation the human would go first," Sunny commented softly.

"Usually—I've only known one case where a faerie guardian passed on before her human charge," she answered, her eyes clouding over with memory.

I felt nauseous. Not only was this my fate if I didn't find a way out of the contract, but it would be Lorien's fate as well. And it wasn't lost on me that by asking for Ophelia's help to keep Balthus imprisoned, I was effectively asking her to doom herself and her faerie guardian to unimaginable misery.

"What's your name?" I asked quietly.

The sprite blinked at me as if she'd forgotten I was there. "Emily, honey, I'm Emily."

"Emily," I began, forcing myself to continue past the lump of guilt in my throat, "I know I have no right to ask this of you, but will you help me find out what Ophelia knows about the goblin?"

Emily studied me for a long moment, the wisdom and weariness of ages heavy behind her dull violet eyes. Then her face erupted in a smile, and it was almost as if a small portion of the weight she carried had been lifted from her shoulders. "I have a spell, cast by Lauringer herself, that I sometimes use when Ophelia gets really bad—to help remind her who she once was. Let's see if it can de-fragment her memory long enough to find out what she remembers about your goblin."

"Thank you," I replied, knowing it wasn't enough.

"You're welcome, honey. This is no way to spend eternity. You remember that."

"Who wants black currant scones?" Ophelia trilled, oblivious to the charged atmosphere in the room. She reappeared from the kitchen, carrying a rose-patterned china plate piled high with the warm pastries. She set it on the coffee table with care and delicately placed three of them on matching smaller plates, distributing them between us.

She looked at Emily and frowned, then her eyes lit up and she said, "I know, Emily, you can share mine." She crumbled off a small piece and gently nudged it toward the rim of her plate.

Ophelia watched us expectantly until we all took a bite, as if she was a child who had just tried out her Easy-Bake Oven for the first time. The scones smelled delicious, and tasted even better—soft enough to melt in your mouth and with just the right amount of sweetness. Ophelia glowed with pleasure at our chorus of deliberately happy chewing sounds.

I tried to savor mine, but the effort of forced enjoyment turned it into a tasteless paste in my mouth.

"These are perfect, honey," Emily complimented.

"Thank you, Emily," Ophelia answered primly around a mouthful of scone. "Would you like some tea?"

"Not right now, honey. I have a happy spell I want to try on you. You remember our happy spells?" asked Emily.

"Oh, yes! That would be lovely!" Ophelia clapped her hands.

"Alright, honey, here we go." Emily glided up to hover above Ophelia, reaching inside her drab dress to pull out a tiny pouch. She sprinkled a heavy golden dust over Ophelia, who blinked, and then shook herself as if awakening from a dream.

She gave Sunny and me a startled look, and then shifted her attention to Emily. "Was I getting bad again?" she asked worriedly. There was a light of awareness in her eyes that hadn't been there before, and she seemed to glow faintly golden with the spell.

"Not too bad," Emily grinned, some of the dullness lifting from her eyes as well. "These ladies need your help. That's mostly why I cast the spell. But it's worth it just to see you like this."

Ophelia smiled affectionately at Emily before turning her attention back to us. "I must apologize—I'm not myself lately. And I fear Emily's spell won't last very long. What can I do to help you?"

"Uh, no need to apologize," I stuttered, trying to get past my shock over the radically different woman the spell had revealed.

"I just appreciate you being willing to help. I wanted to see if you remembered anything about a goblin that you and Balthus met several weeks ago. Apparently Balthus won some sort of bet with him and took a soul as payment?"

Ophelia gave me a quizzical look. "As a matter of fact, I do remember that goblin. Balthus and I were having a drink at a tavern on the outskirts of the goblin territories. There were quite a few goblins at the gaming tables that night, but this one approached Balthus directly. He said he was feeling lucky and offered Balthus good odds on a wager.

"Balthus wasn't really there to gamble, but when the goblin offered a soul to secure the bet, he decided he couldn't refuse. The goblin seemed desperate, like maybe he was on a gambling binge or something." Ophelia shook her head. "Sometimes they get like that. They won't stop until they win big or lose everything.

"Anyway, he lost. And he didn't even put up much of a fuss about it. He just handed over the soul and walked away." She shrugged, as if to say that there was no accounting for the actions of goblins.

"Did you happen to catch the goblin's name?" I asked hopefully.

Ophelia shook her head slowly. "No, sorry. And you know goblins—they really do all look alike. They take pride in it. Although, if I recall, there *was* something different about him…that's right, he had a tattoo or a mark of some kind on his hand!" she recalled with excitement.

"It was on his palm. I think he was trying to keep it hidden, but I caught a glimpse of it as he tossed the dice. It looked like the number eight." She traced the symbol on her own palm with a manicured nail, one loop flush with her index finger and the other with her pinky.

"Sideways like that? Looks like the symbol for infinity," I said, frowning in thought.

"Does that mean anything to either of you?" Sunny asked them. "An infinity symbol tattooed on a goblin's hand?"

Ophelia and Emily exchanged mystified glances, both shaking their heads in the negative.

"Oh, and one more thing," Ophelia added with an uncertain grimace at Emily. "I overheard him talking about the Unseelie Court."

"The Unseelie Court! Oh Ophelia, Balthus hasn't been associating with them, has he?" Emily groaned in alarm.

"No, no—of course not!" Ophelia exclaimed anxiously. "I just happened to overhear the goblin bragging to some of the others about his connections. He claimed to be a regular guest on the Hell Ride. And maybe that's all it was—bragging. I wouldn't even have mentioned it, except for that I thought it might somehow help you find him."

She looked uncomfortably from Emily back to Sunny and me.

"Okay, I've heard of the Seelie Court—but what's the Unseelie Court?" I asked in confusion.

Both Ophelia's and Emily's gazes shot to me in disbelief. Emily was the first to offer an explanation. "The Unseelie Court is the opposite of everything the Seelie Court stands for. They're the largest organized force for evil in the faerie realm. Their sole purpose is to upset the balance of good and evil, with the hope that chaos will take reign and evil will come out on top. They pose an ever present threat to the Seelie Court's efforts to keep the balance in check."

Sunny and I exchanged glances.

"And what's the 'Hell Ride'?" Sunny asked.

"That's the Unseelie Court's idea of a fun way to spend an evening," Ophelia answered in distaste. "A bunch of them get together on the Hell Barge and fly through the night sky, kidnapping unsuspecting mortals that are unlucky enough to cross their path. Then they torment and terrorize their victims until they grow bored, and deposit them unconscious back where they found them.

"People who have experienced it usually wake believing it was all a horrible nightmare. Creatures called gleaners are responsible for erasing the memories—but sometimes they don't do a good enough job of it. Most of the people who claim to have been abducted by aliens are probably just remembering being taken on the Hell Ride."

"Great—now I have to worry about evil faeries kidnapping me for an anal probe," Sunny muttered under her breath.

"So, basically what you're telling me is that I'm looking for a goblin with a tattoo on his palm, and the only places we know he's been are at a tavern near the goblin territories, and possibly on this Hell Ride," I reiterated, trying not to sound as bleak as I felt.

"That's all I know," Ophelia grimaced apologetically.

"Well, it's more than I knew before." I sighed. "Can you tell me the name of the tavern, and how to go about finding the Hell Ride?"

"The tavern was 'The Grimy Goblin'. Any of the pegs who work near the goblin territories should be able to get you there. And as for the Hell Ride, I don't know of any way to find it—but your friend has the right of things," Ophelia said with a nod in Sunny's direction. "Trust me; you don't want anything to do with it."

"Maybe you could request an audience with Lauringer," Emily suggested tentatively. "She's pretty reclusive, but she's always been sympathetic to the plight of mortals who've lost their souls. She's the one who gives me this spell for Ophelia. If anyone can help you, it's probably her."

"How would I go about requesting an audience with Lauringer?" I asked.

Emily gave a hesitant shrug of her small shoulders. "I keep in contact with her to request refills for Ophelia's memory spell. If you want, I can explain your situation and let you know what she says."

"I'd really appreciate that, Emily. Thank you," I agreed gratefully.

Ophelia let out a soft moan. "I'm sorry," she gasped with a pained smile. "It's starting to hurt again." A tremor passed through her pale form and sweat began to bead across her forehead.

"Thanks for all your help, Ophelia," I said softly. "I'm so sorry about this."

She gazed up at me in reassurance. Then, as I watched, the light in her eyes dimmed and her expression faded to blankness, the golden glow of the spell winking out of existence.

"It's okay, honey, I've got you," Emily cooed in a comforting tone as she sprinkled silvery healing dust over Ophelia.

"Thank you, Emily, that's much better," Ophelia said, her voice turning child-like once more. "Would you like some more scone?"

"No thank you, honey, I'm full. They were very good, though." Emily smiled, but I could see the pain behind the renewed dullness in her eyes.

Ophelia glanced at Sunny and me sharply, as if she was just noticing our presence. "What are they still doing here?" she asked in annoyance.

"We were just leaving," I assured her. "Thank you for your hospitality, Ophelia. The tea was lovely and the scones were delicious."

"Oh. Yes, they were good, weren't they?" she said, humming as she poured herself another cup of tea.

"And thank you, Emily—for everything," I whispered as Sunny and I rose to leave.

My throat ached from holding back tears as we got on the elevator. "That was horrible," I said shakily.

"It was certainly no Sunday afternoon chat with Angelica." Sunny dropped a sympathetic arm around my shoulders. "I'm glad I came with you, though."

"Me too." We rode the rest of the way in silence.

"I think I'll take a shower," I mumbled when we reached the penthouse. I excused myself to my bedroom. Nothing so far had brought home the severity of my situation the way meeting Ophelia and Emily had. I had to *do* something. I couldn't let myself—or Lorien—end up that way.

I drifted by the gauzy curtains of my neatly made bed, stopping short when it dawned on me that I hadn't made my bed. Upon closer inspection of my pillow, I discovered what appeared to be a thin, oblong figurine depicting two frogs in an intimate embrace. It was made of a soft, rubbery material and was smooth except for the slightly raised curves of the embracing frogs. I noted the round plastic knob on the bottom and suddenly realized what it was.

I turned the knob for confirmation, and the figurine came to buzzing life in my hand.

I turned it back off and stared at it for a moment, torn between shock and amusement. I did love frogs, but it was rather more of a platonic love. *Gee, thanks Angelica,* I muttered, having no doubt that she was the one responsible for leaving me the erotic device. I shrugged and dropped it into the drawer of my night stand.

Who was I to turn down a gift? These were desperate times, after all.

<u>Chapter 11 - Faerie Tale</u>

"Syd, will you please talk to me? I know you're angry, but you can't avoid me forever. We have a house together; we had a life together. I'm still your husband. I understand your need to punish me, but I love you Sydney. I didn't mean to... Please—just talk to me, okay? Call me on my cell. I'll pick up. Bye."

I jammed my finger into the button that would erase Jeremy's message and hung up, staring out past my bedroom's balcony toward the rhythmically rolling ocean. Jeremy's tone was calm and rational throughout the message, but somehow that only served to piss me off more.

Let's see, it was 10:30 on a Monday morning. He'd definitely be at work now. I called the house and got the answering machine, as hoped.

I waited, tight-lipped, for the beep as I listened to my recorded voice cheerily proclaim that I'd reached Sydney and Jeremy.

"Hi Jeremy—it's Sydney. I got your message. I am not trying to punish you; I simply don't want to talk to you, seeing as the only relevant topics of conversation that come to mind are divorce and selling the house, neither of which I am currently prepared to deal with. If you're in more of a rush than I am to go ahead with either of those things, let me know and I'll do my part. But other than that, I have nothing to say to you right now. I'll let you know when I do."

I hung up. *I wasn't trying to punish him,* I fumed. I really didn't want to talk to him. If it felt like punishment to him...well, too bad. I had more important things to deal with. Besides, he should have known that before noon on a Monday was the absolute worst time to throw some emotionally coercive psychobabble at me.

Although, I supposed it was partly my fault for listening to his message during that particular time frame...

"Ouch." Sunny's comment interrupted my musings.

I turned to find her leaning in the doorway of my room, cradling a steaming mug of coffee in her hands. Apparently she'd been there long enough to hear my message.

I sighed. "Too harsh?"

"Well, that depends on what you were trying to accomplish. If, for instance, you were hoping to scare the man off calling you back for a while, I'd say it was probably a pretty good bet. Succinct, to the point—I liked it. But yes, I'm afraid it was rather harsh. Effective though—harsh, but effective. Personally, I like this side of your personality." Sunny grinned.

I couldn't help my answering smile. "So you don't think I'm a bad person for wanting to use a certain detective to distract myself from thinking about my husband?"

Sunny cocked her head at me and gave me an appraising look. Then she shrugged and offered, "Hey—Jeremy was the one who opened the door on the whole affair thing. He really can't claim to be too shocked if you happen to wander in after him. Besides, how could you be expected to resist Patrick Sparrow?" she teased.

"With that muscular body, and those sexy tattoos, and that whole trying to save you thing—I get hot just thinking about it." She stretched languorously, reaching upward with one arm until her back popped, carefully holding her coffee stationary with the other hand as a relaxed smile spread across her face.

I narrowed my eyes and studied her more closely. She was practically glowing with satisfaction. "You wouldn't happen to have received a visit from an incubus last night, would you?" I asked suspiciously.

Her smile widened and she breathed a little sigh of pleasure. "Two, as a matter of fact. They were twins. Beautiful twins, with long, dark hair and lean, muscular bodies, and huge, hard…"

The phone rang, interrupting Sunny's fulsome description of her nocturnal callers.

"How the hell did I sleep through all that? I am so jealous!" I shot her a look of disgust as I glanced down at the caller ID, noting with surprise that it was Hannah. Hannah always waited until she saw me to ask questions about her paperwork. There was only one reason she ever called me. I groaned.

"Good morning, Hannah! How are you?" I asked, feigning cheerfulness.

The call waiting beeped. It was Cindy. I ignored her, wondering if her ears were about to start burning.

"Sydney—so nice to hear your voice! I am doing fine, thank you. How are you? Did you have a good weekend?" Hannah asked.

Now there was a loaded question. "Uh, I kept busy. And you?"

"Very nice, very nice. An old flame flew in from Paris for the weekend—we had quite a lovely time together," she said, her voice filled with smiling innuendo.

Great. Apparently I was the only one who wasn't getting any.

"It would have been nice if he could have stayed longer, *toutefois c'est la vie,* yes?"

"I suppose so," I chuckled.

"*Oui,*" Hannah sighed dramatically. "Well, perhaps you know why I am calling, Sydney. Cindy is now three weeks behind on her payments. I hate to bother you at home, but she does not take my calls, and I know you speak with her often. Will you please mention it to her? Even a partial payment would be helpful, with business such as it is."

"I'll mention it to her, Hannah, but you know D.J.D.—they never seem to have enough money to go around."

"Yes, I know," she said with a sigh. "Well, thank you, Sydney. I will see you later this afternoon?"

"Yes, I'll be by before you close," I answered.

"Very good. I have a gift for you," Hannah said, her voice perking up.

"Oh, you don't have to do that, Hannah," I argued.

"*Oui,* but I want to. So I will see you later then. *Au revoir!*"

She hung up before I could say another word, leaving me with an uncomfortable feeling closely approaching guilt. I knew it wasn't my fault that D.J.D. wasn't paying her, but whenever she asked me to talk to Cindy about it, I felt like it was. The fact that she was nice enough to get me a present just made me feel worse.

"What doesn't Hannah have to do?" asked Sunny, interrupting my disgruntled musings.

I looked up to find her still lounging in the doorway, with a smile that wouldn't quite disappear, and the boneless fluidity of someone who'd just had a really good, really long massage. I shook my head and repressed a wave of longing and jealousy. Maybe turning those incubi down hadn't been such a brilliant move after all. Oh, well—at least I still had my frog vibrator. Joy.

"She says she has a gift for me when I come by this afternoon."

"Oh, that's nice. I wonder what it is. I hope it's not a bottle of her perfume." She grimaced, but a sip of coffee quickly renewed her contented smile.

"I don't know. I wi…I mean, I'd prefer it if she wouldn't do stuff like that, though."

Sunny's smoky green eyes sparkled with laughter. "Good save, Syd. And why? I think you should accept a gift when it's offered, and simply enjoy it."

"I'm sure you do," I smirked.

Sunny blew me a kiss.

The phone rang and I saw that it was Cindy again. Better answer it or she'd start to get frantic. "Okay, time to go back to work," I said, rising from the bed and shooing Sunny ahead of me as I jogged toward my dining room/office. Our habitual morning Salsa pulsed softly from the flat-screen's speakers as I passed.

"Hello?" I said, answering the phone just before it rang to voicemail as I dropped into the chair in front of my laptop. We'd already been through the morning banking, so I waited with baited breath to see what other delights Cindy had in store for me today.

"Oh, Sydney! Good—you finally picked up. I need you to go online and check Mickey's bank account to see if a deposit's come in," Cindy rattled off, sounding panicked.

As I typed in the bank site, Leslie's hateful voice pierced the waiting silence.

"THAT MONEY BETTER BE IN THAT ACCOUNT. THE CUT-OFF TIME FOR BETTING ON THE RACE IS NOON."

"Did you find it yet?" Cindy asked me anxiously.

"It's coming up now," I assured her. "Let's see. The balance is…$50,000.00."

Wow—where had that come from? On second thought; I didn't want to know.

"Oh, good!" Her relief was palpable. "IT'S THERE, MR. HOROWITZ," she reported cheerfully. A grunt of response sounded from somewhere nearby.

"There's this new sports betting site—maybe you could check it out for me," she suggested. "Let me see…where did I put that web address?" I heard her rustling through papers in the background.

I made a face, and then said in a pleasant tone, "While you're looking, I have a few things to go over with you. Hannah has been asking me about her payments. She says they're three weeks overdue now, but that anything you can give her would help. I also wanted to remind you that the electric bill has to be paid this week or they'll turn the lights off. And we got another 'Final Notice' from the IRS…"

"Never mind, I'll just look the site up later," Cindy interrupted. "Maybe we'll hit it big at the track today!" she added, presumably in response to my concerns. "Just remind me about the electric bill again before the end of the week. Gotta go!"

Ah, Cindy. So predictable, it almost wasn't even fun anymore.

I looked up to find Sunny sitting on the couch, absorbed in whatever her laptop screen had to offer, as she blew on steaming mug of black jet fuel number three.

"I need to talk to Lorien about the stuff we found out yesterday," I announced.

"I thought we were going back to work," she said distractedly.

"Well, what's the fun of working from home if you don't play hooky every once in a while? Besides, I'm reasonably caught up at the moment, so my time will be better spent figuring out how to save my soul. If I lose that, somehow I don't see myself keeping my job."

"Good point," she agreed, taking one last look at her screen and then relegating her computer to the coffee table. "Studying ancient terms was getting tedious anyway. I can seize the day without Latin." She pulled Jasper into her lap, who complained at first, but then nestled in and began purring in response to her stroking. "So, how do we call Lorien?"

"Not entirely sure, but I have an idea," I grinned. "I WISH…" I began loudly. I immediately erupted into a sneeze, and then held my breath as I waved away a warning cloud of red faerie dust.

"Sydney! You know you're not supposed to say that!" Lorien chided.

"Impressive. It's like you have your very own faerie doorbell," Sunny chuckled.

Lorien's tilted violet eyes narrowed. "Meaning you tricked me?"

My wince of guilt answered her question.

"Of all the sneaky, underhanded…what if I'd been in the middle of something important?" she demanded. "Haven't you ever heard of the girl who cried 'troll'?"

Sunny snickered.

"I'm sorry, Lorien," I said, instantly contrite. "But I had to talk to you and I didn't know how else to reach you. I wouldn't have bothered you if it wasn't important."

Lorien glowered at me and muttered something about ungrateful, lumbering humans. "What is it then?"

"Well, I came across some information yesterday—with regard to the goblin that supposedly gave Balthus the unaligned soul," I said carefully.

"Did Agent Sparrow find something?" Lorien asked sharply. "He's supposed to keep me posted!"

"No, it wasn't Sparrow. It was someone else."

"Who else do you know that would know anything about goblins?" she scoffed. Then she looked at me hard, something akin to alarm straining her features. "Who have you been talking to, Sydney? Not another death djinn—you know they can't be trusted!"

"No, nothing like that," I assured her quickly. "It was a human, but I promised not to reveal her identity." Oops—there went half the possible population.

"*Her?*" Lorien repeated. "And how do you know *she* was human? There are female death djinns, you know. And they're just as underhanded as the men—maybe more!"

I sighed in frustration and glanced at Sunny for support.

"Oh no, I don't wanna be in the middle of this. Besides, I thought Lorien just magically knew about everything you did." She wrinkled her nose and went back to stroking Jasper. The white tip of his fluffy, black tail twitched as he gazed unblinkingly at the faerie.

Lorien blew out an irritated breath. "I *do not* spend every minute of my life watching Sydney. I sense when she's in imminent danger, and I look in on her from time to time to help her out."

I gave an impatient wave of my hand. "Trust me; I'm pretty sure this woman was human. And even if she wasn't, you know I didn't slip up and say anything I shouldn't have, or you would have shown up with your sneezing powder."

"Faerie. Dust. And what's with the sudden secrecy?" Lorien exploded. "I'm your faerie guardian—I've been trying to help you out of this mess from the beginning!"

I chewed my lip, debating internally. I didn't like keeping secrets from her. "Alright. I guess I didn't promise not to tell *you*—but I did promise not to reveal her identity to the Seelie police. That means you can't tell Sparrow, okay?"

Lorien shook her head at me in disbelief. "I can't promise you that, Sydney. If you've discovered something that will impact Agent Sparrow's investigation, we have to tell him."

I let out an annoyed huff. "Of course I wouldn't keep anything important from Sparrow! I just can't tell him who gave me the info. And if you can't promise not to tell him who she is, then I can't tell you either. But I'm betting when you hear the story, you'll agree he doesn't need to know anyway."

Lorien sighed in agitation. "Sydney—what have you gotten yourself into now?"

"Nothing—Sunny and I just went on a little information reconnaissance. Now, promise me you won't tell Sparrow and I'll tell you all about it." I grinned.

"Fine," Lorien agreed, the word coming out on a breath of aggravation. "I'll keep your secret. You know my first priority is to protect you."

"Thank you," I said in a more penitent tone.

I moved to the loveseat and settled into the cushions before beginning the story. Lorien floated to a seat on the glass edge of the coffee table in front of me. "The woman's name is Ophelia; Balthus told me about her. Apparently, she traded her soul to him a couple hundred years ago. And she was with him the night he won the unaligned soul from the goblin."

"When did Balthus tell you about this woman?" Lorien asked with a frown.

"When I spoke with him at the prison. He made me swear not to tell the police about her—and when you hear what she's like, you'll see why it wouldn't do any good for them to interview her anyway. She already told me everything she knows about the goblin—and it wasn't much."

Lorien was shaking her head. "I watched your entire interview with Balthus on the screen in his cell. He never said anything about anyone named Ophelia."

"He spoke to me in my head just as Sparrow was pulling me out," I explained.

Lorien's eyes widened in shock. "I'd heard that death djinns have that ability, but it's said they only use it to communicate with their chosen mates," she murmured.

"Well, maybe he did it out of desperation, hoping I'd prove his story and get him out of jail," I said uncomfortably. I didn't want to consider the ramifications of Balthus deciding I was his 'chosen mate'.

"I don't like it, Sydney," Lorien said, concern painting her features.

"What's to like," I grumbled.

"Why would Balthus think you could prove his story and get him out of jail?" Sunny interjected. "We're going on the premise that he's guilty here, remember? That's how we're going to get your contract cancelled. That bastard is *not* going to use you to prove he's innocent!"

"I don't know why he told me about Ophelia," I groaned, rubbing my fingers hard over my face. I breathed deep, trying to collect my thoughts. "Maybe he thinks that by proving he won the soul from someone else, instead of stealing it himself, people will be more likely to believe that he didn't know it was illegal."

"And he'd probably be right about that," Lorien muttered.

"But even if he got the soul from the goblin, it doesn't mean he didn't know it was unaligned. Sparrow will realize that," I said. I could hear the edge of desperation in my voice.

"Of course he will," Sunny soothed. "Patrick Sparrow's mind is one of the sharpest tacks in his very well-appointed tool box." She winked at me cheekily.

"Agent Sparrow is the top detective on the Seelie squad," Lorien agreed, joining forces with Sunny to ease my escalating panic. "And you're right, Sydney. We don't know Balthus' motives for telling you about Ophelia—so there's no use worrying ourselves with speculation. Why don't you go ahead and tell me what you found out about the goblin."

"Okay," I breathed, trying to quiet a fresh bout of anxiety.

I related the entire Ophelia experience, with Sunny interjecting whenever she felt I was leaving something out. At the end of the tale, Lorien appeared to be just as disturbed as I had been.

"I can see why Balthus wouldn't want Ophelia questioned by the police," Lorien stated with a sad shake of her head. "She probably wouldn't handle it particularly well, and who knows what secrets of his she has running around in her brain after two centuries. It *does* sound like she told you everything relevant to the case that she was capable of telling."

"So you agree there's no reason to tell Sparrow about her, then," I reiterated for confirmation.

"I said I wouldn't tell him, didn't I?" Lorien answered, flashing me a look of irritation.

"Did you know that's what happens after a couple of centuries with a death djinn—I'd start to go bonkers and you'd be tied to my crazy ass forever?" I asked her with forced levity.

Lorien looked at me for a moment, her plum-colored eyes softening. "I'm your faerie guardian, Sydney. I chose you at birth. I'll never abandon you."

My lower lip wobbled, just a little.

Then Lorien smiled, her wings beginning to flicker faster. "I can't believe we might actually get to talk to Lauringer! Emily was right—if there's any magical help to be had, she's the one to give it. I've always wanted to meet her!"

"Hmm, I guess I could bring you along. Although, with her being so reclusive, maybe it would be better if I talked to her alone…"

Disappointment flared in Lorien's eyes, but when she noticed the teasing twitch of my lips, it transformed into a look that promised reprisal. "Very funny," she mumbled.

I laughed. "Of course you're coming with me! That is—if she agrees to see me at all," I added. "What about the Grimy Goblin and the Hell Ride, though?"

"And the infinity tattoo on the goblin's hand," Sunny piped up. "Do you have any idea if that means anything?"

Lorien's brow creased in thought. "I'll have to ask around. It doesn't tweak my wings, but I'm not really familiar with the various goblin societies and organizations. It's surprising that a goblin would mark himself in such a distinctive manner, though—as a race, they pride themselves on their physical similarities.

"As for the Grimy Goblin, I think it would be best if we left that up to Agent Sparrow. The goblin territories are notoriously unfriendly to outsiders. And I'm sure Agent Sparrow has some goblin connections. He should be able to send someone in to poke around without attracting any attention.

"Don't even think about trying to find the Hell Ride," Lorien added bluntly. "You don't want to have anything to do with the Unseelie Court."

I wasn't going to argue. I had already decided the Hell Ride would be my last resort.

"If that's everything, I think we should call Agent Sparrow and let him know what you found out. The more help we have, the better. And he and I made a deal to exchange information. When he sees I'm keeping my side of the bargain, he'll feel obliged to keep his," she said, sounding pleased.

"*You* can tell him the info came from an anonymous source." The unrestrained glee in her voice triggered warning bells, but before I could comment, she disappeared.

I grimaced at Sunny. "You don't think he'll be too mad about me not wanting to tell him, do you?"

"Good afternoon, ladies," a warm Irish brogue drawled behind me. "Lorien claims you have some urgent information for me."

I made a strangled sound. Goddess criminy—she could have warned me! I was suddenly and keenly aware that I was still in my pajamas. Embarrassment warred with a perverse thankfulness for my choice of sleeping attire. In place of my usual ragged t-shirt and oversized boxers, I wore a loose tank-top of thin white cotton that emphasized my breasts, and fell just short of the low drawstring waist of my cotton sleep pants.

I hurriedly sat up and sucked in my stomach, restraining the more obvious urge to smooth my hand over my tousled hair. I didn't remember it sticking out at any weird angles when I'd glanced in the mirror earlier.

Lorien reappeared and resumed her seat on the edge of the glass coffee table, her avid expression making it plain that she intended to enjoy the effects of Sparrow's unannounced presence.

"Patrick—so nice to see you again!" Sunny exclaimed, noting my reactions with an amused gleam in her eyes. "Please forgive our casual state of dress—Lorien didn't tell us you were coming," she continued. "Would you like a cup of coffee?"

"Thank you, Sunny, coffee would be perfect—black please," he accepted gratefully. "And my pleasure to see you again as well," he added as Sunny rose to get his drink. She gave him a pleasant smile, and then shot me a smirk behind his back on her way to the kitchen.

"I apologize for blinking in like that. Lorien's message led me to believe that you needed me here directly," Sparrow said in a wry tone, his gaze fixed on Lorien. She shrugged in feigned innocence.

"It's nice to know the Seelie police have such good response time," I joked, having somewhat recovered from his sudden appearance. "Please, have a seat."

His blue eyes traveled over me, growing hot above the small smile splayed across his lips. "It's my pleasure to protect and serve you, Sydney."

A jolt of response traveled through my body, every nerve ending coming to life beneath his gaze. I felt my nipples harden beneath the thin cotton of my tank-top and I forced myself to breathe. "Such dedication," I bantered.

"You have no idea," he grinned. He joined me on the loveseat, his proximity heightening my senses to an almost unbearable level. His elbow brushed my arm as he leaned back, and his woodsy scent stole over me, intensifying my reaction.

All I needed to complete the sensual torture was taste—and he definitely looked good enough to eat.

His aura was fresh and vital, the day's stubble not yet having begun to shadow the expanse of his jaw. The sleeves of his white, long-sleeved cotton work shirt were rolled up to his elbows, revealing tanned, tattooed forearms. And his dark slacks hinted at muscular hips and thighs.

Lorien watched our exchange in silence, looking like an extremely small and unrepentant cat that had swallowed an even smaller canary. I could almost picture the telltale tiny yellow feather sticking out of her mouth.

"Sydney came across some information about the goblin who gave Balthus the unaligned soul," she said with a crooked smile.

"I see," Sparrow replied, looking from Lorien back to me. "What sort of information?"

"Well, it's not much," I began, pausing while Sparrow accepted a steaming mug from Sunny. He murmured his thanks as she dropped onto the couch opposite us. "For one thing," I continued, "we found out that Balthus met the goblin at a tavern called the Grimy Goblin on the outskirts of the goblin territories."

"Balthus already told us that and we've put feelers out there, but it's almost impossible to track down a goblin without a name," Sparrow said evenly. "Anything else?"

"Oh," I said, a little crestfallen. "Well, I wasn't able to get the goblin's name, but I found out that he has a tattoo or mark of some kind on the palm of his hand. It looks like the symbol for infinity."

I lay my palm out flat before him and traced the shape that Ophelia had indicated. "Does that have any significance for you?"

"Like this?" he asked with a frown, retracing the symbol on my palm with his own finger and looking at me questioningly.

"Mmhm," I breathed in answer, reclaiming my hand and closing my fingers over my tingling palm with a shiver. Out of the corner of my eye I saw Sunny and Lorien exchange amused glances.

"No, I don't recall that symbol being associated with any particular group, but I'll ask around. Distinguishing marks are rare amongst goblins. It's not as good as a name, but it may be the next best thing. Did you learn anything else?" he asked with interest.

"The goblin was overheard claiming that he'd been on the Hell Ride."

"The Unseelie Court." Sparrow's exhalation was harsh. "Trading in unaligned souls is just the sort of thing they'd be behind. And the Seelie Court won't stand for the death djinns having dealings with the Unseelies. It's worth pursuing—something like that could nullify their soul contract altogether."

Sunny, Lorien and I grinned happily at each other.

"Is there more?" Sparrow asked intently.

"That was it about the goblin," I said, still smiling. "But I might be able to arrange a meeting with Lauringer. Maybe she could use her magic to help us find out what's going on."

Sparrow whistled. "I'm impressed. You've been busy since I saw you last."

I beamed at him.

"Just one more question," he said.

"Hmm?" I tilted my head in inquiry.

"From whence did this small wealth of information, and a possible introduction to the famous Lauringer, come?"

My pleasure dimmed and I bit my lip. "Sparrow, do you trust me not to keep anything from you that would help your investigation?" I asked, my gaze begging for his understanding.

His eyes narrowed and his irises darkened to cobalt. "I trust you not to *knowingly* keep anything from me that would help, Sydney. Who gave you this information?" he repeated firmly.

My hackles rose at his tone but I reminded myself to remain calm. "Sparrow, the person who told me this is innocent and needs to remain uninvolved. I *swore* I wouldn't reveal their identity. And I swear to you now that I would tell you anyway if I thought it would help you. But they told me everything they knew, and further questioning might harm them."

"You really think an innocent person would come to harm at my hands?" Sparrow demanded.

"I don't think you'd ever intentionally harm anyone who didn't deserve it."

Sparrow's expression softened.

"But I do think that further questioning by anyone, including myself, could harm this person. Please Sparrow—I need you to trust me. And don't be angry. I hate it when you're angry."

He looked surprised, and when he spoke his accent was noticeably thicker. "Have you seen me angry so many times then?"

"A few," I shrugged hesitantly. "Maybe irritated is a better word. Although it's not as if we've ever met under anything less than stressful circumstances."

His gaze was intent upon mine. "I didn't realize I was reacting so strongly," he said. "There are things about this case, Sydney—things about your situation in particular—that hit a nerve with me..." he trailed off.

My heart beat faster as I stared back at him.

"May I speak with you in private?" he asked, his eyes flickering toward Sunny and Lorien.

"Sure," I answered, feeling unaccountably nervous as I stood and motioned for him to follow me. "We can talk in my room." I glanced back at my friends before entering the kitchen and saw Lorien hovering above Sunny's shoulder, both of them grinning.

"Don't do anything I wouldn't do," Sunny mouthed at me.

Ha Ha—this coming from the woman who had spent last night with twin incubi.

I led Sparrow down the hallway to my bedroom, intensely aware of his presence close behind me. Closing the door with a soft snick, I gathered my courage to turn and look at him. He stood watching me, emotion flickering in his sapphire eyes.

"I feel I owe you an explanation, Sydney."

"I'm not sure you owe me anything, Sparrow," I said, "but an explanation would help."

He sighed. "Do you mind if we sit?"

I nodded and strode past him to perch on the edge of the bed. He followed my lead and sat near, but not touching me. His weight caused the mattress to dip and the silver coin he had given me slid out from beneath my pillow.

He retrieved the coin, rubbing it between long fingers as he shot me a questioning look. I flushed in embarrassment, trying to formulate an explanation that would make sense. I couldn't think of one that didn't sound utterly lame, so I said nothing.

"My mother gave me this coin," he stated softly, "when I was but a small lad. I haven't much left of her but this, and a single photograph of her and my father."

My embarrassment faded to surprise as he continued.

"My father was a sidhe warrior, well-respected for his loyalty and fierceness in battle. And my mother was human—a beautiful, fiery young Irishwoman. In their time, the barrier between our realms was a bit less solid, and many mortals still believed in the faerie folk.

"As my sidhe kin tell it, my mother discovered my father bathing in a shaded pool on her family's property one summer afternoon. Taking him for a vagabond, and bravely ignoring his nakedness, she grabbed the nearest weapon she could find—a large tree branch—and began to beat him soundly with it, calling him indelicate names and demanding he vacate the property immediately." Sparrow chuckled and shook his head.

"Sounds like love at first sight." I grinned.

"Yes, well, much to my mother's surprise, the young man disappeared into thin air right before her eyes. She knew immediately that she must have encountered one of the fae, and decided the pool must be enchanted, so she resolved not to go near it again, thinking that would be the end of it. But my father had other ideas. He was fascinated by the fierce young woman with the fair skin and shining, dark hair. He began to spy upon her, knowing it was wrong, but wanting to learn something more of her."

"So you're telling me your father was a stalker?" I teased.

Sparrow laughed. "A stalker with the most honorable of intentions. And it worked out in both their favors in the end—as you'll see if you'll let me tell the tale."

"I think it's sweet that you lured me into the bedroom to tell me a story, Sparrow," I said, a whisper of wickedness in my smile.

Sparrow's eyes blazed and he gave me a warning smile in return. "Just listen, little witch."

I snorted.

"My mother was from a large family and was the sixth of eight children."

"Ouch," I whispered.

Sparrow shook his head, fighting a grin.

"They were poor, having little more than their modest piece of farm land in the country. It had become my mother's responsibility to tend the vegetable garden, and she did so without complaint, but she found that her harvest lacked the ripe abundance that the garden had provided for her sister before her.

"In truth, it was caused by overuse of the soil on the small section of land, but her family teased her mercilessly about her 'black thumb'. Although they were kind about it, she sensed their disappointment and it saddened her. They often relied on the garden to provide for their own table in hard times.

"It is not difficult for faerie folk to cast simple cures, especially those akin to nature. And seeing how the poor harvest distressed my mother, my father cast a healing spell upon the earth of the garden. Not only that, but he returned often in the misty hour just before dawn to secretly cast strengthening spells upon each stalk of corn, head of cabbage or kale, and upon each vine of beans."

"Lorien told me about dryads and how they sometimes ask faeries to cure their blighted trees," I nodded, getting into the story.

"Yes, that's right. And my father's cures worked so well that soon my mother's garden was providing the most ample crop the little patch of land had ever brought forth. The vegetables were ripening so quickly and in such great supply that her family was able to begin selling and trading some at the town market for the extra coin and supplies they so desperately needed. Everyone who tasted that corn and those beans agreed they were the sweetest, most delicious they'd ever eaten.

"No longer able to claim she had a 'black thumb', my mother's family began teasing her over the sudden turn-about, asking if she hadn't struck a deal with the fae to bless the garden. My mother laughed, but she wondered at the unusual change herself, their teasing reminding her of the young man she'd encountered at the nearby pool. She decided to set a watch upon the garden one night, just to see if anything out of the ordinary could be observed."

"It's like he bought all her chairs," I said dreamily.

Sparrow looked at me askance. "What?"

"Did you ever see that movie where the woman made the chairs and tried to sell them, but no one would buy them, so the man who loved her secretly bought all of them himself?"

"Uh, no. I don't watch many movies," he said uncertainly.

I laughed. "Never mind. Go on."

He cleared his throat. "Where was I? Oh, right—so my mother watched the garden all night. When dawn approached and naught had happened, she began to feel foolish and resigned herself that there was nothing to see. But just as she rose to abandon her perch by the window, my father appeared in the midst of the garden patch. She watched as he moved amongst her rows of vegetables, sprinkling his silvery strengthening dust over each of the plants. And with shock, she recognized him as the man she'd chased from the pool.

"She stormed outside, angered and frightened by his interference. But when she looked into his eyes, she knew that he had meant no harm, and that she had nothing to fear. It didn't take long for her to realize that it was actually quite a romantic thing for him to do, and he was rather a handsome young rake, so she allowed him to court her properly.

"They fell in love and eventually decided to marry, making their home on a small tract of land near her family's farm, where they had a modest but happy life together."

"That's a beautiful story, Sparrow. I think you have a bit of the bard in you," I said softly.

"Well, that's thanks to my sidhe kin, who raised me." Sparrow grinned. "My uncles told me the story of how my parents met many times while I was growing up. It's become like a fable in my mind."

"Did you have any brothers or sisters?" I asked.

"I was my parents' first and only child. I believe they tried to give me a sibling or two," Sparrow winked, "but the coupling between a faerie and a human will rarely produce more than one offspring."

"I was an only child too." I gave him a rueful smile. "I'm guessing your fable turns sad at this point, though."

"Yes, I suppose it does. But I'd like for you to know the rest, if you don't object to hearing it."

"Tell me," I agreed solemnly.

Sparrow nodded, the look in his eyes sparking a curiously warm sensation in the region of my heart. "It was when I was about six years old that rumblings of trouble began in the faerie realm. A new leader had come to power in the Unseelie Court. An ambitious young goblin named Nugratz had gained a large following of the younger members of the court. They were dissatisfied with what they viewed as the Unseelies' cowardly obeisance to the laws of the Seelie Court.

"Nugratz staged a coup and murdered the old leader of the Unseelies, promising his followers that if they made him their new chief, he would lead them to victory against the Seelies. The Seelie Court called forth their army of loyal warriors to crush the uprising before it could get out of hand, and my father joined his sidhe kin in battle. The clash was short but bloody, and although the Seelie Court triumphed, they lost many brave fighters. My father was among them."

I had been expecting it, but he said it with such a lack of emotion that I didn't know how to react, or even if I should. Sparrow's voice remained toneless as he continued, like he was distancing himself from the words.

"My mother was heartbroken and wept for days, becoming despondent and listless. Soon after, a strange gentleman showed up on our doorstep, asking to speak with the lady of the house. He appeared refined and gave me a kindly smile when he bade me fetch my mother, but I was overcome by a fear of him I couldn't explain. My mother dried her tears and agreed to see the man, shooing me off to play outside. But I remained by the window and listened.

"That man was King Moab, Sydney."

I immediately flashed back to the coldly elegant king of the death djinns, who had taunted Sparrow in the police station, and whose power had filled me with such bitter desire and fear. My dread for the six-year-old boy that Sparrow had once been grew.

"My mother had heard of the death djinns and their ability to grant wishes. She knew that she must first make a heartfelt wish for death—which was no difficulty for her after the loss of her love—and that she would then be able to make two wishes of her choice without reprisal, losing her soul only upon the completion of the third. She intended to make the first two wishes and cheat the djinn out of the third wish, retaining her soul. In her innocence, however, she did not realize that some wishes cannot be granted even by a death djinn.

"She wished for death and King Moab gladly accepted her contract, for although she had no spell crafting talent, she was very beautiful. Her eager first wish was for the return of my father's life. When Moab explained that not even a death djinn can return life to the dead, and that she must choose another wish, she flew into a rage and drove him from the house.

"But it was too late; she had already entered into the contract. And he didn't stay away for long. He began courting her, bringing flowers and small trinkets to woo her. My mother was strong, resisting him for over a year, but she gradually began to succumb to his seduction. I hated him, for I knew that he was slowly taking her from me. I could see it in her eyes when he finally broke her spirit and she was no longer able to resist."

Anger and futility burned in his gaze—the same anger and futility I'd seen every time he saw me near a death djinn.

"Sparrow..." my voice faltered past a tightening throat.

But Sparrow continued as if he hadn't heard me.

"At last she agreed to make her wishes and complete the contract. Her first two wishes were to see that I was taken care of: that I would grow up to be healthy and strong amongst my sidhe kin, and that I would always be protected and guided by the force for good.

"Then she told Moab that the third wish would be for herself, but that she hadn't quite settled on what it should be. She asked that he return the following day so that she could spend one last night with me while making her decision, for she intended to send me to live with my father's kin after giving up her soul.

"She gave me this silver coin that night, promising me it would be my good luck charm and that everything would be alright."

Sparrow rubbed the coin between his fingers again, as if the contact gave him the courage to continue.

"I remember falling asleep, weeping in her arms, begging her not to leave. When I awoke the next morning, she was gone. I wandered outside, calling for her. I made my way toward her family's property, for I had the thought that she might have wanted to say goodbye to them as well.

"I came upon her in the pool where she had first met my father. She had drowned herself, choosing to end her own life so that her soul could not be claimed, and would return to its rightful place in the Sea of Souls to be reborn. I was taken in and raised by my sidhe kin, for though my mother had cheated Moab out of her soul, he could not renege on her first two wishes."

The pain in Sparrow's eyes seemed ancient and diluted by long acceptance, but it tore at my heart. It flowed into me, making me angry and sad and breathless with injustice. I hadn't even realized I was crying until he reached up to gently brush a tear from the corner of my eye. His hand remained, cradling the side of my face.

"Don't cry, Sydney. All souls pass, and enough tears have been shed over my parents already. I needed to tell you this, not because I wanted your sympathy, but because I felt you should know why I have been so angry around you. The thought of watching you lose your soul to the death djinns infuriates me. Do you understand?"

I nodded mutely, my tears falling faster.

"Damn it, Sydney, don't cry like that," he whispered, leaning forward to press his lips to the thin rivulets staining my cheeks. "I'm sorry, I should have known better than to lay that on you." He groaned and cupped my face in both hands, his mouth traveling unhurriedly across my jaw. My eyelids fluttered shut as his lips reached mine and began a gentle tasting, making me forget everything but his touch.

I opened my mouth to him and he deepened the kiss, my tears salty on his tongue. A slow, profound force moved through me, different from the quick stabs of desire I had felt before. It left me dizzy and reeling as I returned Sparrow's kiss with a passion approaching desperation. I clung to him, feeling as if I would lose myself if I let go.

His hands left my face, traveling restlessly down my shoulders. Warm palms moved to lift my breasts in a teasing embrace, his thumbs brushing enticingly over the fabric above my nipples. I arched into him reflexively, drawing his breath into my mouth as liquid pooled low and hot within me. I wanted him so badly I ached. A deep wave of need moved through me and I moaned, reaching to free his shirt from the waistband of his slacks so that my hands could roam his skin.

"You have no idea how much I've wanted to touch you like this, Sydney," Sparrow breathed into my mouth.

"I think I might have some idea," I disagreed, my smile melting into a haze of desire as Sparrow's kiss became more demanding.

My fingertips brushed firmly up over the unyielding muscles of his back, splaying wide to take in as much of his coveted flesh as they could. I gently raked his smooth skin with my fingernails on their journey back down, before moving my hands around the solid mass of his waist and pushing them up between us so that I could caress his chest.

Sparrow's hands left my breasts to stroke my hair and he grasped the nape of my neck to fit my mouth closer to his.

My hand wandered across his chest, making him gasp when I found his nipples. I rubbed them with my fingertips, creating a gentle friction, and he retaliated by breaking our kiss. I sounded an objection that quickly turned into a moan of pleasure as he pushed up my tank-top and his mouth found my breast, teasing one thoroughly with his lips and tongue and then kissing a path over to the other.

He tore his mouth away with a groan and pulled me into him, stroking my back as we both caught our breath.

"I have to get back to work," he gasped unsteadily.

Seeing the disappointed look in my eyes, he grasped my hand in his and brought it to his lips, then slowly guided it down between us, pressing it firmly into the thickness of his erection. Goddess, I wanted him inside of me.

"I want you, Sydney—so much it hurts." He grimaced. "But I didn't intend for it to happen like this. I have to stay focused on the investigation and getting your contract cancelled."

I wanted to tell him that having incredible sex with him would probably go a long way toward strengthening my resistance to the death djinns, but it didn't seem like the prudent response. Instead I said, "I appreciate that, Sparrow; I really do. And you can be sure that I'm focusing on getting my contract cancelled as well. *But I want you too.*"

He smiled. "A compelling argument—one which we'll have to explore later, because they really are calling me back to the office."

"Your tattoo is glowing again," I commented, brushing my fingers over the white fabric concealing his upper arm. A mild shock of awareness warmed my hand, sparking along my already aroused nerve endings. "I can see the red pulsing through your shirt," I whispered in fascination.

He answered by leaning forward and taking my lips in a swift kiss, his tongue tasting them gently at first, then thrusting into my mouth suggestively, bringing us both back up to the boiling point.

"I can't seem to get enough of you, Sydney," he murmured as he pulled me closer, nipping at my earlobe and sending a delicious shiver down my spine. A soft growl of frustration sounded deep within his throat. "I have to go. But I'll talk to you soon, okay?"

"Soon," I agreed. I wanted more. I wanted him to tear my clothes off and take me right there. But I wasn't about to beg for it. If he'd rather go back to work instead, that was fine.

Not.

He stood and tucked his shirt back into his slacks, then leaned down to brush his lips across my forehead. His fingers skimmed lightly over my cheek in a caress that left my flesh tingling for his touch long after he disappeared.

I sank back into the bed with a groan of frustration. When I grabbed my pillow, I discovered that Sparrow had replaced the silver coin beneath it.

I squeezed it tightly in my palm, cursing all death djinns.

<u>Chapter 12 - What Lies Hidden</u>

Figuring that I'd wallowed in my frustration for long enough, I trudged through the kitchen to rejoin Sunny and Lorien in the sitting room. I turned the corner to find the tawny leather couch occupied by Angelica. She wore her French maid's uniform with her long blonde hair piled neatly atop her head.

She sat next to Sunny, who was still in her pajamas, with her dark curls spilling over the shoulders of her silky black robe. A sparkling Lorien hovered excitedly between them, and Angelica was listening attentively as she and Sunny gave a joint update on my death djinn predicament.

Jasper seemed to have taken a liking to Angelica without the offending presence of her vacuum, and had stretched himself out on his back beside her so that she could rub his belly. I thought I'd heard the sounds of cleaning earlier, but I'd been a little too preoccupied to acknowledge it.

Sunny stopped mid-sentence as soon as she caught sight of me, a knowing grin spreading across her face. "Did Patrick just now leave?"

"No," Angelica answered sadly. "Sydney's lover left almost an hour ago. He continues to withhold his beautiful erection from her, merely teasing Sydney with caresses of his hands and mouth. She has been alone, attempting to quiet her longing since he left."

Sunny and Lorien looked from Angelica to me with similar expressions of disbelief.

"That's about the size of it," I confirmed as I dropped onto the vacant loveseat. "But maybe next time you'll let me tell them myself."

"I am sorry, Sydney," Angelica said, her blue eyes anxious. "It is just that I feel your unfulfilled desire so strongly. I was barely able to keep myself from coming to you."

"It's alright Angelica, really." I felt guilty for chastising her. It wasn't her fault that my frustration affected her almost as much as it did me. And it wasn't news that anything involving sex was a natural topic of conversation for her. A person could learn a thing or two from Angelica about releasing their hang-ups.

"It's good that you were able to keep yourself from popping into my bedroom, right?" I asked encouragingly. "I mean, unless you popped in and then left before I saw you." I tried not to show my discomfort at the thought.

"No," Angelica said brightly. "I was better able to control my response this time."

"Have you had sex since we talked yesterday?" Sunny asked with an unabashed grin.

"Oh yes!" Angelica nodded enthusiastically. "I went to a man in his dreams last night and we shared very hot and satisfying sex for many hours. I had weeks of pent-up desire to spend, so I brought all of my favorite toys. I think he especially enjoyed the swing."

"*Swing?*" Lorien muttered under her breath. I giggled.

"So, do you think you'll see this man again?" I probed.

"Well, I did think about your suggestion," Angelica hesitated, the topic of monogamy making her uncomfortable in a way that openly discussing the use of sex swings couldn't.

"I do not wish to return to the unsatisfying lifestyle of endlessly answering countless calls of passion. And I *was* drawn to something in this man, even though his call of passion was not particularly strong. I think its lack of strength allowed me to fulfill my own desires as well as his.

"There is something that feels strangely familiar about him," she continued, a troubled look in her eyes. "I think that maybe I will visit him again tonight," she admitted, sounding embarrassed. "I am still finding it difficult to control my urges, after all.

"But we should be discussing Sydney's situation, not mine," Angelica insisted. It was an obvious attempt to change the subject.

"Yeah—what happened with Patrick, Syd?" Sunny propped her elbows on her knees and dropped her chin into her hands, fixing me with an impertinent grin. "Other than him teasing you with his hands and mouth and leaving you longing for his beautiful erection, that is?"

My cheeks warmed and I shot her a dirty look, but remembering Sparrow's kisses brought an irrepressible smile to my lips. "He told me how his parents died, and then we made out."

That got a mixed reaction. Angelica leaned back into the sofa cushions with a thoughtful expression; Lorien gave me a sad smile of understanding; Sunny just looked concerned and a little horrified. My gaze fixed on Lorien.

"His dead parents? That was his idea of a romantic prelude to your first kiss?" Sunny asked in disbelief.

"In my long years as a succubus I have learned that desire can be sparked by many different things," argued Angelica. "Some lovers never feel so alive as when they are reminded of their own mortality. Maybe Sydney and her lover used this topic as a way to incite their passions."

The absurdity of that theory registered distantly in my mind as I continued to stare at Lorien's sad expression. "You knew."

Lorien shrugged, her bare feet twitching in a nervous rhythm beneath the edge of the coffee table. "The details of Agent Sparrow's past are no secret to anyone who's interested enough to find them. And his bias against the death djinns and their contract was one of the reasons I was so happy to have him on our side. Nonetheless, I didn't feel like it was my story to tell."

She raised her violet eyes to mine, adding, "And I don't think Agent Sparrow would have told you if he didn't care about you, Sydney."

I nodded, my heart leaping at her words.

"The death djinns had something to do with Patrick's parents' deaths?" Sunny asked sharply.

"King Moab did," I said with a nod. I pulled a squashy throw pillow into my lap and pulled absently at the fringe. "Sparrow's father was killed in a battle to subdue an uprising of the Unseelie Court. His mother entered into a contract with King Moab thinking she could wish his father back to life. She never intended to use her third wish and give up her soul. But she had already wished for death when she realized that Moab couldn't bring back Sparrow's Dad.

"Moab tried to seduce her into completing the contract, and when she was afraid she wouldn't be able to resist him any longer, she killed herself. Sparrow found her. He was only six years old. After that, he was raised by his father's sidhe relatives."

"Poor Patrick," Sunny murmured.

"Yes, that is very sad," Angelica agreed sympathetically. "Was his mother a spell caster or would she simply have become one of the harem King Moab keeps to satisfy his sexual desires?"

"Uh, she wasn't a spell caster," I answered delicately.

"He desired her sexually then." Angelica nodded, oblivious to my discomfort with the topic. "As I was telling you before, some of my kind will also use their powers of seduction to convince mortals to give up their souls in return for pleasure. It is a nasty business." Angelica wrinkled her nose.

"Do your people have a contract for taking souls like the death djinns do?" I asked.

"No!" Angelica exclaimed, sounding horrified. "My people consider the soul trade to be an abomination. It is only those living on the fringes of our society—who would deal in dark magic and perhaps even align themselves with the Unseelie Court—who engage in the taking of souls."

"What do they *do* with the souls, anyway?" Sunny asked, frowning as she took a sip from her blue ceramic mug and tasted coffee that must have gone cold.

She replaced it on the table, careful not to disturb Lorien. "I mean, I know that death djinns use humans as sex slaves or for any spell casting ability they have. But it sounds like anyone in the faerie realm can buy or trade for spells, and I'm sure there's a pretty much endless supply of humans who would be willing to exchange sex for wishes. So why take on the responsibility of owning a stable full of souls and having to keep up their human hosts for eternity?"

Angelica shrugged and shook her head sadly. "The death djinns have created an entire societal structure where owning souls is a symbol of power and status. Those from other races who engage in the soul trade generally do not hold onto the souls that come into their possession for very long. They merely keep them until a suitable opportunity to trade them presents itself.

"But for the death djinns, the more souls they acquire, the higher their status within their society. They will trade souls to gain goods or services that are of greater value to them—but above all, they are collectors. The more valuable a soul is, either because of the host's spell casting power or their sexual desirability, the more the other death djinns will covet possession of it for their own stable."

"It's about control," Lorien added softly. "A death djinn trading something of their own for a spell or for sex wouldn't give them anywhere near the sense of power they gain from the possession of a human who can provide it for them."

Angelica nodded. "And even if they choose to be kind to their charges, death djinns are still nothing but slave masters. Choosing to bestow kindness instead of cruelty makes the slave master no less powerful—and although a kind master may seem more pleasant than a cruel one, it makes the charge no less a slave.

"That is why you must not give in to the seduction of the death djinn to complete your contract, Sydney," she said, giving me a sober look. "Better to choose death, as your friend's mother did, and return your soul to the Sea of Souls so that it will remain free to be reborn."

"We're not going to allow it to come to that," Sunny insisted, crossing her arms and extricating herself from the indention she'd made in the tawny cushions.

"What exactly is the Sea of Souls?" I asked. I didn't even want to consider having to make the kind of choice that Sparrow's mother had made.

"It is the natural resting place of unaligned mortal souls," Angelica answered. "It is my understanding that when a mortal dies, their soul is returned to the Sea of Souls until it is time for the soul to be reborn. This happens over and over, throughout a soul's many lifetimes, until the soul has progressed beyond the bounds of mortality."

Angelica looked to Lorien for confirmation.

"That's pretty much what I was taught as well," Lorien agreed. "Each soul's progression toward immortality is determined by the wisdom it gains through its interactions with kindred souls throughout its mortal lifetimes. Family, lovers, friends, enemies—all of these relationships provide opportunities for the soul to progress. And certain souls are fated to experience specific relationships together before either of them can progress."

"Yes." Angelica nodded. "This is the main reason why the soul trade is such an abomination. Not only is it a slave trade, but it inhibits the progression of mortal souls. A soul that is prevented from returning to the Sea of Souls by an unnatural immortality cannot progress. Nor can any of its kindred souls progress to immortality while they yet await a shared lifetime with the captive soul."

Sunny whistled. "Wow. You guys just calmly sat there and explained what a lot of people would consider to be the meaning of life."

Angelica grinned. "Maybe so, but the knowledge of it does not necessarily make the lessons any more easily learned."

"Wait, I'm confused," I cut in with a frown. "If a soul's value is based on the desirability of the human it's aligned with, then what's the point of owning an unaligned soul?"

"The soul would need to be realigned before anyone could make use of the host," Angelica clarified. "This forcible stripping and realigning would leave the mortal at the beck and call of whoever held the soul. But without the soul contract, the holder would not be required to grant anything in return."

Lorien nodded. "Claiming supposedly 'willing' slaves through a soul contract is bad enough. But taking them this way is truly horrendous. Stripping a mortal of their soul without granting them immortality puts them into an unconscious state of limbo until their soul is realigned."

"So that's why the woman in the hospital is in a coma," I realized. "But why can't they just realign her soul?"

Lorien winced. "Sparrow told me they tried. But whoever stripped her soul botched the spell too badly."

I sucked a sympathetic breath through my teeth.

"So for every unaligned soul they've found, supposedly there's a human out there, lying unconscious somewhere, waiting for their soul to be restored?" Sunny asked with a scowl.

Lorien nodded in puzzlement. "But according to Agent Sparrow, the woman we saw is the only human they've found so far with a connection to one of the unaligned souls. And they believe they would have eventually been able to trace her soul to her body, even without Balthus' help. That's why it's so odd that they haven't been able to trace any of the other souls to their human counterparts yet.

"They're still working on identifying the magic used to strip that woman of her soul, but haven't come up with anything helpful so far. They need to find the other victims in order to compare magical signatures and look for more conclusive evidence."

"And how do they plan to find these people?" asked Sunny.

"Well, they're still hoping to figure out a way to trace the magic. But detectives have also been visiting hospitals all over your world to look for other coma patients without their souls intact. Nothing so far, but the investigation is ongoing and it takes time." Lorien shrugged helplessly.

"It does seem strange that none of the other souls have been traceable to their owners." A small crease marred Angelica's smooth forehead. "And the Seelie Police must be under a time constraint as well. If they are unable to restore those unaligned souls soon, they will surely be required to return them to the Sea of Souls."

"But…that means they'll all die," I said.

Angelica gave me a sad little smile and a chill of unease shivered through me. "It is unfortunate, but still better than living as a slave."

Lorien nodded in confirmation, and a morose hush fell over us.

As if in protest of the uncomfortable silence, Jasper got to his feet and leapt to the floor. He fixed his unblinking gaze on Lorien, and she cooed at him half-heartedly, and sprinkled him with green faerie dust. He purred and flexed his paws against the textured carpet.

"He is a very sweet creature," Angelica said, her contagious smile helping to lift some of the gloom. "His coloring is quite unusual. I noticed it the very first day I met you, Sydney. Did you know that there are certain spells that can only be completed with seven hairs from the white-tipped tail of an all black cat?"

I widened my eyes at her in disbelief. "You're kidding."

"No, it is true. Let me know if you ever need to cure a genital wart, stop a bed bug infestation, or perform an exorcism, and I will find the spell for you."

"That's quite a range of maladies," Sunny choked, staring at Jasper in wonder.

Angelica grinned as she rose gracefully to her feet. "But I have abandoned today's work for long enough. I will finish up Sydney's bedroom now, if she doesn't mind."

I nodded my thanks and she stepped into the outer foyer to grab some supplies from her cart.

"She's on a roll today," Sunny informed me. "She even took off all the vent covers and cleaned the vents out."

"We made her sit down and take a break after that," Lorien added.

"You're truly amazing, Angelica." I twisted around to look at her as she passed.

"It is something that should be done periodically—I will do the same in your bedroom." She smiled and disappeared through the kitchen.

"Did you know about those cat spells?" I asked Lorien.

She shook her head with a bemused expression.

"Genital warts, bedbugs and exorcisms." Sunny shuddered. "Does that mean we have to worry about demons too?"

Lorien snorted. "Don't be silly—there's no such things as *demons*.

But technically any creature that can take on spirit form is capable of possession."

"Oh sure, like demons are such a stretch from faeries, succubi and djinns," Sunny grumbled.

I grunted a laugh as I watched Jasper blissfully rub his head against the driftwood base of the coffee table. Hopefully possession wasn't on the list of things I'd have to deal with. He'd probably lose some of his good humor if I started plucking hairs from his tail.

"Maybe I'll go pick up my paperwork a little early," I mused. "I think the rest of this day's pretty much shot for work anyway."

"Ooh—let's grab an early dinner at that Indian restaurant, and then go for a Starbucks and browse the bookstore," Sunny suggested. "I'm almost out of new reading material."

"Sounds good. What about you, Lorien? Do you have any plans for the evening?" I asked.

"As a matter of fact it's my nephew Obie's birthday and his party is in a few hours." Lorien's wings fluttered in excitement, sprinkling dust on the glass table-top. "I was just on my way to pick up his present, when I sensed you wishing and came here instead."

I winced apologetically. "Sorry about that. Like I said—I didn't know how else to get your attention."

"Well, maybe I overreacted a little. You *did* have important information. And it was worth it just to see the look on your face when Agent Sparrow blinked in here." Lorien grinned. "But next time, all you have to do is concentrate and call my name."

"Oh," I said, chagrined.

"Oh," Lorien mimicked.

"So what are you getting Obie for his birthday?" I asked, ignoring her sarcasm.

Lorien brightened. "There's a woman in North Carolina who handcrafts the most beautiful wooden furniture and toys. I've ordered him a rocking horse and I'm going to pick it up before the party. He thinks horses without wings are the funniest thing." She giggled.

"A woman in North Carolina? Won't a rocking horse made by a human be a little big for your nephew?" asked Sunny skeptically.

"Well, no," Lorien answered, looking embarrassed. "She specializes in making miniatures. She trades some of them to faerie folk for garden spells and strengthening spells for the wood she carves."

"Uh huh. And what does she do with these miniatures when she's not trading them to faeries?" Sunny asked with a growing look of understanding.

"Humans buy them for…" Lorien's voice dropped to an inaudible murmur.

"For what?" I asked, still not catching on.

"Dollhouses—humans buy them for their children's dollhouses, alright! But they're the perfect size for us," Lorien retorted.

I let out a helpless titter. "I'm sorry, Lorien. I'm not laughing at you, really. I think it's sweet that you use dollhouse furniture."

"It's not sweet. It's practical," Lorien grumbled, "more practical than wasting it on a fake house for a fake family of dolls."

"You're absolutely right," I agreed, trying not to give in to the smile that kept wanting to twitch up the corners of my lips.

"Anyway, I've got to get going," Lorien said with forced dignity. "Give me a call if anything else comes up."

"Thanks Lorien. And tell Obie 'Happy Birthday' for us, okay?"

"Will do." She smiled, thoughts of her nephew overruling her embarrassment. She waved goodbye and disappeared.

"I'll get dressed as soon as Angelica's finished in my bedroom," I said to Sunny. "Then, when you're ready, we can go."

"Mmm...Indian food," she intoned happily as she jumped up from the couch. "Give me fifteen minutes."

I bent down to tease Jasper with one of his toys—a fuzzy white mouse whose felt tail was sticking out from beneath the couch. He batted at it lazily with one black paw, for the most part ignoring me. Apparently he was too relaxed to move after his magical catnip high.

He'd always been more interested in rubber bands and paper clips than in any toy I'd ever bought for him anyway.

"Sydney," Angelica said in a hushed voice, "I have found something that you must see."

She rushed into the living room, her cotton apron askew, and what appeared to be a small glass vial in her hand.

"What's that?" I asked with a frown.

She dropped onto the loveseat next to me and presented it for my inspection. It was a sphere-shaped bottle of forest green glass, about an inch and a half in circumference. The bottom had been leveled so that it could stand upright, and the tiny opening at its top appeared to be stopped with a rounded wedge of gold.

As I stared at it, it seemed that a faint glow resided within its depths, like a dim star that could only be glimpsed from the corner of my eye.

"What is it?" I repeated.

"I do not know, Sydney. If I had more dealings in magic, I might be able to tell you. But I can feel that it contains great power," Angelica said in a hushed tone. "I found it inside one of the vents in your bedroom."

I gazed at it dumbstruck for a moment before the gears of my mind began to spin and caution kicked in. "What if this belongs to Balthus? Sparrow searched the penthouse the night he arrested him, but I don't think he looked inside the vents. Could it be dangerous?" I asked worriedly.

Angelica studied the little vial intently. I got the impression that she was probing the glass in the same way she had probed me the day before to determine that my soul was still intact. Finally she looked up, her eyes luminous.

"No, Sydney. It does not feel dangerous. It seems as if it is a vessel for some power that lies dormant. I do not think you would be successful in any effort to open it or break it without the appropriate release spell."

I gingerly took it from her hand, and when nothing happened I blew out a caged breath. "Well, thank you, Angelica. Lorien's already gone, but I'll tell her about it the next time I talk to her. I'm sure she knows someone who can tell us what it is."

Angelica nodded and smiled. "Very well. I will see you Thursday then," she said as she stood to leave. "I look forward to our visits—you are one of my most interesting clients."

I laughed. "Thanks. You're pretty entertaining yourself."

∞∞∞∞∞∞∞∞∞∞

"I'll just stay in the car this time," Sunny said dryly.

I hadn't been quite so lucky with parking today, finding no empty spaces on Hannah's block. Oh well, I supposed Lorien was busy watching Obie blow out birthday candles right about now, or whatever it was that faerie children did at their birthday parties. Besides, I could use the exercise.

"If it's Hannah's perfume you're worried about, you could just practice breathing through your mouth like I do."

"Or I could just wait here," she answered with a winning smile. "That way you can leave the keys in the ignition so the car's still cool when you come back."

"Fine," I huffed. Sunny grinned at me as I left the wagon.

The blazing summer heat began wringing moisture from my pores as soon as I stepped onto the sidewalk. By the time I reached the immaculate glass door of Haute Hannah's, I was more than relieved to step into its cool, bright interior. The sparkle of well polished gems within their glinting glass cases, and the soft sounds of French jazz, assailed my senses. I glanced around for Hannah, who came bustling from the back at the tinkling of the doorbell.

"Sydney, how lovely to see you! You look beautiful today. I have just finished pulling your papers together. Good timing, yes?" Hannah's energy left me smiling, as always.

"Yes—thank you, Hannah. You look lovely as well. Could it be that you have a certain glow about you after your weekend with your friend?" I teased.

"Ah!" she tapped me on the arm playfully. "It is the glow *d'amour!*" she sighed, the back of one be-ringed hand drifting across her forehead in an exaggerated gesture.

"Well, it suits you," I said with a laugh.

"*Amour* suits every woman, my dear." She smiled. "Oh—and I have a gift that I believe will suit you, in particular, quite beautifully!" she exclaimed, turning to hurry behind one of the display cases.

My face fell; I had forgotten about the gift. I tsked at her. "Hannah, you know you shouldn't have done that," I complained half-heartedly to the back of her well-coiffed head, knowing it would have no effect.

"Now, none of that, Sydney," she chastened me, pronouncing the second syllable of my name with a heavier emphasis than usual. "If I wish to give to my favorite employee a gift, I shall do so. And here it is!"

She beamed with triumph as she rose from behind the display case. In her hand she held a large, irregular chunk of fused crystal. It was dark amber in color and accented with gold in a pattern that made it look a bit like a deranged flower. The crystal sparkled beneath the shop's concentrated lights as if it was alive, and I used that one positive thought as fuel for my effort to conjure a delighted smile for Hannah.

It might actually have been pretty, if its natural beauty hadn't been mutilated by the gaudiness of the gold. And if it were sitting on a shelf with someone's crystal collection, instead of attached to a pin designed to sit heavily above a woman's breast. It was a brooch—the most massive and ornate one I had ever seen. And Hannah was grinning at me expectantly, waiting for my reaction.

"Oh, Hannah, it's...unbelievable."

"It is, is it not? The amber shading—it reminded me of your beautiful golden brown hair and your lovely russet eyes. I thought to myself, Sydney must have this piece!"

"That's very sweet of you, Hannah. I can't tell you how touched I am." And I was. No one had ever called my eyes—which I thought were a rather plain shade of brown—anything as exotic as 'russet' before. "But I can't accept this—it must be worth a fortune!"

Hannah frowned at me and threw her hands up in a gesture of dismissal. "Nonsense, Sydney. I am surrounded by beautiful jewels that beg to be worn every day. My greatest joy is to bestow them upon women who will flaunt them. I also greatly enjoy my fee, of course," she added, smiling at me from beneath lidded eyes, "but this piece—it is meant for you. Here, I will pin it on you. It will look nicely against your black blouse."

She brooked no argument, and I gave in, allowing her to fasten the heavy crystal formation to my shirt. Luckily, it was a sturdy cotton knit fabric that would most likely recover from the pin holes and the weight of the thing.

She stood back and gazed at it with a critical eye. "It is beautiful on you, Sydney, just as I knew it would be!" she reported.

"Thank you, Hannah. I don't know what to say," I told her.

"You are welcome, Sydney," she replied in a satisfied tone. "Now, let me get your papers so that you may be on your way, *oui?*"

She disappeared into the back room, returning with my work for the week and smiling indulgently as I thanked her again before I left. The brooch pressed through my shirt and into my skin like a burden of guilt. I was grateful she hadn't chosen that moment to ask me about the money D.J.D. owed her.

As I walked back to the car, an itch rose up between my shoulder blades. I rubbed at it and glanced around nervously. It was more a feeling than a physical sensation, and not so much a warning as the sense that I was being watched. But I saw nothing out of the ordinary—only the usual Worth Ave crowd of languidly moving shoppers with too much time on their hands and too much money to spend.

Maybe someone had been staring at the enormous rock formation above my breast, in awe that I hadn't yet toppled forward with its immense weight.

As I approached the car, Sunny was leaning against the rear door, legs crossed and feet resting on the edge of the curb. She smiled and waved, motioning for me to join her there. My forehead creased as warning bells sounded in my brain, her posture seeming forced and out of place. Why was she sweating out here instead of waiting in the air conditioned car?

"What's up?" I asked when I was closer.

"That is some hunk of rock. I'm surprised you don't have a bunch of little rocks swirling around you, being helplessly pulled into its orbit."

"Give it time," I said, only half joking. "Is something wrong?"

"Well, don't look now, but I'm pretty sure someone's following you. Just lean against the car and pretend like we're talking."

I smoothed my frown and moved to Sunny's side.

"Smile and try not to look so worried," Sunny advised.

I immediately spread my lips in what I hoped was a convincing semblance of a smile.

Sunny chuckled. "Now laugh like I've said something funny," she encouraged.

I feigned an amicable laugh.

"Good," Sunny smiled cheerfully. "Now do the hokey pokey and turn yourself around."

I glanced at her in confusion. Her voice was so deadpan that it took a second to register that she was kidding. I scowled and elbowed her in retaliation.

"I don't have to take this abuse you know," she complained with a smirk.

"If you didn't want to do the hokey pokey, all you had to do was say so."

"Just tell me who's following me," I snorted in exasperation.

Sunny's eyes glowed with amusement. "Look across the street and a few doors down at the woman standing in front of the window with the sunglasses. She's wearing black slacks, a silky beige blouse and a big floppy black hat. She's kind of short with curly brown hair and she's got a white shopping bag in each hand."

"I see her." I eyed the plump little woman in the ridiculously large hat with skepticism. "But she's not even looking over here. What makes you think she's not just shopping?"

"Don't stare!" Sunny hissed. "She may be able to see our reflection in the window. I saw her follow you down to Hannah's and then wait nearby until you came out. Then she started to follow you back here. I thought you were going to spot her when you stopped to look around, but she stepped into one of the shops. She came back out as soon as you started walking again, and she's been staring at those sunglasses for an awfully long time now."

"I did feel like someone was watching me before. I'm going to talk to her." I pushed myself away from the car, realizing that I was angry. Now people were following me?

"Wait!" Sunny demanded, grabbing my arm. "What if she's a death djinn? Lorien said they could be women too."

"You have my permission to tackle me if it even looks like I'm starting to make a w-i-s-h—just watch out for Lorien and her sneeze dust," I warned drily. "But death djinn or not, I'm going to find out why that woman's following me. Come on." I tugged her across the street and down the sidewalk, stopping close enough to touch the woman. I was sure she saw my reflection in the window beside her, but she gave no sign of a reaction.

"Excuse me," I said loudly.

She turned to look at me with a polite question in eyes that were an even deeper shade of brown than mine. "Yes?" she asked. She had dark, ruddy skin and a compact torso that looked out of proportion to her height—even though she was barely pushing five feet tall.

"Do we know each other?" I asked.

She studied me, her eyes alighting on my unwieldy brooch. "Uh, no. I don't think so. Should we?" she inquired. Her speech was rough, and colored by an accent that I couldn't place.

"Well, my friend saw you following me, and we thought perhaps it was because you recognized me from somewhere." My tone bordered on accusation.

She tore her gaze from the chunk of crystal to my waiting stare. She looked from me to Sunny in silence for a moment, and then sighed. "Beautiful. First day on the job and my cover's already blown." There was a wry twist to her sturdy lips. "My name's Galena. Pat Sparrow asked me to keep an eye on you, Sydney."

"Agent Sparrow didn't say anything to us about having Syd followed," Sunny said suspiciously.

Galena's dark eyes twinkled with humor. "Well, I could flash you my Seelie badge, but I don't suppose that would mean squat to you. And I assume he didn't say anything because I was supposed to stay out of sight—you know, not interfere with your daily routine or give you any cause for concern—just make sure you didn't get into any trouble. You can ask him the next time you see him."

"I will," I asserted with a mutinous expression. "I'll ask him why he felt it was necessary to have someone spy on me."

Galena let out a gravelly chuckle at the annoyance in my voice. "I could see how that might make a girl a bit temperamental—but take it easy on him, Sydney. I've known Pat for a long time, and I've never seen him this personally involved in a case. I get the feeling he's just worried about you."

My anger deflated, but I still couldn't help wondering if this had anything to do with my earlier refusal to tell Sparrow about Ophelia.

"And since my cover's blown anyway, I have to tell you," Galena added, "that brooch is absolutely fantastic!"

Sunny flicked me a comical look of disbelief.

I glanced at the sparkling monstrosity weighing down my shirt, shocked by the envy in Galena's tone. Then my eyes settled on the colossal onyx earrings sandwiching the sides of her face, and her elaborate matching gold and onyx necklace, and I decided maybe I shouldn't be so shocked after all.

"It was a gift from the woman who owns Haute Hannah's, down the street. I do some work for her," I explained. "It's actually kind of... overstated for my usual wardrobe. I'd give it to you, but with my luck Hannah would find out and be eternally insulted. If you really like it, you should take a look in her shop. She designs all of the jewelry herself, and she's kind of pricey, but this is a good example of her style."

"It's just gorgeous," Galena admired. "Maybe I will stop by her shop some time."

"Just watch out for her perfume," Sunny muttered.

Galena gave Sunny a questioning look, and I took the opportunity to study her. I couldn't figure out why her proportions seemed off.

"What are you?" I blurted. "I mean, I assume you're not full human since you work for the Seelie police—or maybe you're not human at all. Although I guess I don't really know much about it..." I trailed off, hoping that whatever race she was, I hadn't just insulted her.

Galena looked amused by my discomfort. "I'm a dwarf."

"Aren't you a little tall for a dwarf?" asked Sunny. "Not that I've ever seen one—but I've read about them. Although I suppose that was fiction.

Regardless, *dwarf*—doesn't that denote, you know, someone *smaller*? You must be, what—five feet tall?"

"I saw a dwarf once, at the Seelie Police station," I put in, "but he couldn't have been more than three feet tall."

"That would have been my brother, Galen." Galena nodded. "He usually works the front counter."

"Yeah," I said, recognition dawning at the similarity in their names.

Galena glanced around and then lowered her chin to direct our attention downward. She bent to drop her bags on the sidewalk and, pretending to look inside one, quickly lifted the hem of a pant leg to reveal the strangest 'shoe' I'd ever seen.

It was black lacquered wood that had been carved to mimic the contours of a normal sized shoe. A two foot wooden stilt extended above it, at the top of which rested a second, smaller shoe that held Galena's foot.

Grinning at the expressions on our faces, she released the fabric of her slacks so that it fell in a curtain to once more conceal what had to be the monster of all high heels.

"Impressive. How long did it take you to learn to walk in those?" asked Sunny.

Galena laughed. "It took a little getting used to, but it's not as hard as it looks. They're dead useful for undercover work in your realm, especially since glamour spells can be unreliable and that type of magic doesn't come naturally to dwarves."

"I never would have guessed," I marveled.

"Not bad, right?" Galena looked pleased.

"So, do you do a lot of undercover work here?" I asked curiously.

She shrugged one silk-clad shoulder. "Now and then. But these baby's are only for when I really want to blend in. It's not as if dwarves have trouble passing for human." She winked. "You'd be surprised how many faerie folk walk among you every day—mostly for purely harmless reasons. Although fugitives will sometimes defect here in an attempt to avoid capture in the faerie realm," she added more soberly.

"And we try to keep an eye out for immortals frequenting your realm in the hopes of taking advantage of humans. Take this nasty unaligned soul business, for instance." She sighed. "Everyone's had to put in extra over-time on this one. Although, I have every faith that Pat will crack the case eventually. That boy's got mad skills, and he's not too hard on the eyes either, if you know what I mean."

Galena grinned impeniently.

"If he thinks protecting you will help, sweet thing, I'm not about to question it. Speaking of which, I should probably get back to pretending to secretly follow you. If you don't mind, just ignore me and keep doing whatever you were planning to do." Her voice was tinged with chagrin.

"Are you sure?" I asked, uncomfortable with the thought of her trailing us all night while we enjoyed our drinks, dinner and shopping. Not to mention that I wouldn't have minded hanging out with someone who had some history with Sparrow.

"We're going to this great little Indian restaurant. You're welcome to join us," I offered.

"Thanks, but I'm supposed to be on the job. Besides, I think I need to spend some time practicing my stealth techniques." Her lips twisted in self deprecation. "Just remember—if you run into any trouble, I'll be around."

Galena bent to pick up her white shopping bags, pushing the tissue paper aside for a moment to reveal twin, short-handled axes with gleaming half-moon blades. "Mithrium," she said proudly. "Light as air, but they'll cut through anything—and anyone. Just give a holler if you need me." Then she rose and strode away, black pant legs swishing above her hidden two-foot heels.

I watched her go, trying to picture the jewelry-laden dwarf wielding those double axes with that huge hat flopping around her ears. Somehow I had no doubt that she'd be a force to be reckoned with.

"Never a dull moment," Sunny commented as we crossed the street toward the station wagon.

I blasted the A/C to dry our sweat and then pulled out into the late afternoon traffic.

"Do you think Sparrow's spying on me because he's hoping to find out who told me about the goblin?" It hurt to think that Sparrow mistrusted me so much that he'd have me followed without telling me about it.

She held her long curls up off her neck and glanced at me thoughtfully. "I think Patrick Sparrow wants to protect you, Syd. And sure, it probably bugs the crap out of him that you won't tell him where you got your information." She chuckled. "But unless I've completely misread him—I'm pretty sure you can trust him."

I frowned as I considered that. I was pretty sure Sparrow could be trusted too, but it eased my mind to hear it from Sunny. I'd trusted Jeremy and look how that had turned out. Just thinking about his betrayal hurt like hell, so I pushed it back into the numbest corner of my heart again, telling myself I'd deal with it later.

All I knew for sure was that I needed to be careful.

Chapter 13 - Milk And Honey

Relaxed and happy from exotically spiced Indian food, and laden with bags containing new novels for our bedside tables, Sunny and I returned to the penthouse for the evening—only to be assaulted by a frantic faerie.

"Oh, Sydney—thank Titania you're home! Come on, we have to go right now or we might not make it!" A frazzled Emily greeted us at the door in her dress of drably shifting colors, tattered wings abuzz. She motioned anxiously for me to follow her.

"Go where?" I asked in alarm.

"Lauringer's agreed to meet you, honey, and if we keep her waiting, we likely won't get another chance!"

"Lauringer? Now?" I repeated, panic crowding my pleasantly spice-muddled mind.

"I'll transport you; you'll just make it—I hope." Emily reached into the dull folds of her dress and pulled out a tiny grey pouch. She flitted up to hover above me. "Keep your eyes closed, honey, and try not to fall when you land."

I shot Sunny a helpless look and found her expression hovering somewhere between encouragement and fear. "Oh, wait!" she cried.

Emily made an impatient noise as Sunny dashed into the kitchen. I heard the rattling of metal pans being shifted inside a metal drawer, and realized what she was up to.

We had decided to hide Angelica's mysterious, dark green vial inside the drawer beneath the unused stove. I didn't want it anywhere near where we slept in case it was dangerous (never mind the fact that it had been in my bedroom all along). We had settled on the kitchen as the safest place.

Sunny sprinted back into the foyer with the small vial wrapped in a thin, blue and white striped napkin. "Here," she said breathlessly as she took my bag of newly bought books and folded the object into my hand. "Good luck, Syd." Her eyes held mine for a moment, lending me an unspoken strength.

"Thanks," I said softly. I looked up at Emily, still hovering above my head. "I'm ready," I told her, my calm tone belying the trembling in my midsection as I closed my eyes and stiffened my knees.

I grasped the hidden vial tightly. If anyone knew what the strange object was, Lauringer would. If anyone could lend the magical help to prove Balthus guilty and get me out of my contract, she could. I told myself I should be excited about this meeting—not terrified.

My wobbling insides weren't convinced.

A familiar iciness swept down over my body and I held myself rigid as the gut-clenching loss of gravity overtook me. I was beginning to feel as if I might lose my already questionable grip on reality unless the falling stopped, when I abruptly slowed, as if cushioned by some immense force that lowered me the rest of the way to the ground.

I kept my feet this time—only just—and vaguely registered the crackle of something being crushed beneath them as they accepted my full weight.

I took a deep breath and opened my eyes to a dim world of lush green. I stood in a shadowed clearing, leaves and small branches cluttering the woodland carpet beneath my feet, and the untamed forest closing in thick around me. Barely enough light remained in the deepening dusk to filter through the intertwining branches above and illumine the spaces between the trees.

A milky blue orb, the size of a large marble, sprang to life in the darkness before me. Emily called in a hushed voice, "Follow me, quickly now!"

There was nothing for it; I began to pick my way through the snarled vegetation behind her, alternately thankful for my jeans and cursing the open toes of my sandals. I was too out of breath, and concentrating too hard on not losing sight of her bobbing blue faerie lamp, to ask questions. It was almost pitch black now, and I stifled an expletive as my big toe caught on another tree root and I miraculously managed not to fall and break my neck.

Head down in an attempt to see where I was stepping, I thought about how I was going to have to soak my aching toe in peroxide when I got home. It was probably a good thing it was too dark to see the abused appendage. I was definitely going to have to redo my pedicure.

I looked up just in time to keep from careening into Emily, who had stopped short. She was staring into the blackness ahead, mumbling to herself.

"Why did we stop?" I hissed after a moment, as much to fill the growing silence as anything else.

Actually, silence wasn't really the right word. There were rustlings and chirrupings and the crackling of branches and the hum of the forest coming to life all around us. And the more silent we were, the louder it seemed to grow. I thought I recognized the song of the tiny golden-brown frogs mixed into the forest's cacophony, which made me feel a little better. But those cracklings made it sound as if larger things were moving nearby as well, and it was freaking me out.

"Aha! There it is!" Emily exclaimed, her voice mingled with triumph and relief. "This way honey—I was afraid we'd missed her."

A glowing light appeared, shining through the trees ahead of us. I could just make out the shape of a cabin beyond the columns of thick, gnarled trunks. I got the strange feeling that it hadn't been there a moment before. I followed Emily toward the structure, my now throbbing toe thankful for the assistance provided by the light.

We cleared the last of the trees, and spread out before us was a large, rustic-looking A-frame log cabin. Its exterior was well-tended, the numerous picture windows clean and trimmed with fat flower boxes spilling over with vibrant blooms. A heaping pile of firewood rested to one side of a cobblestone path leading up to a front door painted grass green.

"Well this looks cheerful," I commented grumpily. "Why didn't we transport straight here? I could have done without the nature hike."

"Magical protections, illusion charms and location shifting spells," Emily panted as she flew up the path at a breakneck pace. "Hurry—put your hand on the door before it shifts again!"

I stared at her uncomprehendingly for a moment before sprinting forward after her, as quickly as my complaining feet would carry me. The entire cabin seemed to go a bit hazy, fading into more of an apparition of a cabin than a solid structure, and I expended my last ounce of adrenaline to move faster. I collapsed hard against the door, wheezing, thankful to find it a physically substantial mass beneath my fingers. It made me wonder if I hadn't imagined the whole fading thing.

When I finally stopped puffing long enough to spare a glance for Emily, she was smiling down at me in weary relief. "You'll be fine now, honey. Just take a minute to collect yourself and then go ahead and knock on the door. I'm sure Lauringer already knows you're here. She'll send you back home when you're done—by a much more direct route, I'll wager. And sorry for the trek through the forest, it really was the only way. Good luck, Sydney—I know if anyone can help you, Lauringer can."

She gave me a warm wink of encouragement and began a slightly unsteady flight back up the path toward the trees, dull yellow faerie dust trailing behind her.

"Wait!" I choked out, overwhelmed by a surge of panic. Emily turned to look at me questioningly. "You're not coming with me?"

"No, honey," she answered, her eyes sympathetic. "This appointment was for you. Lauringer doesn't mind making sure I have Ophelia's memory dust when I need it, but with the way she is…I just think you're better off meeting with her alone."

"But…Lorien!" I said, concentrating hard and turning her name into a call as I spoke it.

Emily stared at me in confusion.

"My faerie guardian, Lorien," I explained breathlessly. "She'll never forgive me if I meet with Lauringer without her. Lorien!" I called again.

Emily just shook her head. "Not a good idea, honey. Besides, this entire place is warded—she can't hear your call. You'd have to go all the way back through the forest to escape the wards—and if you did, you'd never find this place again. You'll just have to meet with Lauringer without her. I'm sure she'll understand."

I seriously doubted it. I slumped against the door with an unhappy groan.

"Chin up, honey," Emily said bracingly. "Now you listen to me—you'll be fine. You just remember what can happen if you don't find what you're looking for. Okay?"

I took a steadying breath. "Okay," I repeated, standing up straighter. "And thanks again, Emily—for everything."

Her smile was weary as she nodded and turned to fly away once more. I stood against the door, restraining the urge to call her back as I watched her disappear into the forest. When she was no longer visible, I grimaced and glanced down to take inventory of myself. I was a mess.

My jeans were streaked with dirt, my sandals were beyond filthy and my toe was bleeding. My black shirt appeared to have escaped without much damage, although it was slightly askew and Hannah's ridiculous brooch was still pinned to it. Sunny had dared me to wear it to dinner and during our trip to the bookstore. I unpinned it now and pushed it into my pocket, where it created a large rock-shaped lump.

I pulled the edges of the napkin containing the glass vial from my other pocket and clutched it in my hand as I knocked on Lauringer's green front door. It opened immediately to reveal an attractive young woman in a smart navy business suit and matching fitted gloves. She stood before me in her stocking feet, her waist-length golden-blonde hair hanging loose about her shoulders.

Although the suit and the rustic cabin made an odd contrast, her appearance would have seemed relatively normal—if it weren't for the color of her skin. Every inch of exposed flesh glowed golden. Not as in goldenly tan, but as in glittering, sparkly golden, as if it had permanently absorbed a layer of gold dust.

Her eyes were also infiltrated by the strange phenomenon. What should have been white was a pale shimmering gold, and although the irises retained a trace of what appeared to be cornflower blue, both they and the pupils were so heavily tinted with specks of gold that barely any other color remained visible.

When she smiled at me, even her teeth gleamed faintly golden. "I was wondering how long you were going to stand outside before knocking. Come on in, Sydney. I'm Lauringer, as you've probably guessed." She closed the door behind us and motioned me toward a snug kitchen nook with a carved table of raw wood and four matching chairs with thick, green cushions. A set of green glazed canisters were lined up neatly along the length of the table.

"I really appreciate you seeing me," I told her when I found my voice.

The interior of the cabin spread out in an open design. It was sparsely furnished and filled with soft, warm lighting that left no corner shadowed.

The living room furniture, arranged cozily before the sprawling fireplace, was informal. The cushions and the few scattered throw rugs, like the accents in the kitchen, were in shades of green. A wide staircase framed one side of the kitchen nook and led up to an unseen second storey, which I assumed contained the bedrooms.

The kitchen was comfortable and functional. Fat bunches of dried herbs hung from a rack spanning the length of the enormous window above the sink, their pungent aroma permeating the room. Another larger rack hung along the opposite wall, displaying numerous pots of varying size and thickness, some made of copper, some of steel, some of cast iron.

Lauringer went to remove a whistling tea kettle from the stove as I took one of the chairs at the wooden table.

"I must admit that Emily's description of your plight interested me. It is rare for a human to attempt to escape a death djinn contract. Suicide has been the generally accepted method for many. Would you like some tea?"

I started at her bluntness.

She blinked her strange golden eyes at me, and then they widened in comprehension.

"I'm sorry, Sydney. I'm afraid that I may be a bit lacking in the social graces. You've probably been told that I'm something of a hermit. The truth is—I don't think I've had a guest in my home for at least half a century. Please forgive my unthinking comment."

I cleared my throat. "Uh, I'm feeling a little out of sorts myself. I've heard so much about you. My faerie guardian practically worships you."

She studied me as she dropped teabags into two earthenware mugs and poured steaming water over them. "Milk and honey?"

"Please," I answered, grateful that I hadn't had to ask. I was so nervous I probably would have suffered through drinking it bitter if she hadn't offered.

"So, you have a faerie guardian?" She placed one mug in front of me and settled into the opposite chair with her own. She opened one of the green glazed canisters and scooped out a heaping tablespoon of dense golden powder, which she stirred into her tea before taking a sip.

"Yes," I said. "I just found out about her a few weeks ago, when this whole death djinn thing started. Her name's Lorien."

She noticed my eyes on her hand and said, "You're probably wondering why I'm wearing gloves. It's a precaution of my trade. I handle many potent substances which could have decidedly...unpleasant effects if they were to come into contact with my skin."

Then she smiled. "You're very lucky to have a faerie guardian, you know. Only a small portion of the human population is chosen. She'll be the best friend you'll ever have—don't take her for granted."

She sighed and took another sip of her tea. "I'm sure you've seen the effect that Ophelia's decision has had on poor Emily."

"Yes," I answered, my brow creasing in a frown. "I was pretty horrified to learn what a couple of centuries without my soul could do to both me and Lorien. I know that getting Balthus discredited is a long shot, but I have to try. Although, I'm not sure where it will leave Emily and Ophelia if I succeed." I searched Lauringer's face for her opinion on the matter.

After all, she had been providing Emily with the spell to keep Ophelia intermittently sane.

Her glittering eyes revealed nothing as she continued to study me. "Maybe if you succeed, it won't only be your contract that is cancelled. And if not—well, a life without your soul is no life at all."

Lauringer glanced down at the wrapped vial in my hand. "I don't require payment for my services, you know."

I looked at her in confusion.

"That vial of immortality," she explained, "I assume you brought it as payment."

I stared at the thin, blue and white napkin in dawning amazement. I unwrapped it carefully and set the forest green vial containing the faint glimmer of light on the table between us.

"My friend found this in my penthouse. Balthus was staying there before I moved in, so I suspected it was his. But I didn't know what it was, or whether it might be dangerous."

She chuckled and picked up the vial to examine it. "No, it's not dangerous. And it happens to be extremely valuable. Immortality is a rare and expensive commodity on the death djinn market. Balthus won't be pleased to have lost it."

I gnawed my lower lip, my mind churning. "Is it valuable enough to get me out of my contract?" I ventured hopefully.

Her golden eyes turned hard. "Not likely, Sydney. There is very little that would persuade a death djinn to abandon the pursuit of a soul contract. And although immortality is harder to come by than a human soul, I doubt a djinn would consider it an equal trade.

"I do, however, believe that you're on the right track as far as trying to discredit Balthus. Why don't you tell me how you think I might be able to help you with that?"

Lauringer folded her gloved hands together on the table top and looked at me expectantly.

I did my best to keep the events in some semblance of coherent order—from the woman in the coma with the unaligned soul, to the goblin with the tattoo on his palm and his possible connection to the Unseelie Court, to the death djinn arrests for possession of other unaligned souls, to the Seelie Police's inability to trace the souls to their human counterparts or identify the magic that had been used on them.

Lauringer remained silent and expressionless as I spoke. When I was finished, she continued to watch me for a moment, as if coming to a decision.

"I would like to examine the unaligned souls, and in particular, the soul of the woman in the coma."

"Uh, do you want me to ask my friend at the Seelie Police Department about getting you in to examine them?"

Her face lit with amusement. "That won't be necessary, Sydney. I am well enough known that I shouldn't have a problem getting myself in."

"Right." I felt my cheeks color. Of course the most powerful mage in the faerie realm didn't need my connections. "Um, how about the infinity tattoo; does that mean anything to you?"

The humor in her expression died. "I'm sorry, Sydney, I can't say that it does. And even if you found the goblin that supposedly has this tattoo, he would most likely deny Balthus' story, and it would be the word of a criminal versus the word of a goblin—neither one being a particularly reliable source.

"Although it shouldn't matter anyway." Her jaw clenched and her voice grew agitated. "What I can't understand is why the police haven't made more of a move against the death djinns already, with so many of them found in possession of unaligned souls. Of *course* they're pleading ignorance—it would be foolish to admit such a thing!"

She took a calming breath.

"I'm afraid I have rather strong opinions on this issue," she said apologetically. "I've seen what happens when a death djinn controls a human soul. I've watched Ophelia and Emily suffer. And others.

"I will examine the unaligned souls myself to see if I can't find something that the Seelie investigators have overlooked. But in the mean time, my advice to you is simply to sit tight and keep your guard up. Even without further evidence, the sheer number of death djinns involved should be enough to get a conspiracy conviction against them. And that, in turn, will hopefully be enough to get your contract cancelled.

"You're strong, Sydney. You can get through this. Just hold out a little while longer."

Her voice was filled with quiet conviction. And as her eyes held mine, I had the sense that she understood what I was going through, even though she was a stranger to me.

"If I could do something to help you resist them, I would," she added. "But you probably know by now that the death djinn contract forbids any such interference."

"Yeah, convenient little clause," I said with a crooked smile.

"Isn't it, though?" she replied in a bitter tone. "So how would you feel about accompanying me to the Seelie Police station to take a look at those souls?"

"Now?" I asked, surprised.

"No time like the present," she answered briskly. She swallowed the last of her tea, then gave me a quick once over and grinned. "You're a bit of a sight aren't you? Here, let me fix that. After all, it was my penchant for privacy that put you into such a state."

Before I could form a response, she reached into one of the green canisters on the table and pulled out a palm-full of fine silver dust. In a single smooth movement she sprinkled it over me, while softly mumbling an incantation. Warmth spread through me, and my clothes shifted against my skin as if they had been disturbed by an ethereal wind.

The dull throb in my toe disappeared, and when I looked down, it was as if nothing had happened to it. There was no trace of blood and my toenail polish looked fresh. My filthy jeans and sandals had also been returned to like-new status.

"Wow," I breathed. "You should bottle that stuff and sell it. Most women would kill to have something like that on hand. You'd make a fortune."

Lauringer gave a wry chuckle as she stepped into a pair of navy, high-heeled pumps that had been discarded near the stairs. "I've found that fame and fortune can have a way of backfiring on you. Ready, then?"

I nodded, rewrapping the vial of immortality before I stuck it back in my pocket. "Uh, just one more thing. I know you don't think finding the goblin will help, but just in case, would you be able to tell me how to find the Hell Ride?"

Lauringer's golden eyes clouded. "Oh, Sydney. You don't want to do that."

"You're right—I probably don't," I replied on a mirthless laugh. "But I'd like to know anyway."

"You remind me a little of myself," she said softly. "I only hope that your determination doesn't end up getting you killed...or worse."

She pursed her lips, looking torn.

"Please," I requested with quiet resolve.

She sighed in resignation.

"Alright, Sydney. If you insist on pursuing this course, I suppose I can't stop you. Calling the Hell Ride is frighteningly simple, although only those belonging to the Unseelie Court dare to do so," she warned.

"During the hour between midnight and one a.m. you must stand in a 'tween place and recite the following incantation: 'Unholy Court, I call you this night; Come bear me away in the absence of light; I surrender to darkness as clinging as soot; Light's goodness lies shadowed and evil's afoot.'"

"Could I borrow a pen and paper to write that down?" I asked, knowing I'd never remember it correctly.

Lauringer gave me an unreadable look and then snapped her gloved fingers. A green marble pen appeared on the kitchen table next to a small pad of textured paper. I shook my head and smiled, amazed at her casual use of magic, as she bent down to write the incantation for me.

"What's a 'tween place?" I asked, wedging the folded paper into the pocket with the crystal brooch.

"Places where two realities meet—it can be as simple as a doorway, a window, or even the edge of a shadow, where dark and light meet. But the Hell Ride is no joke, Sydney. The Unseelies delight in the torture of mortals and, although it happens rarely and the incidents are well-concealed, there have been...accidents. By choosing to join them, you surrender a part of your will to them. I would not advise this course of action."

"Duly noted. I'd probably be too scared to do it anyway." I grinned.

"You should be." My grin evaporated at her serious tone.

"Ready?" she asked after a moment.

I nodded again.

Lauringer spoke a single word. One second we were standing in her kitchen, and the next we were standing in the lobby of the Seelie Police Station. I gasped in amazement. Galen, the grizzle-bearded dwarf behind the counter, looked equally shocked.

"Good evening, Master Dwarf," Lauringer said pleasantly. "I would like to speak with the officer in charge of the death djinn investigation. Please tell him or her that Lauringer wishes to offer her services with regard to the inspection of the unaligned souls. And I would appreciate you making it clear that I am pressed for time and will need to conduct my investigation immediately, if I am to do so at all."

"Right away, madam," growled Galen. "We would be honored to accept your offer of assistance." He bowed from atop his stool, and then hopped to the ground. His head disappeared below the long counter as he hurried toward the door leading to the back offices.

Lauringer grinned at my bemused expression. "Despite my inclination toward privacy, sometimes celebrity has its perks."

It wasn't long before the door behind the counter opened again, and Sparrow strode out to meet us. His dark hair was tousled, as if he'd been sleeping, and his button down shirt was absent of its tie. He greeted Lauringer with deferent professionalism, his dark blue eyes registering surprise when they saw me.

I imagined him warm in his bed moments before, and the image was so enticing that I wanted nothing more than to crawl into his arms and join him there. My mouth went dry at the thought, and I gave him a shaky smile. His eyes held mine as he extended his hand to Lauringer.

"Lauringer, I'm Agent Sparrow. I'm the detective in charge of the death djinn investigation. It's a great pleasure to meet you, and I would personally like to thank you for your generous offer of assistance. I understand that your time is precious and I would be more than happy to escort you to our containment room immediately."

He gaze roved over my face. "Sydney, I'm glad you're here. Full of surprises as usual, I see."

I smirked at him. "Speaking of surprises, there's something I'd like to discuss with you in private."

Despite the fact that I wanted to crawl into bed with him, and run my hands through his hair, and explore the tattoos inked into the muscled contours of his chest...I hadn't forgotten about him sending Galena to spy on me.

"I see you two know each other," Lauringer observed with a faint smile. "Well, thank you for coming so quickly, Agent Sparrow, and I apologize for disturbing you after hours. When Sydney explained the situation, I felt compelled to come immediately. As you know, magical signatures fade with time. It may already be too late for me to glean any new information from the unaligned souls, but I will do my best."

"Much appreciated," Sparrow said with a nod. "Follow me, please."

He led us through the door into the back room. Only a few of the wooden desks were occupied at this time of night, but the smell of coffee was still thick in the air. It seemed a permanent fixture of the room, an aroma that was probably never absent long enough to fade completely.

One of the desk's occupants glanced up as we passed, then did a double take at the sight of Lauringer. He nudged his co-worker, who nearly fell out of his chair when he realized who she was, and in turn threw a wad of paper at the officer several desks over. She looked up in annoyance, which faded as her eyes widened and then followed Lauringer across the room.

Lauringer either didn't notice the commotion she was causing, or she simply chose to ignore it.

Sparrow continued down the hallway that led to the outer courtyard. He stopped to unlock one of the doors lining the passage with a long, silver key. Then he pulled it open and flicked on an overhead light to reveal a large, perfectly round room whose dimensions seemed impossible from the outside.

Rows of shelves lined the walls around the entire circumference, the jewel-like twinkle of hundreds of multi-hued crystal vials winking out from their depths, like the hoard of some obsessively organized dragon. The dull gleam of copper and bronze oil lamps added to the effect. Wooden work tables with careful spaces around each one occupied the center of the room. When I stepped inside, the padded floor felt soft and spongy beneath my sandals.

"I'm sure you're familiar with the procedures and organization of a containment room," Sparrow said to Lauringer, waiting for her to nod as a formality. "The unaligned souls that have been rescued from death djinn possession are in this area." He indicated a sprawling section of shelves to our left.

"That many?" I whispered, amazed and saddened at the sheer number of vials there.

Both Sparrow and Lauringer turned to look at me. "I'm afraid so, Sydney," Sparrow answered quietly.

Lauringer pursed her lips, an angry light filling her golden eyes. "Sydney's right. The number of unaligned souls you have found is astounding. Which begs the question, Agent Sparrow—what more do you need to prosecute the death djinns for this outrage?"

Sparrow ran an agitated hand through his dark hair and sighed.

"Believe me; I would like nothing more than to see the death djinns prosecuted for this. But certain questions have come to light that must be answered before the case can be satisfactorily closed. King Moab insists that none of his people would deal in unaligned souls and has demanded a more detailed investigation into this matter. And he is not someone that can be ignored—his influence extends to certain high ranking members of the Seelie Court." He gave Lauringer a pointed look.

"I would think that such blatant disregard for mortal life would be more important than the friendship between two heads of state—no matter how high they rank," she said stonily.

"And I assure you that once I can prove the death djinns' guilt, it won't matter who's in bed with whom," he answered in a heated tone. "However, as long as the question of their innocence remains, I have no choice but to keep digging for more proof."

Lauringer gave him an unreadable look and then turned toward the shelves. "Thank you, Agent Sparrow. I would like to begin with the soul belonging to the woman you found."

"Certainly, it's this one in the red vial," he said, removing it and handing it to Lauringer. "There should be a file attached to each of the vials detailing any information we have discovered. Though I'm afraid the files are rather slim."

She turned her attention to the vial. "I will have to examine the woman as well," she mumbled. "I will be a little while in looking these over," she said, glancing at us. "I don't wish to be rude, but I concentrate better when I'm alone. Would you mind? I'll let you know when I've completed my examinations."

"Of course," Sparrow agreed politely. "We'll be in my office—turn left when you exit the containment room, and it's the last door on the right."

Lauringer nodded absently, her interest already reabsorbed by the vial she held. Sparrow motioned for me to follow him back out into the corridor and he shut the door behind us. Then he grasped my hand and pulled me down the hallway at a fast walk until we were ensconced in the privacy of his office.

He pushed the lock flush against the knob and dragged me into his arms with a soft, "Come here, Sydney."

His lips tasted mine gently, almost questioningly, at first. I welcomed him into my mouth, and he pushed me against the door with the warm weight of his body. His fingers twined with mine and he slowly raised both my hands above my head, imprisoning them there as he began a questing invasion of my mouth. The kiss was hot enough to fry my brain and make me forget my earlier displeasure over him sending Galena to spy on me.

He hardened, pressing into me through the barrier of our clothing, and I writhed against him, wondering if he might have a couch hidden somewhere nearby. He groaned into my mouth, his Irish brogue husky as he muttered, "Not that your outfit isn't quite becoming, but I preferred what you were wearing this morning."

I pictured the thin tank-top and soft cotton sleep pants. Then I pictured us kissing on my bed. I smiled against his lips. "And I preferred the location."

He chuckled and pulled me into his arms, placing a kiss on the top of my head. "I've been thinking about you all day. And what in the realm are those lumps in your pants?" he asked, leaning back from me and staring dubiously down at the bulging front pockets of my jeans.

"Oh, yeah." I put my hands over my unshapely pockets, flushing with embarrassment. "We can't all have magical disappearing pockets, you know."

His brow rose in question.

"The night you captured Balthus in the lamp," I explained, "you stuck it in your jacket and it disappeared. When I put something in my pocket, on the other hand, it tends to stay there as a thing-shaped lump."

"Relocation spell," Sparrow supplied in an amused tone.

I pulled the crystal brooch from one pocket, hastily shoving the paper with the Hell Ride incantation deeper into the fabric compartment. I had the distinct feeling that Sparrow would be none too pleased to discover my continuing interest in that subject. I held the huge crystal formation up against my shirt and flashed Sparrow a wide smile. "How do you like my new brooch?"

He visibly struggled with his expression before answering, "It's quite an eye-catching piece."

"It was a gift from one of the women I work for." I grinned. "Don't worry—it's not really my style."

I snorted at Sparrow's look of relief.

I shoved the thing back into one stretched-out pocket, then pulled the napkin with the vial out of the other. "Here, I guess you should have this. We found it hidden in my penthouse. Lauringer says it's a vial of immortality and I'm guessing it belongs to Balthus. I suppose it's too much to hope that it might actually help with the investigation?"

He took the forest green vial and held it up to the light. "This is very rare, Sydney. I'll perform a detailed examination of it just in case, but I can't think how it would be connected to the unaligned souls."

He glanced back down at me. "If an immortal is foolish enough to trade away their immortality, that's their affair—the rules designed for the taking of souls don't apply. You'd think Balthus would have kept something this valuable in his containment safe, though."

Sparrow looked thoughtful. "It's not really the type of thing I was looking for when I searched your penthouse, but I'm still surprised that I didn't find it. Where was it?"

"The vent," I answered with a smirk.

"Sneaky," he said, humor coloring his expression. "I'll have to remember to look there next time. Of course, I was a bit distracted that evening." His sapphire eyes turned wicked.

"Oh, no," I laughed, stepping away and scooting behind his desk. "We have things to discuss. And don't even try to tell me that you felt anything other than annoyance with me that night."

He gave me a rueful look. "I was angry that night, Sydney—angry that such a beautiful young woman almost traded her soul to a death djinn—angry that I cared enough about stopping you to allow it to interfere with my job.

"I was only supposed to be following Balthus; I hadn't intended to make an arrest until I had more evidence against him. But I couldn't allow you to ruin your life."

My gaze landed on a faded photo in an elegant gilt frame on the corner of Sparrow's desk. It portrayed a lovely woman with long, dark hair, standing beside a roguishly handsome man. She appeared to be laughing at something he was whispering to her out of the corner of his mouth. A heavy sorrow settled over me as I raised my eyes to meet Sparrow's.

"You saved me that night, Sparrow, and I'm going to find a way to get out of this." My voice held a quiet strength that I was surprised I actually felt. Then I smiled at him teasingly. "But it's nice to hear that you were helpless to resist my charms from the beginning."

"I've got some very definite plans for your charms, Sydney—plans that mostly involve you writhing helplessly beneath me," he said in a silky tone as he pursued me around the edge of the desk.

I gasped with laughter and turned to flee to the other side of the small room, but Sparrow was too quick. He grasped my shoulder, and placing the vial of immortality safely in a desk drawer, he turned me around to face him.

Then he lowered himself into the rolling leather chair behind his desk and pulled me forward until I had no choice but to straddle him. He eased me down on top of him so that the length of his erection pressed directly into the fabric of my tautly stretched jeans, right where it grazed the sensitive spot between my legs.

"Is that a promise?" I breathed, intoxicated by the feel of him and his heady aroma of woodland spice. I ran my fingers through the softness of his hair and looked into his eyes.

"Yes, Sydney, it is." The certainty of his words sent a cascade of desire spilling through me.

He touched me unhurriedly, first cupping my face with his palms, then allowing his fingertips to explore the contours of my jaw and my neck, before slowly gliding down to tantalize my nipples and cup my breasts. I grasped his thick shoulders in my hands and arched toward him as his fingers traveled lower, down the planes of my stomach, past my hips and over the tops of my thighs in a leisurely discovery of my curves.

I moaned softly as those questing fingers moved, with maddening slowness, back up the insides of my thighs, tracing little circles until they reached my aching center. He pressed one finger lightly into me, stroking me through the denim until I bloomed for his touch.

"Oh, Goddess, Sparrow," I breathed. My eyes fluttered shut and I leaned into his hand, my head tilted backward. I felt him swell as he shifted against me, and I smiled. "It feels like *you're* the one who's writhing beneath *me*."

"We'll be exploring both of those options," he whispered hotly as he traced little circles over my clit. He seemed to know exactly how to touch me—and if he kept it up I was going to come right there, fully clothed.

He leaned forward and captured my mouth with his, increasing the pressure of his fingers as his tongue teased mine. "Come for me, Sydney," he urged, his voice a seductive command. A helpless sound escaped my throat and I strained against him as an explosion of mind-numbing pleasure expanded throughout my body.

I shuddered and clutched his shoulders so that I wouldn't be swept away. His arms banded around me and he stroked my back, nuzzling me with his lips. "You are so damned sweet, Sydney," he murmured. "You have no idea what you do to me."

I felt him still rock-hard beneath me as I regained control of my watery muscles. I opened my eyes and stared into his bright blue ones, my body still on fire for his. "I want you inside me," I stated, the words stark with need.

He groaned and pulled me against him, muttering what sounded like a prayer in Gaelic. "I'm taking you to my bed tonight, Sydney," he said in a roughened tone, "just as soon as Lauringer leaves."

Anticipation swept through me, leaving me edgy and tense. As if in answer to our thoughts, a knock sounded at the door and Lauringer called out that she was finished. Sparrow lifted me to my feet and pulled his shirt free of his waistband so that it concealed the evidence of his desire.

I reached up to straighten my hair and smooth my clothing, wondering if it was obvious that I'd just experienced one of the most intense orgasms of my life.

Lauringer stood outside the door, looking dazed and exhausted. She forced a smile and shook her head, her lips tight with anger and disappointment. "I'm sorry," she said. "I'm afraid I can't tell you anything new."

Sparrow cleared his throat and donned his detective persona. "Well, on behalf of the Seelie Police department, I'd like to thank you for your efforts. Personally, you have no idea how much I appreciate your help. You can imagine how much pressure we've been under, with the need to release these captive souls one way or the other.

"I'm sure it will ease the minds of everyone involved to know that we've exhausted every possibility in our attempts to discover these souls' human counterparts before returning them to the Sea of Souls."

Lauringer nodded.

"Yes, Lauringer, thank you so much for being willing to help," I said, stepping forward. "I'm grateful that you took the time to see me."

She blinked at me with glazed eyes, and Sparrow took her arm when she swayed unsteadily.

"Are you alright?" I asked in concern.

"I need..." she mumbled, her words slurring together. "I have to get home." And then she was gone.

I stared at the empty hallway.

"Do you think she'll be alright?" I asked, turning to Sparrow with a worried frown.

"Spell fatigue can make you weak and disoriented like that. But if the tales are true, Lauringer is more powerful than either of us can imagine. I'm sure she'll be fine as soon as she gets some rest," he reassured me as he shut the door to his office with a soft click.

"And at least we know we haven't overlooked anything now. She must have expended a great deal of magic to tire her out like that."

He crossed his muscular forearms over his chest and perched his hip on the edge of his desk. "I still can't believe that you were able to get her involved," he said with a smile. "Do you have any idea how amazing you are, Sydney?"

My own smile grew as I moved toward him. "You think so?" I asked, stopping just out of reach.

Sparrow nodded, his eyes blazing brighter.

"Let me ask you something then," I said, raising my hands above my head in a languid stretch that thrust my breasts forward.

"Mmhm," he agreed, his eyes riveted.

"Why did you have Galena spy on me?" I lowered my hands and took a step back, watching him expectantly.

His gaze traveled to mine and an expression of self-deprecating amusement crossed his features. "I was wondering when I was going to have to answer for that—Galena said you looked less than pleased."

I gave him a saccharine smile.

"Look, Sydney," he said uncertainly, "despite what you might think, the only reason I had you followed was for your own protection. I don't want any of the other death djinns trying to hone in on Balthus' uncompleted contract. I'd keep watch over you myself, if I wasn't responsible for heading up this damned investigation.

"And just so there are no misunderstandings, I *did* tell my superiors that you gave me information pertinent to the case, but were unwilling to reveal your source. So on record, it looks like you're being followed in an attempt to discover your informant. But I swear to you—my sole motive was to protect you."

I stared at him.

"Not that I think you can't take care of yourself..." he added haltingly.

He looked so anxious that I almost laughed. It was a good enough explanation for me. And a lot could be forgiven for an orgasm like the one he'd just given me. But I still let him sweat it out for a few moments more, before I smiled and walked forward into his arms.

"Didn't you say something about taking me to your bed?" I whispered, nipping at his earlobe.

His arms tightened around me and he muttered something low and fast in Gaelic, followed by a growled, "Little minx of a witch."

<u>Chapter 14 - Passing Time</u>

Sparrow's apartment was cozy and tidy. It was a small one bedroom in Seelie City with a wall of windows overlooking the leaf-canopied main thoroughfare. A worn, but comfortable, beige leather couch and matching recliner took up most of the living room—a large entertainment center took up the rest. The carpet was dark blue and the pictures on the walls were mostly nature scenes, both photographed and painted.

It felt neat, but lived-in, and faint traces of Sparrow's scent lingered in the air—a spicy forest musk that sent tendrils of awareness curling through my veins. I paid a visit to his bathroom to freshen up, the clean towels and spotless floor reinforcing my initial impression of how he kept the place. I was happy to find that he wasn't a slob.

"I like your apartment," I commented as I padded up behind him in the kitchen. He was staring into the open door of the refrigerator, his tanned feet bare against the tile floor. I'd never been inclined toward foot fetishism, but there was something sexy about Sparrow's feet. They were long and well-shaped, with small symbols tattooed in diagonal lines across the top of each one.

He smiled at me over his shoulder. "Thanks. It's not much, but it's home. I'm afraid the strongest thing I have to drink is beer." He gave me a rueful look. "I can pour you a glass of water or juice. Or I could make coffee…"

"What kind of beer do you have?"

"Triple A—Argyle's Aerie Ale. It's a local brew made from hops grown in the nearby valleys. It's kind of a lighter version of your Sam Adams. Are you a beer drinker?" he asked in surprise.

"Actually, yeah," I said, playfully mimicking his surprised expression. "Sam Adams is good—I'll give it a try."

He snorted. "I guess I'd just pegged you more as a wine kind of girl." He grabbed two bottles and reached up to retrieve a couple of tall pilsner glasses from a maple-wood cabinet.

"I like that too, although I usually stick with reds—or champagne. But I've been hooked on tasting obscure beers since I was sixteen. My godmother used to go camping cross country every summer and she'd always bring back lots of funky microbrews for us to try."

I accepted a glass of the golden liquid, tiny bubbles of carbonation chasing each other up its length to the surface. I inhaled the fresh aroma of hops and took an experimental sip. "Mmm…that's good."

"It's my favorite—I'm glad you like it." He grinned. "You were saying about your 'godmother'? Who's that?" He placed a hand on my back as he led me to the sofa. His touch sent warmth radiating down my spine and my body tingled to life.

"My mother's best friend," I explained, intensely conscious of his knee brushing mine as we settled onto the couch. "It's kind of a tradition, I guess. When you have a baby, you choose a close friend, or couple, to be the godparents as a sort of honorary acknowledgment."

"Are your parents still alive?" Sparrow asked.

"Yes. My mom and my step-dad live in New York, and I see them every few months. My real dad, though…we haven't spoken for years." I shrugged. "We send cards during the holidays. I got a birthday card a couple of months ago, so I won't hear from him again until December."

Sparrow gave me a questioning look.

"It's a long story." I sighed. "My parents got divorced when I was a baby. My dad was emotionally and physically abusive toward my mom. I had a relationship with him off and on when I was younger, but he started the emotional shit with me and I eventually came to realize that I was better off without him in my life. It's not something I spend much time thinking about."

I nibbled my lip in silence for a moment and gazed searchingly at Sparrow as I continued. "Maybe that's hard to understand for someone who grew up without their parents. But I believe life's too short to force yourself to be around someone who treats you badly, no matter who they are. My mom and I have a great relationship, and there are a few other relatives I keep in touch with. But better to create your own family than stay with one that causes you pain.

"I have close friends who are more like family to me than any blood tie could ever make them. Like Sunny—and a few other people I've been lucky enough to find."

"I can understand that," Sparrow said softly. "I've kind of created my own family, too. I have my sidhe aunts and uncles and cousins on my father's side, but the people I'm actually closest to, who I call Aunt and Uncle, aren't related to me by blood.

"When my parents died, all of my aunts and uncles were already focused on raising their own families. Uncle Connor and Aunt Shea never had children, and they kind of adopted me after I came to live with the sidhe. My closest friends, who are like siblings to me, aren't my blood relatives either."

"You said they live in Ireland. Do they live in the faerie realm or the human realm?" I asked, eager to hear more about his people.

"Everyone pretty much makes their home in the faerie realm, except for my friend Doyle. He's always been fascinated with the human realm." Sparrow grinned. "When he turned eighteen, he surprised everyone by taking a job as a bartender in Dublin and enrolling in a human university. Now he's leading snorkeling tours for a company in the

Keys. He said he got sick of the cold and the rain and needed some sun and sand for a while."

"Is he full sidhe? And is that unusual—for a sidhe to choose to live in the human realm?"

"Yes, Doyle is full sidhe—and it's not unheard of, but I think his parents are still getting over the shock." Sparrow's eyes crinkled in laughter as he shook his head and downed a long draught of his beer.

"Are sidhe immortal?"

"Yes, they are," Sparrow nodded, giving me an appraising look. "They can be killed if the physical trauma is severe enough, but barring that, they can live forever."

"So do they just stop aging at a certain point, or what?" I asked slowly.

"Like many immortals, the sidhe age at the same rate as humans until about their twentieth birthday, at which point the aging process slows significantly. After that, it can take decades for them to age as much as humans do in a single year."

"Wow," I breathed. "Are half-sidhe immortal?" I asked, my stomach sinking in disappointment at the thought.

I frowned inwardly. So what if Sparrow was immortal and I wasn't? Forever should be the last thing on my mind. I had yet to deal with the fact that Jeremy and I weren't going to be together 'til death did us part.

"Children born to one immortal and one mortal parent will inherit different traits from both," Sparrow answered. "Some are immortal, some mortal, and others fall somewhere in between. As for me, let's just say I'll age better than the average human, but no, I am not immortal."

I pursed my lips at him, "So when I start to get wrinkles, you'll probably still be young, hot and muscle-bound. That hardly seems fair."

He grinned and reached over to twirl a thick strand of my hair between two long fingers. "So you think I'm young, hot and muscle-bound," he stated, his expression dripping with satisfaction.

I snorted. "Don't get cocky—just because you were born with the fountain of youth, and we mere mortals can only aspire to it through hard work and surgery."

"I can't help it if I'm genetically superior."

I scoffed.

Sparrow gave me a mischievous smile as his fingers traced my jaw and his thumb brushed over my bottom lip. "By the time you're old and wrinkly, you probably won't want me around anyway. You'll most likely be sick of me in another week."

"Keep it up and I might," I said, trying to hide my laughter. "It's probably for the best."

"You're likely right, Sydney. After all, I can be extremely annoying," his voice dropped to a husky whisper as he slid forward and pulled me toward him. "Overbearing," he breathed against my mouth, briefly claiming it with his own before trailing his lips across my cheek. My eyelids fell shut and I stifled a moan. He kissed my earlobe and my neck, his tongue a soft promise of pleasure. "Demanding, even," he murmured.

I breathed a groaning laugh. "Sparrow, I'll give in to whatever demands you have—just don't stop."

"Stop? Why would I do that? I've barely begun," he intoned wickedly. He raised his head and waited for me to open my eyes before unhurriedly leaning forward to take my lips in an excruciatingly slow kiss that sent a thick, molten wave of desire rolling through me.

He deepened the kiss, his tongue brushing mine in a leisurely dance that coaxed and teased, until I was trembling with hunger for him. I grasped at the tails of his shirt, too needy to bother with the minutia of buttons, and pushed it up his sides, his flesh warm and firm beneath my palms.

I ran into the obstacle of his arms and groaned the word, "Off!" into his mouth. He chuckled and pulled away to lift his shirt over his head, the break in contact eliciting another groan of protest from me.

His shirt hit the carpet and my eyes drank him in. His skin was lightly tanned and covered with tattoos—from his flat stomach, to his well-defined chest, to the muscles of his shoulders and arms. When he turned, I saw that they covered the broad expanse of his back as well. They were all Celtic knots and symbols, mostly in black, but with some traces of color. It could have looked messy and chaotic, but it didn't. It looked sexy and masculine, shaped by cunning intention.

I stared at him, riveted, my fingers splaying out to play over his body in fascination, touching firmly here, grazing lightly there. "You are so much hotter than any man has a right to be, Sparrow," I breathed, my hands continuing their mindless journey across his feverish, ink-imprinted skin.

He shuddered and exhaled in a rush at my words and my touch, visibly struggling to remain still beneath my fingers.

"Your Aegish-thingy tattoo—it's glowing red again," I mumbled, enthralled by the warmth and the tingle of electricity that teased my fingertips as they traced the design.

"Aegishjalmur. It does that around you," he said, his voice a husky brogue. "It's your turn, Sydney."

He reached for the hem of my top, his hands gentle but insistent as they pulled it higher. His fingers grazed my breasts in a lingering caress as he pushed the silk over the thin cotton of my bra, transforming my world into an edgy torrent of sensation. He palmed my nipples and then slowly pushed my arms above my head, the silk becoming a soft torment against my skin.

The cool air whispered over my heated flesh as my shirt hit the floor atop Sparrow's. Then he lowered my arms, moving in slow motion, his muscular forearms encircling me as he reached behind me to deftly unhook my bra. He kissed me again, his mouth demanding my response, and I melted into him, answering with my own insistent need.

He slid the straps down my shoulders, never breaking our kiss as he discarded the scrap of fabric, and then his lips were at my breast, his tongue laving, his mouth suckling, as he pushed me back into the yielding cushions of the couch. His fingers caressed my belly and sides as they moved downward to find the button of my jeans, slowly undoing the little metal tab and sliding my zipper down as his mouth followed the path of his fingers.

"So beautiful," he whispered, his tongue swirling around my belly button in a warm, languid spiral. The ache in my core was becoming painful and I whimpered a pleading objection to the sweet torture of his unhurried pace. He tugged my jeans over my hips and sucked in a breath.

"Sydney, you're not wearing panties," he groaned.

"More comfortable without them," I said breathlessly, wriggling to help him work my jeans down my legs.

"That's...that's just..." he began in a strangled voice as my jeans finally came free.

"Does it bother you?"

"I've never been so turned on in my life," he growled, forcing my knees apart with his. He lowered himself atop me to take my mouth in a scorching kiss, his hand questing down my body to find the triangle of aching flesh at my center.

My hips arched helplessly upward at his first soft touch, and I moaned as he pushed my knees further apart, his finger stroking a slow path between my swollen labia. His mouth left mine, his lips trailing over my collarbone, and down to my breast. His tongue gently flicked my nipple before drawing it into his mouth, and my back bowed, my body wound wire tight.

"You're so wet, Sydney," he whispered thickly.

"Please, Sparrow." As the words spilled from my throat in a husky plea, he slid one finger deep inside me. I gasped a cry of assent, my head falling backward as my hips raised to meet his stroke.

I was already mindless with the pleasure of his finger moving inside me, when his lips began trailing down my stomach. He continued, lower and lower, until he reached my clitoris, his tongue swirling gently around it as he slipped a second finger into me, filling and stretching me with his slow stroking.

My fists clenched in his soft, dark hair, my body straining, winding ever tighter as his fingers and his tongue moved faster. A tidal wave of ecstasy began to build and roll, sweeping through me, and I was suddenly opening wider to take him within me, and clenching rhythmically to pull him deeper, as I cried out in pleasure.

His hand stilled and he murmured soothing words in Gaelic, fluttering lazy kisses over my belly as he waited for me to come back from the oblivion into which he'd sent me. When I finally opened my eyes, I smoothed my palm through his hair.

He smiled up at me, his eyes bright pools of blue, as he gently released his fingers from me, his tongue toying with my belly button. "I love making you come, Sydney. I think it's my new favorite pastime."

I swallowed and stared at him. "Then I must be the luckiest woman in all the realms," I chuckled, my voice cracking.

"Would you like for me to make love to you properly now, or would you rather relax and have another pint first?" he inquired with a devilish grin.

I smiled and crooked a finger at him, urging him up my body to my lips.

"Make love to me, Sparrow," I whispered heatedly, leaning forward to take possession of his mouth.

His erection pulsed in response, pressing into me through the fabric of his clothing, and I moved to unfasten the bothersome material and free him. I pushed his pants down his hips, running my hands over firm buttocks and thighs above close-fitting briefs. When I couldn't reach to push them any lower, he sat up to assist me, and they quickly joined the clothing heap on the floor.

His legs, also heavily inked with tattoos, were thick with lean muscle, his thighs taut and solid beneath my roving fingers. I rose and climbed between them, pushing him into the back of the couch and leaning forward to part his lips with my tongue, my hands braced against his shoulders.

His arms came up to band around me, pulling me deeper into his mouth, and I lost myself in sensation, forgetting my intent to finish undressing him. His hard length pressing against the tops of my thighs reminded me, and my hands began a slow slide down his chest.

His muscles tightened as my fingertips grazed over his nipples, before moving down the flat plane of his stomach. I teased his tongue with mine as my fingers found the elastic waistband of his briefs and slipped inside. He drew my breath into his mouth when I cupped his restrained length with one hand beneath the clinging fabric.

I brushed my lips against his, and then pulled away, lowering myself to the carpet to kneel before him. I smiled up into the luminous depths of his eyes as I pulled at the last scrap of clothing that remained between us. "Off," I demanded softly. Sparrow reached out to cradle my chin in his palm and complied by tightening the muscles of his thighs to lift himself off the couch.

I eased his briefs down his hips and he sprang forward, fully erect—and beautiful, just as Angelica had predicted. Sparrow brushed his thumb against my lips, parting them, and I nibbled at the pad, drawing it into the heat of my mouth in an erotic promise.

He tasted of salt and spice.

When the briefs lay discarded by his feet, I took him gently in my hands to stroke him, suckling at his thumb as my own brushed a bead of liquid across the head of his penis. He groaned and his eyes fell shut as his head dropped back into the couch cushion.

His shaft was long and smooth, and so thick that I couldn't quite close my fingers around it. I watched in fascination as he jerked with pleasure against my touch. I drew my mouth away from his thumb and leaned forward to slowly slide my tongue up the bottom of his hardened length, taking the head between my lips when I reached the top.

Sparrow shuddered and breathed my name, followed by something in Gaelic that sent desire pooling low inside me as I took him further into my mouth. My fingernails grazed his scrotum as my hand rose to stroke him in time with my lips, my tongue swirling around his swollen head on each slow pass. I realized that my hips were moving helplessly to the same rhythm and a haze of exquisite sensation filled my brain as I went a little faster, sensing the pace that would drive him over the edge.

I heard a distant ringing sound, but was too caught up to care as I felt Sparrow tensing beneath me. I could feel the rush of pleasure that was about to overtake him—it seemed to move through me a split second before it rolled into him, and he grasped at my shoulders, pulling my mouth toward his as he exploded into climax.

He claimed my lips in a long, lingering kiss, as we both floated in a dazed after-glow.

Sparrow finally rose and disappeared into the bathroom, returning with a towel and a warm washcloth. He set about gently bathing my sensitized skin, pausing to kiss me again and again as he dried me. Then he pulled me close and cradled me to his chest, his fingers playing through the length of my hair, igniting shivers of pleasure across my nerve endings.

"That was incredible, Sydney."

"Ditto," I murmured against his chest, my tongue flicking out to sweep across his nearby nipple. He sucked in a breath and chuckled.

I lifted my face to look at him, a question in my eyes. "It was the strangest thing, Sparrow, but it was almost like I could feel what you were feeling while I was touching you."

He reached out to brush a strand of hair back from my cheek. "I know, Sydney. I felt it too. There's obviously a connection between us…"

A muffled ringing sound interrupted him and Sparrow cursed softly. He bent down to extract his pants from our pile of clothing and pulled a cell phone from his pocket.

"I'm sorry Sydney—it's my emergency line. I have to take this." He gave me an apologetic look as he flipped open the phone.

"Sparrow," he answered curtly, his expression growing grim as he listened. "I'll be right there."

He flicked the phone closed with an aggravated snap. "There's been another mass death djinn arrest. I have to go back to the station, Sydney. I'm truly sorry."

I grinned, trying to hide my disappointment. "Well, maybe one of them got sloppy and you'll be able to find something to crack the case. Will you come by tomorrow and let me know what happened?"

He pulled me into his arms with a groan. "Yes, I suppose tomorrow will have to do. Let's get dressed and I'll blink you home."

He released me and we untangled our clothes from their heap. He finished dressing before I did—pretty much on par with men and women everywhere.

"I'll probably be at the station for the rest of the night and then I'll need to come home and grab some sleep. Is tomorrow evening around 6 pm okay?"

"That would be great." I smiled at him as I attempted to straighten the layers of my silk top.

"I'll call first."

"Okay, I'll give you my number."

"I already have your number," Sparrow said with an amused expression.

I curled my lip at him. "I don't have yours."

"Lorien knows how to contact me. Phones don't exactly work between the realms."

"I'll bet you say that to all the girls." I smirked at him as I pulled on my sandals. I combed my fingers through my hair and self-consciously patted the pocket bulging with the crystal brooch.

"Am I a complete mess?" I asked with a crooked grin.

"You're beautiful," he said softly, stepping forward to embrace me. I closed my eyes as his mouth descended toward mine, a familiar plummeting sensation jarring my stomach as he coaxed my lips apart with his tongue. I clung to him, kissing him back, suddenly feeling like I was flying rather than falling. Then all too quickly he was lowering me to my feet as we floated to a stop.

"I regret not having the opportunity to make love to you properly this evening," he whispered against my mouth. "But hopefully we can remedy that soon."

When I opened my eyes again, we were standing in my living room. He stepped away, giving me a heated smile that left me tight and breathless, and then he blinked out. My knees felt weak, but I didn't think it had anything to do with the inter-realm transport this time.

∞∞∞∞∞∞∞∞∞

Sunny had fallen asleep, sprawled on the couch with one of her new books lying open on the coffee table next to her. Jasper was curled into a fluffy black ball at her feet. I grinned at the picture they created, wondering if I should disturb them. It was almost 2 am, and I was already going to be hating life when my alarm went off in the morning. I dimmed the overhead lights and tiptoed toward the stand lamp that was shining down onto Sunny's cheek.

As I clicked it off, she opened one eye and groaned, turning her face to blink blearily up at me. "You're back," she croaked, wincing as she sat up. "Ugh. Need coffee."

Jasper glared at the disturbance.

"It's two o'clock in the morning, Sunny. If you have coffee now, you'll never get back to sleep. How about if I make us some nice herbal tea instead?"

She shot me an offended look and I chuckled.

"So what happened with Lauringer?" she asked on a yawn. "You were gone for hours."

"It's been a very long, very strange night," I said with a smile. "I suppose you want me to start from the beginning?"

Sunny blinked at me. "No. Why don't you start somewhere in the middle, then you can skip around, and I'll try to guess the correct order of events."

I winged a throw pillow at her.

"So?" she demanded, catching my missile and placing it behind her head.

I dropped onto the loveseat with a sigh. "Well first, Emily took me on a twenty minute nature hike in the pitch dark to find Lauringer's disappearing cabin in the woods..."

I told her all about my meeting with Lauringer and the trip to the containment room in the Seelie Police Department. When I concluded with Lauringer's lack of success, Sunny frowned and shook her head.

"After all that, she didn't find *anything*?"

"I'm afraid not. But at least now the police don't have to waste any more time examining those souls, and they can concentrate their efforts elsewhere. Plus, there was another big death djinn arrest tonight, so hopefully this time something more conclusive will turn up."

"Really?" Sunny's eyes lit with interest. "They found *more* unaligned souls? That can't be good for the death djinns."

"I'm not really sure what they found, but Sparrow promised to come by later and let me know what happened."

"You saw Sparrow again? And he's coming by later?"

I bit my lip, trying to temper the wickedness from my grin. "I saw Sparrow—I saw him in his office, and then I saw even more of him at his apartment afterward."

Sunny's mouth dropped open. "You had sex! I was wondering why you weren't more upset by the Lauringer thing. Oh, just wait until Angelica hears that you finally had yourself some of Sparrow's beautiful erection. How was it?" She looked as excited as a kid on Christmas—a kid with an expression naughty enough to earn her a lump of coal.

"Well, technically we didn't get around to actual sex, since he got called back to the office to deal with the death djinn thing. Come to think of it," I frowned, "I didn't even get to see his bedroom. I saw lots of the living room and the couch, though."

Sunny huffed out an amused breath. "Didn't even make it to the bed, huh? In a hurry, were we?"

"Not at all. On the contrary, Sparrow seems to be extremely proficient at taking his time." I smiled at her from beneath heavily lidded eyes.

"Oh, you are a bad, bad girl, Syd," Sunny said on a choked laugh. "So, is hot tattoo boy everything you'd hoped?"

"All that and more," I breathed, a shiver running through me at the remembrance of Sparrow's touch.

Suddenly I wasn't sure how I was going to survive the wait until 6pm.

<u>Chapter 15 - Deceptions</u>

The blaring of my alarm gradually penetrated my sleep-fogged senses and my brain groaned a curse that I was too tired to verbalize. I managed to cast a heavy arm in the general direction of my nightstand, intending to hit the snooze button just once—just to get those extra nine minutes—but my hand found only empty space before coming into contact with the wooden surface. I tried again, scooting my complaining body all the way to the edge of the bed and stretching my arm out further, but I still couldn't reach.

I grumbled and cracked an eye open. My alarm had been moved to the far side of my nightstand. Lorien hovered above it, her arms crossed and a perturbed look pinching her small face. I forced my other eyelid up and stared at her warily.

"I can't believe you went to see Lauringer without me!" Her tilted violet eyes sparked with resentment.

"How did you know...never mind," I croaked. I wearily pushed myself into a sitting position and leaned over far enough to turn the blasting alarm off, ignoring Lorien's glare of outrage when she was forced to dart out of the way. I was willing to bet that my bad mood rivaled hers. I was *so* not a morning person.

I groaned and rubbed my hands over my face. "I had no choice, Lorien. Emily was in a frantic rush to get me there before Lauringer's cabin could do its crazy disappearing act to keep people from finding it. I tried to call you, but apparently there are all these protection spells around it so no one can blink in or out—just like in Seelie City. Emily said you couldn't hear me calling from there, and if I tried to get far enough away to reach you, I could have missed the meeting."

I rose and stumbled toward the white marble vanity sink to splash cold water on my face, making a mess all over the countertop in the process. When I looked up from toweling myself and the counter off, Lorien was floating behind me in the mirror. Her anger appeared to have faded into resignation and disappointment, and I winced, unsure which was worse.

"I was *really* looking forward to meeting her."

"I know. I'm sorry," I sighed, squeezing a blob of toothpaste onto my toothbrush. "How was Obie's party?" I asked, hoping to distract her with thoughts of her nephew. It worked, kind of.

"It was fun," she said with a gloomy half smile. "All the neighborhood kids came and they played 'pin the tail on the hobgoblin' and 'musical toadstools'. I think Obie really liked his rocking horse." Her smile brightened.

"That's good," I said with a tired grin as I finished up at the sink. "Listen

Lorien, I'm really sorry about you not getting to meet Lauringer. I'll tell you all about it, but I need caffeine first. And I'm going to have to get some work done on my computer before my boss calls. I'll make some tea. Do you want some? Sunny makes coffee, if you'd rather have that." I trudged toward the bedroom door, Lorien trailing behind me as I made my way to the kitchen.

"I guess I could use some tea," she answered, still sounding disheartened.

Sunny stood watching the progress of the coffee pot, humming to herself and looking a lot livelier than I felt. "Morning Syd; morning Lorien," she intoned when she saw us.

"How come you're so cheerful?" I asked as I pulled my favorite red mug from the dishwasher.

Lorien perched on a clear section of counter next to the sink and conjured her own tiny earthenware mug out of thin air.

Sunny smiled serenely at both of us. "Incubi rock."

I snorted as I dropped a tea bag into my mug and filled it with hot water from the dispenser. "So does a certain half-sidhe detective—but getting barely four hours of sleep still sucks. And there's nothing like waking up to a pissed off faerie who's decided to move your alarm clock out of your reach. Milk and honey, Lorien?" I asked in a syrupy tone.

"Yes please." She ignored my complaint. "You saw Agent Sparrow last night too?"

"Mmhm," I answered. A helpless grin stretched my lips, despite my determination to hang onto my sleep-deprived grumpiness. I looked down to hide it as I stirred my tea.

"How did that come about? No wait—tell me about your meeting with Lauringer first. What was she like? Was she brilliant and mysterious? Does she really glow golden?" Lorien's wings buzzed with excitement as she dipped her tiny mug into my larger one and then followed me out to my makeshift office.

"Well," I answered thoughtfully as I waited for my laptop to fire up, "she definitely glowed golden. Her skin, her teeth—even her eyes looked like they were coated with gold dust. What's up with that anyway? Is she part faerie or...what is she?"

Sunny appeared and plunked herself into one of the dining room chairs, a ridiculously large ceramic latte mug of steaming black coffee in her hand. Her eyes were trained on Lorien as she awaited a response to my question.

Lorien practically quivered with enthusiasm at the chance to discuss one of her favorite topics. "It's a mystery—no one knows for sure." A conspiratorial gleam lit her eyes. "She won her fame for casting the binding spell over Seelie City, and in the beginning, everyone assumed she was a human mage who came to train in the Faerie Realm. But that was around two hundred years ago, so she either has immortal blood, or she gained immortality somewhere along the way."

Lorien's wings slowed to a flutter and she took a sip from her mug. "Of course, I doubt she'd have a problem casting a permanent illusion spell to make herself look however she wants," she mused.

"Anyway, she's managed to avoid publicity quite well, and there are precious few pictures of her to be found. I came across one in an old book where she didn't seem to have that golden glow. But the strongest faerie magic is cast with golden dust, and I suppose prolonged use could eventually make the caster appear golden. It sounds like the revolving protection spells around her house alone would require a constant use of power."

"Huh," I grunted. "She had a bunch of canisters on her kitchen table and I saw her stir some golden powder from one of them into her tea. Then later, she used some silver powder from another one to heal my stubbed toe and clean me up. I didn't see what was in the rest of them."

"Really?" Lorien said with interest. "Faerie healing dust is silver. It sounds like at least some of Lauringer's magic has been influenced by ours." She looked pleased by the thought.

"Do you think she's part faerie, then?" asked Sunny.

Lorien shrugged. "Not necessarily. She could have just studied our magic. Tell me more about her Sydney. What was she like?"

I looked up from the banking spreadsheet I was half-concentrating on. "Well, she looked like an attractive young woman in a business suit. She was professional, but friendly, and she seemed pretty upset about the whole unaligned soul thing. I was surprised she was so willing to help, considering how reclusive everyone says she is. And she didn't think finding Balthus' goblin would be of much use, but she agreed that proving the death djinns' guilt might get my contract cancelled."

Sunny frowned. "Why didn't she think finding the goblin would be of use? I mean, we don't have much to go on, and he supposedly gave Balthus the unaligned soul, so I'd think he would at least be worth questioning."

I nibbled my lip. "I think she believes a goblin's word would be useless against Balthus' from a legal standpoint. But I'm with you—I think any new info would help. Not to mention that the infinity tattoo still seems pretty mysterious."

"Did you get to see her do any major spell casting?" Lorien probed hopefully.

I grinned. "Personally, I thought it was pretty amazing when she healed my toe and cleaned my clothes with a handful of dust."

Lorien looked unimpressed.

"Okay, what else?" I mumbled, blowing a breath up into my bangs as I thought. "Oh—she also did this neat trick where she made a pen and pad of paper appear out of thin air so she could write down…some notes."

I still wasn't ready to admit to having the Hell Ride incantation.

Sunny raised her eyebrows above the rim of her coffee mug. "Hey, that's pretty cool," she said when she finished swallowing. "You didn't tell me about that one last night."

I bobbed my head. "Yeah. She doesn't even seem to have to think about using magic; she just wants something and it's there."

Lorien's wings drooped and I sighed. "I'm not really sure what you're expecting to hear, Lorien. I mean, isn't it amazing enough that she has a friggin' disappearing cabin in the woods?"

"I guess." She gave a disheartened shrug. "It's true that not many other mages would be able to maintain those types of protection and dislocation spells. I just thought that maybe she'd have performed some more active magic while you were there."

"How about when she transported us to the Seelie Police Station and I didn't feel as if I was falling to my death." I gave her a pointed look.

"One second we were standing in her kitchen, and the next we were at the station. I think Galen—that's Galena's brother, who works the counter there," I reminded Sunny, "about crapped his dwarf shorts when the great Lauringer appeared out of thin air in front of him."

Sunny and I shared a snigger.

Lorien sputtered and began zipping up and down like a demented hummingbird bird. "Lauringer went to the Seelie Police Station?" she finally managed in a shocked chirp.

"I was getting to that part," I said smugly, "but you seemed so much more interested in how Lauringer acted than in the actual results of the meeting."

"You got Lauringer to go to the Seelie Police Station with you?" she gurgled again. "Lauringer hasn't made a public appearance in decades! Why didn't Agent Sparrow tell me this?" she demanded.

I lifted my hands in the universal sign for cluelessness. "When did you see him?"

"Earlier this morning. I stopped by the station to see if he had any new developments to report and the first thing that came out of his mouth was that you'd met with Lauringer last night. I was so upset you'd gone without me, I came straight here."

I snorted. "Well, there's your answer. You didn't give him a chance to tell you anything else."

"I…" she stammered defensively, then she puffed out an annoyed breath. "Never mind. Just tell me what happened!"

"She wanted to examine the unaligned souls. She was particularly interested in the woman they found in the coma," I began.

"Makes sense since she's the only one they were able to connect one of the souls to," Lorien interjected.

I opened my mouth to continue and she pre-empted me with another observation. I rolled my eyes at Sunny, who was sitting back and grinning into her second monster-sized mug of coffee.

"That was also the soul they found the strongest traces of magic on," Lorien mused. "Agent Sparrow had really hoped that would lead somewhere. Did she find anything?"

"Actually no." My expression turned sober. "She wore herself out looking for clues and by the time she was done she could barely stand. But she didn't find a thing."

Lorien sank to her feet in the middle of the table. "Nothing?" she asked, her wings drooping.

"No, but there was another big death djinn bust last night. Maybe they'll find something on one of the unaligned souls this time," I said optimistically.

"How could she not find anything? She's *Lauringer*. She's the most…"

"…powerful mage alive," I finished for her. "I know. But apparently there was nothing to be found. We'll just have to keep looking. Besides, if death djinns keep getting arresting for having unaligned souls, even old King Moab won't be able to keep the blame off them forever, right? That's what Lauringer seemed to think, anyway."

Lorien gave me a worried look. "I hope you're right, Sydney."

The phone rang and I wrinkled my nose at the caller id—it was Cindy, and I hadn't finished the morning banking update. "Sorry Lorien, but I've got to get some work done. You can hang out if you want. It shouldn't take too long."

I pushed the button to answer the phone and Cindy started talking before I finished the word 'hello'.

"I have an emergency. Mickey has a big summer school exam this morning and his Hummer won't start. I need you to pick him up and take him to school. The exam starts in forty-five minutes!"

I mouthed a silent curse. "Give me his cell number and I'll call him for directions," I said, my placid tone belying my annoyance.

"Perfect, Sydney," she breathed in relief. "But hurry!"

I hung up and dialed the number.

"This is Mick," drawled a male voice.

Mick? Since when? "Uh, hey Mickey, this is Sydney. Your Mom asked me to give you a ride to school. Can you give me directions from the store to your house?"

"Sydney, long time no see. How's it goin'?" he asked, his unhurried manner ratcheting my level of annoyance up another notch.

"I'm fine, thank you Mickey. But apparently if you want to pass the eleventh grade you need to be at school in forty minutes, so maybe we can talk in the car on the way?"

"No prob, Sydney." His nonchalance scraped against my last nerve. He gave me the directions and was telling me that he was looking forward to seeing me when I hung up on him.

"Apparently I've got bus duty this morning," I grumbled as I stalked toward my bedroom to throw on some jeans.

"Be sure to tell Mickey I said 'hi'," Sunny called after me. The sounds that followed bore a suspicious resemblance to laughter. But I must have been mistaken, since my friends would *never* find humor in my aggravation.

∞∞∞∞∞∞∞∞∞

I pulled my station wagon into a circular driveway behind Mickey's massive black Hummer. A sprawling, two-storey stucco and river-stone house rose to my right, surrounded by lush greenery. I had never been to the Horowitz home before, and though it looked nice, I hoped to never have the occasion to come here again.

I beeped the horn, and a few minutes later Mickey stepped out and waved at me. He locked the front door, grinning as he sauntered toward the car in pressed slacks and a crisp polo shirt.

"Hey, Mickey," I greeted as he got into the passenger seat. "Lead the way. I hope it doesn't take more than fifteen minutes to get there." I began backing out of the driveway as soon as his door was shut. "And buckle your seatbelt, please."

"It's not far," he assured me as he fit the metal buckle into its slot. "Sorry to put you to the trouble, Sydney. Stupid Hummer wouldn't start. I wish the car manufacturers would make something guaranteed to never break down, don't you?"

"It would be nice, but if they did, they'd run themselves out of business," I said drily.

He made a face. "Turn here," he grumbled.

"So…are you ready for your big test?"

He gave me a blank look.

"The one that starts in ten minutes?" I prodded.

"Oh, right. Yeah. I've been studying real hard."

"Any of your friends going to summer school with you?" I asked, trying to keep up the polite conversation.

"No…yeah…" He seemed to be struggling with his answer and I gave him a questioning look.

His face smoothed out and he smiled. "Not really. A couple of kids I used to be friends with, but I've decided not to hang out with them anymore. It's easier to get things done without your friends bugging you."

I raised my eyebrows. That didn't sound like a normal sentiment for a seventeen-year-old. When I was seventeen, my life revolved around my friends. "Well, it's good that you're serious about passing summer school. I'm sure when the regular school year starts you'll have more time to relax with your friends again."

After a moment of silence I glanced over at him. I was startled to find his face an alarming shade of red. His mouth worked soundlessly, his eyes pleading for help. My foot couldn't decide whether to brake or go faster.

"Mickey, are you alright?" I demanded, my mind racing for the location of the nearest hospital and coming up blank. I'd have to call 911 from my cell phone if there was something really wrong with him. Mickey made a choking noise and my panic escalated. *Please, oh please, do not let anything happen to him—and especially not in my car!*

"Mickey, what's wrong?" No answer. He was still goggling at me with that silent, helpless expression. Should I stop and try to give him mouth to mouth? I was scrambling for my cell phone when he gasped and started coughing.

"Missed the turn," he choked.

I gaped at him. "Are you okay? What happened? You scared the crap out of me!"

He shrugged, recovering his composure with abnormal speed, while my pulse was still doing cartwheels. "Spit went down the wrong way."

I whipped the station wagon into the median to make a u-turn. "That must have been some spitball," I muttered in an incredulous tone.

"Turn left and it's about a quarter mile up on the right," Mickey recited calmly.

I did not get paid enough for this. I spotted the high-school and turned into the fenced parking lot. A few kids made their way up the grass-lined sidewalk in small groups, all headed for the same double glass doors leading into a rambling, red brick building. I pulled against the curb near the entrance and stopped.

Mickey hesitated, his eyes following a couple of kids swathed in what appeared to be black rags.

Their clothing might have looked like second hand goods, but I knew better. This was an exclusive private school. All these kids' parents had enough cash to keep them in the most expensive fashions and driving the flashiest cars money could buy. The parking lot looked more like a mini Fortune 500 than a summer school.

The raggedy pair consisted of a boy and a girl about Mickey's age, and they were unmistakably part of the school's Goth contingent. By the way Mickey was looking at them, they were also his former friends.

"Those the kids you decided not to hang out with anymore?" I asked.

Mickey looked as if he was struggling to rein in his expression. "Yeah," he answered. "We used to be really good friends. But they got me into some stuff, and well...I probably wouldn't be in trouble if I hadn't listened to them, you know what I mean?"

My eyes softened. "At least you realized it in time to do something about it."

I wondered how hard it had been for him to make all the drastic changes he'd made recently. I remembered the way he'd looked at the two sexy Latin guys outside the coffee shop, and realized how difficult it must be for him if he was trying to come to terms with being gay, as I now suspected.

He gaze turned sad and my heart went out to him. "Sometimes I just…" he began, his eyes going cloudy as they searched mine. "Sometimes don't you just wish you could go back in time and do things differently?"

I thought about the crazy turn my life had taken over the past several weeks. If I'd just stayed home to nurse my broken heart that night, instead of going to the bar and meeting Balthus, I might have avoided the mess I was in now. But I'd probably never have met Sparrow. Or Lorien. I *did* wish I had done things differently, but sometimes avoiding the bad things meant missing out on good things as well. And maybe it would help Mickey to know that. "I wi…"

I clamped my lips together, realizing in horror that I had let my guard down and almost wished aloud. As that knowledge passed across my face, something akin to disappointment, laced with anger, passed across Mickey's. A sudden chill of shock and suspicion settled into the pit of my stomach as I stared at him.

"Well, I guess I'd better go." His grin was mocking as he reached to open the car door, an alien flash of emerald burning in the depths of his blue-grey eyes. I gasped softly in recognition.

Emerald like Balthus' eyes. Emerald like King Moab's eyes. The emerald eyes of a death djinn.

I stared after him, frozen in disbelief, as he disappeared through the double doors of the brick building.

∞∞∞∞∞∞∞∞∞

"Lorien!" I called, trying to remain calm and obey the speed limit, despite the disturbing certainty that was growing within me.

She appeared beside me, and in the next instant was shooting backward through the air. I tried to watch what was happening in the rear view mirror, while still paying attention to the road. There was a high-pitched buzz as her wings worked furiously, streaking into a near invisible shimmer. She paused in a drunken tilt over the backseat, layers of purple faerie dust sifting down from her agitated wings. Then she finally gained control over her momentum and darted forward to join me in the front seat again.

"Do you have any idea how hard it is to blink into a moving vehicle?" she grumbled in an acid tone.

I tried hard not to smile. "Sorry Lorien, I'm afraid I wasn't familiar with that rule."

"It's not a rule," she sighed irritably. "All the faerie guardians have to learn to do it in case of emergencies, since you humans spend so much time in transit these days. It's just a bit disconcerting to blink somewhere and suddenly find yourself flying backward, about to become a faerie splat on a rear windshield."

My lips twitched in mirth, but she was too busy straightening nonexistent wrinkles in her dress to notice. A bright melon-colored dust sprinkled from her wings and I realized that she was embarrassed.

"Can a death djinn possess a human?" I asked, jumping right into the reason I'd called her.

Her small hands abruptly stopped their fussing and her tilted eyes shot toward mine. "Well, they can shift into smoke, which could be considered a sort of spirit form, so I suppose so. Why do you ask?"

"I think my boss' son is being possessed by a death djinn," I said grimly.

She gave me a doubtful look. "It's next to impossible, not to mention illegal, to possess a human unless they have consciously invited the possession. What makes you think he's been possessed by a death djinn?"

"Oh, only that he started showing a strange interest in me right around the time that this whole thing with Balthus began. And since then, his entire personality and appearance has changed so drastically that it borders on psychotic. And he's tried on several different occasions now to trick me into making a wish out loud. And today when he almost succeeded, his eyes turned that fiery green color I've only seen in Balthus' and King Moab's eyes." I curled my lip and sent her a sideways glance that asked what other proof she could possibly need.

"Still, it could just be a coincidence," she faltered in disbelief. "How old is he?"

"Seventeen."

She puffed out a relieved breath. "Teenagers are always doing crazy things, no matter what race they are. And lots of people have green eyes."

I sighed. "Exactly, teenagers *are* always doing crazy things. And the ones who dress all in black and question every convention and authority, like Mickey did up until a few weeks ago, might even be inclined to experiment with spells and witchcraft. I went through a phase like that myself—the witchcraft, not the dressing all in black. Anyway, what if he decided it might be cool to try some dark spell he found and unwittingly invited in a death djinn?"

"That scenario has a lot of 'ifs'." She sounded more like she was trying to convince herself than me.

"Mickey's eyes are bluish grey—not even a hint of green," I added blandly.

Her mouth thinned into a grim line. "Call your succubus friend Angelica and find out about that spell to perform an exorcism."

∞∞∞∞∞∞∞∞∞∞

"You didn't tell me my racetrack account check was trying to clear this morning!" Cindy accused, her voice rising and fraying around the edges.

"Cindy, you told me to drop everything and get Mickey to school."

"I told you last week that check had to clear!" she insisted in a clipped wail.

I could have told her that most people didn't write checks unless they had the money in their account to cover them. But it would have been a waste of breath.

I heard voices in the background and the slamming of a door. "We'll just have to wire the funds before Mr. Horowitz finds out," she whispered. "Remind me."

I made a note on my legal pad, growling deep in my throat as the line went dead.

"I don't think I've ever heard you make that particular sound before," Sunny commented from the couch, her eyes dancing with laughter above the rim of her laptop.

"You should try it," I grumbled. "Next time someone really pisses you off, just start growling at them. It's highly effective."

"Is that so?" She smirked.

"As a matter of fact, it is," I bantered, my mood improving. "Not only does it make you feel better, but it makes them think you're crazy, which in turn makes them question whether they want to fuck with you. It's a win-win situation."

A knock sounded at the door. "That should be Angelica," I said, jumping up to answer it. Sunny's laughter floated in my wake.

"Hi Sydney," Angelica greeted me in her usual cheery manner. She pulled a scrap of paper from the front pocket of her uniform and handed it to me. "I found that exorcism spell for you."

"Thanks Angelica. Can you hang out for a while?"

"Certainly. I just finished my last cleaning job for the day."

She followed me into the living room and Sunny swung her legs over the side of the couch to make room for us.

"Pretty crazy that Syd figures out she knows someone who might be possessed right after you tell us about an exorcism spell, huh?" Sunny grinned at Angelica as she leaned over to set her laptop on the coffee table.

"Synchronicity," Angelica agreed as she lowered herself onto the couch, crossing her long legs in an unconsciously sensual movement. "It is the positive forces of the universe working in tandem to match seemingly unrelated circumstances with perfect timing."

She nodded toward the paper in my hand. "These are the instructions for performing the spell. Read it over and let me know if you have any questions. It does not appear to be too complicated, compared to others I have seen."

"That's a relief," I said as I perused the step-by-step directions. Apparently all I had to do was pluck seven of Jasper's tail hairs and burn them in a small, enclosed room with Mickey. The hardest part was going to be getting Mickey into a small, enclosed room.

Well, that and getting Jasper to forgive me for plucking out his tail hairs.

"So, how are your adventures in monogamy going?" Sunny asked.

Angelica blushed. "I find that I like the human man I have been visiting very much. I would have thought to find myself becoming bored, having sex with the same person over and over. But strangely, my fondness for him grows. Our physical intimacy has begun to take on another dimension and seems to become increasingly...meaningful to me." She sounded ashamed.

I smiled down into the piece of paper I held and Sunny snorted with laughter. "Try not to sound so horrified by the prospect, Angelica," she said. "That's exactly what's *supposed* to happen when you're in a monogamous relationship."

"But I sense that he is hesitant," Angelica continued worriedly. "Although it is obvious that he enjoys our sexual relations, he seems to become more and more resistant to me entering his dreams. It is as if he is torn by some need to deny his desire for me. When I went to him last night, he appeared almost frightened to see me—even though I wore my most appealing pink lace bra and matching crotchless panties. No man has ever attempted to resist me, much less in my best lingerie!"

She looked from me to Sunny, her blue eyes wide and troubled.

"Maybe it's time to tell him it's not a dream," I suggested. "If I were having recurring dreams of mind-blowing sex with some fantasy guy, I might start to wonder what was going on after a while too. I might even start to think that I was going a little crazy."

"Do you think it would ease his mind if I changed my appearance so that he would not recognize that it was me?"

Sunny sputtered. "You mean if he started having vivid sex dreams about a different woman every night, instead of the same woman? That does sound like every guy's fantasy, but somehow I don't think it'll help convince him that there's nothing unusual going on."

Angelica sighed unhappily. "I do not wish to cause him distress. I only hope he does not react badly to discovering that I am more than just a figment of his imagination."

I gave her a sympathetic look.

"If he can't handle it, it's his loss, Angelica," Sunny said firmly. "Your friends, the twins, are two of the smartest, nicest guys I've ever met. Sure, it took a little while to get used to the idea of having intimate relations with a pair of incubi…"

I let out a mirthful snort. As far as I'd seen, she hadn't had any trouble embracing that concept at all.

Sunny shot me a dirty look. "It did! And for them too—they'd never been with a human who knew it wasn't just a dream. My *point*," she rolled her eyes at me and focused on Angelica, "is that if this guy rejects you just because you're a succubus, then he isn't good enough for you anyway."

"That's very sweet of you to say, Sunny. And I'm so glad that you and the twins are enjoying each other." Angelica's face brightened and she turned to study me. "What about your lover, Sydney?"

Heat suffused my cheeks beneath her probing gaze. "I sense that he has finally brought you to satisfaction, but that he has not yet fully surrendered his beautiful erect…"

"Yes, Angelica," I said quickly. "We're still working on that last part. He's due over here around six, though, so hopefully we'll get to it tonight."

Sunny sniggered and glanced at the time display on the cable box. "By the way, it's 5:30."

I leapt up, flustered. "I still have to shower!"

"Do you mind if I stay to meet him?" asked Angelica.

"That'd be nice!" I answered as I sprinted for the hallway.

"What about the spell?" she called after me. "Do you have any questions?"

"Seems pretty straight-forward!" I yelled as I reached the door to my bedroom. Then I paused. "Just one thing. It says you need to capture the spirit form in a vessel to prevent repossession. What type of vessel?"

"Traditionally, a crystal vial, but I suppose you could use any object. Just make sure it's not too fragile or too unwieldy to transport."

"Thanks! Speaking of vials, Sunny, why don't you tell her about the vial she found in the vent while I'm getting ready?" I didn't wait for a response as I rushed toward my closet to find something flattering to wear.

Twenty minutes later I put down my brush and was spritzing myself lightly with my favorite perfume, when the phone rang. I briskly smoothed some moisturizing gloss onto my lips and rushed across the room to pick up the receiver.

"Hello?"

"Miss Corrigan? This is Peter at the front desk. You have a guest, a Mr…"

"Send him up. Thank you, Peter." My heart quickened with nervous excitement.

I skipped back into the living room, where Sunny and Angelica still reclined on the couch, giggling conspiratorially about something—probably to do with sex. Jasper was curled up on Angelica's lap and they had cracked open a bottle of champagne.

"He's on his way up," I announced breathlessly. "I love punctuality in a man. It's a sign of consideration, don't you think?" I added with a grin.

"I wonder why he didn't just blink in, like usual," Sunny commented.

"I don't know." I shrugged. "Maybe he thought announcing himself at the front desk would be more date-like?"

He's ten minutes early," Sunny observed. "What do you think that means? Maybe it's a sign of his eagerness to share his beautiful erection. What's your take, Angelica?"

I glared at Sunny, but was saved from Angelica's response by the knock at the door. Butterflies winged through my mid-section and I felt like a giddy teenager as I raced to answer it. The butterflies transformed into a leaden weight and dropped into the pit of my stomach.

"Jeremy," I said in a strained voice, "what are you doing here?"

He stared down at me, disbelief coloring his eyes. He looked a little thinner than usual, but other than that he appeared well. He wore dress slacks and a silk shirt, as if he'd come straight from work.

"Syd," he breathed. "It's so good to see you. When Hannah told me you were staying here, I almost couldn't believe it. Why did you tell me you were staying at her apartment? And how can you afford to stay in a place like this?" He gazed past me into the penthouse.

"It's just something I happened into," I answered haltingly. "Jeremy, this really isn't a good time. You should have called first."

His eyes shot back to my face and he ran his fingers through his short golden hair in agitation. "Damn it, Syd, that's not fair. I've been trying to call you for weeks and you refuse to answer. All you ever do is leave messages. When will it be a good time? We need to talk."

"I know, Jeremy, and I'm sorry." Misery made my voice wobble. "I just haven't been ready to deal with it. And I'm going through some other pretty heavy things right now, things that aren't related to us, but as soon as I get past them I promise we'll talk."

He didn't seem to hear me, his attention focusing instead on the voices spilling from the living room. "You have company," he murmured. "Who is that?" He brushed past me to enter the penthouse.

I trailed helplessly behind him as he followed the sounds of Sunny's and Angelica's laughter—which faded abruptly as we came into view.

"Jeremy," Sunny said after a tense moment, "how are you?"

He didn't answer. My nerves were wound so tight it felt like I was about to shatter.

"Sunny," he mumbled finally. "I'm fine. How did you..." he broke off, shaking his head as if to clear it. Sunny and Angelica watched him, both of them looking frozen with discomfort.

My mind raced in a useless loop as I tried to figure out what to say to break the tension.

An Irish brogue broke the silence. "Your door's open, Sydney, were you expecting me?"

I turned to find Sparrow standing in the front doorway with a beautiful bouquet of wildflowers. My brain spun faster. "Sparrow," I whispered, trying to smile at him.

"I think I should go," Jeremy muttered behind me. I cringed at the anguish in his voice. He dodged around me, pushing roughly past Sparrow's more muscular frame on his way to the elevator.

No one spoke. Sparrow's eyes roved over my face, as if trying to read it. I jumped when the soft ping of the elevator broke the suffocating quiet. And then Jeremy was gone.

"Who was that?" Sparrow asked.

"My husband," I answered, numb with the shock of Jeremy's unexpected visit.

Sparrow stared at me. "You didn't believe it was worth mentioning you were married?" he queried with a furrowed brow.

He strode to the dining room table and put down the bouquet of flowers. "These are for you," he told me, his tone flat. "I'm afraid I have to cancel our plans for the evening, but I'll be sure to let Lorien know the pertinent details of last night's death djinn arrest so that she can keep you updated."

I finally found my voice. "Wait, Sparrow. Jeremy and I are separated."

He blinked out before I finished speaking the words. I suddenly realized how awful it was that I hadn't told him. I had been doing such a thorough job of hiding Jeremy's betrayal from myself, it hadn't occurred to me that Sparrow deserved to know about it.

Tears rolled down my cheeks and I hugged my midsection. It hurt to see Jeremy. But it hurt worse to imagine what Sparrow must think of me now.

Oh Goddess. I was starting to fall in love with him.

A sob shuddered through me, and Sunny was suddenly there, her arm tightening around me as she led me toward the couch.

I barely heard Angelica's whispered, "I'm so sorry Sydney," before she disappeared too, leaving Sunny alone to comfort me in my misery.

<u>Chapter 16 - Playing With Matches</u>

"What happened last night?" Lorien asked in a hushed voice.

I looked up from a blank study of my laptop screen. I'd been attempting to focus on work for over an hour. But my mind seemed determined to keep floating off into space. At least it had ceased its insistent, torturous replay of last night's Sparrow and Jeremy fiasco. I'd tossed and turned all night with those images on a loop in my brain.

I felt tired and drained, but blessedly numb. I lifted the corners of my lips in a smile that I knew didn't reach my eyes. "Sparrow and Jeremy showed up here at the same time, and I don't think either one of them was too happy about it."

The expression on her face was so sympathetic that it nearly broke through my numbness to the pain buried beneath. I quickly looked away.

"Where's Sunny?" she asked, her voice gentle.

"In the shower."

"Oh. I just thought you'd both want to know what happened with the latest death djinn arrest. I talked to Agent… well anyway, they arrested about thirty more death djinns and found almost a hundred more unaligned souls."

I winced. "That's terrible. What are they going to do now? Surely that's enough to prove the death djinns have been conspiring together on this thing."

Lorien grimaced. "So far, they're claiming no knowledge as to how the unaligned souls got into their containment safes—just like the others."

"Of course they're not admitting it!" I exploded. "Why would they stop pleading ignorance now? Lauringer's right—this is ridiculous. They've got over a hundred death djinns in custody and who knows how many hundreds of unaligned souls that were found in their possession. What more do they need?"

The anger felt good—much better than the emptiness. A sudden reckless need to *do* something pulsed through me.

"It's not that simple," Lorien reminded me. "King Moab is using every ounce of his considerable influence to fight this. And the Seelie mages haven't been able to determine that any of the djinns are lying."

She frowned as she continued. "It gets worse, Sydney. Apparently, after the first mass arrest, Agent Sparrow ordered that death djinn containment safes be secretly monitored for suspicious activity. The unaligned souls they confiscated last night were all deposited some time within the last week. The problem is that, according to the records, at least half of the death djinns arrested didn't access their safes within the last week."

I groaned in aggravation. "Someone else? Could they have had someone else make the deposits for them? Or could they have figured out a way around being recorded?"

I ground my teeth. The frustration and lack of progress made me want to crawl out of my skin.

Lorien sighed. "Agent Sparrow is wondering the same thing, but so far this is more proof in King Moab's favor. Mages are examining the new unaligned souls for any connection to their mortal hosts, as well as any traces of the magic used to extract them. They're not letting the arrested death djinns go, but with the king leaning on the Seelie Court, they still can't convict without further proof."

"And a conviction is what it's going to take for your contract to be questioned."

"So more waiting," I spat in disgust. I watched Lorien fidget with the skirt of her color-shifting dress, the restless action signaling that there was more she hadn't told me. "What else?" I demanded.

When she looked up at me, there was sorrow in her eyes. "It's just that now the general consensus among the mages is that the human hosts belonging to the unaligned souls are probably dead. They can come up with no other explanation for the fact that they haven't been able to trace any of the souls to their owners."

"But you and Angelica said the souls were of no use if the people were dead!"

"They aren't," Lorien said on a vexed exhalation. "If the mages could only get a better fix on the magic used to extract them, maybe they could figure out what's really going on."

I managed a bitter smile. "Did the Seelie mages at least get any fresher traces of magic on these new souls?"

Lorien shook her head. "So far the strongest traces of magic they've found are still from the soul of the woman in the coma."

It kept coming back to Balthus' unaligned soul. And the only lead we had was the mysterious goblin with the infinity tattoo on his palm. Apparently Sparrow's mages weren't coming up with squat on any of the others. *Then again, it wasn't their souls that were on the line if the death djinns went free*, I thought bitterly.

A niggling voice in my brain insisted that there was still one connection no one had bothered to explore—the Hell Ride. And in my current mood, I was feeling just rash enough to do it myself.

Sunny wandered out from the hallway, the edges of her skirt swirling above her pink polished toenails. She dropped into one of the heavy dining room chairs and began pulling a brush through her long, damp curls.

"Hey Lorien. What's up?" she chirped.

Lorien glanced my way and said, "I was just telling Sydney about the latest death djinn arrests."

Sunny paused mid brush stroke, her expression intent. "Tell me the bastards are going down."

I let out a derisive snort and she scowled. "Why the hell not?" She yanked the brush through a tangle in her hair.

"Same old, same old," I intoned. "Nobody can trace the magic used to illegally extract the souls. Nobody can prove the death djinns are lying about having nothing to do with it. Forget the fact that they had them in their own containment safes. Some justice system, huh?"

"Be fair," Lorien chastised. "They have proof that at least half the death djinns arrested didn't access their containment safes during the times when the unaligned souls were deposited," she told Sunny.

Sunny's brows knitted in surprise and confusion.

"Whose side are you on, anyway?" I muttered resentfully at Lorien.

She gave me a hurt look and her wings began sifting purple dust. "I'm on your side, Sydney. I've always been on your side."

"Well then maybe you could stop defending the damn death djinns for a minute!"

I regretted my words immediately. My only excuse was that I was tired and hurt and apparently itching for a fight. Lorien's wings buzzed faster, sounding a high-pitched noise of protest, and then she disappeared. I stared after her, my chest constricting with shame.

I was such an asshole—first Sparrow, and now Lorien. Maybe I could work on alienating Sunny next.

My best friend's expression was neutral as my gaze drifted to her face. "Way to shoot the messenger, Syd." Her tone was sympathetic, despite the accusation in her words.

I closed my eyes and sighed, then pulled my legal pad in front of me and picked up the phone.

"Who are you calling?" she asked.

"I've got an exorcism to perform. Think it might count as atonement?"

"Say three hail Mickeys and call me when it's over," she said dryly.

I smiled at her quip. "Here goes nothing," I muttered as Mickey's cell phone began to ring.

"Mick here," he drawled.

"Mickey, hey there! It's Sydney." Silence. "I, uh, wanted to ask how your test went yesterday. Did you get there on time?"

"Yeah, yeah. Thanks," he answered, sounding surprised.

"Good, that's good." I rushed ahead before I lost my nerve. "Well, the reason I'm calling is I was wondering if you'd like to come by my place for that cup of coffee we've been talking about."

"Really?" he asked.

"Yeah," I faltered, grasping for a reason to explain my sudden change of heart. "My friend, Sunny, you remember her from the coffee shop?"

Sunny's eyes narrowed on me.

"Sort of," he answered uncertainly.

"Well, she remembers you. And she's teaching a college class next semester on, um, trends and modern society," I invented. "She wants to interview you about being Goth."

Sunny smacked my arm with the back of her hairbrush.

"Oh. Well, I'm not really into that anymore," he said.

"I know," I rushed on, "but you used to be, and that's exactly the perspective she needs. You know—someone who can look at it from the outside, who's already been on the inside." Wow. I really hoped that hadn't sounded as lame as I thought it had.

"Alright, I guess," he answered slowly. "I'm at my parents' store, but I was just leaving. I can come by now if you want. Where are you?"

I swallowed a lump of panic. "Uh, I'm in the tenth floor penthouse of the big beachfront hotel up the street. I'll tell the front desk to buzz you up when you get here."

"'Kay—I'll see ya in a few."

The line went dead and I jumped to my feet and darted toward my bedroom to find tweezers.

"Why did you tell him I wanted to interview him?" Sunny hissed behind me.

"Sorry!" I exclaimed breathlessly. "It just popped into my head!"

"Couldn't something else have popped into your head? Something that didn't involve me having an intimate conversation with a death djinn possessed teenager? I can't think of two beings I'd rather spend less time with!"

Her reflection glared at me in the vanity mirror as I dug through a drawer for the tweezers. When I didn't respond, her hands flew up to rest on her hips, and I flinched, knowing I was in trouble.

Fantastic. I was batting a thousand today. Next stop: pissing off Jasper. Where were those friggin' tweezers? Aha!

I stuck the metal tips into my pocket and whipped around, folding my hands into a pleading gesture and giving Sunny a desperate look as I picked up the phone to dial down to the front desk.

"Please Sunny!" I begged. "All I have to do is get him into the bathroom and burn some hairs from Jasper's tail in there with him. It'll be okay, I promise, but I have to get the hairs before he gets here. Worst case scenario, you just sit with your laptop like you're taking notes and ask him a few questions about the Goth scene, and I'll keep feeding him coffee 'til he has to go!"

She shook her head at me in disbelief. "Are you delusional? That is far from the worst case scenario, Syd—more like the *best* case scenario. And what if you're wrong?"

I blinked at her as the front desk answered and I told them to buzz Mickey up when he got here. I nibbled my lip as I put down the phone.

"Well, then he'll tell his parents I'm a freak who lured him to my hotel room, locked myself in the bathroom with him, and proceeded to burn a dish of hair. No doubt I'll be fired, and quite possibly arrested. But I'm not wrong. Now help me find Jasper!"

I sprinted back toward the living room with Sunny following grudgingly in my wake. Neither of them looked happy as I plucked him from the couch and deposited him into her arms.

"Can't you just snip the hairs with scissors?" she asked in exasperation as Jasper flinched away from me and she had to adjust her grip on him for the umpteenth time.

"Sorry guys—spell says 'plucked' not 'snipped'." I retrieved the last two hairs and dropped them into a small dish with the rest as Sunny gladly released Jasper. He darted behind the couch with a hiss and a highly accusatory meow.

"I'll give you a whole can of tuna after this is over, buddy," I called. Sunny arched one dark brow at me and I fought a smile. "And I'll buy you dinner," I promised.

"If he gets a whole can of tuna, I get sashimi tuna and sake at that posh new sushi place," she informed me with pursed lips.

"Done." I grinned.

There was a knock at the door and I cursed. "Be right there!" I called out.

"I'll put more coffee on," Sunny muttered in resignation as I dashed to the guest bathroom with my dish of cat hairs. I grabbed the matches from their place by the scented candle on the sink and dropped them into the dish, which I hid on a shelf next to some towels.

Mickey was just reaching up to knock a second time when I pulled open the front door.

"Sorry—I was in the other room," I apologized. "Come on in. If you need the restroom it's down that hall, first door on the left."

He nodded, but showed no sign of heading that way. Oh, well. I guessed it was too much to hope it would be that easy. "Wow, nice crib!" he exclaimed as he followed me toward the living room.

"Thanks. It's only temporary, though." I didn't want him blabbing to his parents that I was living less than five minutes away.

Sunlight spilled through the sliding glass doors, making the space feel clean and bright. The soft tones of a baroque flute rose from the TV speakers as I motioned for Mickey to have a seat on the tawny leather couch.

I took a deep breath and tried to internalize the calm atmosphere.

"So how come you're staying in a hotel?" Mickey asked.

I attempted to read his face, thinking he knew damn well how I'd come to live here, but his expression was innocent.

"It's a long story," I said, skirting the topic. "Ah, here's Sunny with coffee."

"Hey Mickey, nice to see you again!" she said cheerfully. "Thank you so much for taking the time to be one of my interviewees. I really appreciate it. I can't wait to hear your perspective."

"No problem," mumbled Mickey, his face turning red.

I had a moment of doubt at his shy reaction. If I was wrong about this possession thing, I was about to embarrass myself badly.

Sunny curled her lip at me as she placed a bamboo tray on the coffee table and we settled onto the couches. The tray held three over-sized mugs of coffee, a white ceramic pitcher for milk, and a dish of sugar. Serving me coffee was payback, since she knew I hated it without the Starbucks syrup. But I was too relieved that she was playing along to complain. Maybe if I added enough sugar and milk it would be tolerable.

"Please help yourself, and we'll get started," Sunny offered. She took hers black, while Mickey and I diluted ours.

"So Mickey, how old were you when you first became interested in the Goth scene?" Sunny traded her mug for her laptop and watched Mickey with an inquisitive expression over the top of the screen.

Mickey fidgeted, drumming the heels of his sneakers into the carpet beneath his gangly, jean-clad legs. "Um, I guess I was about fifteen."

"Mmhm." Sunny managed to imbue the sound with fascination as her fingers clicked against the keyboard. The silence stretched out until Mickey took a few nervous sips from his mug. Sunny smiled faintly as she asked the next question.

"And what would you say it was, about becoming Goth, that drew you most—the look, the attitude, the way you felt you would be perceived by parents and/or peers? Something else, perhaps?" she suggested.

"Uh, all of that, I guess."

"Uh huh," Sunny drawled. I hid a smile as her fingers clicked into the silence again and Mickey self-consciously gulped more coffee.

"Could you be more specific?" she asked, just as the hush was becoming uncomfortable. "What was it, exactly, about the look and the attitude that attracted you? And how did you imagine you would be perceived, both by peers and adults, by adopting those attributes? And what, if anything, else would you say influenced your decision to become Goth?"

Mickey looked overwhelmed.

"Sorry." Sunny grinned. "Let's take one thing at a time. What was it that you liked most about the look?"

"Well, just that it was different," Mickey said hesitantly, fingering the hem of his white polo shirt. "I guess I was tired of looking like everyone else, you know?"

"So you felt you needed an outlet to express your individualism," Sunny suggested.

"Yeah." Mickey appeared heartened by her assessment. "And I thought the black clothes and the piercings looked cool and kind of tough."

"That's good feedback, Mickey," she encouraged. "Let me just take some notes here." Sunny began typing away again as she gave Mickey time to drink more coffee.

At this rate, his mug would soon be empty.

"So you said you perceived the look as being cool and tough," she reiterated a moment later. "Does that also describe the general attitude you associated with the Goths?"

"Yeah, I guess. Goths tend to be above all the petty popularity stuff that most high-school kids care about. They hang out with each other and don't care what anyone else thinks about them." He sounded proud, but there was frustration beneath his bravado.

Sunny pressed on. "And once you decided to become Goth, did you find that you were easily adopted into that group, or was there a period where you felt like an outsider?"

Mickey shrugged. "There's only a few Goth kids at my school. And I was already kind of friends with Derrick." He paused and fiddled with a string hanging from his jeans pocket. "And I had a few classes with Kelly, so I used to talk to her sometimes."

His face flushed a blotchy red that traveled down his neck and disappeared beneath the crisp white collar of his shirt. He tried to disguise it by taking a long, two-handed swallow of coffee.

Sunny and I exchanged a knowing glance. Kelly had obviously been a big part of Mickey's decision to go Goth. So much for my theory about him being gay. Sunny cleared her throat and looked down to type. When she looked up again, an interested smile was pasted on her face.

"Would you like some more coffee, Mickey?" I asked when he placed his empty mug on the glass tabletop.

He patted his stomach. "Uh, no thanks. I think I've had enough."

"Yeah, me too," I agreed. "I need some water, though." I stood up. "Sunny, Mickey?"

"Please. Coffee always makes me thirsty," Sunny chimed.

"I'll get us all some," I said quickly, not giving Mickey the chance to refuse. A double-sized mug of Sunny's extra strong rocket fuel and the biggest glass of water I could find, and Mickey would be running to the bathroom any minute now. I hoped.

I kept one ear to the living room as I pulled down three of my tallest glasses from the top shelf of a cabinet. I used them for beer and they were big enough to fit two whole bottles a piece.

I could just make out Sunny's voice as she said, "Mickey, thank you again for helping me out with my research—I really appreciate it. Let's see, you were saying that you already knew a couple of the Goth kids, so it wasn't that difficult for you to become part of their group. Did the other kids begin to view you differently when you became Goth?"

I strained to hear Mickey's response as I filled the glasses from the dispenser.

"I guess a few of the jock assholes started making fun of me more, but they were jerks to begin with." He shrugged, his tone turning defensive. "Besides, like I said, Goths don't care what other people think of them."

"Mmhm. And parents and other adults? Did you feel that they viewed you differently?"

Mickey sniggered. "My parents? They hated it. My dad's favorite nickname for me went from 'useless idiot' to 'useless zombie faggot', and my mom just wailed about how I'd never date a cheerleader or join the football team. Like I ever wanted to hang out with those jerks anyway, wasting all my time on after school practices," he said with rancor.

I set the water glasses on the coffee table and resumed my place on the couch. I schooled the sympathy from my face, doubting Mickey would appreciate it.

Sunny spent a good amount of time typing and Mickey finally picked up his water and downed a few gulps. His expression remained sour.

"Some people look at Goths and automatically think they're into vampires, satanic worship or the occult," Sunny spoke into the silence.

Her choice of topic made me nervous. I didn't want Mickey, or rather the death djinn that I was ninety-nine percent sure possessed him, becoming suspicious about what we were up to.

I was suddenly and uncomfortably aware of Jasper's unknown whereabouts. I thought he was probably still nursing his grudge behind the couch—but what if he decided to come out? And what if Mickey's djinn knew about the white-tipped tail thing? My plan would crumble and I probably wouldn't have another chance to get this close to him.

But Sunny's tone was all innocent detachment, and Mickey's expression only turned more darkly inward.

"Kelly had this Ouija board we used to play around with. It got kind of spooky," he answered, his blue-grey eyes going dull and distant.

And then I saw it—that eerie flash of emerald green burning in their depths. My entire body tensed as I tried to conceal the shock of fear that echoed through me.

"Spooky?" Sunny asked.

I didn't think she'd noticed the change in his eyes. She did, however, begin to frown as the silence lengthened and she looked up to find his face contorting as if he was struggling to speak.

"Mickey? Are you okay? Why don't you drink some water," she suggested in concern.

Mickey made a strange gurgling noise as if he was choking. Sunny put her laptop down and started to rise, looking at me in confusion, as if she couldn't believe I was just sitting there doing nothing. And then suddenly, Mickey reached for his water glass, took a few sips, and smiled at her as if nothing had happened.

Sunny slowly sank back into the couch cushions, retrieving her laptop as she continued to stare at Mickey. "Are you alright?"

"Just a tickle in my throat," he answered.

"Uh *huh*." Sunny sounded skeptical, but continued with the interview. "So, you were saying the Ouija board got spooky?"

"Well, Kelly and Derrick tried to make like it was all spooky, but it was actually pretty dumb. When I told them so, they got mad." Mickey rolled his eyes. "I was done with the Goth scene anyway. It was lame. I wish I'd never gotten into it."

Sunny raised her eyebrows at his abrupt change of attitude.

"What?" he asked her, his tone turning sarcastic. "Didn't you ever do something when you were a teenager that you wished you hadn't?"

"Well, yeah," she said slowly. "When I look back at the pictures, I kinda wish I'd never worn my hair in that big, ridiculous poof in the eighty's."

I chuckled in commiseration.

"But I guess it was in fashion back then and it would have looked even more ridiculous if I hadn't gone along with it," Sunny continued. "I suppose I'm just surprised that you went so quickly from thinking the Goth scene was cool, to thinking it wasn't."

Mickey shrugged. "Everyone makes mistakes. What about you, Sydney? Isn't there anything you wish you'd never done when you were my age?"

"Hey! This interview is supposed to be about you. Let's not drag up my sordid past," I evaded with a joking smile. Any doubts I'd had about Mickey being possessed died with his newest, less than subtle attempt to get me to make a wish.

Mickey didn't look amused. He let out an exaggerated yawn and said, "So are we done? I've got someplace to be."

Sunny glanced at me as she answered, "Well, I do have a few more questions."

"Sorry. I really have to jet. Maybe next time." Mickey rose from the couch and headed for the door.

"Do you need to use the restroom before you leave?" I asked, trying to sound gracious instead of desperate.

"Nah," Mickey answered.

My heart sank as he reached for the door knob. "Catch ya' later, ladies," he said.

"Oh, wait!" Sunny called, jumping up from the couch. "Before you go, there's a case of expensive champagne in the laundry room, but we can't get to the damned thing because it's stuck tight between the wall and the washing machine. You're a strapping young man—could you just take a quick look and see if you can wedge it out for us?"

I stared at her in confusion. Then I realized that the laundry room should work just as well as the bathroom for the spell's purposes. Sunny was a genius!

"That would be great!" I exclaimed. "If you can get it out for us, there's a fifty dollar bottle of champagne in it for you. Just don't tell your parents!"

Mickey's face perked up at that. What teenager refuses free alcohol—even if they are possessed by a death djinn?

"I've gotta run to the restroom," I glanced meaningfully at Sunny. "Can you show Mickey where that case of champagne is?"

I darted toward the guest bath as Sunny made a show of doing something with her laptop to give me time to get the cat hairs and matches. I closed the door behind me and turned the faucet on as I felt along the shelf for the hidden dish. My fingers tipped it over the edge and my heart plummeted into my stomach as it began to fall. I caught it at the last second and brought it down safely with a panicked gasp.

When I went to stick the matches into my pocket, though, I saw that most of the white hairs were stuck to the matchbook. Holding my breath, I picked them off, one by one, and re-counted the tiny wisps...thank Goddess, still seven! The matches went into my pocket as I snapped off the faucet and cupped the dish in my hands so that its hard-won contents wouldn't blow away.

"Sorry, Mickey," Sunny was saying. "Since you took the time to answer my questions, I want to make sure I save our interview. But the stupid computer keeps freezing up."

She and Mickey glanced up at me as I walked back into the living room with my hands wrapped around the glass dish.

I chuckled nervously. "I keep telling Sunny to bring her dishes to the kitchen. Other than that little habit, she's the perfect houseguest." The look she gave me was dry as the desert, and I mentally tacked on another bottle of sake to the dinner I owed her.

"Follow me, Mickey, and maybe you can budge that monstrosity of a washing machine for us."

My heart tripped in excitement and fear as I led him to the laundry room. It was dark, and my trembling fingers brushed across the cool metal wall-plate to find the light switch. Most of the space was taken up by the huge, stainless-steel washer and dryer. Varnished wooden shelves lined the walls above the two machines, and a thin blue runner rug that matched the wallpaper ran the length of the room.

It smelled of my favorite jasmine and water lily dryer sheets. A box of them lay open atop a laundry basket piled high with my dirty clothes. I inhaled, trying to calm myself, and schooled my features into a smile before I turned to face Mickey. He was right on my heels.

"Close quarters," I said with a mad titter as he backed up. "The washing machine's right there. Just see if you can't pull it forward away from the wall a bit."

"Where's the case of champagne?"

I could see that this was the point from which the plan was rapidly going to deteriorate.

"Uh, don't ask me why, but someone left it behind the machine. Crazy right?" Mickey was looking at me as if I was a little crazy now. Well, if you squinted, it kind of looked like there was enough room to fit a few bottles back there.

"Anyway, if you could just try to pull it forward away from the wall?" I insisted.

He moved past me into the room and paused before the machine, testing its weight with the strength of his arms. It didn't budge. He bent his knees and pulled harder. I silently swung the door closed and set the dish of cat hairs on top of the dryer behind my laundry basket. I fumbled with the matchbook, nearly dropping it when Mickey spoke.

"This *is* heavy."

I stifled the urge to laugh insanely as my fingers steadied around the matchbook and I plucked a match from its bed. "Try to use your leg muscles. I don't want you hurting your back."

Mickey grunted with effort as I struck the match against the flint strip. The sour smell of sulfur drifted up into my nostrils, but it didn't catch. I struck again and the smell rose stronger, but still no fire. I prayed the third time would be the charm as I struck it again, fast and hard. A tiny point of blue flame sprang to life and I cradled a shaking hand around it as I lowered it toward the scant pile of cat hairs.

I was so focused on the match that I nearly shrieked when Mickey suddenly said, "Sorry, Sydney, I think you're going to have to get a couple of guys in here to move this thing." He rose and leaned over the top of the machine, his neck craning as he tried to see behind it.

My eyes shot back to the miniscule trail of smoke floating up from the now dead match. I fretfully ripped at a fresh match, accidentally pulling out two that stuck together.

"I'm not seeing anything back there, Sydney," Mickey said in confusion. He looked toward me. "Is that smoke?"

I frantically struck the matches, not caring that my fingers were too close to their heads. I felt the instant bite of white heat as both matches caught and the sparks flared against each other, flashing brightly and joining into one larger flame that licked eagerly down the paper strips. I dropped the conflagration into the dish, bringing my singed fingers to my mouth as I anxiously watched for the cat hairs to begin burning. I fervently hoped the match getting burned in there with them wouldn't interfere with the spell.

Mickey stepped toward me, now looking angry and suspicious. "What are you doing? Why is the door closed?" he demanded.

The acrid aroma of burning hair filled the small utility closet and I backed up against the door, staring wildly at Mickey for some sign that the spell was working.

"I don't know what you're playing at, Sydney, but you'd better let me out of here right now." Mickey's voice dropped low in warning and a chill swept through me as emerald fire took over the blue-grey of his eyes.

I stood motionless, my back flattened against the only exit. He grabbed my shoulders with surprising strength, and I squeaked in denial as my eyes flew to the guttering flame in the now blackened dish. His gaze followed mine, falling upon the flame just as it snuffed out of existence.

A look of rage constricted his features and his grip tightened painfully on my shoulders. I instinctively executed a move that's been hard-wired into the female brain since the times of being hit over the head and dragged off by cavemen. I kneed him in the crotch.

His face went slack with surprise, then rigid with pain as he backed away from me and doubled over, clutching his groin. Shit. I was in so much trouble if this didn't work. Mickey panted as he looked up at me with accusatory fury. I gasped—his eyes were swirling with color, eerie green flickering angrily through the blue-grey of his irises.

A ghostly form began to take shape in front of him, its substance fed by an other-worldly smoke that seemed to pour from Mickey's skin. I stared in shock as the distinctively willowy figure of a woman materialized.

"You bitch!" she wailed, rushing at me.

I threw my hands up in a feeble defense, but my back was already against the door—I had nowhere to go. I closed my mouth, afraid of what would happen if I inhaled the figure's smoky form, but it only scattered harmlessly around me. A faint keening of frustration echoed through my ears as the smoke slowly began to re-gather.

"What's going on in there?" Sunny's muffled voice demanded through the door. I felt the knob turn against my back and I activated the lock to keep her from opening it. "What the hell? Syd? If you don't answer me I'm breaking this door down!"

True to her word, she started banging against it so hard that the force of her blows vibrated through me. "It's okay, Sunny!" I called in a strangled voice. "But I can't open the door just yet!"

The banging ceased, but I could feel her there, hovering behind me in worried indecision.

The shapeless smoke reformed into the amorphous outline of a woman. She was several inches taller than me, thin and long-limbed, with dark hair and high cheekbones. A sophisticated dress swathed her slender body in hunter-green, and her earlobes were lined with small glittering studs. Almond-shaped eyes peered at me sullenly through the smoky veil of her gathering form.

"Who are you?" I asked in a stunned voice.

"I am the princess Amalia." She crossed her slowly solidifying arms over her chest in an imperious stance.

I stared at her dumbly.

She narrowed her eyes. "Certainly my dear brother has mentioned me."

I shook my head and a look of surprise flitted across her face before it darkened with irritation. Her fists clenched and she swore. "That bastard has always underestimated me—he and my father both. I am the eldest; it should be me who is next in line to Father's throne. Not that ingrate, Balthus.

"But I have my own plans," she spat, "and I will not be shunted aside simply because I was not born a son! I *warned* Balthus that he would be forced to bargain with me for possession of his chosen mate."

"Chosen mate?" I repeated weakly.

She paused in her tirade to stare at me, an unpleasant smile spreading across the sharp vee of her lips. "Did you not know Balthus has marked you as his chosen mate? Regardless of who completes your contract, he means to have you in the end. It is merely a matter of how hard a bargain he will be forced to drive to claim you. My price will be delightfully high." Her smile widened to show even rows of small white teeth.

"I could include something for you in the bargain as well," she added slyly. "Perhaps a clause that would prevent him from passing you around for the pleasure of his friends?"

I swallowed in revulsion.

Amalia chuckled. "No. As his chosen mate, he would likely guard you too jealously to share you in such a manner. However I know my brother well. He likes to think of himself as a Casanova—a great lover and a giver of pleasure rather than pain. But he revels in power just as much as the next man.

"Unlike our father though, who takes his satisfaction from the more obvious tortures, Balthus is a master at the subtler art of mixing pain with pleasure. He will take you against your will, but force your body to enjoy it, taking his satisfaction from your shame as you begin to crave his touch. I could add a clause to your contract that would give you more control over the physical aspect of your relationship."

I stared at her in speechless horror as the emerald flames burned brighter in her eyes.

"Just one wish, Sydney. Anything you want—I can grant it," she offered soothingly. "And when my brother comes to claim you, I will drive a bargain that will make your eternity with him far easier to bear." She gave me a look that approached sympathy. "We are both women. We have both suffered at the hands of men. And I know how hard it's been not to make your third wish. It's only a matter of time, I'm afraid, and I fear you won't receive such a generous offer from another."

My brain clouded with doubt. Oh Goddess. It was even more hopeless than I'd thought. I was so tired of worrying and wondering when I was finally going to slip up. Maybe she was right; maybe I should take what she was offering now, while it was still on the table.

"I…" I croaked.

The simultaneous sounds of Sunny's renewed banging and Mickey's pained groan broke the spell she had begun to weave around me. "Syd, goddamn it! You listen to me! Don't you dare listen to that demon skank!"

A vexed growl issued from Amalia's throat and I suddenly noticed something that should have registered long before now. The entire time she had been talking, she had been growing less hazy. There was barely any smoke left to her nearly solid form. My eyes flew wide as I remembered the last step of the spell—I needed to capture her spirit in some type of vessel!

I looked around frantically, dismissing the washer and dryer—way too big, not to mention there was no way that could be good for the laundry. The bottle of detergent on the shelf? I could always buy more. And maybe she'd accidentally drown in it. No—no matter how satisfying a thought that might be, it probably wasn't a good idea to drown the princess of the death djinns in laundry soap.

Then I caught a faint amber glimmer atop the heap of clothing in my laundry basket. Hannah's hideous brooch peeked out from the edge of the front pocket in my discarded jeans. Good enough—it was even made of crystal! I made a grab for it and Amalia lunged at me, realizing I'd caught on to my mistake.

I grasped the rough-edged rock just as she made contact with my arm. Her touch was vaguely solid for a moment, but then it evaporated into insubstantiality. Amalia howled with fury and I held the crystal out in front of me, my arms shaking, gripping it with both hands as if it was a sword. There had been no words of incantation with the spell Angelica had given me, only instructions. I prayed that my mere intent to use the crystal as a vessel to capture Amalia would be enough.

We stared at each other in frozen silence, and then the crystal began to glitter with a weird inner light. Amalia's form grew cloudier, and then her lower body lost substance, became smoke, and drifted toward the brooch. The rest of her quickly followed, her head disappearing last as her disembodied voice wafted past my ears with a faint parting shot of, "You'll be sorry you didn't cut a deal with me, you little bitch!"

The crystal grew warm in my hand, trembling violently and emitting a single, bright strobe of light. Then it fell quiet and still. I stared at it in awe, afraid to move, but it remained cool and lifeless against my palm. I looked up to find Mickey struggling to his feet. He winced as he moved, but his eyes held something akin to worship.

"Did you kill her?" His voice was a mixture of hope and fear.

"Uh, I captured her." I sounded as stunned as I felt.

"Hello! Can you open the freakin' door now?" Sunny demanded, with what sounded like a kick for good measure.

I grinned. "Are you alright?" I asked Mickey as I reached to pop open the lock.

He nodded. "I am now." He moved gingerly, but didn't say a word about my knee shot to his groin.

"Did it work?" Sunny nudged open the door with a pink-tipped toe, holding a butcher knife in one hand and a steaming pot of coffee in the other.

I blinked at her. "What were you planning to do with that?" I asked, my lips twitching in hilarity.

"Stab! Burn! Scald! Whatever!" she exclaimed, looking wildly from me to Mickey. Then her gaze narrowed in on Hannah's brooch, still clutched in my hand, and her face crumpled in disgust. "I knew that thing was evil from the moment I saw it. Where's the demon death djinn skank?"

"You mean Princess Amalia? You're looking at her new home. This is where I trapped her."

Sunny lowered the butcher knife and her eyes became thoughtful. "You know, I think that brooch could start to grow on me after all." She dropped the knife on the kitchen counter with a clatter as she made her way back out to the living room, still grasping the coffee pot. "It's too early for alcohol. I need more coffee," she muttered.

I smiled wanly at Mickey. "Why don't you come sit down and tell us how this happened."

"Are you a witch or something?" he whispered uncertainly as we followed Sunny toward the welcoming comfort of the couches.

I chuckled. "Why do people keep asking me that?" A pang shot through me at the reminder of Sparrow's favorite taunt, and I sobered.

"No, Mickey," I sighed. "I'm just a regular person like you, who got caught up in some crazy shit. How did Amalia manage to possess you anyway? From what I've heard, you had to invite her in." I collapsed onto the couch next to Sunny, who was refilling her mug, and left Mickey the loveseat.

"It must have been that Ouija board," he said with a grimace. "It was Kelly's grandmother's. She said we couldn't use it, so Kelly would sneak into her room to get it. It wasn't like those board game ones you buy at the store—it was carved out of real wood and the symbols were so faded you could barely see them. I think the pointer thing was made out of bone. It looked really gnarly and old."

I exchanged an interested glance with Sunny.

"So what did you guys do?" Sunny probed. "Ask it questions? Invite the spirits to speak through you? How many times did you use it before you got possessed?"

Mickey shrugged. "I don't know—we used it a few times. We asked it questions, just screwing around really. It didn't move, so I guess we started taking turns spelling out stuff to mess with each other. Kelly and Derrick both knew my parents were riding me hard about my grades and the way I dress. I asked how I could get my parents to leave me alone."

Mickey frowned and rubbed his temple, as if he was trying to remember. "At first, nothing happened. Then I think Kelly made the pointer spell 'TURN 18'." He smiled faintly. "But then…I don't know, it just started going crazy. It was moving real fast and jerky all over the place, and it finally spelled 'I CAN HELP'. I thought it was Derrick fucking with me, so I played along. It said 'INVITE ME IN', and Derrick and Kelly were staring at me, waiting to see what I'd do, like it was a dare or something. So I pointed to 'YES'."

He shrugged again and shook his head. "Nothing happened. I mean, I kinda got the chills, and it felt real spooky and silent all of a sudden, but nothing happened." Mickey looked down at his jeans and began rubbing his fists against the tops of his legs.

"Until that night—when I got home and went to bed. I had this crazy dream that there was someone in the room with me." He gave us a troubled look. "Some kind of presence, weighing down on me until I couldn't breathe. I've never been that scared before. I woke up, but I was too afraid to move. It felt like it was still there, pressing down on me. It was dark, but the room seemed kind of smoky and wrong, and I tried to yell, but I couldn't make a sound."

He shivered. "That's all I remember. When I woke up the next morning—she was there, inside me. After that, sometimes it was me, but sometimes it was her, making me do stuff." He groaned. "She totally wrecked my life."

I gave him a sympathetic look. "She was the reason you stopped hanging out with your friends?"

Mickey nodded, his face falling into disgust. "That was her way of getting my parents to leave me alone. She thought it was funny, making me take out all my piercings and dye my hair and dress up like a Prep." His fingers moved over his nose and eyebrows and he scowled. "Some of those were new, too. Now I'm gonna have to get them redone." He dropped his head into his hands and made a sound of utter revulsion. "She even had me ogling dudes!"

Sunny sniggered softly.

"And she must have been the reason you started talking to me." I was almost afraid to ask what she'd told him. Although he seemed grateful for my aid in curing his possession, he was still my boss' son.

He spread the fingers he was hiding behind to peer up at me. "She wanted to trick you into making a wish real bad." His voice was muffled by his palms, and he dropped his hands, still looking miserable. "She'd been spying on people who knew you, trying to get info about you, and I guess she figured I'd be a good 'in' since you work for my parents. She was totally pissed that her plan wasn't working, too.

"When she wasn't bitching about that, she was bitching about her brother and her dad—dude, she *really* hates them. She sure seemed to be having a good time taking it out on me, though." He hid his face again. "She made me do stuff I'd *never* do. Ugh. I still can't believe she had me checking out other guys."

Sunny grinned. "Aw, don't be so upset, kid. Just think how cool your friends will think it is when you tell them you were actually *possessed*."

Mickey blinked at her in disbelief. "You really think they'll listen?"

Sunny flapped her hand at him. "Sure—it's a great story, even if they don't believe it. Just pick yourself up some black hair dye, put on your shabbiest clothes, stick some metal back in your face, and go find 'em. You might have to grovel a little, but I bet they'll take you back."

Mickey sat up straighter and gazed at Sunny hopefully.

I chuckled. "She's right. Just don't let them talk you into using that Ouija board again," I cautioned.

"Hell no, Kelly's not gettin' me anywhere near that thing," he agreed.

"Good. So everything's okay, right?" I asked, wanting to be sure. "You feel like you're back to normal now?"

He shifted himself delicately as he sat. "Pretty much."

I bit my lip. "Yeah. Sorry about the knee to the groin."

Mickey shrugged and Sunny raised her eyebrows at us in question, having been on the other side of the door during that part of the excitement.

"And just, uh, one more thing," I said. "I would appreciate it if your parents didn't find out about this."

The look on Mickey's face was comical. "Are you kidding me?"

His expression of disbelief made me breathe easier as I added, "Including the fact that I happen to be living five minutes away from their store."

"Dude, I barely even talk to them unless I have to. As far as I'm concerned, I was never here." His gaze seemed to request my agreement.

I smiled and nodded. "Good deal." I should have known he'd be just as keen as I was to keep the whole episode from them.

"Uh, I guess I'll be going, then," he said in a tentative voice.

I nodded, unable to think of a reason to keep him any longer. "Yeah. Let me know if you have any weird side effects or anything. I might know someone who can help." I stood and walked him to the door

"Okay." His eyes darted around as we stood in the foyer waiting for the elevator. Finally they settled on me and he said, "Thanks Sydney, really. I don't know what I would have done if..." he trailed off, embarrassed.

I smiled and reached up to hug him. He stiffened, and then sort of hugged me back. "It's okay, Mickey."

I released him and he stepped into the elevator. "Just be more careful with the occult stuff. And remember, other things will start to get easier soon too." I grinned. "After all, you're almost eighteen."

The doors slid shut on his answering smile.

A reckless energy bounded through me, almost as if I was on a magical high. I was surprised at how easy the spell casting thing had turned out to be. And it felt good to take action, instead of waiting for the Seelie Police to come up with something.

I suddenly knew what I wanted to do next. I slipped into the laundry room and felt inside the pocket of my dirty jeans until my fingers found the slip of paper Lauringer had given me.

"Whatchya doin'?" asked Sunny as she passed behind me on her way to return the coffee pot to its base on the kitchen counter.

I jumped guiltily. I was pretty sure Sunny would think calling the Hell Ride was a bad idea. "Thought I'd throw this load in the wash," I answered, starting to do just that.

She moved into the doorway and propped herself against the frame as she watched me. "Whatchya planning on doing with the demon skank brooch?"

I laughed. "Not sure yet. Maybe I'll wear it to dinner. Nothing like a little demon skank to jazz up an outfit."

"Or maybe she's worth enough to someone that you could trade her for the cancellation of your contract."

I slowed my transfer of clothes into the washer and looked up at Sunny's calculating expression. "Ya' think?"

She shrugged. "Maybe. Apparently she's royal family. It's worth a try."

"You really are a genius," I said with a grin. "And I couldn't have captured her without you. I especially liked the way you kept Mickey drinking with those long pauses in the interview. And getting him to come in here at the last second—that was inspired."

"Yeah, well," she answered with an embellished flip of her dark curls, "I guess I should have known better than to doubt you—faerie girl." She winked and turned away. "I'll leave you to your laundry. I've got a class to plan…you know, other than my 'trends and modern society' one."

I smirked at her retreating back as I finished stuffing my clothes into the washer. As soon as I turned it on and added the soap, I headed for the pantry. Jasper came running at the whir of the electric can opener and was soon purring in contentment over a full dish of tuna, allowing me to stroke his back as he ate. Apparently I had been absolved for his tail plucking.

"Oh, and by the way—don't think I've forgotten about sashimi and sake," Sunny called from the living room.

"Wouldn't dream of it," I answered.

Jasper finished licking his dish and head-butted me happily. "If only all my trespasses were so easily forgiven," I whispered with a sad smile.

Chapter 17 - Lessons Relearned

Unfortunately, I couldn't just perform an exorcism and call it a day. I was still on call for work and sales figures needed to be entered into the computer. My abandoned paper stack lay piled on the dining room table like a disapproving reminder. My eyes glazed over at the mere thought and my brain drifted back toward the far more exciting topic of spell casting.

Actually, come to think of it, Mickey's exorcism wasn't my first spell. Back in my own Ouija board days I remembered tinkering with the odd spell here and there.

Two in particular came to mind. I'd performed a pretty cool spell to make the cat I had before Jasper my familiar. I never knew if it worked, but we'd always been particularly close.

And then there was the spell I'd performed when my first love broke up with me. I burned a candle down in increments every night, as I visualized our astrological colors intertwining and repeated an incantation to bring him back to me. And he *had* come back to me—with stories of how I'd appeared to him in his dreams with those same colors swirling around me.

Of course, not too long after that, I caught the bastard cheating on me and we broke up for good. I should have been more careful what I wished for then too.

I sighed as I finished making an extra large mug of tea, then planted myself in front of my laptop and buckled down into work mode. Sunny was doing the same, sitting on the couch with her laptop and coffee, working on the syllabus for her medieval literature class.

Jasper, with his belly full of tuna, had settled in for an afternoon nap. He was curled up on his favorite sunlit chair by the sliding glass doors.

I was just getting into my data entry stride when the phone rang. I stifled a groan at the interruption. It was Hannah. And mid-week calls from her usually meant guilt-inducing D.J.D. money questions that I couldn't answer.

"Hi Hannah! How are you?" I asked with forced cheer.

"Oh, Sydney! Bon, bon, mon ami! Life is good, yes?"

I chuckled at her contagious enthusiasm. "I suppose it is, Hannah. What can I do for you?"

"I am so sorry to bother you," she said, her tone sincere, "but it is time for the annual business renewal, and I have forgotten to give it to you in your papers on Monday. I would save it for next week, but the deadline is Tuesday, you understand? Could you possibly come by this afternoon and pick it up? You know how hopeless I am with paperwork!"

I let out a breath of relief that she hadn't asked me about the growing balance D.J.D. owed her. It wasn't as if I could do anything about it, but

I knew she could use the money. Her meager sales figures revealed how painfully slow summer business had been.

"Of course, Hannah—no problem. I'll be by before you close."

"*Merci beaucoup*, Sydney—you are the best! Also—I wanted to let you know I received a call from your Jeremy yesterday. He said he wanted to drop off some of your things but could not remember your apartment number and could not get hold of you. I told him you were in the tenth floor penthouse at the hotel, which seemed to confuse him. I hope I did not make a problem for you."

I had a flashback to sixth grade and the time I told my mom I was going to my friend's house, when I was really riding my bike to go meet a boy. I neglected to warn my friend and she showed up at my house looking for me.

Never use someone as an alibi without telling them so they can cover for you.

"No. It wasn't a problem, Hannah," I lied.

"Very good—I am glad to hear it. So I will see you later then!" She hung up.

I managed a self-deprecating smile and shook my head. "Looks like we'll be stopping by Hannah's on our way to sashimi and sake tonight."

"I'll stay by the car and watch for suspicious activity," Sunny returned with a distracted grin.

I snorted as I went back to my stack of sales figures. Unlike Hannah, D.J.D. seemed to be doing relatively well for off season, which made me feel even worse that they were getting so far behind on her balance again.

A timid knock at the door interrupted my attempt at concentration. I rose to open it and found Angelica hovering there with a look of distress twisting her features. Her blue eyes were dull and glassy in her pale face, and her perfect skin was blotchy, as if she'd been crying.

I reached for her slim shoulders and pulled her inside, putting my arm around her as I closed the door and led her toward the couch.

"Angelica, what happened?" I asked as tears began silently coursing down her cheeks.

Sunny looked up, her questioning gaze transforming into a worried frown. "Hey, what's the matter?" She sat up straighter. "Did that guy you've been seeing do something to upset you? I told you if he couldn't accept you for what you are he doesn't deserve you!" she insisted with staunch sympathy.

"No! He...I..." She looked at me in desperation and her tears began to flow faster. "I'm afraid I have done something unforgivable, Sydney," she whispered, her voice cracking.

"I doubt that, Angelica," I denied gently. "What is it? It can't be *that* bad," I said with a teasing smile.

She blinked at me, tears clinging to her lush eyelashes in tiny droplets. "You must believe me. I did not realize until last night. I would never have knowingly betrayed you."

A sinking trepidation settled low in the pit of my stomach as I waited for her to continue.

Angelica seemed unable to hold my gaze and looked down at her hands, her graceful fingers wringing anxiously in her lap. "The man I have been seeing, the one I have been telling you about…"

My dread grew heavier as my mind whirled through unpleasant scenarios involving her lover having a connection to the death djinns, and her unwittingly revealing something they could use to compel me or sabotage Sparrow's investigation.

"It's your Jeremy," she finished on a quiet exhalation of anguish.

I blinked at her in confusion, wondering what Jeremy could possibly have to do with anything. Then her meaning hit me and the breath left my body in a rush. Sunny and I both stared at her in shock. My hand flew to my mouth, muffling the disbelieving word that spilled from it, "How?"

Her eyes flew to mine, their hollow blue depths imploring my forgiveness. "I am so sorry, Sydney. From the beginning I felt that there was something familiar about him, but I had no idea he was yours. I have grown so close to you over these past weeks, and I have felt your sexual frustration and desire for your Agent Sparrow so strongly—I must have unconsciously followed your connection with Jeremy." Her head dropped.

"I .." I began faintly, struggling to break through the stunned vacancy that fogged my brain.

"It's not your fault Angelica," I said finally. "You didn't know. I mean, it's not as if he hasn't cheated on me before."

She cringed at the note of bitterness in my voice. "But that's just it, Sydney," she rushed on. "You mustn't blame Jeremy for this—he did not know until last night that I was anything but a dream. He was terrified when he saw me here!"

I remembered the haunted look on Jeremy's face and his sudden departure began to make more sense. I'd thought it was because of Sparrow, but Jeremy couldn't have known that he was my date. He could just as easily have been there for Sunny or Angelica.

"When I appeared to him afterward, it took me long hours to calm him and explain. When he finally accepted the truth, he was greatly distressed that he had shared sexual pleasure with someone other than you—especially someone who you considered a friend!

"Jeremy is consumed by a terrible guilt. This is the reason he resisted me, even in his dreams. He fears that you will never forgive him, Sydney… and I fear that he will never forgive *me*," she added softly, her eyes drifting away from mine.

"But there is more that you should know," she insisted, taking a deep breath as her expression settled into a pained resolve. "Jeremy and I spoke long into the night, and much of our discussion revolved around you."

I squeezed my eyes shut, envisioning mortifying discussions about the intimate details of our former sex life, and wondering just how much she had told him about my current situation.

"Do not misunderstand me, Sydney," Angelica interjected. "I told Jeremy nothing about your death djinn involvement, nor did I mention anything about Agent Sparrow. He very much wanted to know what had been going on during your separation, but I told him that as a friend I could not abuse your confidence in such a manner."

I beamed a grateful look in her direction.

"It was his feelings for you and the events leading up to his betrayal of your monogamy which he described to me. He told me about the woman from his office with whom he shared sexual pleasures—the one you called 'tramp'?

"He described his confusion and guilt afterward, and referred to the entire experience as having been dream-like and unreal, saying that he couldn't believe he had done such a thing."

I felt my lips pucker in an expression of disgust and Sunny rolled her eyes at me in commiseration. I wasn't impressed by Jeremy's sob story. Confusion and guilt were the least of what he deserved.

"Angelica, I know you don't really believe in monogamy, but Jeremy and I were married—and that's supposed to mean something," I told her, my tone sharper than I intended.

"Please Sydney, hear me out," she entreated. "There was something that didn't seem right to me about Jeremy's story. So I went to his office today, to satisfy my own curiosity and see this woman for myself.

"Her name is Edie. She is a succubus, Sydney—and not a very nice one. She chooses to live and work in the mortal world, as I do, but for her own twisted purposes. She takes pleasure in seducing married men outside the dream state. The more they resist her, the harder she tries to break their will."

I gaped at her. "Are you telling me that she *forced* Jeremy to have sex with her?"

Angelica's fingertips skimmed lightly across her forehead as she sighed. "No. I wouldn't put it that strongly. What I'm saying is that I know her, and she would not have stopped trying to seduce him until he gave in. She could not force him, but as he continued to resist her advances, she would have increased the intensity of her seduction.

"It is true that at least a part of him had to want her and be willing to experience the pleasures she offered—but you must realize how difficult it is to resist a succubus intent upon seduction. It is our specialty and we

have refined the art over millennia. Even more so than the death djinns."
She gave me an apologetic but pointed look.

I dropped my head into my hands as the implication of her words sank
in, a humorless little laugh escaping my lips. This changed everything. Or
at least it made everything more complicated.

"What a mess," I mumbled hoarsely.

"I did not tell Jeremy about Edie," Angelica stated.

I gave her a quizzical look.

"I have interfered enough," she said in a resigned voice. "But despite
what you may feel toward me, you should talk to Jeremy. He suffers greatly,
Sydney, and truly did not mean to hurt you. It is up to you whether to tell
him this thing or not."

I sank back into the couch cushions and closed my eyes, allowing silence
to fall between us.

"What are you gonna do, Syd?" Sunny ventured after a long moment.

I scoffed limply. "I have no idea what to do. Everything's so confused.
On the one hand, knowing that Jeremy was unwittingly seduced by a
damn-near-impossible-to-resist succubus makes me feel a whole lot better.
But on the other hand, things would have been much simpler if he had
remained the cheating asshole I thought he was."

I opened my eyes and tilted my head toward Angelica. "I don't blame
you for any of this, you know."

She blinked at me uncertainly as a wordless sob shuddered through her
slender frame. Then she broke into a teary smile and leaned over to hug
me tight. "I was so worried that you would hate me," she whispered with a
delicate sniff.

I squeezed her back and hummed a rueful murmur of denial. "I
could never hate you, Angelica. You know you'll always be my favorite
succubus."

She exhaled a fractured laugh. "You are sweet, Sydney. But I think I am
also the only succubus you know."

Sunny snorted mirthfully under her breath.

I wondered whether Angelica intended to continue her relationship with
Jeremy, but I couldn't quite bring myself to ask. My emotions were too
mixed up to deal with intimate images of my friend and my not quite ex-
husband.

Nor was I particularly eager to initiate the Edie discussion—although
Jeremy did deserve to know he'd been magically seduced.

I comforted myself with the morbidly amusing thought that, if things
went wrong with the Hell Ride tonight, I wouldn't have to deal with any
of it. I felt guilty for not telling Sunny or Lorien what I was planning, but
I'd made up my mind, and I didn't want to be talked out of it. Knowing
Jeremy hadn't been completely at fault for cheating only strengthened my

resolve.

I was through being a helpless pawn of the magical forces around me.

∞∞∞∞∞∞∞∞

"I'll be right back." I left Sunny in the running car and jumped out to dash into Hannah's shop. It was almost five, and not only was Hannah about to close, but we had twenty minutes to make our reservation at the hot new sushi place Sunny wanted to try.

I reflected on my luck in finding a parking space in front of Hannah's, but decided with a grimace that Lorien was probably still too pissed at me to be assisting with such menial comforts. It had to be the time of day and the fact that it was off season.

I nearly ran right into a tall, well-dressed woman who was exiting the cool interior of Haute Hannah's. My face erupted into a chagrinned smile as I looked up at her. "Sorry about that!"

"Not to worry, dear," she answered, winking at me as she passed. I stopped dead, staring after her as unease blossomed through me. She had striking hazel eyes, but there were unmistakable green flames burning within their depths.

"Hannah?" I called as I stepped into the sparkling ambiance of the deserted shop. There was no answer and my heart skipped a beat. I rushed toward the back office in panic.

The door swung open to produce Hannah, humming to herself as she counted an impressive stack of hundred dollar bills. I was so relieved to see her that I gasped, and was inundated by an overwhelming cloud of French perfume. I made a choking noise as I attempted to exhale the cloying scent. She looked up at me in surprise and quickly stuffed the cash in a drawer.

"Oh Sydney! Good, I was just about to close up for the day! I have the forms right here. They are Greek to me, but I am sure you will figure them out in no time. I thank you again for coming by on such short notice." She smiled as she handed me the papers, seeming even more chipper than usual.

"It's no problem, Hannah," I murmured, studying her with concern. "So did the woman who just left buy something?"

Her smile faltered.

"I thought I recognized her from somewhere," I added, watching Hannah for any sign that she was in trouble. "Has she been here before?"

Hannah licked her lips, appearing nervous all of a sudden. "She comes in now and then."

I did my best to conceal my disquiet. "Oh. Maybe that's why she looks familiar."

I wanted to warn her, but what was I going to say? *Gee, Hannah, were*

you aware that you've been consorting with a death djinn? If not, don't
worry. She could just be after me. You'll be fine as long as you don't wish for
death around her.

Hannah blinked rapidly. "Well, I am sure you are eager to be on your
way. You must be going out this evening—you look so pretty in your little
red skirt!"

I glanced down at the silky fabric floating above my knees and mumbled
my thanks. Before I could form another thought, she was bustling me
toward the door. "So I thank you again for coming and I will not keep you
any longer! See you Monday!"

She closed the door between us and turned the lock with one hand as
she fluttered the be-ringed fingers of the other at me in a hasty farewell. I
stared through the glass after her retreating back with growing misgivings.
Was I imagining things?

Ever exuberant, enthusiastic Hannah, who had always been so sweet to
me, couldn't be involved with the death djinns. Could she?

"That's weird," Sunny responded with a frown when I told her about
the peculiar experience. "I did see that woman leaving the shop—I was
trying to see if I could spot Galena following you again." She grinned.
"But nothing looked out of the ordinary from here. Maybe it's just another
death djinn trying to spy on you."

"Hannah seemed like she was in such a rush to get rid of me after I asked
about her, though." My hands gripped the steering wheel in apprehension.

"You don't think she'd help them, do you?" Sunny asked incredulously.

I gave her a troubled look. "She had a huge wad of cash in her hand and
she wouldn't answer me when I asked if the lady bought anything." It hurt
to even think about Hannah betraying me like that.

"Well, we'll definitely have to keep our eyes open," Sunny said with a
frown, "but it's probably not the best idea to start grilling Hannah about
death djinns just yet. You should at least wait until you figure out a spell to
alter her memory afterward. You know, in case she decides you belong in a
mental ward with a Thorazine drip attached to your arm."

"Now there's an interesting idea," I mused.

"Yes, it's supposed to wash all your worries right away. And I promise to
bring some coloring books and the biggest box of crayons I can find when
I come to visit you. I'll even get you the ones with the sharpener built into
the box!"

"I meant the memory spell, not the mental ward," I growled, shooting
her my dirtiest look.

"Oh, sorry. Yeah, I guess that would be pretty cool too." She snickered at
me with an annoying lack of intimidation.

I tried to let it go and simply add Hannah and her suspicious 'customer'
to the growing list of things I needed to put out of my mind for the time

being.

But a renewed sense of helplessness began gnawing at my insides. It was lighter fuel to the reckless fire of my resolve. I would call the Hell Ride tonight—despite the danger. I would do whatever it took. Because Sparrow's mom was right—death was better than giving up my soul.

∞∞∞∞∞∞∞∞

"Heavenly!" Sunny exhaled on a contented sigh as we headed home several hours later. "That was so worth an interview with a death djinn possessed teenager. It was even worth kissing up to that snotty little hostess."

We'd caught the draw bridge as we left Hannah's, run into construction on the street beyond, and to top it all off, one of the two parking garages had been closed.

I was still feeling too guilty to even consider asking for Lorien's help.

As a result, we'd been a half hour late for our reservation and had to beg the manager to fit us into the packed seating schedule. He put it off on the overwhelmed hostess, and she was still in a huff about it when she came to retrieve us from the bar over an hour later.

Her ire was obvious from the way she scowled and flipped her hair at us, not to mention the way she stormed off after handing us our menus, her satin kimono swishing angrily with her strides.

Oh well. After an hour at the bar we had no difficulty finding humor in the situation.

And the sushi was fantastic—unbelievably fresh cuts that melted on our tongues and the most wickedly spicy wasabi I'd ever put in my mouth. Not to mention a bean sprout salad and a ginger miso soup to die for.

Sunny had performed a taste test of three brands of sake in order to determine her favorite. She was still giddy from the liquor, even though we'd walked around afterward and made our usual pit-stop by Starbucks.

I was more clear-headed, having opted for Japanese beer. Sake always put me in mind of a combination of warm vodka and sweet white wine—neither of which held any appeal for me, much less mixed together.

Back at the penthouse, I bid my best friend a good night and watched her stumble off to bed before heading to my own room to dial Cindy's cell phone. I sighed with relief when it rang to voicemail, and left her a message that I wouldn't be able to work tomorrow because a family emergency had come up and I had to fly out tonight. It was sort of true.

Instead of changing into the sleep shirt and shorts I had put aside earlier, I donned my thickest pair of jeans and a red shirt with the logo 'Women Who Behave Rarely Make History'. I needed all the encouragement I could get. Then I laid out a pair of socks and sneakers by the bed (having learned my lesson about wearing sandals on expeditions to the faerie realm), set my alarm for midnight, and tried to relax.

The buzz of the alarm pulled me into a groggy state of awareness what seemed like only minutes later. I reached across my nightstand to make it stop, hoping the sound hadn't woken Sunny.

I staggered over to splash cold water on my face, refusing to look my mirror image in the eye for fear that one of us would talk some sense into the other. Then I slipped on my shoes and socks and pulled Lauringer's slip of paper from its new resting place next to the frog vibrator in my bedside drawer.

I smiled forlornly at Sparrow's bouquet of wildflowers, springing up from a tall crystal vase on the nightstand. As an afterthought, I reached beneath my pillow for his silver coin and stuck it in my pocket for luck.

I was used to bare feet, and the carpet felt oddly springy beneath my sneakers as I treaded across the room to open the sliding glass door. I stood balanced in the middle of the frame, the warm sea-breeze brushing my face as the cool inside air caressed my back. Before I could change my mind, I began to read:

Unholy Court, I call you this night.
Come bear me away in the absence of light.
I surrender to darkness as clinging as soot.

I paused, squeezing my eyes shut as I breathlessly forced out the final line:

Light's goodness lies shadowed and evil's afoot.

I stared into the night, frozen and waiting. The ocean crashed restlessly onto the shore and the moon shone bright and almost full. It rode high on the horizon, its glowing reflection glinting off the endless ripples masking the deeper water below. The spiky outlines of palm trees were scattered silhouettes along the edges of the beach, their fronds swaying in the breeze.

A strange electrical charge permeated the air and the underlying silence became almost painful as the blood rushed past my ears. Then a low-grade hum began to pulse through me. It grew louder and stronger, a disturbing vibration that expanded until it felt as if it was coming from inside my own head, drowning out the crash of the waves.

A shadow passed across the moon, blotting out its milky white glow in a mass of inky blackness that stained the midnight sky. It spread like a contagion, swelling rapidly to choke out the stars. Suddenly, a hulking behemoth was hovering before me, cloaked in writhing darkness.

A thick beam of light shot out to pin me, throwing the balcony into stark relief. It was blindingly bright, but it seethed with a pestilent taint that seeped into my skin like oil. I nearly retched at the vileness of it.

I fought down the twisting in my stomach, panic ripping through me as I realized my feet were rooted to the spot. I tried to open my eyes against the virulent intensity, managing a squint that allowed me to discern a cloud of dark motes drifting down over me. It might have been faerie dust, but instead of sparkling and reflecting the light, it seemed to absorb and distort it, hurting my eyes as much as the sickly brightness.

In the space of one rapid heartbeat I was sucked violently out and upward, as if by a great whirlwind. It stole my breath along with my balance, and before I could scream, I was tumbled roughly onto a hard, unforgiving surface.

Tears sprang to my eyes as jagged splinters abraded my palms. My entire right side went numb as it absorbed the impact, and then abruptly exploded into searing pain. A dreadful wheezing sound escaped my throat as I tried to suck oxygen into my stunned lungs.

In the sudden stillness of fear and the clarity of pain, I was struck by the stupidity of what I had just done. Ever since talking to Ophelia, I'd kept this idea in the back of my mind, thinking of it as a brave last resort in my search for the mysterious goblin. It had seemed the only move left open to me after being blocked and checked at every turn.

But there was a fine line between bravery and foolishness. And against all advice from those wiser than me, I had called the Unseelie Court and invited them to take me on the Hell Ride. I had surrendered control to the greatest force for evil in the faerie realm.

And now it was too late to turn back.

Don't miss the exciting conclusion of Sydney's
adventures in the Faerie Realm!
Soul Seduction - Book 2 of
The Third Wish Duology
Available now in print and for e-readers!

If you enjoy this author's books, she would truly
appreciate it if you would take a quick moment to add
positive reviews to Goodreads.com and/or the website
for the store where you purchased them!

An excerpt follows from **_Passionate Magic_**, which
features Sparrow's best friend, Doyle. It is more of a
traditional romance than _The Third Wish_ Duology, but
still has plenty of fantasy. I hope you enjoy it!

- Dawn Addonizio

Chapter One of _PASSIONATE MAGIC_

The summer sun blazed down onto Violet's upturned face, soaking into
her body to melt away the tension that had been building since she'd arrived in Key Largo two days ago. Dazzling points of sunlight glinted across
countless rippling waves as the boat sped toward a nearby coral reef, the
rush of wind softening the heat and sending her long, dark hair fluttering
out behind her. The sweet scent of orange and coconut tanning oil teased
her senses.

She was on summer vacation from her job teaching fourth grade, although it didn't feel like much of a vacation. She'd been putting off this
trip, but with the end of the school year she'd run out of excuses. She
couldn't believe it had already been two whole months since the day she'd
stood beside the ugly upturned earth that marked her parents' graves.

Vicki and George Hendrickson had always loved the ocean, reveled in its
mystery and magic, and they had instilled that love in their only daughter.
Even now, being on the ocean soothed and calmed Violet—despite the fact
that, in the end, it had been this very expanse of water that had stolen her
parents' lives.

Violet sighed. She'd thought she was almost at peace with the unfair
way in which they'd been taken from her. But two days spent alone in their
cozy garden villa, going through closets scattered with Hawaiian shirts that

carried traces of her dad's aftershave, and her mom's eclectic collection of hats, had stirred her grief back up to the surface.

She needed a break, intending to go for a walk down by the docks and maybe a swim on the beach. But she'd happened past this snorkeling tour just as it was leaving and joined it on a whim.

Maybe it was the boat's name that called to her—Ocean Magic—painted in bright, glowing blue against the vessel's crisp, white-washed stern. Or perhaps she was drawn by the challenge of embracing the ocean again after what had happened; proving that she held neither fear nor blame for it.

Violet couldn't help a small smirk as she admitted to herself that it also might have had something to do with the sexy boat captain rounding up customers from the dock as she passed. The husky timbre of his voice had lured her over, Irish if she wasn't mistaken. She was a sucker for that particular accent. Of course, it didn't hurt that he was built like a Celtic god.

She stole a peek at him through the dark lenses of her sunglasses. He stood at the polished mahogany captain's wheel, the wind ruffling his short honey-brown hair, all easy self-assurance as he chatted with a pair of women who sat nearby.

Just her luck, they both looked like supermodels. She inhaled the brisk salt-air and turned away to stare out at the fathomless aquamarine water, determined to enjoy her adventure with or without the attention of the handsome boat captain.

As the boat coasted to a halt, she peeled off her shorts and top, bending to retrieve her fluorescent orange snorkel vest and mask. She sucked in a breath as she rose in time to see the mouth-watering captain casually pull off his shirt, revealing a wide, well-defined chest and abs with just a hint of a six-pack. The pair of women beside him appeared to appreciate the view as well.

Violet refused to join them in their ogling, doubting he needed his ego inflated further. When he began instructing them on water safety, however, he drew her attention once more. He had the loveliest voice, with that rich Irish brogue of his, and his sea-green eyes sparkled with warmth when he smiled.

He caught her gaze for a moment, holding it as he finished his speech, almost as if he was speaking to her alone. He seemed to start toward her, and heat rose to her already flushed cheeks. Flustered, she looked away and hurried to the back of the line to await her turn to descend the ladder into the water.

∞∞∞∞∞∞∞∞∞

Doyle forced a smile at the scantily clad young woman sitting in front of him. She was tracing a manicured fingertip over her glossed pink lips in what was obviously meant to be an enticing manner. She and her giggling, gum chewing friend had rushed to sit by him as soon as they'd boarded the boat.

"Brittany and I were giving each other belly button shots at the bar last night. It was a blast." She gave him a coy look from beneath lashes thick with mascara. "You should come hang out with us tonight. If you buy the shots, we'll feed them to you."

Brittany giggled and Doyle laughed politely. "That's quite an offer, ladies."

They were certainly pretty enough, but he met the same type of girl day in and day out. He'd enjoyed his share of them, taking advantage of what they were only too willing to give, but he wasn't in the mood for another meaningless romp with a tourist.

It was his last snorkel trip of the day and he was eager to be done with it. He loved his business, but he was wiped out from the brutal heat and his four earlier groups. It wasn't so bad when he had a turn in the water and his partner, Manny, stayed on the boat to supervise the scene from above. But it was Manny's turn to swim.

He'd never thought anything could make him miss Ireland's wet, aching cold until he experienced mid-summer in the subtropics.

The flirtier of the two girls leaned into him. "That's not all I have to offer, handsome," she whispered on a drawn out breath. The cloying aroma of smoke and cloves nearly made him choke. "Come swimming with me and I'll show you."

Doyle gave a noncommittal chuckle and hid a grimace. Maybe sweating on the boat was the better alternative after all. He reminded himself that he couldn't complain. He'd said he wanted sun and sand, and he had it in spades here in the Florida Keys.

He'd never regretted his decision to leave Ireland. Although he wasn't sure his poor parents would ever get over the shock of it. That he'd chosen to venture so far from home was only a part of their dismay; it was more that he'd bucked convention and decided to live in the human world. Because, despite appearances, Doyle wasn't human.

I wonder if knowing that would be enough to make these two leave me alone, he thought dryly. But he would never reveal his secret, the satisfaction of chasing away overbearing tourists notwithstanding. He hadn't even told Manny, and they'd been friends and business partners for ten years.

Doyle steered the boat alongside the reef, giving his first-mate a nod to indicate they were stopping. Manny winked in salute as he dropped anchor, the wiry muscles of his arms and bare chest shifting beneath summer-darkened skin that had started out a deep, Costa Rican brown. Doyle stripped off his t-shirt with the Ocean Magic's logo, ignoring the increased giggling from the college girls, and began to give his rote safety spiel before he sent the group into the water.

He almost stumbled over his words as his eyes fell upon the beautiful young woman watching him solemnly from the aft railing. He'd been busy piloting the boat and fending off advances from the 'girls gone wild', but he couldn't believe he hadn't noticed her.

She had a solitary air, standing apart from the couples who were helping each other with their lifevests, and not joining in the laughter of the other clustered groups of passengers. But she didn't look like she minded being alone. Her posture was selfpossessed and confident, though a veiled sorrow seemed to linger beneath the tranquility of her expression.

She was several inches shorter than he, with a firm but curvaceous body. Her breasts and hips were full and ripe, her pale golden skin clear and sun-blushed. Her long, dark hair fell in waves to frame a soft face with extraordinarily blue, almost purple, eyes. She locked gazes with him as he finished speaking, and he began to move toward her, as if in a dream. But at the last moment she turned away and joined the queue to get in the water.

Disappointed, he faltered to a stop, oblivious to the giggling blonde who threaded her arm through his and asked if he would be her snorkel partner. He mumbled something about having to stay on the boat as he disentangled himself, earning a pretty pout.

Absorbed with thoughts of the mysterious brunette, and determined to introduce himself on the return ride, he picked up the clipboard with the passenger roster and tried to guess her name. As he scanned the page, he smiled in triumph. Hendrickson, Violet. The name reflected the color of her eyes. And she was the only passenger traveling alone.

∞∞∞∞∞∞∞∞∞

Violet admonished herself for being foolish as she waited, her mask looped around her wrist and fins dangling from her fingers. The captain was far too good-looking for his own, or her, good. Out of the corner of her eye she saw one of the blondes hanging on his arm, and she turned away, shoving him resolutely from her mind. What had she been thinking? There was no way he'd been about pass up that free lunch to come talk to her.

She reached the ladder and was soon lowering herself into the warm, soothing water; all other thoughts forgotten as the buoyant swells welcomed her into their embrace. She had forgotten how good it felt to be out here in the middle of the ocean. It was far different from swimming near the shore with the rolling whitecaps crashing onto the beach. Here it was like another world, with only an unbroken expanse of blue-green serenity as far as the eye could see.

She quickly donned her snorkel mask and fins, and worked her way out over the jumble of pitted and maze-like corals that made up the reef. Lacy sea fans waved lazily in the currents and multitudes of colorful fish flitted every which way. She lost herself in exploring the teeming marine life, following a couple of parrot fish that were chasing each other for a while, and then stopping to admire a large anemone with purple-pink tentacles.

She floated past a school of butterfly fish, flashing silver and yellow in the water-muted sunlight, and held her breath to dive down for a closer look at a huge grouper that she'd nearly missed. Its mouth gaped open and its fins barely moved as it hovered in a dark crevice, waiting for prey. Trigger fish darted by as she returned to the surface to clear out her breathing tube.

Violet's gasp of delight sounded hollow inside her snorkel as she caught sight of a sea turtle in the distance. She hurried toward it, trying to minimize her movements so as not to startle the creature. A large shadow moved past, and she blinked, jerking her face around to see what it was.

Something smacked hard against the side of her head and her vision went grey. She was stunned for a moment, and then pain crashed over her. She realized suddenly that she could no longer breathe. Her mask was filling with water, blinding her, and something was dragging her down, down, away from the air and the light. She panicked, struggling and flailing against its merciless pull.

Her lungs burned and tightened until they felt as if they would implode. No longer able to stop herself, Violet inhaled seawater.

∞∞∞∞∞∞∞∞∞∞

Doyle paced from stern to bow in frustration. The group had dispersed out over the reef, and from this distance he couldn't tell who was who. They were just a collection of bright orange blobs. They would be floating around out there for another half hour before he would get the chance to talk to the lovely Violet Hendrickson.

Who was she? And why would someone like her be vacationing alone? With his luck, she had a fiancée waiting for her back at her hotel room.

He continued his pacing, staring moodily out over the water, and then he went stock still. That was odd. He could have sworn he'd just seen a merrow's tail break the surface out beyond the reef, its large, silvery green scales sparkling in the sunlight.

The merrow were mer-folk, and notorious for keeping to themselves. There had been tales of sailors spotting them throughout history, but he'd never seen a hint of their existence in all his years in the Keys. It was strange that one would be anywhere near a place that was so populated by humans. His eyes scanned the water, searching for another glimpse.

Instead, he saw something that made his blood run cold despite the blazing afternoon heat. There was a single orange jersey floating about a hundred yards off the starboard bow, like so much abandoned flotsam.

Without a second thought he dove over the side of the boat and began a furious swim toward the empty snorkeling vest. He realized too late that he should have donned a mask, as he squinted through blurry, salt-stung eyes to gauge his surroundings. As soon as he reached the solitary jersey, he plunged deeper.

This was where the reef started to become the territory of divers. The seafloor dropped and the coral became a rocky landscape of peaks and valleys, jutting out to create hundreds of miniature caves. Many were large enough to conceal a human body. Had some fool decided to go exploring on their own and gotten stuck? Inadvisable though it was, he began feeling around inside the dark dens with his ungloved hands.

A perturbed moray eel shot out at him, its jagged teeth nearly clamping onto his fingers. He jerked his hand back and moved onto the next opening, growing frantic. The human brain could only go without oxygen for about five minutes. It must have been at least two since he'd jumped in the water. And though Doyle wasn't human, whoever had been wearing that orange snorkeling vest was. And they were running out of time.

A large, sleek shape rushed past him, creating its own wake beneath the surface. Doyle squinted at it, thinking it was a shark. But then he glimpsed something that seemed out of place on the seafloor below and he dismissed the creature as he lunged toward it.

A clump of dark wisps floated at the edge of a recess of rock, disappearing into a hidden cavity beneath. His fingers tangled in the mass, identifying the clinging strands as human hair. He reached deeper, past the curve of an unmoving head, to grasp a lifeless body beneath the shoulders. He tugged, and found himself holding an unconscious Violet in his arms.

He felt as if he was looking at her in slow motion. Her beautiful face was pale and eerily still, her long hair hovering in a weightless raven cloud. Then time caught up with him and he pushed off the rock, his leg muscles stroking for the surface.

"There they are!" someone shouted.

Doyle barely registered the sound as he rolled onto his back, pulling Violet's limp form with him, desperate to get her to the boat where he could perform CPR. His arms tightened beneath her ribcage as he struggled to position her, and suddenly she was choking and sputtering as she coughed up water and gasped for breath.

Doyle didn't think he'd ever felt such stark relief in his almost two hundred years of existence.

His first mate reached his side and began trying to pull Violet from him. Doyle's grip on her tightened reflexively, some primal instinct roaring to life, unwilling to relinquish her to another.

"Easy now," Manny soothed.

Doyle wasn't sure whether the calming words were meant for him or for Violet, but he relaxed his hold and allowed Manny to slide her down so that she was supported between them.

"We'll have you out of the water soon," Doyle assured her gently as they began working their way back to the boat. She murmured a sound of gratitude between coughing sputters.

The rest of the group bobbed in loose knots around them, treading water and staring. Doyle knew they were only concerned, but it was all he could do not to shout at them to get out of the way. He heard a faint, agitated buzz and looked up to find a distraught faerie hovering overhead, her wings sifting sparkling purple dust that scattered behind her on the wind.

She was a sprite, approximately three inches tall with dark shining hair that fell past her knees. Her skin glowed with silvery light and her pastel dress shimmered in shades of pink, blue and yellow. From the anxious stare she was directing at Violet, Doyle guessed that she must be the young woman's faerie guardian.

Faerie guardians bonded with certain mortals at birth, following them throughout their lives to bring them aid and protection. Most mortals had no idea of the existence of the faerie realm or any of its denizens. If they had a faerie guardian helping them they simply attributed it to luck, when they noticed it at all.

Doyle had a bone to pick with this particular faerie. Where the hell had she been when her charge was drowning, and why hadn't she steered Violet away from the danger?

"How the devil could you let this happen, little sister?" he muttered up at her, his jaw set in a grim line.

Her tilted eyes widened a fraction. "You're sidhe," she gasped in surprise.

He was just about to let loose a scathing reply, when he realized that Violet was trying to speak, her voice coming out stilted and hoarse from a throat raw with saltwater.

"Excuse me?" she managed finally. "I didn't let anything happen," she croaked. "Something knocked into me and dragged me under!"

She sent him a how-dare-you scowl and looked to the other group members for support.

"Of course it's not your fault, sweetie," a plump, motherly woman cooed. Her flowered rubber bathing cap was askew, leaving her kindly expression lopsided, but Violet smiled back at her in gratitude.

Some of the others nodded their agreement, staunchly remaining nearby, but several people were rapidly working their way back toward the boat. No doubt it had something to do with Violet's announcement that something had tried to drag her beneath the waves.

"I didn't mean you," Doyle assured her quickly. He directed an aggravated glance at the faerie as he realized his mistake. Of course Violet had assumed he was talking to her.

Violet shot him a disbelieving look. "Who did you mean, then?" she demanded, her voice still husky. "I'm fairly sure you weren't calling your friend here 'little sister'. He looks manly enough to me."

Doyle was forced to tamp down an unreasonable surge of jealousy toward Manny. "I didn't...I'm sorry, okay? Let's just get you back on board," he said with an irritable sigh.

"Captain Doyle's just a little hot with me for no keeping a closer eye on things," Manny said in a smooth tone. "He only wants to keep you safe, lindita." He gave Violet a reassuring smile, but a question flickered in his dark eyes as they traveled to Doyle's.

Doyle shook his head in silent apology and concentrated on guiding Violet to the ladder. He ignored the faerie now flitting back and forth in front of them. Apparently she found the situation humorous, her attempts to stifle her laughter with her small hands failing miserably. The dust from her wings changed from purple to green, and it drifted into his face as the wind changed direction, tickling his nose.

He sent her an irate glare. Most types of faerie dust made humans sneeze, and right on cue, Violet and Manny erupted in unison.

"Bless you," Doyle said, unable to keep the sourness from his tone.

The faerie shot upward with a muffled chortle.

"Just a little salt water in the nose, eh, lindita?" Manny chuckled.

Violet tilted a smile in Manny's direction and Doyle fumed.

They reached the ladder and Manny managed to ascend it first, helping Violet up and leading her to a bench. Doyle scrambled after them and hurried to Violet's other side.

"Thank you, Manny. Can you get everyone back aboard while I tend to Miss Hendrickson?"

Manny gave him another questioning look, but rose and did as he asked.

Doyle placed a hand on Violet's shoulder. Though he felt her stiffen, he couldn't seem to make himself stop touching her. Her skin was warm and satiny beneath his palm. His gaze dropped to the rounded tops of her breasts where they peeked from the scooped neckline of her bathing suit. They rose and fell gently with her breath, the sight making his throat go dry.

He jerked his eyes back to her face and found her studying him with a puzzled frown. He swallowed. "I'm sorry." His voice sounded rough and he swallowed again. "I was just checking to make sure you had no visible signs of injury."

One delicate sable brow lifted. "Whatever it was hit me in the head." Violet reached up to gingerly explore her scalp.

"Of course." Doyle nodded quickly, his fingers brushing hers as he began his own examination.

Violet winced and sucked in a breath as he found a tender spot.

"Sorry," he said again, lightening his touch. "The skin doesn't seem to be broken, but you do have quite a bump. Does it hurt anywhere else?"

He gave the faerie, still hovering above them, a meaningful glance. She pulled a small cloth pouch from inside her dress and darted down to sprinkle silvery healing dust over the area he was probing with his fingers.

Violet shook her head. "No. I think I'm alright. It's already starting to feel better."

Doyle smiled and Violet's rosy lips quivered upward in response. She smelled of the ocean and sun-ripened fruit. Her hair was drying into shining ripples of silk beneath his hand, and he longed to run his fingers through its length. She was so close, her eyes like wide pools of liquid amethyst. A man could lose himself in their crystalline depths. If he just leaned in a few inches, he would be able to taste her…

An annoying chorus of giggles broke the spell. Doyle shook his head to clear it and reluctantly pulled his hand back from Violet.

∞∞∞∞∞∞∞∞∞

Violet wasn't quite sure what had just happened. First the handsome captain had blamed her for almost drowning. Then he'd insisted on taking care of her himself and sent the other, friendlier man away. She could have sworn she'd caught him ogling her cleavage, but he'd insisted he was only looking for injuries. Her head had been throbbing. But when he'd touched her, his fingers had literally soothed away the pain, as if by magic.

To make things even more confusing, just now there had been a moment when she was sure he was about to kiss her. A shiver went through her, her lips still tingling at the enticing thought. His sea-green eyes had held such heat as they stared into hers. But he'd pulled away when his two girlfriends showed up.

"Are you okay?" gasped the woman in the red bikini. Her voice dripped with concern, but her eyes roamed the captain's muscular chest as she spoke. It was the clingy blonde he'd had on his arm earlier.

"What happened?" her friend asked in an anxious tone, steadily grinding a piece of chewing gum between her teeth.

Captain Doyle straightened and crossed his arms over the width of his chest, as if to distance himself from Violet. She felt a bright flash of annoyance at him, mingled with a touch of disgust for herself. She reached down to pull a towel from her backpack, using it as an excuse to scoot away from the fickle captain.

"Something big knocked into me from behind. It was probably a shark," she replied briskly, enjoying the discomfort that flitted across both women's faces as their eyes traveled from her to the water in which they'd just been swimming. "I felt it dragging me down before I passed out."

"Did it bite you?" asked the one with the gum, grinding it harder as she stared at Violet in horrified fascination.

"I..." Violet looked down to make sure she wasn't bleeding. It suddenly occurred to her that the only way a shark could have pulled her down was with its teeth. But all she found were a few light abrasions where her skin had rubbed against rock. Although relieved not to find any more serious injury, she discovered, with a surge of disappointment, that her favorite silver anklet had fallen off.

She looked up to find the woman still looking at her expectantly. "No, I wasn't bitten," she said, feeling foolish. She must have imagined being dragged down.

"Thank Gawd!" the woman exclaimed, appearing not to spot the inconsistency in Violet's shark story.

Violet glanced at Captain Doyle, sure he'd catch it right away. But he was staring off into space, not even listening to her. Apparently she no longer merited his attention. Miffed and a little hurt, she stood up and wrapped her towel tighter around her midsection. "Excuse me. I need to use the restroom."

∞∞∞∞∞∞∞∞∞∞

"It wasn't a shark," the faerie piped up as soon as the word left Violet's mouth. "It was a merrow. That's why I wasn't able to warn her away in time. Sometimes my signals get crossed when other magical beings are involved."

Doyle stared at her, frustrated with his inability to reply.

"I don't think this was an isolated incident. A couple of months ago...oh, Titania's wand!" she cursed.

"I have to go. My son found his way out of his playpen. Little tyke's getting much too clever. I'll find you later, when you can talk." She gave him an apologetic grimace and was gone.

Doyle blinked and realized that Violet was no longer at his side. He rose, skirting around the college girls, and began walking toward the bow in search of her. He thought he'd seen a merrow. But why would one of the mer-folk want to harm Violet?

Violet exited the head, pointedly avoiding his gaze as she returned to her seat, and Doyle sighed. Apparently he'd upset her again. He'd have to figure out how to make it up to her later. Right now, he needed to get his passengers back to shore.

"Ready to pull anchor, amigo?" Manny clapped him on the shoulder.

"Let's take her in," he grumbled.

PASSIONATE MAGIC is available now in print and for e-readers!

<u>About the Author</u>

Dawn Addonizio lives in South Florida with her wonderful husband, who is a science teacher, and their beloved menagerie of pets.

When she's not working her day job, or staring into space, she spends her time writing fantasy and making jewelry, wine accessories, and all manner of other sparkly things.

You can visit her store at DawnsBoutique.Net, "like" her on Facebook/D.Addonizio, and read some of her musings at DAddonizio.blogspot.com. You can also follow her on Twitter @DawnAddonizio